Curves, Kisses and Chocolate Ice Cream

D0495658

www.southdublinlibraries.ie

Curves, Kisses and Chocolate Ice Cream

SUE WATSON

bookouture

Published by Bookouture
An imprint of StoryFire Ltd.
23 Sussex Road, Ickenham, UB10 8PN
United Kingdom
www.bookouture.com

ISBN: 978-1-78681-203-2
eBook ISBN: 978-1-78681-202-5

For Lesley McLoughlin and Cocoa.

Chapter One

The Cabbage Soup Diet

Diet Diary: April 2001; Fell in love with the barista in the nearby Starbucks. Ate 100 tonnes of cabbage, drank gallons of tap water. I Never. Left. The. Bathroom. Lost 3 days, gained 4 pounds. The barista left Starbucks and I never saw him again.

'You're VERY fat,' he said.

I didn't know where to put myself.

Having worked hard all day at Caprioni's Cafe serving up delicious ice creams with orgasmic toppings to happy customers, one of my final requests of the day was from a cute little boy with green eyes and a lisp. He can't have been more than five years old, and as he licked his lips and lisped his way through an order of strawberry ice cream with raspberry sauce, he'd decided to supersize his order with an unsolicited comment regarding my size: *You're VERY fat.*

Not just *fat*, but *VERY fat*, with the emphasis on *VERY*. He was a little boy, he wasn't passing a judgement, or being mean, he was merely making an accurate observation about the lady behind the counter. It was just unfortunate that lady happened to be me, and the words had continued on a loop in my head ever since.

It had taken me by surprise, and I was hoping I may have misheard, though there was nothing I could come up with that might have been mistaken for fat. I tried, oh God I tried, desperately convincing myself he may have just said you're VERY 'bat' or VERY 'hat' but I was kidding myself. I just wished he hadn't said it so audibly, and the cafe hadn't been so quiet at the particular bloody millisecond he said the 'F' word. In fact, for me it would have been less of an issue if he'd said the other 'F' word. This wasn't the first time someone had felt the urge to share with me my body image, like I didn't know I was at least two stone overweight. I'd spent many years of my childhood hearing the cruel remarks regarding what I optimistically referred to as 'my curves' – but when you're an adult, people usually keep their comments about other people's weight to themselves. Colleagues might have whispered behind my back, and discussed the state of my increasing arse as it left the room, but never in front of me. And shop assistants might have given me pitying but knowing looks outside the changing rooms as I handed back the small tent I couldn't squeeze into muttering something about 'the wrong colour'. But on the whole, being an adult is easier because people have, in theory, learned to keep their comments to themselves. But kids are different, and this one was keen to make his feelings known.

I attempted to style it out, smile and ignore what he'd said. If by any chance someone within a five-mile radius hadn't heard his loud remark, then perhaps we could just move past it? But no, his mother had other ideas.

'You can't say that to people,' she started, looking at me with guilt, embarrassment and the inevitable pity. 'Say you're sorry, Josh,' she continued, while I feigned an indulgent smile and wafted my hand in the air like it didn't matter and there was no need for an apology or a bloody inquisition that now seemed to be drawing everyone's attention. I wanted to forget about it, but she was making quite the spectacle and people were muttering, their glances drifting across my body as my face flooded scarlet. Then everything escalated even more as she raised her voice, repeated that he mustn't say 'things like that', thus alerting anyone in the vicinity who may not have already heard how fat I was, to prick up their ears.

'Say you're SORRY,' she yelled, as his chin puckered and he burst into tears. I didn't know where to look or what to do, it now seemed that whatever was going on between the VERY fat lady and the little boy had caused him to cry and not only was I corpulent I was cruel too.

'Please, it's fine,' I said, aggressively squishing strawberry ice cream onto a cone and attacking it viciously with raspberry sauce. Needless to say, it wasn't fine, and by the time I handed him the cone the little boy was in a full-on tantrum and pushed it sharply away so that it hit the counter and landed on the floor. This sent him into paroxysms of ice cream grief and I now looked like the fat, and *cruel* lady who made him drop his ice cream!

'What's going on?' Marco, my miserable colleague said with a frown. 'You causing problems, Dani?' He wasn't joking, Marco was permanently miserable, pretty monosyllabic and never joked.

'I'm… I'm not causing anything…' I said, close to tears and wishing I'd pushed the bloody cone in *his* face. Everyone was looking, the child was sobbing and the remains of strawberry and raspberry were now sliding down the side of the counter and puddling in a bright pink heap on the floor.

'That'll need cleaning,' Marco observed.

'Thank you for pointing that out,' I rolled my eyes, now brimming with tears. When he wasn't being rude he had a talent for stating the obvious.

I couldn't bear the thought of now walking around the counter so everyone could see me. I felt like a circus freak, and perhaps it was my paranoia, but I swear the whole cafe was holding their breath, just waiting for me to emerge from behind my ice cream wall to see just how VERY fat I was.

I couldn't face it, so made like I had urgent business in the kitchen and did an about-turn left centre stage, leaving Marco to handle the mess. It was bad of me to leave like that, but what else could I do? I knew I was overweight, I didn't need reminding, and I didn't need to stick around to watch a single scoop turned into a knickerbocker glory.

I spent the next hour in the cafe kitchen, I couldn't face going back out there and as it was almost closing time Marco could deal with the last few stragglers. I spent the time consoling myself with various titbits and swearing I would start my diet tomorrow. But when tomorrow came I couldn't diet because my best friend Karla was staying for a few days. I loved having Karla around, even though she was pretty and slim and clever. I should have hated her, but somehow, against all the odds, we'd become friends.

ing something fabulous with lavender sprigs and I want you to taste it.'

'I couldn't fit any more ice cream in,' she sighed, sitting back and patting her washboard stomach like it was huge. She just wasn't trying. 'I know you love working here in the cafe, but joking aside, I'm not sure it's the right place for someone who's addicted to sugar,' she raised her eyebrows.

'Spoilsport. I love it here and not just because I can pretend eating ice cream all day is research… though that is a big part of it,' I smiled, brushing over the truth. Yes, I did love whipping up a batch of new flavours and tasting them, but I didn't need a couple of large scoops of each. The ice cream wasn't the problem, it was me – and we both knew it.

'As I said, it doesn't matter to me what you weigh, but please don't stuff yourself silly then call me at two in the morning telling me how greedy and disgusting you are. Sleep has become precious and rare with two kids and a snoring husband, so if you're going to eat, then eat, just don't be whingeing at me with strawberry sauce round your mouth and guilt in your heart.'

'As if I'd call you in the middle of the night to talk about myself…' I said, knowing this to be the case, poor Karla had been the sounding board for my whole life since we'd met.

'You did it last night, and I was in the same bloody room.'

'Ha, I forgot you were staying,' I said, shaking my head at my own mistake and getting up from my seat to waddle over to the counter. I ran the scoop across my freshly made lavender ice cream, shiny lilac heaven curling softly onto my silver scoop, finding it hard to resist putting the loaded scoop straight to my mouth. It wouldn't have looked pretty, especially as people were walking past. I could only imagine the faces as they spotted that vision through the windows of Caprioni's Ice Cream Cafe. 'The thing is, Karla, I'm almost forty and it's not about vanity any more, it's about my health.' I was feeling like this a lot at the moment. I'd initially put this down to the insecurity of leaving London and coming back to where I'd spent my childhood. Change always unsettled me, but as I'd been here a few weeks and was actually very happy why the hell couldn't I stop inhaling ice cream?

'You're not thinking too much about the past are you... I wouldn't blame you after everything that happened here?'

I shook my head, by now my mouth was full of lavender-flavoured ice cream, not too sweet, just creamy and aromatic, tasting of lavender fields and sunshine. I'd discovered many years before that the best way not to think about the past was to fill my mind and my mouth with lovely things – like this sublime ice cream. And with this in mind, I added one more scoop to my bowl; one more wouldn't do any harm, would it?

'Have you seen anything of that Jude guy since you came back here?' Karla asked, as I put down her bowl of ice cream and settled down with mine.

'Not sure I can eat all this, I already ate one bowl,' she sighed. For God's sake she'd only had a thimbleful! She played around with it and tasted it, said all the right things then gently pushed the bowl away. Was she really going to leave that? I ate mine quickly wondering if it would be so bad if I finished hers off, after all it was wicked to waste food.

'No. I heard "that Jude guy" moved to Barnstaple, and that's miles away,' I said, through lavender ice cream, wafting my hand in a dismissive gesture like he was nothing. Though once he'd been everything, and back here I was reminded of him too much. The memories weren't all bad, we started out like Romeo and Juliet, that's what they called us in the cafe; 'Romeo's here, Juliet,' my friends would cry as he swaggered in. But that was a long time ago, and it wasn't good. Perhaps we were a bit too much like Romeo and Juliet, minus the stabbing and the poisoning of course.

'Dani, you might bump into him,' Karla said, and I gratefully dragged myself away from the bittersweet memories. 'I hope you have your armour ready, girl. You know how weak you are in the face of a man with intentions... and sweet treats.'

I put down the scoop and broke a wafer in half in what I hoped was a slightly threatening 'leave it alone' kind of way. This, of course, left me with a problem, a handful of homemade wafer, buttery, crisp and sweet – so I did what any decent human being would do, I popped it in my mouth.

'So, you haven't stalked his Facebook or googled him?'

'Hell no.' I had.

'So, you're completely over him?'

'Hell yes.' I wasn't.

I averted my eyes, and mounted a full-on attack on my bowl of lavender ice cream. It was the only way to avoid answering Karla's questions, this woman could see into my soul, she knew when I was happy, sad and when I was telling fibs. Okay, so I may have casually glanced at my teenage boyfriend's Facebook page and inadvertently googled him when I was bored. I also may or may not have been checking births, deaths and marriages in North Devon and surrounding areas for the past twenty years since I left here. Obsessed? Moi?

I gave a sidelong look at slim, beautiful Karla with the figure to die for and I swallowed a mouthful of cold, sweet ice cream; 'I told you, I was over him twenty years ago when I last saw him, why would I ever want to go back to a teenage fling? Anyway, I think he might be married.' I knew he was married, but there were no photos of her on his Facebook page, which in my book said *estranged*, at the very least.

'What makes you think he might be married?'

'I just… heard… on the grapevine.'

'Facebook?'

I nodded shamefully.

'Oh, Dani, I told you, leave it all behind.'

'I couldn't resist. It doesn't make me a bad person, I was just… curious.'

'Well, I'm glad he's married, it means he's ruining someone else's life and not yours.'

'Karla, I'm a grown-up now. You're so sweet to worry about me, but honestly, I'm good. God, I was just a girl, a nineteen-year-old child; I'm a fierce woman now.'

'Mmmm well that fierce woman has ice cream dribbling down her chin,' she said, with raised eyebrows like she was talking to her kids. 'I hope you're not heading back in the Jude direction.'

I assured her I wasn't, said I didn't want a difficult conversation about my first love, so wiped my chin and suggested we move on.

'Let's speak no more of my long-gone ex – he's just the first of many dickheads I've had to suffer over the years.'

'He started a pattern, that's for sure.'

Karla was a child psychologist – she said her work had made her realise we didn't change even when we grew up. She said that, emotionally, adults were merely children with pubic hair and a mortgage. This seemed rather cynical to me, but for her third year at uni she'd worked in men's prisons and said she defied anyone not to be cynical after that. Anyway, as my best friend she gave me free impromptu therapy 'sessions', whether I wanted them or not. Given my background, Karla said I was a brilliant case study; 'an accident waiting to happen' was the phrase she'd used. She'd also been heard to remark that after my childhood, she was surprised I wasn't a serial killer, which was nice.

She agreed that my weight was probably a result of my up-bringing, which gave me the excuse to avoid any responsibility for my burgeoning waistline. I tried to blame everyone and everything, including my mother's drinking, my father's desertion and the feckless person who created the concept of doughnuts. Apparently blaming others was something people like me did. I was 'textbook', according to Karla.

Now, over fresh lavender ice cream and frothy coffee with Karla, it was my dad's turn to take the blame, and why not? When he walked out on my perfect, beautiful skinny mother thirty years ago, I grieved for the rest of my childhood. First came the tears, then comforting my mother by pouring her gin and the Sunday-daughter guilt when I left her alone as he came to collect me. This was all followed by a good long ride on the doughnut train, a journey I was still on at almost forty years old.

'The thing is, that my problem is out there, for everyone to see and judge. I'm a constant reminder of my own weakness, my lack of control – and when someone – even a little kid – points it out, I just want to run away and hide, it's like being bullied all over again. Alcoholics ruin their families' lives, sex addicts hurt their partners and smokers fill the air with cancer – but they can at least attempt to hide their addiction. I'm not hurting anyone but myself, but it's there for everyone to see, comment on and judge. I can't hide my body...' I said, taking a final mouthful of lavender ice cream.

'You shouldn't have to hide your body. Stop being ashamed, Dani, you're not fat, I told you, you've got curves...'

'Mmmm. Thanks sweetie, but "curves" is just a nice word for fat as far as I'm concerned. I wish I was more like you, and I could eat anything and everything without putting on an ounce. I just have to glance sideways at an ice cream sundae and I put on half a stone.' I lowered my gaze and looked at her; 'I mean, who in their right mind could sit in the Ice Cream Cafe in Appledore, home of Thee Chocolate Heaven Sundae, the Rocky Road Horror and the Elvis is Dead Long Live the Peanut Butter Explosion, and eat only one scoop of vanilla?'

I'd been through the whole ice cream menu here already – three times to be precise. Always thorough in my work, I felt it was my duty as assistant manager to know my product – but it was hard to convince Karla that my ice cream consumption was not a decline into depression, but a professional requirement.

But as much as I loved ice cream and I loved working here – even I had to admit I was eating too much.

'The thing that gives me the most pleasure always gives me the most pain, and currently ice cream and doughnuts are top of both lists.'

'And as I always say, we have choices. I don't see anyone force-feeding you,' she raised her eyebrows.

Karla was a wonderful friend and I didn't really blame her for sometimes being a little judgemental about my approach to my diet and my lack of (ugh) exercise. I hated doing anything physical other than opening the fridge. Having lived in London for the past twenty years, with the sheer stress of work and the hustle, bustle and sardine-like tube journeys I felt permanently sweaty and exhausted. My daily 'workout' had been exactly 546 steps from the tube to my flat – and I was so out of condition, anything more than that and I'd have had to call for medical intervention.

So, I'd handed in my notice, got the dream job in Appledore, working as the assistant manager for the newly refurbished Ice Cream Cafe. It was beautiful, a pink and peppermint-painted ge-lato palace looking out to sea – and with the job came a lovely flat over the cafe. I opened the curtains each morning, and instead of inner city grime and a veil of grey, I looked out onto acres of long shoreline, pastel painted houses and blue sunshine skies. I'd escaped the 9–5 world of living and working like a lab rat in a small cage and was now free to live the life I'd always dreamed of. The fact it only took me ten steps to get from my bed to work each morning was an added bonus, but clearly wasn't helping my weight.

It was lovely to live over the cafe and not have to get the tube or the bus or stand in queues. I just went downstairs and there it was, no dusty office, no boring people in suits, just a pink and peppermint-painted ice cream palace. I was literally sitting on top of an ice cream emporium so who could blame me for popping downstairs in the dark of night to soothe my mind and delight in creamy snacks? It was like being a drug addict living over a chemist – the pull was too hard to resist.

I'd worked at the cafe many moons ago for several summers as a teenager, and even then, my lust for ice cream and toppings knew no bounds. In those days, Ella's late aunt Sophia had owned the cafe and I'd come back here half hoping Sophia would still be standing at the helm and everything would be as it used to be, the way I'd preserved it in my memory. But Sophia had died months before and now her daughter Gina and Ella, her niece, were the co-owners. I had mentioned in passing to Ella that I'd worked at the cafe years ago, but she lived up north and had stopped coming to Appledore for holidays by the time I worked there, so we'd never met before. She asked me why I'd left Appledore, and I said it was for my career; it wasn't, but I didn't want to say too much about the past. I worked on the theory that the fewer people who knew my old business, the easier my new life would be.

I liked Ella, and her mother Roberta was hilarious and a bit mad, and there was also Ella's best friend Sue who had followed her from Manchester and was settling in like she'd lived here for ever. Ella's kids, both teenagers, had been abroad most of the summer but her daughter Lucie was now back living in Appledore. She popped into the cafe sometimes, and even did the odd shift, but said she liked the 'bright lights of Barnstaple', and had a summer job there. In the cafe, everyone did their bit, and it was a lovely atmosphere with each person mucking in according to their talents. Even Marco had a talent; as miserable as he was he made the most amazing bread and cakes that melted in the mouth.

The cafe was always buzzing, Sue wiping tables vigorously (while talking just as vigorously!), her sequins fluttering and glittering in sync with her earrings as she scrubbed and put the world to rights. Roberta, who must have been in her seventies, would be texting or tweeting, and always on her phone like a teenager. When Lucie, her granddaughter, came into the cafe she teased her nan, asking her who she was sexting. 'Daniel Craig of course, you numpty,' she answered back, which made me smile. 'You think she's joking?' Lucie said, hugging her nan and rolling her eyes.

Gina, the glamorous blonde co-owner and cousin of Ella, was in her sixties, but looked like Ella's sister, she was so young-looking. Gina was lovely, but did very little work in the cafe, she'd spend most of her time sitting on a stool at the counter waxing lyrical about her life in Hollywood.

'Oh Dani, did I tell you about the time Sylvester Stallone asked for my phone number?' she'd say, and I would be fascinated by every little celebrity morsel she dropped my way.

'Don't take any notice of our Gina, Dani, the nearest she ever got to Stallone was the cheap seats at the Odeon,' Roberta would counter. I couldn't decide if they loved or hated each other, but they made me laugh. I loved 'the girls', their chatter, their giggles and the way they included me in everything; it was good to be alive... and if I could just lose some weight, my life would be perfect.

I'd booked a couple of days off work for Karla's visit, but the following day I'd agreed to work the morning.

I was happily piling rainbow-hued scoops into a tall sundae dish and making polite conversation with the customer, when all the loveliness of the morning collapsed like melted ice cream. All it took was four little words.

'When is it due?' the customer asked, with a smile.

'Due?' I said, wondering what she was referring to, but knowing in my heart what she meant. She gestured to my stomach, and I felt it drop to the floor – and given my recent food consumption, that was quite a landing. Inwardly I groaned. Not again? Why couldn't people (and little kids) keep their comments to themselves? Karla was right, people remained immature, insensitive gauche little kids even when they grew up. What kind of person would ask a woman about her pregnancy without actually having that pregnancy confirmed first? Although I had to admit, looking at me she probably had all the confirmation she needed. I was devastated, I'd hoped after the lisping child I'd at least be given some respite, but no, here it came again like a tsunami, she might as well have just shouted over the counter; 'Oi, fattie, when are you going on a diet? You look nine months gone with twins love.'

I wanted to die, to climb into a cupboard under the counter and just be left in peace to fade away. I didn't know how to handle this, and she was looking at me 'expectantly' (excuse the pun) for an answer as to the due date, baby's sex and some boring diatribe about maternity leave followed by a few clichés about 'making the most of it because you'll never sleep again'.

I almost went along with it; if I'd been in London and some faceless commuter had asked me about my pregnancy on the tube I'd have gone along with it because it was easier and I never had to see them again. But here, in Appledore, where I intended to stay, I couldn't possibly pretend I was pregnant, I'd have to continue the charade and that would be creepy. So instead I did the next best thing and feigned deafness.

I looked at the woman, my face scarlet, unable to respond to her endless baby enquiries. I desperately hoped she'd get the hint, and move away to be served by vibrant Sue or monosyllabic Marco further down the counter, but no, she merely stood her ground and repeated the question more loudly. So I frowned, pretended I didn't speak English and lifted my head jerkily in a nodding, vaguely aggressive 'what d'ya mean?' gesture, hoping she'd think I was French and move on. But this backfired, because she merely turned up the volume and yelled in my face, enunciating every word of 'I SAID, WHEN IS YOUR BABY DUE?' This was accompanied by elaborate miming, which ranged from pointing theatrically at my tummy to rocking an imaginary baby, and covered the eventuality that there may have been a deaf patron in the cafe who had perhaps missed the loud, verbal questioning.

I can usually laugh at anything, especially myself, and there would have been a time when I'd have dined out on this story, but this was different. I'd always intended to return to Appledore stronger, slimmer, successful, it had been my dream – but instead I'd come back feeling like a failure. I hadn't made it in London and I was now so fat some even thought I was pregnant!

I stood in the cafe, shaking my head; 'No… I'm not… expecting…' I said. The woman's embarrassment at this was even worse than the pitying look that accompanied her red face and I could feel myself tearing up. I left the counter, escaping the woman while Sue took over, apparently unaware of the drama. I wiped tables and tried to make myself busy and disappeared among the customers. I know it's crazy, I hated myself because I was fat and someone had, once again, pointed this out to me. But in my anguish, I had this urge to do what I'd always done and turned to the one thing that gave me comfort. I tried to resist, but soon found myself wandering the kitchen like a feral beast seeking its prey and opening fridges and cupboards. I was a heat-seeking missile, seeking out everything containing fat, carbs and calories – everything I'd tried unsuccessfully to deny myself since I was ten years old. Cheese, bread rolls, cream, chocolate, cake… this was the double-edged sword of working in a cafe, it wasn't just the ice cream. All these delicious foods were always present tempting me – and always there like a big warm hug when I needed it – like now.

I slathered the soft white bread with salty butter and piled on slices of creamy, tangy cheese, adding a little sweet, fruity chutney (it may have been an urgent, emotional need, but cheese still needed chutney, I wasn't a total animal). As the soft roll hit my mouth, I felt my heart swell, my muscles stopped aching, my body went into a state of relaxed pleasure and I forgot about everything. All that mattered was eating that soft roll, and what to eat next, and it didn't take long to find myself at the dessert fridge. I opened it up, the light came on and I swear I heard angels sing as that halo of light hit me.

Pouring cream on chocolate cake, I tasted the deep comfort of rich, creamy cheesecake and temporarily forgot about the bullies at school. The unrelenting sweetness of chocolate smothered my mother's 'fat' accusations and the thick, cool cream soothed away the little boy's comment from the previous day, and the pregnancy enquiring customer. I put the kettle on, always a comfort at times like this, and a chance to take a moment out and either stop myself or carry on. But the sound of the water boiling drowned out the voice in my head telling me to stop. Hot coffee needed company, so I headed for the rows of doughnuts made fresh that morning by Marco, and I sank my teeth into the sugary crisp, yielding to soft squidgy dough weeping with raspberry jam.

As I finished the doughnut, I felt the familiar shadow come down over me, and here were my old friends – guilt, nausea and self-loathing. Why did I do this to myself?

Being mistaken for someone whose baby was apparently due imminently had upset me. I'd hoped my pink uniform at work was flattering and stylishly covered my increasing waist, but clearly I looked like a big, expectant pink marshmallow behind the ice cream counter. Instead of being rational and considering cutting down on the stuff that made me so happy – yet unhappy

– my instinct had been to hide under a duvet of sugary carbs. Surely having been upset by a comment regarding my weight the natural response should have been to turn away from food, the source of my problem? The irony was, I desperately wanted to be slim, always had, more than anything else, but I'd never quite managed it. And here I was, a million diets later, still fighting this demon inside me, while wiping the sugar from my mouth, syrupy sweetness of doughnut made cloying by the salt from my tears. I turned to see Karla standing in the kitchen doorway, the look on her face said it all. I quickly busied myself wiping down surfaces, pretending the cake crumbs were someone else's.

'You okay, Dani? I was in the queue, I heard what happened, I could see you were upset, thought I'd give you a little time alone. People are stupid,' she sighed.

'No, I'M stupid,' I said, tears forming in my throat. 'It's not her fault I'm fat, it's mine.'

She smiled; 'Don't beat yourself up. You've made the first move to changing your life – you've come here.'

'I thought moving here I could be a different person, a better person. And then I find myself back in the kitchen eating bad food and failing again. I just feel like an idiot.'

She walked towards me, concern on her face; 'Dani, you might think you've failed…'

'Don't tell me I haven't.'

'Okay, you failed, if you didn't want or intend to eat that cake,' she said, pointing to the remains of a large portion of chocolate fudge cake, 'then yeah, you failed, girlfriend. But failure isn't a one-time thing; success doesn't have an end date. You only fail when you give up hope… you're thirty-nine and there's still a bit of life left,' she smiled. 'You're too young to give up hope.'

'Oh I know, but I'm not a patient Karla, your psycho mumbo-jumbo might work on kids, but I'm a big girl… a BIG girl,' I said, spreading my arms wide to indicate enormity.

She smiled, as much as she knew me, I knew her too.

'Look, I wanted to be slim and healthy, come rolling back into town looking like a supermodel and throw a big fortieth birthday party looking fabulous.'

She laughed.

'Hey, it's not *that* funny,' I laughed.

'I'm not laughing at the idea of you being a supermodel – though I'll admit that *is* funny. But when you decided to leave London you told me your dream was to live here and work at the cafe – you ticked that box. So stop putting pressure on yourself, there's plenty of time for more box-ticking, just make the next one easy on yourself, have an incentive – use your birthday party in a positive way. Okay, you won't be skinny by October, but you could be *skinnier*, so stop telling yourself "I won't be slim enough for my birthday," use it positively; "I could be slimm*er* and health*ier* and happ*ier* with myself on my fortieth birthday." Forget the supermodel shit as that is not going to happen,' she added cheekily.

'Rude, little do you realise there's a lithe and lovely Cindy Crawford inside this pink blancmange,' I laughed.

Despite my light-hearted approach, I knew deep down this situation wasn't funny. My doctor in London had told me I needed to lose weight and if I carried on eating and not exercising, given my lifestyle and my family history (my dad died of a heart attack at fifty-two) then I may not see my fiftieth birthday. My fortieth birthday was less than three months away, and this had been a wake-up call – well, for about five hours when I ate nothing but kale, then gave up and ate four doughnuts. But I knew if I didn't do it now, I never would. What had happened in the last two days could bring me down, or they could be what spurred me on, in the same way Karla suggested I use my birthday in a positive way, and not as a reminder of failure.

As much as I wanted to be in control and be a healthy weight, so far I'd never wanted it as much as I wanted a six pack of glazed doughnuts. But now I could run along the shore each morning before limbering up on the beach and taking a brisk, bracing swim in the sea… if I wanted to. The problem was, that I didn't; in fact the baggage I'd taken away with me was now back, and bigger than ever! Appledore was already showing on my hips, and the very thought of doing anything brisk before 9 a.m. terrified me. But this wasn't the end, this was just the beginning. This time things were going to be different, because I'd come back to where it all began and from here I could take control finally. I would banish the distant past and use it to grow stronger knowing I could change and be anything and anyone I wanted to be. Gone would be the old dusty life, I was going to open the windows and let the fresh air in, embracing the changes and new challenges.

This was my fresh start, a new job, a new flat, a brand-new life – so why not a new body? I hated feeling out of breath taking the stairs up to my flat and I'd hated being told I was VERY

lowed to meet 'the other woman'. I realised as I grew older that Dad leaving had been Mum's worst fear; 'if only she were fat,' she'd said once, like that would make his abandonment easier. It didn't occur to Mum that perhaps this other woman was more fun, less preoccupied with making everything perfect, including herself. Mum saw my father's departure from the marriage as the result of a ten-pound weight gain when she sprained her ankle – and refused to believe it was anything more. I wondered if she blamed me – I certainly did, after all why would he leave Mum, she was slim and beautiful? I was the disappointment, the overweight child who couldn't control her appetite. Mum meant well, I suppose, by putting me on a strict diet – but this turned out not to be the best way of dealing with what came to be known as 'Dani's problem'. Food suddenly became forbidden fruit – especially the stuff my mother deemed 'bad', which made it all the more tempting.

'If you lose a few pounds I'll buy you a pretty dress,' she'd slurred, 'and a birthday party too.' When you're ten years old, the implication of this 'reward' for losing weight is that you're not slim enough to deserve a pretty dress or a party. It sets you up for a lifetime of feeling unworthy, undeserved and unloved – and makes you prey for every manipulative bad boy that happens to pass by.

Hearing the recent comments in the cafe about my weight reminded me of all the times as a child I'd been made to feel like I didn't fit in. I was the fat girl whose father had walked out, the only one left when choosing for netball sides at school and the teenager who never received a valentine. Despite my mother's promises, I never had a birthday party – and each year I assumed it was because I'd never lost enough weight. It didn't occur to me until recently that it probably had more to do with the fact my mother was never sober long enough to organise a birthday party for her only child. That's why this birthday party – my first and my fortieth – had to be very special and I had to feel at my best. I would lose some weight, wear red and be the centre of attention, the popular, attractive woman I was always meant to be.

'You've done a brave thing coming back here,' Karla said, 'and after everything that happened you have to be prepared to face stuff you haven't faced for years. So be kind to yourself… and so what if someone thinks you're pregnant and a little kid says the "f" word. It doesn't define you, Dani.'

'You're right, but I can't help but be affected by it. The comments about my weight hurt, because they're honest.'

Karla said it wasn't just about 'diets' it was about changing my life, but in order to do that I had to deal with why I'd become like this. Perhaps it was time now to face the past, because only then would I be able to deal with the future?

Later that night I made an eating plan, and vowed to exercise at least three times a week. This time, I was determined, apart from the fact I didn't want to go through the tortuous embarrassment of complete strangers passing comments, this was about my health. I could just about get away with stuffing myself on the sofa (sofa-stuffing) in my twenties and thirties, but approaching my forties with high blood pressure was positively dangerous. I had to take control, understand myself and my actions, consider what motivated me and how I could live healthily without making my life hell. To anyone who's never had a weight problem it seems crazy, how could I do this to myself? I know, I know, I find it hard to understand myself, but that's because it's about more than ice cream and chocolate. It wouldn't be easy to abandon the sheer lusciousness of a double chocolate brownie drenched in white chocolate ice cream but, in truth, the brownie was not my friend. The brownie was killing me.

On Monday morning I woke up feeling hungry as usual. I could smell warm, yeasty bread seeping through from the cafe and longed to cram a fresh warm bagel into my mouth. It was Marco's fault; he was the rudest, most miserable person I'd ever met, but he baked the best bread. But this was the first day of my diet and I wouldn't be swayed by Marco's warm bagels slathered in cold, salty butter.

'I wish I could be like you and eat anything I liked,' I said to Karla as she put two slices of bread in the toaster.

'Not any more. Hell, since I had the kids I only have to look at a bloody Kit Kat and I put on half a stone, but being a healthy weight is more important to me than the temporary rush I get from chocolate. People choose who they want to be, Dani. Perhaps you're just meant to be you?'

'Fat?'

'No, fun and bubbly and…'

'Fat.'

We were both laughing now; we always ended up laughing when we were together.

I made coffee and handed her a mug, watching her eat the hot, buttery toast and wondering if I should have a piece with no butter. I hadn't thought this through, I had nothing in the kitchen that would constitute a low fat, healthy breakfast.

I needed to shop for this diet – at the moment I had a bread-bin full of carbs and a freezer stacked with ice cream, neither of which featured on my 'Flabuless Forty' diet planner.

'What about just eating three healthy meals a day and doing some exercise?' Karla suddenly suggested, like it was a revelation.

'Oh that's brilliant, why didn't I think of that?' I said sarcastically. 'I mean, all these years I've been overweight and I'd never even thought of it,' I added, wondering if she'd notice if I finished off the tiny bit of buttered toast left on her plate.

'I can see you lusting after my leftovers,' she said.

God she was good.

'Mmm, it's a fatties' phenomenon,' I replied. 'Leftovers lusting is a clinical condition, surprised you haven't heard of it, seeing as you're a psychologist.'

I loved Karla, but even she couldn't understand the depths to which I would sink in the pursuit of a sugar/carb fix. I was like a drug addict, secretly ordering pizza at 2 a.m. and telling the guy to 'meet me round the back,' buying groceries with one bag containing 'good food' and another 'bad food'. The 'bad' one would be secreted in the bottom of my wardrobe and redeemed when I was alone and in need of succour. I'd done this from an early age, it made me feel secure to know I had a stash of chocolate and crisps in my wardrobe – and Domino's on speed dial.

It was difficult to explain this complex relationship with food and emotion to anyone who'd never felt like this about food, like Karla for instance.

She might have been a psychologist, but there were times she just didn't seem to comprehend my madness. Yes, I wanted to be slim, but I wanted that bag of doughnuts more… and yes there was more than one doughnut in the bag – I wasn't an amateur! She was a wonderful friend, but the day Karla said she couldn't eat a whole Mars Bar and asked if I'd like to share one, I knew we were on a different page. I'd said a firm no but told her I wanted to slap her in the face because anyone who said they couldn't eat a 'whole' Mars Bar was either lying, or just not trying. As I pointed out (sarcastically) I couldn't eat one either – I had to eat a whole pack of four.

'What about joining a gym?' she asked now as we sipped on our coffee. Again I felt the urge to slap her but restrained myself and lunged at her bit of leftover toast; it was the only lunge I did that day.

'Join a gym?' I said, finishing her toast with a defiant glare. I stopped for a second to savour the deliciousness, moved remembering the good times me and butter and toast had had together over the years. Could we really say goodbye?

'Don't tell me to join a gym,' I said, trying not to think of the loaf in the breadbin just waiting to become more toast lavished with butter. 'I joined a gym in 2004 – I paid for a year's membership, and I went there once! It's actually in *The Guinness Book of Records* as the most expensive gym workout EVER.'

'Oh you do exaggerate, Dani.'

'I don't… it's just that you can't actually comprehend what it's like to be me.'

'Have you thought of hula-hooping?' she said, ignoring my comment.

'Never. And if I ever did I would have to seek professional help.'

'It's supposed to be fun.'

'Fun? Waggling a hoop around your middle vigorously to keep it up? Life's short, why would anyone do that? On me it would be a belt anyway, no room for waggling, so please stop talking.'

Karla shrugged; 'I'm only trying to come up with ideas. Anyway, less talking about it, let's get out there and get started.'

'Mmm.' I was still thinking of buttery toast, buttery crumpets… anything that could provide a warm surface for butter really.

'I mean now. Come on let's take a walk along the beach.' She leapt up with such vigour it made me start slightly – it was far too early for this kind of sudden movement.

I felt quite grumpy and didn't actually want to leave my seat, but having made a big announcement about changing my life I had to show Karla that I meant this. If I didn't she'd go on and on about it. And a stroll along the beach chatting sounded like a nice, civilised thing to do, it was exercise, but not the sweaty, wheezy kind of exercise I hated. So I put on my flip-flops, we headed downstairs and came out behind the cafe.

Seeing Marco toiling away inside, I gave him a friendly wave – which he completely ignored, which amused Karla.

'Come on, stop dawdling and pretending to wave to everyone, we need to get a move on,' she said, crossing the road ahead of me. I waited for a couple of cars to slowly pass and I strolled across, thinking this wasn't too bad after all.

'Dani, I said let's go for a walk, not a wander,' she was saying, as I caught up with her on the pavement.

'I'm power walking,' I said. I really thought I was.

'No, you're not, you're wandering. Just look at that view!' she said, standing there in tight jeans, her hands on small hips gazing out to sea.

We stood together looking ahead, both admiring the loveliness of a seaside morning. The sky was blue, a fresh breeze was blowing from the beach, and seagulls squawked above. This was better than grimy old London, and regardless of old ghosts hanging around here, this was enough to give me the spur I needed. I would be fighting fit and ready for whatever the past had to throw up.

'Can you see over there… that built-up little island-like place?' Karla asked and started walking briskly, while I ran alongside to keep up.

I nodded; 'It's Instow, you need to get a ferry to go there.'

'Let's walk as near to it as we can.'

'It's miles,' I said, wondering if this walk was going to be as civilised as I'd hoped. I'd envisaged going down to the seafront, dipping my toes in the sea, and retiring back to the cafe for a well-earned mid-morning snack.

'It's not miles, come on,' she said, and set off again at quite a pace.

This wasn't what I'd had in mind at all and my T-shirt dress and flip-flops were hardly suitable attire for what seemed to be turning into a bloody marathon. 'Hey, wait for me,' I shouted, tripping over my flip-flops and thinking why did bloody exercise involve sweat and speed? Why wasn't sitting at tables drinking coffee called exercise? I'd be good at that. I kept thinking there must be easier ways to get thinner; I'd read somewhere that drinking coffee can actually help burn fat, admittedly if drunk black and without any accompanying cake, but still…

'You've got to make your heart beat fast at least once a day,' Karla was calling enthusiastically from some way ahead as I staggered along the beach in an ungainly fashion.

'I can make my heart beat faster with a poster of Ryan Gosling,' I shouted back as I tried to catch up. 'And it's more fun than this. Don't go so fast, Karla, I'm dying here.' I wanted to collapse. I had only run a little way, but I just wasn't used to this kind of exertion – well, *any* kind of exertion to be honest.

Karla laughed and carried on marching. 'You gotta move it to lose it, girl,' she was shouting, in a really annoying way. She was also alerting the whole bloody beach to the fact that a fat girl was waddling their way. I flounced (yes, flounced) past a group of sniggering teenagers who shouted something about 'the size of that arse', but I kept going. Yet more people who felt it necessary to point out the bloody obvious. I heard them laughing in my wake and longed to kick sand in their faces and tell them to sod off. But I knew from bitter experience at school that when you tell bullies what you think of them, they're keen to tell you what they think of you – in detail – and it hurts. My face burned and I felt the well of tears begin to erupt – how could I lose weight if people were going to criticise me during the damned process? I felt humiliated, tired and hopeless, and I'd only been walking a few minutes. This wasn't the answer. I shouted to Karla, who was now way ahead of me down the beach, but she didn't hear, so I just crashed there and sat on the ground until she eventually turned round and ran back.

'Sorry,' I said, as she approached me.

'Why are you sorry?' she said, holding her foot in her hand to stretch her leg. It was a simple movement for Karla, but I watched in awe, I'd never held my own foot, probably not since I was in the womb.

'I'm sorry because I couldn't keep up, I'm rubbish at this.' I felt tearful, stupid, a great big lump unable to do the simplest of things, I hated my body and I hated myself.

'Dani, this is the first time you've done a proper walk since… I don't know when. I run every morning, I'm used to it – you just need to fit exercise into your daily life, do your personal best and stop comparing yourself to other people.'

'I know, I know, I just don't think I want to exercise in public,' I said, watching the group of teenagers further down the promenade laughing and messing as if they hadn't got a care in the world.

'Dani, it's not going to be easy, but you must try not to be put off by things and people that don't matter. I'm proud of what you're doing, you're making a change – so stop trying to sabotage your own efforts. Today you came out here and you walked, it doesn't matter how far or how fast, you did it.'

Karla was right, given the choice I wouldn't have left the comfort of the warm toast-scented kitchen. But I did, and now I needed to take more steps.

We walked back to the flat and I waddled upstairs as Karla skipped. We were both the same age by a few months, but I couldn't help but feel like her fat auntie. I was out of breath when I reached the top stair and it scared me, I thought again about what the doctor said about me not making fifty and felt mild panic rising.

Having skipped up the stairs, she jumped on the spot at the top and once inside was dashing around the flat to find the mugs and put the kettle on. Meanwhile, I lay prostrate on the rug, directing her around the flat like a mad satnav and wondering, not for the first time if people could die from 'stairs'.

'Dani,' she called from the kitchen, 'I'm glad you're committed, and I'm with you, but in the past you've set yourself up to fail.'

I knew she was right, but didn't know why. I'd started many diets with real hope and determination, only to fall at the first hurdle.

'I wonder if it's because you've tried to lose weight for a man,' Karla said. 'Sometimes it's been for a boyfriend, and sometimes you've tried to lose weight if there's a man on the horizon… someone you fancy.' She was now standing in the kitchen doorway, her head to one side, looking down at the blob on the rug.

'No I haven't,' I said, my life flashing before me, each diet connected to a love interest. The cabbage soup diet, the mayo diet, the mushroom diet, the standing on your bloody head so you don't eat diet – all for someone I loved from a distance and hoped to snag, or a man I had already snagged who seemed to be losing interest.

'Okay, sometimes, in the past, I'll admit I tried to lose weight for a man…'

'Yeah and if you get the man you put weight on again because you're happy and content – for a while. And if you don't get the man, you put weight on because you feel like you failed, so what's the use?'

'Thank you doctor,' I said, from my prone position on the floor as she went back into the kitchen. 'My relationship with Ryan Gosling wasn't about losing weight – he'd have me whatever I weighed, he just never calls me back,' I laughed.

Despite my joking though, I thought perhaps she might be right, again. Was that why I'd never managed to lose weight in the past, because it was always for someone else? I'd read articles like this in my diet magazines but it never occurred to me that's what I'd done. But now I realised the fact I'd been trying to change for someone else was my whole problem. I'd tried to be someone else all my life and it hadn't worked, this time I had to be me, but more determined, more single-minded. I wanted to live a full and happy life, I didn't want to leave it all behind in my forties as my mother had done. I'll admit I love a bit of drama, and have often been heard to say, 'it's a matter of life and death', even when talking about a haircut or a new dress – but this really was.

'Karla,' I said, still lying on the rug, 'I'm going to do it. I'm going to lose weight, get fit and be the slimmest, sparkliest forty-something in the world…'

I'd never been the pretty one, the cute one, the way I always stood behind people in photographs was the way I'd lived my life up to this point. I'd always stayed low on everyone's radar so they didn't feel the need to make a hurtful comment, or glance at each other 'discreetly', when I'd known full well the meaning of that glance. Achieving better health and a better body would mean more confidence, and I wasn't going to spend my forties hiding any more.

'Good, I've been telling you for years you can be the star of your own show,' Karla said as she walked in with two mugs of coffee. God bless that woman, she'd heard it a million times and was still prepared to take me seriously. 'If it's about you and about being healthy and happy then great.'

'Yep, I'm doing this for me,' I rolled over, onto my tummy, pretending this was an easy move but having to grab the sofa to stop myself from rolling continuously as my weight gathered momentum and I almost knocked Karla off her skinny little feet.

'Out of the way or I'll steamroller you,' I laughed, as she delicately sidestepped me and sat down on the sofa with both hands full.

'I want to be able to walk up the stairs without having to call the fire brigade,' I joked. 'I want to be able to run to catch a bus, to skip everywhere without panting and falling over.' I sighed; 'I want to... actually *like* myself.'

'Oh babe, you don't like yourself?' Karla was saying, watching me with what looked like macabre fascination as I attempted to negotiate my way up off the floor and onto the sofa.

'No. I hate who I am, I hate the self-loathing and fear of imminent death that comes after the delirious joy of a gallon of ice cream taken liberally in a prone position. I want to walk with a sexy swing, not a humping gait...' I landed with a thud on the sofa and took my coffee from Karla.

'One word – yoga.'

'Another word – NO.' Surely, she was joking. Had she not just seen me sprawled on the floor trying to push myself up to my knees in my very own yoga position – the downward pig.

'It's done wonders for me,' she said, stretching out her slim arms like a ballerina. 'It's all about your core; if you get that right you'll exercise right and it does wonders for your balance.'

'No, I can't do all that hippy-dippy downward dogging and facing the moon…'

'The sun.'

'Well I won't be facing anything. I've tried all the gimmicks, they don't last because I either get bored or seriously injure myself. I don't want to go into it, but my pelvic floor has never been the same since the incident with the resistance band.'

'Yeah, I know, and that Aqua Spinning Class.' She was shaking her head at the memory, her face a mixture of horror and disappointment.

'I thought it would be easier than just spinning, the water takes the strain, I assumed it would be like spinning, underwater.'

'It is.'

'Not when I did it, I almost drowned. I died and saw a strange light coming towards me…'

'That was the instructor trying to find you… and the other members of the class you took down with you.'

'Only two others, anyway, stop nit-picking and reminding me of my horrific exercising past. Human beings aren't made to ride bikes under water – in my case human beings aren't meant to ride bikes full stop. So my plan is this – a brisk daily walk along the front under cover of darkness followed by a session going up and down the dreaded stairs. No more gimmicks.'

'Oh God, do you remember when you did that twerking thing?'

I nodded; 'The "twerkshop" wasn't my finest hour. My bum managed to knock out most of the other students, I couldn't go back again, the company wasn't insured for the kind of carnage I could cause. And then there was the hurt locker that was "Diva-fit", emulating the famous moves of dancing divas somewhere in Shoreditch,' I shuddered at the memory. '"All the Single Ladies" routine did for me, I've never walked the same since – every time I hear "put a ring on it," I want to vomit. Beyoncé's got a lot to answer for.'

Karla was giggling. 'Oh, Dani, it's not like you haven't tried, in fact you often throw yourself into things with too much gusto.'

'Mmm well, no more, that's it. From now on, no more mad exercising and no more crazy diets.'

'Okay,' she said, 'I'll get the gallon bottle of vinegar and maple syrup and cayenne pepper ready for that, shall I?'

'No, this time I mean it. No more silly diets, no binges, no blaming my deceased mother, my ex-boyfriend or the mean girls at school who called me "Piglicious". I paused, my brow furrowed at the memory, what bitches! I was so over them all now, but still people like that leave a trace behind them and they'd shaped who I was.

'So tonight let's go out for one last meal before I start my diet,' I said.

'You're always having "last meals",' Karla pointed out. 'And weren't you supposed to start your diet today?'

'I need to build up to it. And the best way to do that is to drink coffee and eat double chocolate chip cookies with my best friend, oh and finish the last of the doughnuts.'

'You don't need dough...'

'I DO. If I wake up in the morning and there's a doughnut or a cookie in this flat I will sniff it out and have to eat it. So I'll clear the fridge out tonight.'

'With bin liners?'

'No, with my mouth.' I gave her a 'don't be silly look', reached for the biscuit tin and munched on a delicious chocolate cookie. 'I'll start tomorrow,' I announced through biscuit crumbs.

'Instead of eating it all, why don't you just throw it away?' she asked.

'Mmm, I could,' I said, still savouring the chocolatey hit and not really listening.

'DO it!' she yelled.

This shocked me slightly and I reluctantly took the biscuit from my lips, gave it one last, lingering look and hurled it into the waste-paper bin. And after a few seconds, when I'd come to terms with what had just happened, it felt surprisingly good. I'd controlled the cookie, and despite its double choc chips and delicious, squidgy interior – for once, it hadn't controlled me.

As you will have gathered, this was by no means my first rodeo when it came to weight-loss action and my diary was filled with detailed notes of every diet I'd ever attempted over the years. Looking through it later that night when Karla was asleep, I realised how connected the diets were to men – the ones in my life or at least the men I wanted to be in my life. I lay there in the darkness going through all the heartache, the self-destruction, the starvation followed by binges, and the epic fails of my dieting past, determined not to make the same mistakes again. Yes, this time *would* be different, this wouldn't be for a man, there were none in my life – this was for me.

And the following morning I was as good as my word, telling myself this was for me, and avoiding warm brioche squidged with ice cream in the cafe and going for crispbread instead. But as I chewed on that dry crispbread I faced a weak moment and asked myself if I could really do this again.

Being a wonderful, insightful friend (and knowing how feeble I was in the face of sugar and carbs), Karla had detected a slight change in my 'can do' attitude from the previous evening.

'So you're going ahead with a birthday party?' she asked.

I nodded; 'It's quite exciting actually, and a good incentive to lose weight,' I said, imagining me standing in the middle of the cafe looking like a film star.

'You can invite the mean girls from school, and the nice girls too of course,' she said, fully on board, not doubting me for one moment or trying to rein me in.

'Yeah, all those people who made me feel like I couldn't achieve anything… like I wasn't good enough. Mmm, I want to see Kathy Parkes who deliberately left me until last when they were choosing sides – I hope she's fat.'

'Me too. But you won't be – you'll be strutting round showing everyone that ever doubted you how fabulous you are.'

'Sadly, my mother isn't with us any more, but I'd love Sylvia to see me strut,' I nodded.

'Yeah, I know, but it's not just our mummies who make us mad. I think if you can meet some of the people who hurt you, then you might be able to work on that self-doubt. These people are still in your head, and they're holding you back. You want approval from people who aren't even worth seeking it from, they didn't care about you, so why care about them? You're not frightened fat little Dani any more.'

'Who are you kidding?'

'You hide behind jokes and humour, you're funny – but inside you're hurting. It's time to let go of the past Dani, so you can stop hurting and move on.'

It was useful having a friend in the profession, but as I said, she could sometimes overanalyse stuff.

'I'm not saying you're mad or there's anything wrong with you, but you've stepped back into a past that made you unhappy, so be kind to yourself'; she sat facing me at the kitchen table, waiting for a response in that 'therapist' way she often did.

'I get it… and as for the mean girls at school, I so need to have them at my party so I can shake some of those bitches off.'

'Exactly,' she smiled, 'out with the old and in with the new,' and we drank our morning coffee in companionable silence watching the sun come up over the sea. I thought about how Jude and I used to sit on the dunes as the sun rose, and I remembered the first time I saw his face, curly black hair, pale blue eyes and the cheekiest grin. He was just seventeen but an 'older man' to my sixteen years. He was my first love, and made such a huge impression on me, as first loves do, but all the lovely memories are bittersweet, and when I think of him, even now, all these years later, it hurts like hell.

It was my first summer working at Caprioni's Ice Cream Cafe. Sophia, the owner, had taken me on during their busy months to help her make the ice cream. I loved doing this, I even invented some of my own. When we ran out of strawberry ice cream once, I blended frozen strawberries with fresh cream and made what came to be known as, 'Dani's emergency strawberry ice cream'. Sophia always said I had a talent for mixing, and Jude said my 'emergency' ice cream was the best he'd ever tasted. He would wink at me as he flirted with the other girls and I would blush behind the coffee machine. I was still chubby, but my puppy fat had turned into curves and I knew he was interested. I could tell by the way he looked at me, creating a spark of electricity only the two of us were aware of. I wasn't confident with boys, but I had an instinct and would open my pink uniform blouse a button lower. I'd had a lonely childhood and becoming a teenager had been no different, I hadn't had many suitors so was flattered by his attentions.

I remember it so clearly, that first summer together, Whitney Houston singing, 'I Will Always Love You' was constantly on the jukebox in the cafe, and even now, when I hear it I think of him. He always bought a Coke and a cone, he varied the flavour, never vanilla and he never stuck to the same thing, he bored easily. I remember the girls I worked with saying they could tell what a boy would be like in bed by the flavours he chose and the way he ate his ice cream.

My best friend Jane was very experienced in that department and if a boy came into the cafe and ate ice cream she would give a muttered running commentary of how this revealed his sexual technique. I blushed at some of the stuff she came out with, partly because I was embarrassed, but mainly because I hadn't a clue what she was talking about. But I remember watching Jude eat a chocolate sundae and wishing it was me.

Sometimes Jane and the others would tease me about Jude; in that awful teenage jungle they didn't believe someone like him would ever fancy someone like me. I'd liked him from afar since I was about fourteen and everyone knew – including him.

The girls made a big fuss about my crush, and if he was in the cafe that they'd heard he fancied me. They hadn't heard any such thing, they were just doing what teenage girls do, lying to each other and trying it on for size. But I had a secret weapon: to girls, I was overweight, and would never be a supermodel, but to boys, I was womanly. There weren't many girls of sixteen with large breasts, and until the other girls caught up, there was a window in the summer of 1993 when I became very popular with the opposite sex.

I sometimes wish now I'd made the most of it, but burgeoning breasts and boys' hormones are wasted on the young. Besides, I only had eyes for Jude, and when he turned up at the cafe one Sunday evening and said he wanted to ask me something, I almost died.

'Will you go out with me?' he asked, just like that. I almost hyperventilated with shock and pleasure and the girls were aghast, even my best friend Jane was jealous. She started making barbed comments about my weight and telling me that Jude was a cheater and to 'watch out'. It wasn't said from a place of kindness or caring, so I stopped caring what Jane said, and when I stayed out all night on the beach drinking beer and swimming naked with Jude, I didn't care what my mother said either. She'd tried to stop me, saying I had to be in by 10 p.m., but when I said 'no' there'd been a shift in the dynamics. I'd never defied her before and she didn't know how to handle it, I was surprised I got away with it, but as long as I did, I just kept staying out. My evenings spent in front of the TV while Mum got slowly sozzled were now replaced with long, hot summer nights with Jude on the beach and it felt like real freedom.

I remember calling Jane and whispering down the phone; 'We did it!'

'Did he put it *right* in?' she asked doubting me, because sex was Jane's arena not mine. Until Jude, I was the chaste, clever one who read books and did Jane's homework for her when she'd been out too late. Suddenly the roles were reversed, I was in a steady relationship, and I knew all about 'positions' and 'techniques', or implied that I did. I'd had sex with Jude, but in reality it was one step beyond a fumble in the sand dunes and I hadn't a clue what was going on. I just lay back and he climbed on top, it was over in seconds, but I loved his arms around me, his kisses and that I finally had someone to call my own.

I wondered now, twenty years later, if Jude had changed. Was he all grown up or still the boy I'd fallen in love with – the same boy who broke my heart?

The Ice Cream Cafe had always been my sanctuary as a young girl, and even as an adult I'd returned here in my head when things were tough in the big city. But now it was finally time to face the memories of those strawberry ice cream summers, even that final one, when I left Appledore with a mashed-up heart.

Jude had an impact on me, on my life, in a way no young love should, but it often does. After him, I vowed never to give my heart to someone who treated it like a piñata, and it had made me wary, too wary perhaps? I still hadn't found that person, and I may never find him, but as soon as I'd returned to the cafe I'd thought of Jude writing my name on his sundae in strawberry sauce. Perhaps that was as good as it would ever get for me? And that was okay because I didn't need a man in my life, I needed a job I loved, some friends and a nice place to live. I had all those things, now I just needed to lose some weight and learn to love myself.

'So a fortieth partay?' Karla asked, bringing me back into the present once more.

I nodded; 'Yeah… and this place would be perfect, and we could spill out into the back yard. I'll ask Ella, but I'm sure she'll be fine with it.'

I loved this idea, it would be the end of October and out of season, so would be fine to open it up for a private party in the evening.

'I'll come back for your birthday, Dave'll be ready for another "Dad and kids" weekend, I can feel it,' she laughed. 'I'll help you decorate the place with bunting and fairy lights… lots and lots of fairy lights.'

It felt right to be back here now, the year I turned forty, a place where I'd spent my childhood summers. It was time to lose weight, take back my life, deal with the past and face the future. And I couldn't wait!

Chapter Three

The Raw Egg and Milk Diet

Diet Diary: June 2003; Had a crush on a guy who worked on a dairy farm, this diet promised 7lbs off in 7 days. Started Monday with raw eggs whipped into milk, vomited for the rest of the day. I lost 2 pounds. He ran off with the farm hand.

It was lovely spending a few days with my bestie. I loved showing her the beautiful little fishing village of my home, and seeing it through her city-jaded eyes reminded me I'd done the right thing to move here. Karla marvelled at seagulls, at pastel-painted houses strung with bunting, little boats on the water, and even the shape of stones on the beach. It made me see the place afresh and appreciate it even more. I'd worried that perhaps leaving London was simply running away, but as Karla pointed out, coming back was the brave thing to do. I now needed to make a commitment to my life here – there was no more running away (or waddling), whatever might happen.

Once Karla had left to go back home to London, I knew I was on my own and went straight to my planner and made a shopping list of good healthy foods. This wasn't as simple as I'd thought – there was a lifetime of bad habits and bad shopping to eradicate – and I was still convinced that a Chocolate Orange could be counted as one of my five a day. At work, I had to keep reminding myself that I couldn't just dip into the ice cream. I had to recommend flavours to customers so needed to make sure I was familiar with each flavour, but that didn't mean three scoops on a large waffle. To take my mind off ice cream and doughnuts and pizza and… I googled for advice and the list of tortuous ways to eradicate unwanted fat made me feel quite panicked – and peckish.

And along the way I felt like my life was flashing before me. It was official, I had been on every single diet known to man. I still baulked at the tapeworm diet – but, quite honestly, if I was guaranteed a beautiful body I'd have closed my eyes and thought of wearing Victoria's Secret's smallest as the worm wriggled down my gullet. So why, you might ask was I still fat? I had a rather naive belief that the diet would work immediately and when nothing much had changed within the first few days or weeks I would decide it wasn't working and be back to square one. If only I applied the same theory to dieting as I did to relationships, believing if I stuck with a man long enough, however mean, stupid, selfish and pointless he was, it would, in time, work. It never worked – on both counts. However, there was something about the air in Appledore, the promise of something sparkling on the water, there was, finally, hope.

This time I wasn't going to starve myself so I could be who I thought someone else wanted me to be. I was going to eat well and move to lower my blood pressure, and if, as a side effect, I looked better, then great. But this was about me taking care of myself for a change, because if I didn't, no one else would, so I took the bull by the horns and did something I'd vowed never to do after the last futile experience: I joined a gym. Again. I tried to manage my own expectations and not go hell for leather on the first visit so that I would never darken the gym doorstep again. And as I slipped into twenty-five yards of black jersey (my workout 'gear'), I told myself if I attended a session only twice it was an improvement on the last time. Well, only time. I could have paid a mortgage on a penthouse apartment for the amount I'd allowed the gym in London to direct debit from my account for twelve months. It was a tidy sum in anyone's money to stand on a treadmill for all of three minutes… even if I hadn't actually turned it on.

Standing in the changing rooms of the 'You Work It Out' gym, I had a few wobbly moments. This was what I wanted, a slim, firm, healthy body – but was this how I wanted to get it? The gym was not my natural home and the smell of sweaty trainers and steam hanging in the air took me back to school, eleven years old, waiting in line to be picked for the netball team. Kathy Parkes was the team captain and official total bitch from primary school right through to sixth form, and seemed to find endless time in her own schooldays to make mine a misery. One by one she would choose, first the sporty girls, then the popular girls, then the pretty ones. And always, always, there were two of us left – me and Leandra Rowbottom. 'Lumpy', as she was known, was big, monosyllabic and mean. But Lumpy had one thing over me – she could catch a ball. And so I was left, the last girl standing, offered as a freakish booby prize to the remaining team, now murmuring their disapproval. 'Oh shit we've got Piglicious, we'll never win with her,' the whisper I was meant to overhear, as reluctantly I joined 'my team'.

Almost thirty years later, I could now see Kathy and her girls in these changing rooms. They weren't literally the same pretty, popular, sporty girls, yet they were made from the same stuff. Just feeling them around me sliding into Lycra and smoothing their perfect ponytails made me nervous and sad. I hurt for the child I'd been. I had few friends back then, and at home I was alone, my mother's only companion being the bottle.

And now, here I was, putting myself through this voluntarily, was I mad? I'd spent longer than I needed forcing on my shiny new trainers, but I couldn't reach the shoelaces. First I tried reaching down, and when that didn't work I sat heavily on a bench in the changing rooms and attempted to bring my foot up to my knee. This made me yelp and drew unwanted attention from several scantily clad gym bunnies who asked if I was okay.

'Yes… I'm just… doing a warm-up,' I said, moving my leg up and down with my hand like I'd seen Karla do. I hoped they bought the lie, but I'd got myself so worked up my muscles had gone into spasm and I felt like a trussed-up turkey, with my leg at a strange angle, my face scarlet and my shoelaces still untied. I seriously worried if I would ever be able to release my leg to the floor again and for a few seconds considered making this an even more expensive gym membership and walking out before I'd even left the changing rooms. But I wasn't going to give in, this was ridiculous, I was behaving like a child, I wasn't back in the school gym, I was at a grown-up gym and was paying good money to be here.

So, after giving myself a stern talking-to (not aloud, that would have drawn even more unwanted attention from the scantily clad model types in my vicinity), I left the changing rooms and nervously headed towards the bit where they do stuff. On entering the workout area with a swinging ponytail (and swinging muffin top), I was amazed to see so much equipment, and so many people working hard and efficiently on that equipment. It was freakish, like they'd been born to it. Great, so I was the only novice in here tonight. However, my lack of experience wasn't the only problem, my laces were still undone and the expensive inner sole that had promised to improve my core was now throwing me forward as I walked. It was an interesting gait, and I'd hoped it was going unnoticed until one of the bloody resident trainers jogged over to ask me if I was injured.

He was dressed from head to toe in electric blue, and clearly very fit, his muscular arms emerging from under a short-sleeved T-shirt. I hid my bingo wings and gave him my biggest smile to distract his eyes from the rest of me.

'Are you suffering?' he asked again.

'You could say that,' I smiled, but it was lost on him.

I couldn't admit that I was walking strangely because I was wearing new trainers and I was too inflexible to tie my laces.

'Oh dear, you're in pain?' he said, which prompted me to go along with the charade and tell a little fib.

'Yes…' I heard myself say, 'it's my foot.'

'Ah I wondered why your laces had been left undone,' he said. 'Is that to relieve the pressure?'

'Mmmm,' I smiled, hoping this would satisfy him and he'd jog on his merry way. But no – he said it was a health and safety issue (first time I've ever been called that) and took my arm like I was ninety-four and edged me across the floor achingly slowly. As everyone watched.

I kept telling him I was fine and would just sit for a while, but he was having none of it. He toured me past the bouncing bunnies who'd just witnessed my footwear debacle in the changing rooms and I couldn't meet their eyes. I felt like I was being paraded round the area as a warning to others – 'if you don't do your workouts, you too could look like this'.

I didn't know what was worse, the fact that I now had to feign a sprained ankle or the pitying looks from 'the beautiful people' on the twenty-mile-an-hour treadmills. Seriously when did anyone ever *need* to run that fast? Did they not have cars?

Everyone was staring as I hobbled past, they'd probably never seen anyone like me, especially not here in these hallowed fitness portals. I tried to make my limp look worse than it was so they would understand what was happening and I wasn't being escorted through the area just because I was so fat and may distress the other patrons. Having said that, I reckoned these superhumans saw injury as 'a challenge'. Where I viewed a sprained ankle as a reason to sit on the sidelines with a sugary snack for shock, they probably considered it something to battle with on the cross-trainer. Awkwardly walking past all this action, their faces shimmering with pity, sweat and sanctimony, I realised not for the first time, this was not my arena. Put me in a library, a nice tea-room or a lovely dinner with friends – that's when I shone – not here among these supermodels with abs and attitude.

To my great relief, the trainer eventually lowered me onto a chair and now had a clipboard and was asking if I needed water. Water? I thought, shaking my head, if I were really injured I'd be demanding a thick shake and a bag of fries – and that would be for starters to deal with the shock. He unclicked his pen and, looking very concerned, asked if my vision was blurred.

I nodded, wanting to add that the sight of all that Lycra running at speed on the treadmills was making my vision blurred.

'Look, there's really no need for this in-depth discussion,' I said, feeling suddenly guilty that I'd fibbed. We all do it, tell little porkies to save embarrassment or someone's feelings. They are usually harmless, but mine often had a tendency to escalate into something more. So much for my determination, for my 'brand new Dani' who was going to smash this. I felt a wave of guilt at letting myself down. Coming here to the church of fitness among all these perfect people was the last thing I needed, and showed up my failings even more. Why on earth did I think it would be any different?

'When did you last eat?' he asked.

'It's okay, I'm not hungry,' I said.

'I didn't mean… I wasn't offering you something to eat,' he seemed surprised at my reaction.

'Oh, I'm sorry. Of course not…' I said, embarrassed. Usually when someone asked me that question they were about to offer me some titbit, or at least give me directions to the nearest canteen.

'I need to know when you last ate, in the unlikely event you end up in hospital,' he said, smiling, trying to put me at my ease, but the word 'hospital' didn't help.

'Oh, of course, yes – I ate about ten minutes ago,' I said. 'I had an apple in the car, I thought I might need a sugar rush to get me inside the building.' This wasn't strictly true; I'd had an apple in the car but had also discovered and scoffed a Twix in the glove compartment. I'd bought it the previous week and it would have been rude and dangerous to leave it there unaccompanied.

'Oh dear,' he smiled, 'you were worried about coming here so ate an apple?'

I nodded sheepishly, thinking perhaps I shouldn't have lied, and the answer was honesty in a situation like this.

'Do you turn to food at times of stress?' he asked, going through the questionnaire.

'Do I turn to food in times of stress?' I repeated, pretending to consider this when I wanted to shout 'do birds fly? Hell YES!' but restrained myself and nodded politely. I wasn't going to mention the Twix fix – I doubt he'd ever eaten one in his life, he'd pass out with shock.

'I know these questions might seem a bit "in depth," as you say,' he smiled. 'But as you're a new member I need to get a picture of who you are. What you are and how we can help you.'

'Oh that's… nice.' I didn't know what else to say, I could hardly answer I'm Dani, I'm a VERY fat lady who apparently looks pregnant and I'm not quite sure how you can help me, unless you want to do my laces up so I can make a swift exit without falling over and head for the nearest kebab shop.

'Now, as you've injured yourself I'll need you to sign something to say you don't hold us responsible,' he was saying, shuffling papers.

'Oh it wasn't your fault, I was… jogging from the car park,' I heard myself lie again.

'Okay, well I admire your keenness, but you need to warm up first before you do any strenuous activity. I know it's tempting, but you must *not* throw yourself into exercise.'

'Oh… okay, I'll resist the temptation,' I said, trying not to laugh at the very idea of my 'keenness' to exercise. I think I was bordering on hysteria by now, I'd been so nervous coming here I had lost sight of my goal and had defaulted into panic/Twix-fix mode.

'Okay, so let's get on filling in this form so we know where we're going.'

I made myself comfy. Perhaps if I just breathed in the air, all that sweat and calorie burning going on around me might penetrate my skin and have a positive effect? I began breathing deeply, and he looked at me concerned, like I was about to pass out – he had lovely eyes, which didn't help my heart rate.

I was disorientated, in a strange place with people moving a lot, but I could see how devastatingly handsome this man with the clipboard was. I was looking at his biceps and imagining him naked when he asked; 'When was the last time you were active?'

'*Sexually* active?' I asked, while thinking, why am I saying this? I will never know what made me say *sexually*. Perhaps it was because I hadn't had sex for years or because I'd spent an hour in the car putting this off and eating an old Twix and too long in the changing rooms trying to get to my feet. I'd also told a great big whopper to a very attractive man who'd paraded me round the gym asking searching questions and announcing me as a health and safety issue. By now I'd officially lost it.

He looked embarrassed, and I immediately realised I'd made a complete arse of myself.

'Oh God no, of course you didn't mean that. You didn't say *sexually* active did you? You couldn't – wouldn't possibly mean that. Did you?'

He shook his head, his face went slightly pink and even in my deep embarrassment I found this quite endearing. He had fair hair that was thick and tousled and his eyes were a really sparkly blue. Yes sex… it had been a while.

'No, not se— just "active",' he smiled and our eyes met, he was cute and it was times like this, when I met men like this that I wished I'd stuck to my diet months ago. 'So, you were last *active…*' he looked down at his clipboard, '…one hour, one day or one week ago?' For some reason I was still thinking about sex and wanted to say, 'three years ago and then he got out of bed and told me he didn't find me attractive any more'. Thankfully I didn't say this, I just pretended/lied and said, 'Ooh a couple of days ago.'

'Oh good, so you're ready to go?'

'No… not really, given my ankle…' I looked down, fake for-lornly. What? No, I wasn't ready in the slightest.

'So shall we say… you last exercised… one year ago?' Oh God, he could read my mind.

'Yes... okay, I'll be honest, I don't actually remember. So make it two, ... or three?'

He smiled; 'It's okay, we can make you better.' Thank God I was sitting down because at this my legs almost gave way, this man was so perceptive, gentle – and the sincerity of his words made my legs turn to jelly. I didn't need my legs doing anything untoward at a time like this, so I grabbed my seat for ballast so I didn't fall off and smiled back at him, thinking, he's so kind and sensitive and lovely. He must be gay.

'Just tell me what you're unhappy with, what you feel you'd like to change?'

'Ha where do we start?' I said, but he didn't laugh, he just smiled and waited for me to answer, like a kind teacher.

'I have a little... high blood pressure and I sweat...' I added unnecessarily. 'And can't get my breath when I go up the stairs, and... I'm pretty irresistible, so form a queue,' I tried to joke. Again.

'Blood pressure?' He looked concerned.

'Only a bit. I mean there's nothing wrong with me, you don't have to "fix" me, I just want to be fitter than I am, which, grant-ed, isn't... at all... fit... Chris,' I added, seeing his name badge. I wished I hadn't mentioned the blood pressure, and yet I felt better for telling him. I'd never had much 'concern' in my life and it felt nice, even if it was just a stranger in bright blue with a clipboard and a job to do.

He cleared his throat. 'Of course,' he said, but I felt like he might be judging me for not doing a hundred sit-ups a day and living on quinoa.

'Look, it's not like I'm a freak because I haven't run a marathon in the last hour,' I said, a little too aggressively perhaps.

He looked at me as if to say 'actually you are a freak and I disliked you on sight, you fat, lazy, quinoa-hating bitch'. Or perhaps I was just being paranoid. It was all so intense, and with the Stepford gym bunnies bouncing up and down in sync like bloody backing singers behind us I was beginning to wonder if I'd landed in the middle of a religious fitness cult. Everyone seemed to find me fascinating and they were all gazing at me under perfect blonde fringes and long, dyed lashes – and that was just the men. I felt like shouting 'go back to your workouts, there's nothing to see here,' but thankfully managed to resist.

After more multiple-choice inanity about my 'preferred choice' of team sports (to which I replied 'none' because I didn't think 'competitive eating' would be acceptable), Chris suggested he take a look at my 'sprained' ankle.

'No, really, it's okay now,' I said, knowing there was no swelling, and wishing I'd fessed up from the beginning about why I was walking like a strange chicken.

'Okay, well you need to get it looked at,' he said. He stood up and, putting down his clipboard, reached out his arm which, assuming it was for me, I grabbed and hoisted myself up with. He seemed a little surprised; 'Oh I was just going to show you some upper body exercises to compensate for your ankle,' he said, gently prising my hand from his arm.

'I'm so sorry,' I gasped, wanting to tell him everything and asking if we could just start again, but I was in too deep. 'I…

I don't think today is a good day for me to start all this,' I said, gesturing towards Stepford's Next Top Models. 'I'll come back next week.'

'There's never a good day,' he said kindly.

'You can say that again,' I smiled, and before he could say anything more propelled myself forwards and let the 'core improver' do the rest, which resulted in an over-important emu-type exit that certainly got the gym bunnies talking.

Once I'd left the arena, I locked myself in a toilet cubicle and cried. I wanted to succeed more than anything else, so why was it so hard for me? Lots of people go to the gym and get so much from it – so why did I find the experience so traumatic? I'd really gathered all my courage to be there and I wanted to embrace it, be strong and committed to the whole concept of healthy living. I'd also paid over the odds for an outsize gym kit and strange footwear that promised the earth but didn't deliver, unless you were hoping for a strange walk that drew lots of attention.

'Is it me?' I asked Karla once I was safely in the car and on my phone. 'I don't understand why it's so difficult. My mother worked out to her Rosemary Conley DVD every day of her life and she stayed at 8 stone 7 until she died.'

'The very fact you know your mother's life-long weight says it all,' she sighed. 'And a lot of good Rosemary Conley and her DVDs did for your mother… look what happened to her?'

'Yeah well, she was on the gin only diet.'

I didn't want to go there, it was all too painful, and I had to get back on track. I promised her I would go back to the gym the following day, and would do sit-ups and star jumps tonight at the flat and prepare my body and my mind for the onslaught that was to come.

'Why not go back to the gym now?' Karla said.

I couldn't go back in there and face that exercise guy again. He'd been patient, even enthusiastic about my quest for a better body – but to go back half an hour after I'd left would seem weird… well, weirder than my first visit, and that was saying something.

I would like to say at this point that I hadn't remembered the leftover doughnuts I'd thrown in the bin the previous night in my quest to start a healthy new life. I would also like to say that the idea of resurrecting them from the deadly waste in my bin hadn't occurred to me, but it had.

'Don't you dare go back to the flat and binge,' Karla was saying. God I hated when she did creepy that mind-reading thing, it was so unnerving. So I just hissed like a cat and put the phone down.

I needed thinking time and wasn't in the mood for laying myself bare to Karla. I hadn't explained to her about my 'sprained ankle' because she'd over-analyse and tell me I fibbed because I hadn't had breast milk or had attachment issues or something equally Freudian – and that was the last thing I needed right now. The truth was, I'd lied about my ankle because I felt scared and foolish, I was in a place that was completely alien to me and it had made me feel eleven years old again. It was like my first

day at high school, everyone else knew what to do except me –
and I didn't fit in. And I didn't need a psychologist to work that
one out.

Pulling up outside the cafe, I could see Ella inside, so I popped
in. The cafe was closed and she was on her own, Italian music
playing on her iPhone and she was just sitting with a cup of coffee. I didn't know much about Ella's life, but I'd heard she'd had a
love affair over the summer with a local guy, Ben Shaw, who had
been in my class at school. I barely remembered him, his dad was
the local solicitor in the village and I think Ben became a solicitor too. I hadn't seen him around since I'd arrived in Appledore
and I didn't like to ask, as I had the feeling he and Ella weren't
together any more.

'Hi Dani, I'm just making ice cream for tomorrow,' she
said, smiling, pleased to see me. 'Having a coffee break at the
moment.'

After spending the evening in a place I didn't fit in, I welcomed being back here in a place where I felt very much at home.
So I rolled up my sleeves and said; 'Can I help? I'd love to learn,
teach me everything you know.'

Ella laughed. 'If I were to teach you everything, it would last
about twenty seconds,' she said. 'I'm just making it up as I go
along, Dani – I've realised it's what Sophia did – and that's when
the magic happens. Making ice cream is as much about whisking
and weighing as it is about just letting it happen; sometimes my
mistakes are delicious.'

I liked that philosophy. 'Just let it happen,' I repeated. Although I knew if I applied it to my weight I'd probably gain

several stone in a few short months and be starring in my own reality show.

As I helped Ella swirl vibrant fruit purees in bright reds and oranges into creamy white ice cream, my mind drifted off, back to my past filled with dark and light. Swirling clouds of white cotton wool on deep blue, chocolate sundae summers, always followed by the rolling grey thunder, the closing in of the final summer when I was nineteen and my life stopped. Jude had hurt me and I couldn't face living here any more without him, I couldn't face a life looking after my mother, listening to the bitterness, the hate, the drink, so I'd left and gone to London. But here in Caprioni's making strawberry ice cream with Ella I was dragged back into the past, like an unrelenting tide. And yet I was conflicted, because here in the cafe making ice cream with Ella, I felt like I'd come home, like I belonged, and I'd never felt that anywhere else.

'I left the gym early tonight,' I heard myself say, as we stirred rich strawberry purée into a thick, creamy canvas.

'I don't blame you,' she smiled, 'I've never been one for the gym,' she looked up at me briefly and continued to stir.

'I know, it's just that I want to be slim, I need to be slim… I want to be healthier, happier, fitter.'

'And you can, you will. But every day won't be perfect, so you left the gym early, you'll stay tomorrow, it doesn't mean you give up.' She stopped stirring and picked up a punnet of strawberries, 'It's like having this beautiful punnet of fresh strawberries and finding a bad one. You wouldn't throw away the punnet, you'd throw away that strawberry and carry on making ice cream.'

I kept stirring and thinking. My mother had tried to stop drinking, and she'd stay on the waggon for days, then one glass became a bottle became a week. One bad strawberry... that's all it took. I would always be one failed gym visit and one salted caramel sundae away from failing – but I mustn't let it stop me. I couldn't give up on life like my mother had. I wasn't going to change overnight, and some days wouldn't be perfect, hell, some days could be an ice cream orgy, but I just had to live them, move on and keep heading towards my goal... and appreciate the good strawberries.

Chapter Four

The Baby Food Diet

Diet Diary: June 2005; Fell madly in love with the guy who plays guitar in the pub. The diet promised me I could lose a stone in two weeks on 16 jars of baby food a day, but after 4 hours, I just wanted chips. I lost a pound, we slept together twice, then he ran away to join the navy. And I gained 7 pounds.

The day after my gym disaster, I awoke with a familiar shadow over me. My failures crowded in, from failing in school, to being a boring girlfriend, and a bad daughter. I could hear my mother's voice, reminding me how I'd let her down when she needed me. I'd been surprised how the past had reached out and taken me back there, it was so unexpected, so vivid.

I looked out onto the beach from my window, which always lifted my spirits, and reminded myself how lucky I was. It was still early, but I could see Ella setting off in Reginaldo, the van, stacked with fresh ice cream, heading for the beach and the last few days of another soon-to-be-forgotten summer, rubbed out by autumn like the sea washing away footsteps on sand.

I think Ella enjoyed the solitude of the van, because her mother, Gina her cousin and Sue were all quite a handful in the cafe – especially if they were doing the same shift. They made me smile; Gina would be quiet unless she was the centre of attention, Roberta could often be heard serenading the customers and Sue would be the unofficial (out of tune) backing singer. Sue also saw herself as a bit of an agony aunt, happy to give advice, share life stories, and crosswords with anyone and everyone who came into the cafe.

One day she'd been sitting on a stool at the far end of the counter doing a crossword. Being Sue, she liked to include everyone in everything and was asking loudly if a limb replacement was a 'prophylactic'. I was busy at the counter but could hear her quite clearly and cringed each time she said the word; 'I know I'm right, but it doesn't matter how I try to do it, I can't squeeze PROPHYLACTIC in,' she yelled. Regardless of how many times I called back that the word was 'prosthetic', she didn't hear me and continued to shout 'PROPHYLAC-TIC' across the cafe. Aware there were young families in the cafe but too busy dealing with a large queue to go over and shut her up myself, I asked Marco to quietly explain that she was basically shouting 'condoms' in the faces of young kids eating ice cream. I watched him wander over, and without smiling say something in her ear, which made her laugh out loud and shout, 'Oh bugger!'

I had a little giggle to myself, I loved the laid-back atmosphere at the cafe and there was always something to smile about
with Sue and Roberta around. And all the women in the group
seemed to mother me – which for a motherless girl was very
comforting. Sue called me sweetheart, Roberta called me love,
and Gina called me honey in her half-American Devonian accent
and I would get hugs and encouragement galore.

Today it was just Sue on the counter, Roberta was clothes
shopping with Delilah, her little dog, and Gina was at a spa. It
was late August, the weather was holding out and we were still
busy, so I set about opening up the shop and mixing extra ice
cream. Sue loved what she called 'a pop of colour' and was looking even more glitzy than usual in a sequined T-shirt with ice
cream cone earrings and bright pink lipstick.

I told her my plans for a brand-new body while mixing Fer-
rero Rocher ice cream and resisting the ambassadorial allure.

'Dani,' she said, 'you're curvy and gorgeous… stop self-defe-
cating.'

I did this a lot – the self-deprecating I mean, I was just getting
used to Sue's way with words – it always surprised and amused
me; 'I know I do, Sue, but when you're overweight you tend to
lose your self-esteem.'

'Don't think I don't know how *that* feels, sweetheart. I've
had my share of disappointments in life and though I haven't
struggled with weight, I've struggled with men and they're bad
for your esteem, I can tell you. My husband walked out on me
for a tart, then a toyboy off Tinder spent all my money, so you
don't have to tell me about low self-esteem. But you have to pick

yourself up and get back on the horse… and ride the bastard hard,' she spat with some conviction before turning to a customer, smiling and saying in a completely different voice, 'Good morning, sweetheart, and what can I do for you?'

Sue was right of course, not about riding bastards, but somewhere in all those words she'd puked at me, there was a kind of wisdom born of pain. She'd been through the mill romantically – I'd heard all the stories as she relayed them to customers – and she was a walking cautionary tale for all single-somethings looking for love on the internet. But I had to admire her, not only did she literally sparkle, with sequined tops, earrings and eye shadow, but she positively shimmered with hope. Sue had been put through the ringer of life but she wasn't giving up – perhaps I could learn something from Sue's steely determination?

I wandered back into the kitchen and did some cleaning, I'd read in a magazine that you could burn up to 500 calories with a good, spirited cleaning session. It also gave me time to think and inevitably my mind went back to the past. Despite my constant joking and apparently light-hearted take on life, I think my biggest fear was that I'd end up like my mother. Due to her addiction, she'd lost everything, including me, and I could see how a person with cravings could become insular, caring only about their next drink – or in my case sugar-loaded trans-fat laced carb. My mum grieved for Dad every day, always believing he'd come back to her and forget about 'the other woman'. She once told me that if she lost a few pounds and had her hair done he would love her again, she was convinced of this, believing she was one new lipstick away from a passionate reunion with him. Then she'd have another drink and her sentences would be laced with gin and bitterness. She couldn't exist without the next drink. Had I inherited the gene that did that to her? There were so many theories, but I had to believe that my need to eat for comfort and solace wasn't inevitable, that it was something I could change.

The worst thing about being my mother's child was the brutal inconsistency; some mornings she'd promise to pick me up after school and 'do something nice'. I'd wait at the school gates, always hopeful, and when she didn't turn up, my child's heart would break all over again. Teachers leaving for the day would ask if I was okay and I'd say 'yes, Mum's on her way'. But before they could ask any awkward questions, I'd set off for home on my own. I got used to the long walk from a very young age, but you don't get used to the disappointment and hurt when your mother isn't there – a cone of hot, salty chips on the way definitely soothed the pain. It would have been easier if she'd always been aggressive, unpredictable and mean – because I wouldn't have known any difference. But to see what she could have been, a glimpse of the mother I might have had, made it all the more painful.

However, my Sunday visits with Dad were a different and much more exciting affair as he'd take me to the Ice Cream Cafe and buy me the biggest chocolate ice cream sundae. Karla reckoned he was punishing my mother by doing this, going against her wishes, feeding me with 'evil' ice cream, and that, as a result, I was comforted and conflicted and unable to trust either of my parents, so took solace in chocolate ice cream.

I was thinking about this now, and I leaned on the counter, gazing out to sea, hoping against hope that coming back here was going to be good for me and I hadn't bitten off more than even I could chew. And trust me I could chew for Britain.

'You okay, sweetheart?' Sue was asking; she'd made me a cup of coffee and was handing it to me. 'That's how you like it, isn't it?' she said, giving me the cup, and her comforting smile filled me with warmth. Here everyone knew how I liked my coffee, it's the little things.

'Thanks Sue,' I said, taking it, feeling vulnerable and trying not to fill up with tears. 'I'm going to take your advice, make a fist of it, ride the horse and go back to the gym tonight.'

'Good girl. I'm proud of you, sweetheart,' she said, putting an arm around me, instinctively sensing my sudden fragility. And I leaned my head on her shoulder, tears falling down my face – my mother had never once told me she was proud of me.

That evening I set off for the gym with some enthusiasm. I was pleased with myself for even setting out there again. 'It'll be my second time,' I'd said proudly to Sue, not mentioning the fact that the first time I hadn't actually done anything but told fibs and mentioned sex inappropriately before grabbing onto a very nice trainer man who probably thought I was a lunatic.

I built myself up again for this second visit, sitting in the car park talking to myself and knowing there were no sweet treats in the glove compartment where once the Twix had lain. I told myself that it was now or never and I had to go into battle, because this was worth fighting for.

I finally girded my loins, grabbed my bag and climbed out of the car, striding across the car park like an Amazonian woman (I'd abandoned the core improvers and the lace-up trainers – they were more trouble than they were worth). I opened the doors and entered the changing rooms to be confronted once more with the tiny-hipped gym goddesses slipping in and out of little bits of Lycra before bouncing around the gym. Catching myself in the huge mirror, I realised I liked the *idea* of exercise more than the reality. I wanted the workout gear, the ponytail, the little bounce as I walked, I just wished I could get it all without having to sweat and chafe. But until someone came up with a sweating/chafing solution I had no choice but to just go for it.

I walked gingerly out of the changing rooms without incident, and consequently no one seemed interested in me, thank God. I continued on past the treadmills, giving myself a silent pep talk – I had everything to live for and not only had I been given the chance of a second life – this was my chance to create a fabulous body to go with that life.

Tonight I was wearing my faithful old pull-on trainers so at least I'd get the chance to actually do something. I looked around for someone in electric blue who might be able to tell me what was what. I hoped to see Chris, after all I'd basically told him everything about my bodily functions; how I sweat and pant, and then there was the awkward moment about being sexually active. As a result, I felt like we were now old friends – though he was probably hiding – he was nowhere in sight and I needed help. I gazed around this large aircraft hangar filled with torture equipment and not only did I not know how to use it, I wasn't sure I wanted to. The safest option was probably the treadmills, anyone could work those couldn't they?

I watched as the others (all svelte people with no body fat and magnificent cores) jumped on and off effortlessly like gazelles. Okay, so it looked like these treadmills were really hardcore and you had to make a run for it, as they were constantly moving. So I stood near one that had just been vacated, it looked fairly slow, I took a deep breath, clenched every muscle in my body and threw myself onto it. But the minute I hit that treadmill it set it off faster, and though one can never be sure when one is hurtling towards space very fast, I didn't think this was the way they did it on *The Biggest Loser*.

I was travelling faster than the speed of light to a certain death, but I had no choice. I ran, and ran, and ran, unable to slow down, because if I did I would be thrown off the back. So I just kept running, and running, until I couldn't run any more and became aware of an electric blue light coming towards me. In my sweating, speed-madness I couldn't tell if it was a trainer and help was nearby or I was having a near-death experience. I couldn't stay on this scary carousel for ever and if I planned to feel the ground under my feet ever again, I had to abandon all thoughts of dignity. So through the sweat and panting and sheer panic, I screamed at the blue light, 'HELP ME!' at the top of my voice, but before anyone could do anything, I lost my grip, and shot off the back of the treadmill.

The next thing I remember was coming to under a rowing machine with lots of skinny people in Lycra looking down at me. This was my worst nightmare, but it was real and I was now being given water (what's with this water thing in gyms? Water's for washing, not for drinking). What I needed right then was a caramel macchiato with chocolate sprinkles, but these people wouldn't even know what one of those was.

In the warren of gym bunnies now crowding me, I felt like I'd died and woken up in the middle of an episode of *Baywatch*. Then I recognised a face, it was Chris, who'd interrogated me the previous day. I lay there dazed and he was telling me not to move. As if.

'Is anything broken?' I asked, almost hoping my injuries would be bad enough to justify the spectacle I'd created. At least if my injuries were fatal people would say 'she died during a tough workout', which was infinitely preferable to, 'she died after being thrown off a treadmill because she was too fat to keep up'.

I looked at Chris, he was checking my pulse.

'Am I okay?' I said weakly, like he'd know and I wouldn't. But that's how I felt in that gym, I didn't feel in control of my own body. To me this was a foreign place with scary machine monsters that were just waiting to hurl you to a certain death while Lycra-clad spectators watched on; some kind of gym Hunger Games.

'Danielle, you mustn't overdo it, I know you're very keen, but what speed were you doing when you came off?' Chris asked a little later as, in the absence of anything more exciting, I drank water while he lectured me on 'use of gym equipment'.

'Call me Dani,' I said.

'Okay, Dani… you mustn't overexcite yourself.'

'Overexcite? Okay.'

'I know it's exciting to start a new regime… after all, I get excited when we have a new elliptical in the gym.'

'I bet you do. I bet you eat mung beans and rise before dawn, too,' I said, ignoring his passionate plea for me not to 'overexcite' myself around the ellipticals – what was an elliptical anyway? He still didn't quite get it that some of us don't 'choose' to go to the gym, and I wasn't banging on the door to be let in so I could literally throw myself around for pleasure. But I noticed then that he looked a bit hurt by my mung bean comment, so I tried to be nicer. 'Okay, I'll try not to… overexcite myself in future.' I continued to sit and pant like a dog, even though the show had been over for at least fifteen minutes. 'Thing is, Chris I'm not sure this is for me… I'm just not comfortable in the gym environment.'

'Ellipticals?'

'I'm sorry?'

'The equipment, an elliptical is a stationary machine, like a treadmill – some people are more excited by other forms of activity.'

'No – I'm not. I'm not excited. At all.'

'Okay, I hear you – but have you considered an exercise class?'

He clearly hadn't heard me. 'No I haven't. Look, I appreciate your suggestions, but you and I are from a different place. You like to get your heart rate going with exercise, I like to get my mine going with a big pizza.'

'Hey, do you know how many grams of fat and calories are in pizza?'

'Yes – thousands of delicious, cheese-soaked calories,' I said, licking my lips and wondering why the hell I'd deleted that Domino's number from my phone.

'But all that saturated… *fat*…' the expression on his face told me he could hardly bear to say the word.

'Oh yes and oh yum!'

He looked at me like I was crazy, he'd clearly never met anyone before who said such blasphemous things about exercise and fat. I had to get out of there, this was my second visit and my career as a gym bunny was over, I had to find some other way of achieving this goal. I tried to envisage myself in a red, fitted dress standing under fairy lights at the cafe on my fortieth, but I was struggling, especially as all I could think about now was a meaty feast pizza and spicy wings.

'We do lots of other fun activities here – it's not all about punishment you know?' he was saying.

'No really… I…'

'I tell you what, go home, relax those muscles, and tomorrow I will show you what else we do. You'll love it, I promise.'

I doubted that very much, but nodded and smiled; I had no intention of turning up again, but he was so nice and trying so hard to be supportive, I didn't have the heart to tell him it was 'over' between us and I was off to get 'carbed-up' at Little Venice.

I said goodbye and got up, turning to take one last look before I left the gym for ever, and he was looking at me and smiled. I smiled back and gave him a little wave, and by the time I got to the car was wondering if it might be nice to come back if only to see that smile again?

I didn't stop at the pizza place on my way home. Chris's commitment had touched me and made me think that if he had faith in me, then why couldn't I? Perhaps I should?

Ella and her mum Roberta were making ice cream for the next day as I limped into the cafe and told them all about what had happened.

'I didn't fall, or trip, I was *projected* across the gym,' I sighed, going red just thinking about it. 'But Chris, one of the trainers, thinks I should go back tomorrow so he can show me what other horrors they have to offer – apparently they have *classes*.'

Ella was laughing; 'Perhaps Chris is planning on showing you what *he* has to offer?'

I laughed, almost hysterically; 'Oh if you saw him, you'd know how funny that is. He's so muscly and SO good-looking, like someone from *America's Next Top Model* – and I'm like someone from *My 600lb Life*. Not sure the two could ever come together.'

'You'd be surprised,' Roberta said, popping her head out of one of the freezers; 'I had a friend once who went out with a male model, and I'm not saying she was big, but when she got on that scale, ooh did the fat lady sing.'

'So you reckon a good-looking guy might just slum it with someone like me?' I joked, fully expecting a flurry of apologies, but she didn't flinch.

'Probably not, but then again, some people have funny taste – and you're quite pretty when you brush your hair and put some lipstick on,' she answered, and went back head first into the freezer.

'Thanks… I think,' I smiled.

'Sorry Dani, you may have realised by now, my mother has no filter,' Ella rolled her eyes, a little embarrassed.

'No, I'm encouraged by her faith, my own mother never said anything as kind and sensitive as that,' I said. They both laughed, but I wasn't joking.

'So you're going back tomorrow?' Karla said when I called her later. She'd just put the kids to bed and was now doing a wash and preparing supper for her husband, who was working late. I didn't envy her life one bit; I was glad I only had myself to worry about.

'I'm not sure, Chris the trainer is very supportive, and I'm wondering if perhaps that's what I need – some one-on-one.'

'He sounds perfect for some one-on-one,' she giggled.

'God, all my girlfriends were trying to make something of this, I was sure he'd be horrified. No, he wouldn't look twice,' I sighed, 'but I just feel so vulnerable around the gym, I need someone on my side.'

'You may have to pay extra for personal training, but it wouldn't be the first time you'd forced yourself on a man by offering to pay for his services,' she laughed.

'That was only because I didn't have a plus-one for my cousin's wedding. And I only paid his train fare… and expenses, and then he got off with one of the bridesmaids… but this guy would *have* to stay with me,' I joked. 'If he charges by the hour, then I can have him all to myself for that hour, and I might be able to avoid any more spectacular slip-ups.' As I said it I realised this might be the answer. The sheer novelty of having someone's attention, someone else's commitment to me, might just be what I needed.

The next day I arrived in a very positive mood, I felt like Rocky running up those steps in Philadelphia before his big fight; I swear I could hear the soul-stirring music as I stepped into the gym and sought Chris out.

'So, Chris, what do you recommend?' I said, almost jumping on the spot, raring to go.

He smiled and produced a set of weights. I'd got this, I could do it. My new life, my new body started here. I was going to be like Rocky and Xena the Warrior Princess rolled into one. But in my keenness to show him I meant business... I concussed myself.

Once we'd left A and E and established there was no brain damage, I decided to cut my losses. Despite having paid a small fortune for membership and actually finding Chris pleasant company and very reassuring in the ambulance on the way to the hospital, I had to drop out of the gym. The gods were clearly trying to tell me something and it would be foolish to continue. There was nothing else for it, I would continue on my weight loss journey, but the gym and all those appliances and skinny people and accidents waiting to happen were one step too far for me. This was the sensible thing to do – it wasn't a bad strawberry, it was a bad punnet and I had to move on.

'Chris,' I said in the taxi home. 'I've been thinking about this and it isn't fair to you, or the gym... or me for that matter. I just can't do the gym any more.'

'No, Dani you mustn't give up,' he said, genuinely surprised and even disappointed at me throwing in the towel. 'I feel like we've failed you…'

'No, no you mustn't. It's just me, I haven't given up, I just think I might need to rethink the exercise part of my plan.'

'Come back, just do a week… try it, I'll help you…'

'No Chris, it's not you, it's me…' I started, then we both laughed. It felt like I was trying to break up with him, when we both knew he was probably glad to see the back of the fat gym member who had spectacular sessions ending in concussion and hospital. Eventually the taxi arrived at mine and we said goodbye, me promising to come back to the gym at some point in the future, him behaving like I'd just dumped him.

For the next couple of days, I tried to eat sensibly and told myself and everyone else that 'my gym will be the beach'. Just because the gym hadn't worked for me I wasn't giving up. I meant what I'd said to Chris and I had this guilt about letting him down, but still the old Dani hung on in there. 'I will do a morning run and lunge and do shreds and all kinds of exercise… tomorrow,' I'd say to anyone in the vicinity. But of course, when 'tomorrow' came I couldn't think of anything I wanted to do less than run up and down the beach. Along with the effort, I was concerned there would be comments, and if I heard someone laugh, I would be straight to the fish and chip shop. I had to protect myself. And so I blamed the weather, my trainers, the tide (which annoyingly was out, leaving the beach looking like a running track but who knew when it might suddenly come rushing in?). I hated myself for slipping back into these old ways of lying to myself and everyone else around me. But it was who I was and it was like two people were having a constant fight in my head. 'Eat it!' 'No, don't eat it!' 'You don't want to be like your mother and give up on life.' And 'Go on have the ice cream/pizza/cheese loaded Nachos they'll make everything okay again… for now.'

A few days after resigning from the gym, I was standing outside the cafe admiring the new awning. I'd just eaten a doughnut and trying not to smell the hot fudge sauce emanating from inside when someone put a hand on my shoulder.

Turning round, I was face to chest (my face his chest – not the other way round, that would be weird!) with Chris. I was amazed to see him here, and immediately wiped my mouth for any traces of doughnut treachery. He looked so healthy and fit and it made me feel bad about giving up and quite angry with myself – and the bloody doughnut.

'I was a bit worried when I spotted you gazing into the window at the ice creams… I remember how much you said you like pizza,' he said the word pizza like it was a sexually transmitted disease and I had to smile. This guy had clearly never chowed down on a Spicy Meaty Feast with cheese crust and garlic sauce.

'Yes, I come here every morning for several large ice creams and a big milkshake,' I said in a teasing way, but he took it seriously, stepping back, aghast. So before he fainted with sheer horror, I explained this was where I worked.

'Wow, no wonder you struggle with trans fats,' he said, in all seriousness.

'I don't struggle with them. I eat them, it's you who seems to have a struggle with them,' I said, perhaps a little too defensively. 'Sometimes a little of what you fancy does you good. Why don't you come in and sample the new flavour, white chocolate and peppermint, my boss Ella created it late last night and it's just gorgeous. Swirly creamy chocolate with a fresh minty aroma – it's totally yum.'

'No, thanks…' the body language said it all, his arms were folded over his body, his legs firm, slightly apart, like a warrior defending his world against the evils of trans fat.

'So, are you going for a run later?' he asked.

'No, I already did a run,' I lied. Yes I know what you're thinking, why tell more fibs and make life harder for myself, again – but having humiliated myself in front of him on more than one occasion I had to try to retain what little dignity I had left. I just felt so inferior in the presence of perfect human specimens. If Chris had known I spent my time sitting behind a counter lusting after ice cream by day and lying on a sofa conducting a detailed survey of local takeaways each night, he'd have probably thrown up on the spot.

'So you already did a run?'

'Absolutely,' I said, and did a funny movement with my legs that was meant to signify running, but looked more like I had a full bladder.

'You can do more than one run a day you know?'

'I can't, not without an ambulance driving alongside me,' I said.

He smiled and sat down on the step of the cafe and I joined him, just hoping I'd be able to get back up without causing a bloody tidal wave.

'How far did you get this morning?' He was looking into my eyes and for a brief and beautiful moment I let myself imagine a life where there'd be something other than pity in those baby blues when he looked at me.

'So…?'

'What?' I said, smiling, intrigued.

'So how far did you get… on your run?'

'Oh *that*.' I wished he'd just drop it. I looked back at him and then at the pavement and then beyond at the sea and I heard myself say, 'I didn't.'

He continued to look out to sea and we stared for a little while and I began to feel awkward. Then he said; 'It doesn't matter that you lie to me, or your friends and family – but you need to stop lying to yourself, Dani.' He said this in a really teacher-like way and I felt thoroughly told off and ashamed, like I was back in my mother's kitchen caught with the biscuits again.

'You don't know me, Chris. You live a very different life with different goals and different ideas of what a person should be. I sometimes tell fibs… who doesn't? And for your information, I'm not lying to myself, I know perfectly well how fat and disgusting and unfit I am. I don't need smug, sanctimonious people like you to tell me what to do and why I should do it.'

He was looking at me, surprised at my outburst, but before he could respond, I carried on.

'This isn't *The Biggest Loser*, Chris, it isn't some intervention to save the fat girl, so just leave me alone and jog back to your gym.' With that I stood up and stomped into the cafe.

How dare he think he could just come up to me like that and start criticising me. People always think they know what you need, what you want, what you should do; I'd had a lifetime of my mother telling me what I could and couldn't do. And that had only led to me taking food from the cupboards when she wasn't looking and hiding it under my bed, in the wardrobe, anywhere it wouldn't be found. That's why the fibs around my weight tripped so easily off the tongue, I was used to lying to my mother about having salad for lunch at school and 'no, Mum, I didn't go to the tuck shop at break', when I'd actually gone to the shop with the fiver I'd taken from her purse when she was pissed the night before. Chocolate Wagon Wheels all round. These were the memories I had to live with and try to move on from, but it wasn't easy when I was constantly being reminded of the past.

Back in the cafe I banged pots and pans in the kitchen for a while, feeling angry and tearful. I was furious with myself for giving up, and for being unkind to Chris, who perhaps just wanted to help me. Talk about looking a gift horse in the mouth! I wanted help, and he wanted to help me – God I was so stupid to be defensive and angry. He'd never help me now.

I was still crying when Ella came in to fill up her van.

'Dani, what is it?' she asked, walking into the kitchen, a concerned look on her face.

'Oh nothing, I'm fine, just told the personal trainer to jog back to his gym.'

'Okay, well, perhaps he deserved it?' She looked doubtful.

I shook my head; 'He was trying to help.'

'I saw him, actually, I had my van parked on the front, I was on the phone and I saw you two chatting on the step. He looked sweet... he's *very* handsome.'

'Yes, but I'm *very* fat,' I heard myself say. She looked puzzled. 'Sorry, Ella, it's been a rough week. You're right, he is handsome. Not that I see him like that,' I added, remembering how nice it felt to be sitting close to him on the steps, the sea in the distance, his big blue eyes searching my face. 'He made me angry, but I feel bad now... and stupid.'

'Look if he made you feel angry, you were probably right to say something. You're a lovely girl, Dani – but you don't have to keep smiling when you're unhappy. Sometimes you have to tell people how you feel.'

Later I went up to the flat thinking about what Ella had said. I had always hated confrontation of any kind, and I'd surprised myself by the way I spoke to Chris. It stuck somewhere in my chest, but perhaps Ella was right and I did need to tell people how I was feeling?

And I suppose I was frustrated too. I'd had such motivation but could now feel it slowly slipping away. I kept thinking about my birthday party and how I had longed to have a new life and a new body for my fortieth, but I just couldn't seem to hold things together. That evening I called Karla, who as always was there for me.

'Girl, you need to sort yourself out,' she sighed. 'Yeah you were right to tell him where to get off, but at the same time, you're not good at hearing criticism. Look, babes, here's someone who wants to help, who might just help you get off your butt, lose some weight and ultimately feel better. It's what you wanted… and okay so he tells it like it is, but he's right, you do lie to yourself. "I'll start tomorrow," and "one piece won't hurt," and "I'm going to run 10k," but you never do.'

I didn't know what to say. She was right, but it stung a bit hearing this; 'I think I say those things to placate whoever's nagging me – I know in my heart I can't do it really.'

'There you go, doubting yourself again. You can do whatever you let yourself do – it's only you stopping you from running a 10k. You need to finally take control. And this trainer guy is just making you look at yourself, and you don't like what you see, that's all about growing and changing – and you need to change if you're going to succeed. Let's face it, you haven't done it so far. And he was just trying to help.'

'People like him want people like me around so they can feel superior.'

'Mmm, I wonder if it's less about his superiority complex and more about your inferiority complex,' she said.

Karla knew me well. But there was stuff even she didn't know. I'd never told anyone exactly what happened the night I left Appledore, the night that changed everything. I could still hear Mum's voice in my head, could still feel the emotional blackmail and guilt manipulating me all these years later, about food, my dad and the way I treated her. But it was all too late now.

Eventually, I put down the phone to Karla and lay awake thinking I might go down into the cafe and make myself the biggest sundae I'd ever had, with strawberry sauce and sprinkles. I wasn't hungry, I'd eaten a healthy, low calorie dinner, but there was always that empty space where my feelings were, and the only thing that could kill those feelings was to eat. I could erase the memories with food.

In Appledore I'd see Mum everywhere, from the beach to the pub to the wooden bench on the front looking out to sea. I wished I could forget, but there she was, always in my head. My mother who sometimes told me she hated me. And always, always, after half a bottle of gin, would tell me how fat I was, how much of a failure I would be, and how I was the reason my father walked out. And through it all I kept her secret for her. When she didn't turn up to parents' evenings at school, I made her excuses. When she 'collapsed' in the butchers, I helped her home, saying it was a virus, my face burning when I saw the looks passed between everyone. And then, when she began staying home, never venturing out, I would say 'her legs are playing up', not really knowing what this meant and hoping to God no one asked for details. But people must have known my mother's secret and Sophia sometimes sent me home from the cafe with little plastic tubs of food. A lasagne or a casserole would appear from nowhere and she'd say; 'Hey we've got leftovers here, Dani, take it for your mum.'

We both knew my mother didn't eat – Sophia was just making sure I got fed properly. The alternative was stale biscuits or whatever I could sneak in my pocket from the newsagents on the way home from school. I always dreaded going home, never knowing how I'd find her, knowing whatever had happened, however well I'd done in school that day I'd probably be in trouble with Mum.

Remembering all this was painful, like waiting for a big wave to wash over you, knowing the next one would hurt just as much and they would keep coming, a relentless remembering of pain. But I had to make it stop; instead of sitting crouching in a corner waiting for the next wave to hit me as she had done, I had to get up and jump over it. I wasn't my mum and I could make a difference for myself, I couldn't change my past but I could change my future. I wasn't a child any more and I had to stop living in the past and take control of the present. Maybe the first thing to deal with in my present was to apologise to Chris?

The next morning I ate a sensible breakfast, no fad, no starvation, just whole wheat toast with a light spreading of butter. I ate it looking out over the estuary thinking about how I must have seemed to Chris. He didn't know me and didn't understand my frustrations, but maybe he was the key to unlocking this block I seemed to have about doing exercise and in turn could help me move forward and become the person I wanted to be.

I decided to call him later to apologise, then have a think about whether or not to go back to the gym.

We were really busy that morning, and I had to run out to the beach with extra supplies for Ella. It was lovely out there and I could see why she liked to stay in the van; there was a small queue and it was ticking over, but it was peaceful too – it felt like quite a refuge.

'How are The Beverly Sisters?' Ella asked, as I handed her the plastic containers filled with ice cream.

'Just like any other day. Singing. Bickering. Dancing.' I smiled.

'Working?'

'In their own stylish way.'

Ella put her head in her hands theatrically and I laughed and headed back up the beach waving.

I was just about to enter the cafe when my phone buzzed, and I answered immediately.

'Hi Dani, it's Chris here, the guy from the gym. I hope you don't mind me calling, you gave your number when we filled in the gym form, so I just thought I'd call you. I wanted to talk to you about something.'

My heart was in my mouth. I still felt so bad about the way I'd spoken to him. 'I'm really sorry about yesterday; I was out of order,' I started.

'No it was me, I shouldn't have been so familiar. As you said, I don't know you and I shouldn't make presumptions about people,' he answered.

'I just think it's two worlds colliding, and I wish I could belong in yours, but I find it frustrating and difficult. It's like I'm watching through a window from the outside and I'd love to be inside... Sorry I'm going on, aren't I?' I sighed. 'But thanks for calling...'

'Can I get a word in?' he said.

I was a little taken aback. 'Oh I see, it's your turn to be rude.'

'No, I didn't mean to be rude, I just want to talk to you. I get how keen you are and I feel bad about the fact you'd sprained your ankle on the first day, and then you fell off the treadmill... oh and then there was you ending up in A and E...'

'I didn't exactly fall... I was ejected,' I said, thinking what a hopeless case I was. 'But it is quite a catalogue of injuries given the small time I've spent in the gym.'

'Absolutely, and yes... you were ejected, though you did *jump* on the treadmill while it was still running and somehow seemed to set it off...'

'Okay, okay, so I shouldn't have got on to it when it was moving but that just shows how out of my comfort zone I was. I didn't even know you had to stop the treadmill before you got on. What comes as second nature to you doesn't to me. I suppose you all had a good laugh about it, you and your gym bunnies?'

'Dani, you're very defensive,' he said, quietly. 'People weren't laughing, they were concerned. I was particularly concerned,' he added. I suddenly felt a bit mushy inside when he said this. 'I was particularly concerned because as the owner of the gym your well-being is my responsibility.'

The mushiness in my stomach hardened. This translated to, 'I'm being nice because my gym doesn't want to be sued by you.'

'So there's really no need to feel so defensive,' he continued.

'Perhaps I am a bit defensive, but do you blame me? You said yesterday that I lied to myself.'

'I admit I shouldn't have said it, but I haven't changed my opinion,' he said. He sounded reasonable, calm and very together, which always unnerved me slightly as I wasn't used to it.

'So, you still think I lie to myself?'

'Yes, but I want to help, that's why I'm ringing, because I want to offer you free personal training.'

'Is this a joke? Why would you do that?' I asked.

'I'll be honest, Dani, there are several reasons; first of all, I'm concerned about your injuries. They may be down to your enthusiasm, but they all happened in my gym.'

So I was right about him being worried that I'd sue him, especially as he was the owner.

'Oh don't worry about my injuries, I won't say anything... I just want to forget the whole episode... well, episodes.'

'Dani, just hear me out – I'm trying to make a go of the gym, but it's the personal training that makes the money and keeps people coming here. You'd be amazed how many people join up, pay for a year's membership, then only turn up a few times.'

'Disgraceful,' I sighed.

'Absolutely. So I'm trying to sell the idea of the personal trainer – but particularly the idea that absolutely *anyone* can be fit... even someone who comes to us as a...'

'Basket case?'

'No... a...'

'Fat pig?'

He laughed, 'Absolutely not. It would just be good for the gym and good for me if I could help you to reach your fitness goal.' I liked that he laughed finally, he always seemed so serious, it was nice that he could let go a little.

'It would be good for me too,' I said. 'But I'm scared it's never going to happen. Look Chris, I appreciate what you're offering me, and there was a time I'd have leapt at this opportunity, but I just feel very vulnerable, like I'm setting myself up to fail, again. I realise in your line of work you don't often come up against someone like me…'

'No I don't…'

'Exactly. So you'd like to make me into a case study, a challenge, then pummel me to death in the gym until I don't know my own name. Don't get me wrong, I want SO much to be slim and firm with a firm, twitching core, I just don't want to be injured again doing it.'

'You won't, because I won't allow it. This time it's my rules, I won't let you throw yourself onto a moving treadmill or jog through the car park and sprain your ankle.'

I felt a little guilty again about my fictitious sprained ankle, and didn't want to dwell on this so moved on. 'I suppose you'll then want to parade me round Appledore at eight stone, saying "I turned fat to fabulous."'

'No, I don't. Firstly, I think "From Fat to Fabulous" is a worn-out cliché used by lazy journalists. And secondly – eight stone? I'm a personal trainer not Jesus,' he said, with a hint of mischief in his voice. So, he had a sense of humour after all?

'Rude.'

'I just want to have you for, say, twelve weeks, we can do a lot in that time. I'll prove to you – and to me – that I can make a difference. I want to take on my biggest challenge – the most unfit, overweight person, lacking commitment, addicted to sugar, no staying power...'

'Ooh, you're making my head swell, keep those compliments coming Chris.'

'Unrealistic expectations... inflexible...'

'You really know how to charm a lady...'

'Doughnut-driven, ice cream-obsessed...'

'Stop, you had me at ice cream. I'm yours.'

'So you'll do it and provide a testimonial and before and after photos too?'

I gave him an uncertain look; did I really want to commit to all this?

'If not for yourself, think about all the other women out there who don't believe in themselves. You could do interviews with the local paper, the radio – you're a great talker, too much sometimes...'

'Thanks, you flatter me too much.'

'But you'll be an amazing challenge. People will say "if he can do that for her what can he do for me?" I'd love you to represent the personal training arm of my gym.'

'No one's ever said that to me before,' I said, sarcastically. But despite my cynicism, what was the alternative, really? I could struggle on alone and lose a pound then gain two, a constant scale rising daily along with my blood pressure. Or I could embrace the idea, take a chance, let Chris have his way with me in the gym? Yes, there was the possibility I may risk killing myself in the process and becoming some kind of weird role model –

or roll model for everyone to scrutinise and comment on, I'd had enough of that. But this was an opportunity to make a real change, with professional help – and for free, could I really say no?

I was desperate to be healthy and slim for my fortieth and I'd only ever done the journey alone but Chris might actually be one of the few people in the Western World who could help me on my crusade. I'd dreamed of being able to afford a personal trainer, and one who looked like Chris might even distract me from the pain of working out.

'I'll be there for you,' he said. 'Every step of the way.'

'You don't need to sell it to me,' I laughed, 'my answer is a big fat YES.'

Chapter Five

The Fruitarian Diet

Diet Diary: August 2006; Truly, madly, deeply, in unrequited love for a vegan at work called Tom. Had to lose a stone before his leaving party so ate fruit, fruit, and more fruit. He left without even saying goodbye. I compensated with crisps and chocolate for a month. Gained 10 lbs. Fruit is evil.

After Chris's phone call I felt very positive and decided to go for a walk on the beach. I was feeling good about myself and what was in store for me, I wanted to drink it all in and enjoy the moment. 'Stop and smell the roses,' Sophia had used to say in her half-Italian accent when I'd complained about something while working in the cafe all those years ago. It's only when you grow up you understand the meanings of these sayings – and now I knew I had to do just that, stop a while and enjoy what life was putting in front of me.

Back then the Ice Cream Cafe had provided a sanctuary, it also provided a kind of family – Sophia and Reg, her husband,

Gina the glamorous daughter who I'd never actually met but seen the photos and heard the stories about. I was only there at weekends and summer holidays while I was at college, but it became a home from home – especially as my own home was such a bleak, unwelcoming place.

And here I was, back again, seeking sanctuary at the cafe all these years later. I loved the solitude, the freedom, no busy traffic, no tubes to catch, no meetings to adhere to. Here in Appledore I simply woke each morning and went downstairs to work, I stirred ice cream, thought up recipes, chatted to and laughed with my crazy workmates, and now there was Chris, my new friend who seemed to make sense of everything.

Best of all, here in Appledore I was back with the sea. When you grow up living by the sea, it becomes part of you – and when you leave it calls you back. I used to hear it in my sleep in London. Sometimes I'd wake in the middle of the night convinced the sea was telling me to go home, but it was a train trundling past. I've never really felt at home anywhere except here – but here was also where the bad memories lived, here in the sand, in the foam of the tide. I could feel them now, on the beach, under the stars, waiting to reclaim me. Along with the happiness, there was always a shadow on my beach. But tonight I wasn't going to think about that, I was thinking about a new life for myself and becoming slimmer, fitter, happier. I was looking forward to helping Ella to realise the cafe's full potential and perhaps even helping her open a second Caprioni's one day. But more than that I was genuinely looking forward to achieving my weight goals, and for the first time ever, it seemed within my reach (unlike my shoelaces).

I walked along the damp sand, the sea was way out and above me was just endless black, dotted with the tiniest stars. Here under this perfect sky I felt as though I was finally healing and growing. Lost in my thoughts, I just kept walking. I marched out further than I intended, but was happy because I'd never walked so far without actually thinking about it, or complaining. And it felt good. I liked the feeling of being energised, instead of hiding in front of the TV with a tray of snacks I'd made a choice and gone walking. There was something in the salty air, something tangible and real – and I felt that this time it was going to happen for me.

Finally, I headed back for the cafe and just as I was crossing from the beach I saw a figure walking down the road. I don't think I'd have picked him out in a crowd, but at a distance I knew him straight away, that swaggering walk, like he owned the whole world… Jude.

I suddenly felt weakened, like he had some superpower that I was helpless to resist. I didn't want to see him, I wasn't ready, not quite strong enough to face him after all these years. Part of me wanted to walk to him, to say hello, how's your life, what happened? But I couldn't because all I wanted to do was escape. For a few moments I stood very still, but then something kicked inside me and I bolted. I couldn't face him, I couldn't face the past – and besides, I was fat, sweaty and make-up-free – and this wasn't how it was meant to be. I'd dreamed of this moment for a long time, and always my hair was down, and I was slim and when he looked at me with longing in his eyes I'd metaphorically grind him into the floor with my stilettos. I wanted to walk up to him and tell him he wasn't worth it, I wanted him to see me and want me and be able to turn on my heel and go, like he had all those years ago. However, my hair was flat, I was wearing a sweaty gym kit, and I still had a way to go with my weight loss.

No, this wasn't the setting to show him what he'd lost – with me looking overweight and ten years older, chip paper flying along the floor, and the sound of a dog barking in the distance. No, when I served him my revenge it would be cold, like ice cream, so I moved swiftly out of his path, already feeling fitter after my walk I ran across the road to the cafe, dashed around the back and stood behind the huge bins. From here I watched him pass, and when he walked under a street lamp, I saw him properly and the memories came flooding in. He hadn't changed, he was still Jude, dark, curly hair, handsome face, cocky walk. Eventually, after I had checked the coast was clear, I trudged back to my flat, thinking about him, and wondering if that unfeeling teenage boy had grown into a different man.

I tried not to think too much about Jude after seeing him. It wasn't like I was still in love with him, but I suppose I still held on to some feelings. He had been my first love, my first kiss, my first everything. But he hadn't taken care of my heart and he'd left me like an empty husk, unable to love anyone else for a long time, if ever. This had made me bitter for a while and though I was over it now, I needed to focus on me and on positive feelings and not let the negative ones drag me down.

I knew the breeze from the sea here would waft back memories and people; I'd seen several girls I'd been at school with taking their own kids to school. The same faces, just crinkles around the eyes, more worn around the mouths. I didn't have any real friends at school, my first friend came later.

I met Jane the same summer I met Jude, we were both working at the Ice Cream Cafe and we'd bonded immediately. She was as skinny as I was curvy, and where I was shy and quiet, she was loud and confident. We'd gone to the same school, but our paths didn't really cross and we'd never talked until we worked together. Our friendship was forged in the fires of post-school euphoria, we both had family issues that made us different and both suffered at school as a result. But at Caprioni's we were free from the bullies and the haters and we could be ourselves. I was doing a marketing course at college and Jane was at art college in Barnstaple, and boy had she changed since school. Where I'd actually put on weight since leaving, she'd blossomed into a beauty, tall and slim and a little bit crazy, she was captivating. She wore tight jeans and bikini tops to show off her midriff, while I covered myself in cheesecloth and black jersey. Jane only had to glimpse sunshine and her skin turned softly golden while mine burned.

For three years we shared our lip gloss and our lives. I thought we'd always be friends, we were so close; she was the only one I told about my mother's drinking. We both knew what it was to live with grieving parents who couldn't nurture us, Jane's mother had died years before and she lived with her dad and brother – so we'd learned to nurture ourselves. We found love wherever we could. I found it in food and Jane found hers in sex. We understood what it was like to have a parent who needed parenting, and even talked about trying to get them together so we'd be sisters, but my mother was filled with too much hurt and hatred to ever open up to anyone, and Jane's father was disabled by grief until the day he died. Consequently, both our childhoods had been sorry affairs we'd had to navigate alone – but now we had each other. And despite still being trapped in the same families, the leftovers of childhood, we lightened our days with secrets, whispered voices, tiptoes upstairs and our nights were spent in midnight escapes from bedroom windows.

I wondered if I might bump into her now. I'd never wanted to get in touch with her when I'd left Appledore because of what happened. I heard she left soon after, and it was only coming back here that had made me feel ready to see her again. I wondered what she was doing, how her life had panned out and if she was happy – in spite of myself I hoped so.

The day after I saw Jude I set off for the gym. Seeing him had been a jolt, and I'd spent a fitful night going over everything, reliving the good and bad bits of our relationship. And the following day I just felt stronger, he wasn't going to destroy me again because this wasn't about him, it was about me. So I set off for my first session with Chris as my personal trainer, and though I was a little nervous, I was filled with determination. My arrival from changing rooms to gym was surprisingly uneventful and, as a result of this, I was expecting at least a high five from Chris when I saw him across the gym. He looked up from a conversation he was having and came over to me.

'Hi Dani, come into the office,' he said. I didn't expect this, for once I genuinely wanted to get started and this all felt a little bit like I was in the headmaster's study.

He took a seat behind his desk and gestured for me to take the one opposite.

'Dani, we need to talk,' he said.

'The last time someone said that he was dumping me,' I joked. He didn't laugh, just looked a bit sorry for me.

'We need to plan this,' Chris continued. 'I want to create a food plan, an exercise plan, and even work through some of the issues that have stopped you getting to where you wanted in the past.'

That sounded sensible, manageable – and as long as it lowered my blood pressure and got me in that dress I would be happy.

'What I'm saying is – it's not just about what you eat and how you move, we have to work on your head too.'

'Yes, well that's been well worked on. My best friend's a psycho… she's always analysing me, she knows all about my childhood, and she's always going on about my mother-centred low self-esteem. I carry it around my middle.' I had to joke about this, the last thing I wanted was to be going all deep with Chris, I hardly knew him.

'You are a funny girl, but give yourself a break, stop beating yourself up,' he said. Looks like he knew me though.

'I'm not… and I don't want to bare my soul, this is about exercise, nothing else,' I said.

'We need to really get to the bottom of this and help you achieve your goals,' he added. 'I just think the first thing you need to do is own up. So, you're saying your mother played a big part in your relationship with food?'

'Yes, she did.' I gave in, I'd told him the first time I met him that I sweat a lot, and he'd seen me concussed and probably dribbling. My mother issues were just one more thing.

'Do you still have a relationship with your mother?'

'She died,' I said, feeling that shadow come over me.

'Okay, so you're blaming someone who isn't even here any more for what's happening to you now?'

I'd never thought about it like that before. 'I suppose…'

'Food is something we often associate with our mothers – it's something that comes with the job. But your mum isn't here now stopping you from working out, she isn't in the Ice Cream Cafe forcing sundaes down your throat, is she?'

'No she isn't, that would be alarming and I'd need to put in a call to psychic Sally.'

'There you go again, joking about everything – but this is serious, it's about your health too. And the first thing we need to do is for you to admit you have a problem and to take responsibility.'

I knew all the psycho shtick, I didn't need Chris preaching at me. 'So where shall we talk about my problem, over cake and coffee in Costa?'

'No that wouldn't be appropriate,' he said, without smiling. 'We're on the same side, Dani. Please don't see me as the enemy. I want this to work, I want to help you realise your potential, and in order to do that we have to be honest with each other, don't take offence when I tell you what I think.'

'Okay,' I said, feeling chastised.

'I'm a professional, and I may not agree with your choices, but I'm not your mother checking up on how many doughnuts you're eating...'

'Thank God for that.'

He didn't smile, not a flicker.

'But... I am your trainer and I've put my name and my reputation on this challenge,' he stood up, moved around the desk and put his hand on my shoulder and lowered his voice slightly. 'Dani, I understand you're scared of making changes and worried about going cold turkey when you give up your favourite emotional sugar crutch.'

'Emotional sugar crutch?' I said, amazed I'd even repeated this ridiculous phrase. 'That sounds like a girl band from the 80s. And anyway, a person can enjoy an ice cream without having to go into rehab.'

'Yes of course. But you told me yourself when we filled in the induction form that your doctor warned you about high blood pressure, so you need to eat healthily and exercise.'

'God, don't you think I *know* all this? Chris, I could tell you the calories and fat grams in that apple she's eating over there,' I said, looking through the glass of his office at one of the gym bunnies; 'and I can tell you how many calories I burn walking to and from the fridge and I can also confirm it doesn't cancel out the chilled Mars Bar in said fridge. It's not about knowledge, it's about the motivation and the staying with it and not saying "sod it" by lunchtime. I knew the calorie count of a Mr Kipling Fondant Fancy when I was ten, so please don't hand me charts and diets and weights... because I KNOW!'

'Okay, okay I get it… so channel all that energy into action, and make the changes you need, Dani,' he said calmly and kindly and at this I saw a twinkle in his eye. Yep, there was definitely more to him than stern trainer, and whoever got to see that was a lucky girl.

Despite being a bit officious at times Chris was soothing, he made me feel calm. I was used to arguing and fighting my corner, I'd done it with Mum and I'd continued to lash out as an adult. Now I needed to focus on my goals and stop fighting everyone.

'So why have you failed in the past?' he asked, going back to his notes.

'I don't know. What drives me? Is it hunger, hurt, emotions?' I'd tried most of my life to work out how my mind worked and what led me to fail again and again. 'Or is it other people?' I asked. 'The world is filled with saboteurs, delicious TV ads for sumptuous, sugar-crazed doughnuts, that bitch in the office who always brings in cakes and trans fat-filled snacks, but won't touch them herself because she's on a bloody diet. Then there's me, I try to cut down and move my arse but my desire for doughnuts always overcomes any plans for so-called "sensible" eating. And since when was a bunch of alfalfa sprouts sensible – they're the most ludicrous thing on the planet,' I laughed.

He smiled at this.

'And then there's the fact that I just *like* food. Why do people think if they put "sensible" and "healthy" before the word food they can ram it down my bloody throat,' my voice was raised now.

'They have to ram it because you don't bloody stop talking long enough to LISTEN!' he shouted in my face.

That woke the Stepford gym up. One or two even stopped their treadmills to see what was happening in the office. You could see them short-circuiting; who could possibly have made the mild-mannered, friendly golden boy of the gym so cross?

'I *do* listen,' I muttered after a few mortifying moments. 'I'm listening now aren't I… so continue your lecture.'

'No, I've said all I need to say for now, and if you're ready – we'll do some work.'

'Okay, so what's first?' I said, the familiar gym dread beginning to take hold.

He gestured for me to follow him out of the office and pointed to a large mat.

'Now, get on your knees…'

'The last time a man said that to me…' I started, about to say something hilarious, but the look on his face said that he meant business. Though it went against all my instincts, I did exactly what he said. We started off with the odd leg lift, which was painful and impossible enough, and then we moved to the weights area where I thought we might have a break and a coffee, but he forced me to lift weights and do lunges. And he wouldn't let me stop. Even when I shouted and cried, he yelled back and told me to get on the treadmill, and keep going until I stopped crying. So I cried again. I was hot, out of breath, in agony, my body was screaming for me to stop and I kept pleading with him to let me have a break, but he just kept going; 'Dig deep, Dani – you want this, you want this SO much.'

'I do, I do,' I was saying, and as I was on the treadmill I couldn't stop anyway so had little choice and just kept staggering on. I was all over the place and Chris kept turning the speed up until it must have looked like I was drunk. I felt wretched and just wanted to get off. Yes of course I wanted to be slim, I wanted to be able to run and skip and have all the energy and lightness of spirit that comes with being a healthy weight. I also wanted to walk along that beach in skimpy shorts and get a wolf whistle like Karla had on her first day here. But all I could see was pain. It became so unbearable I couldn't physically take any more.

'Stop… stop it… STOP OR I WILL DIE!' I shouted into the air, a primal scream piercing the polite silence, gym bunnies scattering as I grabbed the handles of the treadmill and reached to press the stop button, but Chris, unsmiling, was covering it with his hand, preventing me. 'I'm going to die… and when I do I'm going to sue your arse… take you for every penny you've got, you bastard!' I'm sure I spat in his face, the sweat was dripping down the backs of my legs and the swathes of black jersey were now clinging to my flesh. God alone knew the chafing situation I would be left with from this session. Along with the panda eyes from the non-waterproof mascara I'd naively applied before my workout, it would be fair to say I wasn't rocking the 'gym girl' look. It was definitely bordering on 'Fat Goth.'

'PLEASE!' I was calling. 'Please make it stop!'

'One more mile,' he said quietly, no drama, like it was perfect-ly normal to make someone feel this agony and then make them continue without flinching. He was standing by the treadmill, staring at his watch, timing me, looking up every now and then but ignoring my tears and the sheer agony on my face. I hurt all over and the sweat was trickling down my back and I was about to scream STOP for the millionth time, when I thought about *that* dress.

I saw myself standing in the cafe, sparkling in front of a cake with forty candles, all my friends around me, Chris with a new-found respect for his pupil and Jude wishing he could be with me. And something inside me clicked and I didn't stop – I just kept going through the searing pain. My limbs were now scream-ing out, my agonised muscles threatening to stop without my permission at any moment. But I kept on going... I was doing it! It was agony, but for once, Dani wasn't quitting!

Eventually, Chris took his hand off the stop button and I shook my head.

'It's okay, you can stop now,' he said.

'No... let's do five... more... minutes,' I said, and he cheered and clapped and I felt good about myself.

At the end of the five minutes I lunged at the stop button, the treadmill came to a halt and, on shaking legs, I almost fell off the machine for a second time in my gym career. But Chris was there to catch me and he lowered me onto a mat like a dying dog, which is where he left me for quite some time, lying in a pool of sweat in the foetal position, rocking backwards and forwards and feeling like I'd been attacked. I didn't recall any celebrity fitness videos featuring this particular scene, and I was sure as hell that Beyoncé wasn't left to die in a corner of her gym after her work-out. But as I said to Chris later, I was keeping it real.

And later that evening, when I'd finally recovered, I headed home feeling every muscle in my body, and I slept better that night than I had in years.

Over the next couple of weeks I worked out six times, and in between I walked everywhere and ate fresh, healthy food. It wasn't easy, and sometimes I longed for ice cream or chocolate. On the odd occasion I practised what I preached and sampled a small portion of salted caramel ice cream or a little bar of chocolate. But, on the whole, the exercise was so agonising I couldn't cheat on the food because it would render all the gym pain worthless.

My muscles screamed, I went to bed exhausted and my body began to rebel. My left knee started to ache and the doctor wrote that it was 'a sporting injury' in my notes – I was delighted, it was like being handed a medal. And Chris and I worked well together; he didn't flinch when I screamed and swore at him, he took everything in his stride and his calmness was good for me. He still took things too seriously though, often misunderstanding my jokes about doughnut consumption, cake addiction and 'ice cream baths'. Okay, I wasn't completely joking about the consumption and addiction, but an ice cream bath? I gave those up in 1998.

After two weeks and several sessions at the gym with Chris I was feeling so much stronger in every way. I'd test myself by looking around the cafe at the temptation winking back at me in the glittering jars of sprinkles and jewelled sugar toppings behind the counter. I'd gaze at the huge oblong blocks under glass, filled with swirling ice cream in every pastel shade, from pink to lavender to blue, then chocolates and coffees with chips and without. Working here was a huge test of my commitment and, for once, I felt in control. But I couldn't be complacent, I'd been here before.

'I hope I can stay strong,' I said to Roberta, one morning as we restocked the ice cream, it was all so pretty and the flavours so welcoming. Who could say no to sharp and fragrant 'Raspberry Rose', soft yellow 'Bananarama Drama', or 'A Day by the Sea', salted pistachio in sweet, creamy vanilla?

'You probably need to keep the incentive going,' Roberta said, looking from me to the piles of swirly ice cream doubtfully.

'Yes, but how? I have a personal trainer and I'm eating right.'

'You could call the *North Devon News*, tell them you're fat?' she said.

'I could, but then is that something I would want to announce to North Devon?' I asked, sarcastically.

'No, I mean tell them you work in an ice cream shop and you want to lose weight and it's really hard because of your job. It'd keep you on track because you've gone public with your commitment and it would make a nice picture story for this time of year. You could be photographed in the cafe and we'd get some publicity out of it too,' she added.

Roberta was all about the publicity and everyone had been so lovely with me since I arrived, making me feel welcome and included, I wondered if it might help all of us. If I was interviewed by the newspaper that would also be some publicity for Chris and his gym, so here was a way I could repay lots of people at the same time. Roberta was spot on, a public commitment to my weight loss would also spur me on, my health and my future depended on this. I had support from my friends and a personal trainer for the first time ever – and with the local community behind me I couldn't fail.

'Here, this is the phone number for the newspaper – they've been good to Caprioni's, give them a call and say you'll provide a photo opportunity – they'll LOVE it.'

Egged on by Roberta, I called the paper straight away and spoke to a reporter called Rhonda. I told her I'd returned to Appledore, I'd always struggled with my weight and heard myself telling her I was going to lose two stone over the next ten weeks with the help of a personal trainer from the local gym.

'That's twenty-eight pounds, quite a lot of weight in a short time,' Rhonda said.

'Yes, and I work at the Ice Cream Cafe so it's hard to resist the delicious ice cream,' I said, as Roberta nodded and smiled and handed me a list of the flavours which I read out. Rhonda wasn't responding now, she clearly didn't see 'a fat girl tries to lose weight' as a story, so I had to give this a bit of topspin and slipped into my old PR persona from my career in dessert marketing.

'My doctor told me I'm killing myself with carbs,' I said. I was completely misquoting the doctor, but knew this would make a good headline. 'She said I may not live to see my fiftieth birthday,' I added a nice soundbite for good measure.

'Mmm, anything else?' she asked, clearly not taking the bait. What the hell did she want? I'd told her I might die, it didn't get more dramatic than that.

'Anything else?' I repeated.

'Tell her about the 10k run,' Roberta yelped in my ear.

'The 10k run?' I said to Roberta, puzzled.

'Oh right… the 10k charity run in November – that's hardcore,' Rhonda's voice perked up, finally interested.

'Oh I didn't… yes… that's hardcore… but …,' I had no intention of doing this, and was wondering already how I was going to get out of it.

'Well we'd definitely be interested in doing something on that,' Rhonda was saying. 'The 10k is a big deal, and as you know it's for a great charity so we'd be happy to monitor your progress.' There was no stopping her now, I did try to say I might not make it, but it seemed Rhonda only heard what she wanted to and said as it was September and things had gone a bit quiet on the news front regarding tourist incidents and weather, I might make a good picture story. 'I'll be round tomorrow with a photographer,' she said, and the phone was down before I could say anything.

I sat with my phone in my hand and Roberta beaming at my side. What the hell had I just agreed to?

I spent the night before the photo shoot doing lunges, applying face masks and doing my hair. I wanted this to work and most of all I wanted to look good – there were a lot of people in this town who knew mousey, fat little Dani and I wanted to show them I might still be a big girl, but I had a personality and could be glamorous too.

'A couple of stories have gone down so we've got lots of space and we'd like to do something quite big on you for this week's paper,' Rhonda said the next day when she arrived with Mark, the photographer. I said I wasn't sure I wanted 'a splash', just a little piece about the cafe and the gym and their support – but Rhonda soon put me at my ease. 'Absolutely,' she said as we sat together over coffee and ice cream chatting, and Mark the photographer found his light.

I'd always hated having my photo taken, but the fact I'd been working out and had lost weight already gave me the confidence to pose and Rhonda and Mark were great. 'Work it, Dani,' she shouted, as I pouted and posed.

We'd used a corner of the cafe so our customers weren't disturbed, and Roberta made sure the Caprioni's sign was moved onto the wall behind me so we got plenty of exposure. Meanwhile, Sue produced the perfect spread of sundaes which were set on the table in the shoot – it looked like an ice cream heaven.

'As you can see, these desserts are delicious, and a huge temptation,' I said to Rhonda.

'I bet you come down here in the middle of the night and raid the freezers when no one's looking,' she joked. 'I know I would.'

'Absolutely,' I laughed as Mark told me to lie behind the ice creams on the table. I'd been delighted with the way he'd set the scene because it meant most of my body was obscured by the lavish selection of sundaes spread before me. I was feeling better about myself, I wasn't slim and gorgeous yet, but I'd done my hair and Rhonda had helped me with my make-up and I felt good. I was taking those first steps in my journey, and when everyone saw my 'after' photos in the paper, or me in red glitter at my party, they would be stunned. I was going to show them all!

I lay down across two chairs, exhausted when they'd gone.

'I bet you know how those supermodels feel after this afternoon?' Sue said as she wiped down the tables.

'Yes, it's not easy to keep smiling and posing, then having to do it all over again,' I said. 'My face is aching and so are my arms from holding up cones and sundaes.'

'Well I thought you looked lovely.'

'Thanks Sue,' I said, feeling all warm inside, the constant little girl wanting approval from her mummy. 'You sure I didn't look fat and forty?'

'No, sweetheart – you looked classy and extinguished,' she smiled, looking at me with pride.

That evening I went off to the gym feeling quite pleased about the potential newspaper coverage. I wandered into the changing rooms like a real gym bunny (if only in my head), chatting to the other patrons, and even showing someone which buttons to press on the cross-trainer. Who would have thought it? Me giving instructions on the ellipticals.

And as I joined Chris at the treadmills I couldn't wait to tell him all about my imminent media splash.

'I explained about you being my personal trainer and our mammoth quest to get the weight off,' I said.

'That's great that you've got us in the paper, but it might be a little soon to start talking about how much weight you're going to lose this early in the game,' he said.

'I know but I'm keen to throw down the gauntlet for the rest of the world to see that I mean it,' I said. 'I want to be committed, and there isn't a better incentive than telling lots of people that you're going on a diet.'

'Yeah, I know, I just don't want any of this to put pressure on you. And rather than a photo at the cafe – I think it would have been more appropriate for them to take a photo of you working out here.'

He would say that, wouldn't he? But I wasn't convinced a photo of me sweating and heaving in 75 metres of black jersey was exactly the image for me or the gym. Besides, I'd been happy posing at the cafe, I'd worn my new off-the-shoulder top and felt comfortable in my ice cream setting.

'Well, we'd better start working then,' Chris was saying. 'The press love a loser, and if you don't get two stone off, the headline'll be: "Dani's Diet Disaster", or something like that.'

'Oh Chris, I know the press better than you know bicep curls. I used to work in PR remember? This was just a fun thing to do.'

I smiled, recalling Rhonda the sweet, sensitive girl who'd asked me all about my hopes and dreams for being slim. She wasn't like the national press in London – I trusted Rhonda, she was from my home town, and I felt she genuinely wanted to see me succeed. Of course, I'd overshared as always and told her my life story – well the stuff I could bear to share – and she was so understanding it was like talking to a therapist – I even told her about being bullied, the way the mean girls had called me Piglicious and how my first boyfriend had told me I was 'fat'. She laughed when I told her I'd seen him and hid behind the bins at the cafe. 'Oh Dani, you are funny,' she said, 'but I feel your pain, love.'

I felt really good after talking to Rhonda, like I'd lost a tonne of emotional weight along with the real poundage, and I wasn't going to let Chris put a dampener on it just because I hadn't used the gym for the photo shoot.

'Yes, Rhonda was a joy,' I added.

'Journalists are rarely described as "a joy",' Chris said. I was beginning to realise that he could be a bit of a know-all, constantly telling me where I was going wrong.

'Well I know what journalists can be like, I worked with them for many years, Chris – but Rhonda wasn't like any of them, she even paid for all the ice cream.'

'*All* the ice cream… did you eat any of it, Dani?'

'For God's sake Chris, stop being my trainer for a minute. I *had* to eat little bits for the photos. But any of the ice cream consumed on the shoot was included in my daily intake,' I said, though a couple of spoonfuls may have gone astray in my calorie count. But I wasn't going to turn this journey into a prison sentence, I knew me and if I denied myself everything, then I would just want to eat it. For me, the fact I hadn't gone on to ingest the contents of the cafe when I was alone after the shoot was a bonus. 'It's all relative, Chris,' I said. 'I bet if you ate three scoops you'd feel like you'd let yourself down, whereas if I *only* ate three scoops I'd feel virtuous.'

'Mmm not sure you should be feeling virtuous after THREE scoops,' he said.

'We're talking ice cream not murder… and as much as I need to lose weight and eat healthily, I reckon you need to chill out and loosen up.'

'I get it, but as your personal trainer I can't condone…'

'*Condone?* Oh get over yourself, I'm not an approval junkie, I'm a sugar addict,' I said. 'And I'm managing my addiction, it's all I can ever hope to do, so if you can manage the anal aspect of your personality, we'll be okay,' I gave him a smile so he knew I meant this in fun. I was never quite sure how he took me, but I saw a twinkle in his eye. Chris always tried to be professional around me and around the gym, but I imagined he could probably be fun outside work.

The following afternoon I had a few hours off and went into Barnstaple with Gina, Ella's glamorous cousin. She was looking for an outfit for some posh dinner she was going to with her new boyfriend and I said I'd drive her there. I wanted to incorporate movement into my daily life and felt just walking around the town would be better for me than sitting in my flat avoiding the biscuit tin or, even worse, at the cafe lusting after ice cream. Gina was great fun, she filled the car with French vanilla from her vape pen, crossing her long legs and complaining about the lack of eligible men in Appledore.

'So, are you going to treat yourself to something fabulous?' she asked as we entered her establishment of choice. It was an upmarket boutique with designer names and not only couldn't I afford any of it, I'd never squeeze into any of it.

I smiled. 'No, this is *your* shopping spree,' I said.

Gina then spent the next hour and a half trying everything on in the shop, from tight party dresses, to ball gowns, to stuff bordering on bridal.

'I think this little number will be fabulous in Old Napoli,' she said, twirling in a finely pleated midi-dress in green that looked stunning on her. She was 'picking up a few pieces' for the trip to Italy which was pencilled in for the end of October, just after my birthday party, and she was very excited. 'Oh the Italian food, not to mention the men!' she squealed as she grabbed at a silk slip costing a week's wages and holding it provocatively across her. I'd heard all kinds of things about Gina, that she was rich and had a mansion in Hollywood, that she owned the cafe, that she was penniless. Who knew? But if her shopping bags were anything to go by I was putting my money on the mansion in Hollywood – she was spending a fortune.

'I could see you in this,' she suddenly said, whisking a mid-length, red sparkly dress from the rail. It was beautiful, like Dorothy's shoes in dress form, so twinkly and scarlet and lovely, just the kind of thing I would have worn if I'd been slim.

'I love it, Gina, but I'd never get into it.' I loved nice clothes, but never even tried them on because they didn't do my size or because I'd look like a clown in them.

'Go on, try it on. It might not fit yet, but you're dieting, in a couple of months that would look darling on you. This is your colour.'

Gina was convincing, it was a gorgeous red and the 'couple of months' was the eight weeks to my party. I'd always seen myself in a red dress on my birthday, but never one as glitzy as this, but I took it off her, and went into the changing room.

Once I was alone I held the dress against me; Gina was right about the colour, it set off my long dark hair and eyes and I just fell in love. I started to pull the dress over my head, praying I could at least get it on and not be stuck with it there and was pleasantly surprised how it went over my head and that I could actually get it on. I continued to pull it down over my lumps and bumps and I glanced in the mirror. The result wasn't amazing, but it wasn't as bad as I'd thought, the cut was good, it was expensive and it looked so classy – minus a stone or two this could really work. I felt a rush, almost like the kind of rush I got when I saw ice cream or doughnuts – but this was even better. Imagine walking into the cafe for my birthday party wearing this!

'How is it?' Gina suddenly whipped open the curtain.

'It's beautiful,' I sighed, 'and if I work at it I reckon I could squeeze into this by my fortieth... but...'

'But what?'

'I don't know if I'd have the confidence, everyone would look at me.' I longed for the sparkly dress, the party, the attention, and yet I'd been hiding myself away for so long I was scared of these things too.

'That's the point, honey, everyone *should* be looking at you when it's your party,' she said, pushing into the changing room and surveying me in the mirror. 'You HAVE to have this dress, babe... it's DIVINE!' she almost shouted in my face.

'It's probably a divine price too,' I muttered under my breath so the woman who owned the shop wouldn't hear me.

'Oh it's profanely priced,' Gina continued at an audible level, 'but don't worry about THAT! Maureen will let you pay in instalments – won't you Maureen?' she yelled through the curtains.

'Of course,' came Maureen's response.

'That's what I always do – until my millionaire comes along, hey Maureen?' Gina laughed as she went out of the changing room.

I stood in front of the mirror, the dress was £200, and I couldn't afford it, but to pay it off in chunks was possible. And this beautiful, sparkly thing would be yet another incentive to keep going on my journey.

Ten minutes later I'd put down a £25 deposit and my dress had been wrapped in tissue and boxed. I hadn't expected to take it away, but Maureen said she'd known Gina since they were at school and she let her take her purchases away before full purchase so she'd do the same for me. I was excited and delighted, I hadn't bought anything beautiful to wear for a very long time, and this was so special I had to lose enough weight to get into it for my birthday. And with help from my personal trainer I could… couldn't I?

Chapter Six

The Master Cleanse

Diet Diary: March 2007; I wanted someone (anyone?) to put a ring on it, so Beyoncé's diet of choice had to work, didn't it? No solids just lemonade and cayenne pepper, for days. And days. Beyoncé went on to get married and conquer the world. I stayed single and went on to gain 10 pounds.

The following day I headed for the gym – again. I'd done a full day's shift at the cafe, so had a long evening of lunges ahead of me. And to my surprise, I was actually looking forward to it – I needed this and after several weeks of working out I felt more alive and full of energy than I ever had before. I kept thinking about the beautiful sparkly dress and me standing under fairy lights greeting my guests at the party – and it spurred me on.

I think Chris picked up on my buoyant mood that evening and decided to really put me through my paces. It seemed that the minute I was vaguely comfortable with the workout, he immediately switched it up a gear, but that night was brutal. The session was all about a fast-paced series of leaps, jumps, lunges and springs – with weird bicycle movements against a wall. It was fast, sweaty, and probably very funny to the onlookers (and there were a few), but I did it, I pushed through the pain and the doubt and showed them all I was just as good as them. Then while sweating profusely and threatening to do something obscene to Chris with his own equipment, I collapsed in a messy, wet heap.

Sometime later, still in a state of semi-consciousness, I was aware that lights were being turned off and the place was almost empty. I hoisted myself up from the exercise mat, every sinew ready to snap, every muscle letting me know it was there as I got first onto all fours and then tried to get up onto to two legs. It can't have been pretty for Chris to see this bovine move, but I didn't care. All I could think was how everything ached already, so who knew what pain tomorrow morning would bring?

Chris was working on some weights at the far side of the gym, and despite wondering if I was dead, I found a few moments in the afterlife to appreciate his physique. He looked good, lean but muscular with his gym vest and shorts on, the muscles in his legs were firm, but not too bulky, his stomach was flat, his chest rippling.

I eventually gathered my body into a standing position and wandered over to him, stiffly, and when he saw me he stopped what he was doing and looked concerned.

'You okay?'

'Yes – I feel terrible, but good,' I smiled. 'Sorry if I was a bit of a cry-baby.'

'You were good, I wouldn't have made you do it if I didn't think you could.'

'But as my personal trainer wasn't it irresponsible, knowing that workout might actually be the cause of the gym's first, tragic death?' I teased.

'Nope,' he said, still lifting those weights, rippling those muscles, 'the secret is to keep going – and when you're done, go again.'

I wasn't so sure about that. 'So… I guess I could go and eat whatever I like when I go home now, with lashings of cream?' I said.

He looked alarmed.

'I'm joking, Chris.'

'I know, but I'm not acknowledging it, because it seems to encourage you. And when you're working out, you need headspace, and all that joking…'

'Okay, okay, I irritate you,' I said, knowing I could have this effect on people, men particularly.

'No, you don't, you make me smile, but I'm not buying into your flippancy. This is a serious business and we both want the same thing,' he said. I watched his arm muscles undulating and I wondered what it would feel like to touch them.

'Are your muscles hard?' I asked. I couldn't believe I'd just said this, I blame the boot camp workout I'd just done, my head was all over the place.

'Yeah I suppose so, feel them,' he held out a flexed arm and I gave it a squeeze, it was so solid and for a moment I dared to wonder how it would feel to have those arms wrapped around me. I didn't dwell on this, he was way out of my league and it was because of this I felt comfortable with him. I wasn't bothered about Chris seeing me sweat, scream and cry with no make-up on, because in my view he didn't see me as an eligible member of the opposite sex. I was his client, and it was purely business, but the fact he was always so calm and didn't erupt made me feel like I could push him a little. I turned around to see we were now the only people left in the gym, the evening had gone so quickly.

'You leaving soon?' I asked.

'Yeah I don't live far from the cafe, hang on and I'll walk with you.'

'Walk? You're joking it's about two miles from here – I'm in the car,' I laughed like he was being silly.

'I can't believe you'd drive when you could walk.'

'I know, but that's just the crazy shit I do. Wild eh?' I said sarcastically heading into the changing rooms to grab my things, I was too exhausted to change.

'Do you want a lift?' I asked, heading back into the gym.

He looked mildly affronted.

'Oh go on, it's late, live dangerously. I won't tell anyone,' I said, waving my car keys.

He said he would and we wandered out into the car park, my hair matted, my face sweaty and my legs wobbling as I walked.

'I'm not sure I will even be able to drive after that pummelling,' I said. 'You could be in for the ride of your life.' It was suggestive and funny and he laughed and raised his eyebrows and it was all so easy, because it meant nothing. We both knew he was a 10 and I was probably a 5 so all the innuendo in the world could never be misconstrued as flirting, so it was fun. This was the joy of being with an unattainable man – sex or the prospect of it just didn't get in the way.

'I can't believe you brought the car,' he was saying again, as I drove off from the gym car park and headed down onto the front.

'After what you made me do tonight I'm lucky I don't need an ambulance,' I said.

'You have to build fitness into your daily life.'

'I'd rather build ice cream into my daily life.'

'I know,' he smiled, 'that's the problem.'

'No, it used to be the problem, I'm getting on top of things.'

We drove on in silence, and I hated silence so I said: 'I bet you never eat ice cream, do you? Does your body reject it and make you sick?'

'No, I just stop when I'm full.'

'And I don't?'

'Do you?'

'No, well, I do now… most of the time. Having said that, I don't know if I've ever really felt full of ice cream, when you swallow it, it melts and makes room for more. I could eat it any time of the day. I've always loved the calmness of ice cream, cool, creamy sweet. It just soothes me, especially when I'm low or upset.'

'Ice cream for the soul,' he murmured.

'Yeah, that's a nice way to put it. After my parents separated, my dad would come and visit every Sunday and take me for ice cream at Caprioni's, I always had the chocolate sundae. It was divine,' I said, using Gina's expression. 'Crushed meringue, ice cream, warm chocolate fudge, chocolate flakes and a whole cherry on the top. Every time I thought of my dad I would taste that ice cream. He would hold my hand all the way to the cafe and I felt safe and free at the same time, like he'd got my back. And we'd sit at one of the little tables waiting for our order, my eyes darting to the counter every two seconds to see whether they'd made it yet. And when it arrived, I always took my time, savoured every mouthful making it last...'

'Because it was so good?'

'Yeah, it was bloody good, but also because when I'd finished, I had to go home, and I didn't want to. I'd have to say goodbye to my dad and I wouldn't see him for another week,' I smiled at the memory, pulling up outside the cafe. But then I remembered how sometimes my dad didn't turn up on 'our' Sunday. He'd sometimes call and cancel, sometimes he just didn't show. My mother would warn me he wasn't coming, but I didn't believe her and stayed by the window waiting until the night came in and the breeze whipped up the sea. Then the stars came out, and I knew then, and only then, that he wasn't going to take me to the cafe today. I blamed myself for him not coming to see me – after all I was so ugly and fat why would anyone want to be seen with me. How could anyone love someone like me, even my daddy?

'Is your dad still here, in Appledore?' Chris asked.

'No. He died suddenly, I was only twelve, I've never eaten a chocolate sundae since,' I looked over at him. 'Oh it's okay... I didn't give up – I moved onto strawberry sundaes, they don't taste of sadness.'

I glanced at him and he was looking into my face with genuine concern and I was touched. It occurred to me that night that apart from his sadistic tendencies in the gym, Chris might be a new friend, a good friend.

'Sorry… about your dad. That's young to lose him, is that when you started to eat?'

'No, I'd always enjoyed food, always enjoyed soft, warm carbs, sought comfort in the bottom of a bag of Revels,' I said, smiling sadly. 'But Dad left us when I was ten and that's when I really started eating instead of feeling.'

'You said your mum died… when was that?'

'Oh she died when I was nineteen, long time ago now,' I smiled, wanting to dismiss this, to move the conversation on. I still wasn't ready to talk about it. I'd felt a shiver run through me earlier as we'd driven past the road where we used to live, I hadn't been back there since that night. 'What about you?' I said, trying to push the past away; 'Do you still have both parents?'

He nodded, 'Yes, but they weren't happy, and I sometimes wonder if they'd been better off divorcing.'

We sat in silence for a while, both of us lost in our imperfect pasts. Funny how people can be different from each other, yet shared experiences can bring them together. I guessed from his answer that Chris hadn't had a happy childhood either and perhaps we got on so well because we recognised that in each other?

'I'm a couple of minutes down the front, here's great thank you. Will I see you tomorrow?' he asked, getting out of the car.

'Yes – I'll be there,' I said, sad to be saying goodbye, wishing we could keep talking.

He opened the car door and just before he climbed out, he said; 'Dani… when you get inside, go and make yourself a great big sundae.'

I was puzzled; 'Why?'

He laughed; 'Because I think you'll always do the opposite of what anyone asks you.'

I had to laugh, he'd only known me a few weeks and he could already read my mind. Was he clever and knowing, or was I just predictable?

He got out of the car, waved and walked down to the beach and started a slow jog, which developed into a run. I watched until he disappeared over and beyond the estuary and wondered if perhaps I should start jogging along the beach from the gym instead of driving home?

I thought a lot about what Chris said that night. I felt like something had changed between us, in a good way; I felt closer to him and I liked sharing bits of myself with someone who seemed to care. I felt like he knew me better than I did myself and only the day before he'd told me that I had to stop trying to be perfect. It echoed what Ella had said to me about the imperfect strawberry in the punnet, one flaw didn't mean I had to throw everything away. I think my constant strive for absolute perfection (which I was beginning to realise often inevitably ended in failure) was that I was trying hard not to become my mother. I often thought about the way she thought and behaved. I could see reflections of her in my own behaviour, and it scared me. She'd always been morose, quiet, anti-social really, so I strived to be different, like if I kept talking it wouldn't happen to me.

Chris saw this and said I was like a rather noisy butterfly. He said I had to concentrate on my exercise regime and try to put everything else from my head and focus, and I'd achieve more, but focus wasn't a word I knew. So he just kept me sweating and lunging and leaping until I was too breathless to speak, he said it was the only way he could get any peace when I was in the gym.

The original arrangement had been for just an hour a day, but after the first few sessions he gave me far more – I'd arrive at the gym after work and often still be there at eleven at night. He'd be locking up while still timing me on the treadmill and I even stopped taking the car. When we'd finished most nights, we'd walk back into Appledore together, and I enjoyed those walks so much, just strolling along the front, the night air cool and salty as we talked our way home.

'It's only been a few weeks but I'm losing weight slowly and I don't feel under pressure,' I said one evening as we wandered over to the treadmills together.

'I do sometimes cheat on the diet but I'm honest about it – with you and with myself. Besides, having put all the hard work in here I don't want to spoil it, so I don't go mad… and for the first time it seems to be working.' I loved the way I felt more at home in this environment too, though sometimes I'd glance at some of the women who were hard-core gym members and knew I'd never be like that. Karla always said I had to stop comparing myself unfavourably to others, but these women were perfect human specimens and I was still a blob. A fitter, healthier blob – but still a blob. 'I'm no gym bunny, I'll never look like her,' I said to Chris, pointing to a new member who looked like a model with long blonde hair and a body to die for.

'Oh you mean Alex? Oh she's very different from you…'

'Oh thanks,' I laughed, 'I realise that, you don't have to spell it out.'

'No I don't mean it in a negative way – she's just a completely different kind of person. Alex lives and breathes fitness.'

'Well she looks good on it.'

'You're more comfortable with yourself since you started working out, and already that looks good on you,' he said.

'Cheers,' I said, flushing slightly. I know Chris had to build me up, he was my personal trainer and it was his job to help me feel confident and good about myself.

'Don't blush when I say you look good,' Chris laughed.

'I wasn't, it may have escaped your attention, but I'm on a treadmill and it makes me red with exertion,' I said, rolling my eyes. He laughed and looked at his watch to time me, and I gazed briefly at his strong, lean, muscular body. In truth, his compliments made me slightly uncomfortable, they made me want something I couldn't have. I enjoyed spending time with Chris because he was incredibly supportive. I loved talking to him too, we had the same interests, though from different angles, he was keen to see how far he could push a person and I was keen to see how many calories I had to burn before I could eat a guilt-free sundae.

I saw Chris as simply my friend; yes, I'd noticed his glorious biceps, and yes, I could easily have melted into those blue eyes, but I would have been in a queue of millions. I'm also being honest when I say I wondered what kind of lover he would be... for someone else. Chris was so handsome, I knew he was way out of my league but that didn't stop me wondering, when I saw him running along the beach each morning what it would be like to be more than a friend to Chris...

Even though our workout sessions were vigorous, it showed how much my fitness had improved because I managed to talk through the sweat and panting. And after seeing the beautiful gym goddess Alex arrive on the scene, so perfect and cellulite free, I pushed Chris a bit more. It was either that or rush to the nearest chip shop to drown my sorrows in a large portion with salt and vinegar.

'No one is that slim and beautiful without having some hidden flaws... please don't tell me she's a prize-winning surgeon who's kind to animals,' I said in a low voice.

'She's not. She's actually a serial killer, it's how she stays fit, chasing her victims.'

I rolled my eyes. 'She'd probably be able to do that without a hair falling out of place. Just a sheen of sweat sparkling on her décolletage and a "come and get it" look in her eyes,' I said, marching harder on the treadmill. Chris didn't encourage my chatter during a workout and I knew if I kept on he was likely to hurl me into a lunging oblivion. However much I was changing as a person, thankfully I'd always be a rebel and struggled with authority. So I kept talking through the burn. 'So what's it to be, is Alex a bunny boiler? A black widow? Or just a gold-digging psycho with dead bodies in her basement? Go on, tell me what you reckon her flaws are.' I wanted to hear it from Chris, I'd seen them talking and I wondered if she was the kind of girl he'd go for. Who wouldn't?

'Well… she has absolutely… no flaws,' he said, deadpan, and before I could say anything, he took on a mock-dreamy expression making the shape of a heart with his fingers and thumbs. He was only teasing, and I laughed along, but for some reason it made me feel a bit uncomfortable.

'I wonder what it would be like to be her… just for a day?' I mused. 'To walk along the beach in a bikini and know you can have any man you want.'

'Mmm but you never will.'

'Oh thanks for that,' I said in pretend outrage.

'What I mean is, you could, but you won't. You're committed, but she *lives* for fitness, and would rather have an apple than your big scoop of Rocky Road Horror,' he teased. We both knew I wasn't bingeing on ice cream any more, but I took his point, she'd probably never eaten ice cream in her life. The weirdo.

'Yes, well Alex doesn't know what she's missing. Mind you, I'd trade one night with a bowl of Rocky Road Horror with hot fudge sauce for a night of passion with any of her suitors.'

'She doesn't have ice cream or suitors, she's here every hour of the day working out, totally obsesses about her cardio and what she puts into her body,' he said.

'Yeah,' I looked over at her, 'now you mention it, I can't imagine her face-down in a chocolate sundae,' I sighed.

'No, I can't either.'

'I miss inhaling ice cream,' I said this like I was speaking of a long-lost lover, and in a way I was. Let's face it, ice cream had given me the most pleasure and excitement for the past few years.

'A scoop of ice cream occasionally won't do any harm,' Chris conceded.

'Whoopee-do… a whole scoop?' I said, imagining myself in the kitchen in my nightie, whipped cream and sprinkles everywhere, cramming handfuls of ice cream into my mouth. 'Would I be allowed several scoops… with a whipped cream and chocolate button trim too?'

'You are a nightmare – it's time for you to take responsibility,' he said and threw a ball at me hard.

'Ouch, I can't catch.'

'And stop saying "I can't." Take the ball, I've thrown it to you and now you have to decide what to do with it. I'm not leading your journey, I'm next to you, so let's pick up some speed, stop looking at everyone else and comparing yourself unfavourably. Now MOVE!'

He made me jump slightly, and for a moment I was back on that school playing field, but looking over at him smiling, bouncing on his feet and beckoning me to throw the ball back, I knew I was finally among friends.

Chris seemed to care about what happened to me above and beyond the gym. He asked about my day, he told me about his, it was in a way a sort of relationship, the previous evening he'd even asked me when was the last time I had a boyfriend. I'd told Karla on the phone, but she'd said I mustn't read too much into this. 'People often fall for their therapists,' she said, 'and in a way he's like your therapist. You've met him at a vulnerable time in your life and he seems to offer comfort, support...'

I'd assured her I had no illusions about my friendship with Chris, but now, as I climbed onto the rowing machine and he told me how to position my body, I felt a rush of something. Here in the gym he was so authoritative – and so damn hot!

'So... what now,' I said, stalling for time so I could sneak in a few seconds' rest. I hadn't worked on the rowing machine before, I was a little scared of that and the cross-trainer.

'Dani,' he said, as I tried to put my feet into the stirrups and inadvertently caused my whole body to shoot forward.

'I have whiplash,' I said, clutching my neck.

'We just talked about you taking responsibility and you can't even get yourself on the rowing machine – let alone work it,' he said, holding my foot like I was a child and he was putting on my shoe. Eventually, I was 'strapped in'.

'Do we have lift-off?' I asked.

'Yeah, go on, I want to see you do ten minutes on here... it's really easy, just push off with your legs, pull the oars to your chest, bend your knees and start again. And please don't pull, break or maim anything – or concuss yourself.'

'Okay,' I said, reaching for the oars and pulling them back while pushing my feet forward. I did this with some gusto and he just stood by while I threw myself into the whole thing. I was really going for it; I'd show him. After a few rounds, I began to get into a rhythm, but my upper thighs were killing me and my stomach was pulling too. Now I knew how those Olympic rowers felt, it looked so easy but it was agony. 'How many minutes have I done?' I gasped.

'Forty-four seconds,' he monotoned.

'Don't lie to me, Chris.'

'I wasn't.'

Throughout this time, I kept my birthday party at the forefront of my mind. I needed to focus on my goal, so called Karla regularly for advice on invitations, decorations and food – ice cream obviously, I'd allow myself some leeway, food-wise, at my party. Ella and the rest of the cafe girls were behind me on this and Ella said she'd make several gallons of ice cream specially for my party.

One evening when I'd been working out, I went home and tried on the red dress, taking it carefully out of the box, and unfolding the tissue paper. I put it over my head and pulled it down over the lumps and bumps as I had in the changing room a few weeks earlier and to my deep joy there was definitely less resistance. I wasn't ready to wear it out yet, but it certainly fit slightly better – I just had to keep doing what I was doing! Jude always said I suited red – it went with my dark hair, but as I put on weight he'd suggested I should wear black; 'it covers you better,' was what he'd said. I'd worn a lot of black until now.

I wished I could shake off the memory of him. He'd even turned up in my head when I'd weighed myself at the gym at the end of week one and had only lost one pound, I'd heard Jude saying, 'I just don't fancy you any more.' And then my mother's slurred voice telling me I'd always be fat, always fail at everything. This was her mantra, I was her subject of choice after a few drinks; 'You're lazy, that's your trouble,' she'd say. 'And greedy... you're so greedy.'

'I'm greedy, you see,' I said now to Chris as we worked out together. We were doing weights and I was trying to explain why I'd always found it difficult to resist what I referred to as 'the call of Krispy Kreme'.

'No one is greedy, Dani – some people are more hungry than others – but there are reasons for that, as you know.'

'I've had other clients whose parents had been abusive and it's often a trigger to overeat,' he said gently.

'Mum didn't mean to be like that,' I said, my voice cracking, 'she just didn't love me enough. How could she? I was fat and ugly and...' It was late and the gym was almost empty so we both sat for a while, neither of us knowing what to say. I'd only ever shared my mother's alcoholism with Karla, and even then I hadn't told her everything, I was too ashamed about how I'd behaved, and what happened. 'This isn't what you signed up for,' I said to Chris, wiping my eyes. 'You can tell me to sod off, you don't have to stay as my trainer.'

'Why would I do that?'

'You didn't know I'd be like this, when you agreed to train me. You probably thought "Oh she's a laugh, I'll just turn her from a heifer to a hottie and be on my way," but here I am telling you my life story...'

'No one's ever as simple as they seem. When I first met you I knew there was more to you and that you'd probably be all kinds of complicated.'

'Oh yes I'm very mysterious, I cover it all up under this fleshy exterior,' I laughed.

'I reckon underneath all that flesh there's a girl just itching to work out,' he teased.

'And I reckon under that sanctimonious lettuce-eating exterior there's a fat kid just itching to eat ice cream,' I said, and gave him a hard nudge.

'There's a fat kid inside all of us… it's just that some of us have locked him up and thrown away the key,' he said. I detected a sadness in his eyes and wondered why, but before I had chance to utter another sentence I was being handed a very heavy tyre and told to flip it.

As the tyre hurled forward virtually taking me with it, Chris covered his eyes in mock horror, just waiting for the crash.

And as much as I huffed and puffed and retaliated – I liked the attention he gave me, it was fun and affectionate, and until now I'd never really had this with anyone.

Chapter Seven

The Werewolf Diet

Diet Diary: July 2009; Fell for a guy who lived in the flat below who looked a bit like Jacob from Twilight, so I thought why not? Twenty-four hours of hell drinking only water and juice with no solids. After three hours of howling at the moon (and the fridge), I caved in and ate too much ice cream. I lost a pound and he moved out.

I meant what I'd said to Chris about taking a look at things from my perspective. I'd been in his world of lunges, press-ups and low carbs for a while now so it was time he visited my world. As it was Sunday evening and the gym closed early, I invited him over to the cafe for a relaxing post-workout ice cream sampling. I was pleasantly surprised when he didn't leap back making the sign of a cross and start throwing holy water at me.

'That sounds… good, I think,' he said warily, like I'd asked him to do a Bush Tucker Trial. Baby steps.

'We have to have some light and shade, we can't live our lives denying ourselves a little treat now and then.' He was helping to push me into a healthier life and I wanted to push him to enjoy life more. God knows what his idea of enjoyment was after a tortuous workout – probably forty lashes and a freezing cold shower.

'I don't want you to see this as an excuse to eat ice cream indefinitely.'

'As if?' I said, mock-horrified at his suggestion, though there was something about having your trainer with you when you ate ice cream. It kind of gave me permission to enjoy some guilt-free sugar.

'If you overdo it, I'll make you run up and down the beach twenty times.'

I'll admit the threat of running suppressed my appetite for ice cream temporarily, but walking home with him later I was really looking forward to a few scoops.

It was after ten when we arrived at the cafe, it was closed and quiet and we went into the back kitchen where I brought out various delicious flavours.

'Some of these are new, Ella asked us to taste them and let her know what we think,' I said, lining them up on the counter, where Chris perched on a stool. I glanced at him and it made me smile to see him fidgeting slightly, he looked out of his comfort zone – as I had once in the gym. Oh, how the tables had turned.

'Your boss asked you to try the new ice cream flavours?' he said incredulously.

'Yes, honestly, it's my job,' I said, hearing myself and starting to laugh. 'It's vital research, Chris.'

'I've never heard ice cream called research before,' he said, taking small tastes from each of the scoops. 'It's like wine tasting, you should probably spit it out once you've tasted,' he teased.

'Oh too late! Oops I just swallowed it all,' I laughed and then he blobbed some banana nut onto my nose and I responded with a splash of vibrant vodka lime on his.

'Ooh that's nice,' he said, 'really sharp and tastes of alcohol.'

'That's from Caprioni's "Adults Only" ice creams, they are so boozy we couldn't let children near them. I don't like them myself, can't stand the taste or smell of alcohol.'

'Oh… your mum?'

'I think so, but to be honest I'm kind of grateful to her – alcohol would just be something else I'd have to give up for my health, so I reckon she did me a favour.'

'You're right, you have to see the silver lining… hey taste this,' he said, offering me a pink splodge of ice cream on his spoon. He held it while I took it with my lips, it felt like such an intimate thing to do I felt my face flush and was glad we were in low lighting. 'I love this,' he said, 'but it's full of cream and sugar, isn't it?'

I nodded; 'That's what ice cream is – the base of our ice cream is cream, sugar and eggs – the yolks make ice cream creamier.'

'What about sorbets, do you make those, presumably they're healthier?'

'Yes, but they have sugar in them.' God, I wished he'd chill for a moment and forget about the bloody nutritional value of everything he put in his mouth.

'It won't kill you to enjoy the sweet, fruity vibe of "Ravishing Raspberry", or Ella's mum's invention – a "Beyoncé Boost"; cool watermelon with a sizzling hint of hot ginger.'

'What about using the sweetness from the fruit?' he said, ignoring what I felt was quite a seductive sales pitch.

'We do that too, we sometimes make an ice cream I created when I was just a teen,' I said proudly. 'It's called "Dani's Emergency Ice Cream", you just put frozen strawberries into whipped fresh cream and watch it turn into ice cream. It's like magic!'

'That sounds delicious, perhaps there's a healthy alternative?' he said.

'Mmm there might be but it might taste revolting,' I smiled.

'I think it could be a way of you having your cake and eating it,' he said with a twinkle in his eye.

'Mmm, that's been my problem, having cake and eating it.'

'Yeah. That's what brought us here,' he smiled.

'Thing is Chris, I'm a purist, I don't want anyone to bastardise my ice cream,' I said, moving away from the bowl and showing some restraint in the face of several sweet, creamy melting scoops. I was surprised at myself, I wasn't shovelling it in like I used to, just tasting bits here and there – and I wondered if I'd really changed, or was I self-conscious going for it in front of Chris?

'I understand, you want ice cream to be ice cream,' he said. 'And thanks for tonight, I've enjoyed tasting your ice cream, so why don't you come over to mine tomorrow after the gym and I'll show you my version?' he said.

I was surprised and flattered by his offer, that someone like Chris would want to spend time with someone like me outside the gym was lovely. I stopped myself from being carried away by this – I had no illusions, this was all part of the trainer/client thing. I had to remember that Chris saw me as his project, and he just wanted to try to entice me over to the dark side of low fat low carb low bloody trans-fat ice cream.

Despite eating only full fat, carb laden, sugar laced ice cream, I was prepared to see what he had to offer and agreed to join him. It would be fun, I enjoyed his company even if I didn't enjoy his ice cream. The following evening I headed for the gym and despite our new status as friends outside the gym, we were back on his terrain and he was very much the task master. He barked at me, yelled at me, turned the treadmill faster as I was running, almost causing an international incident. While sweating, panting and heaving in my usual glamorous manner, I did wonder if I'd just imagined the evening before. I thought we were friends, but he seemed to be punishing me even harder, probably trying to work off the previous evening's scoops. I wondered if we were still going back to his to try out his ice cream and I have to say I felt a frisson of relief and excitement, when at the end of the workout he said, 'Get dressed, you're coming home with me.'

'I love it when a man says that,' I joked, skipping off into the changing rooms.

So once we'd changed and he'd locked up we headed over to his place (walking! And it was much further from the gym than mine). We arrived at his little cottage on the estuary and before we'd even gone inside I felt it welcoming me from the beach.

It was now dark and there was lamplight in the window, the inside was dark wooden beams and floors, raspberry walls and lovely old rugs. I didn't expect this cosiness, I expected clean lines and minimalism from someone as single-minded as Chris, but this felt like a warm hug. The kitchen was sparse, but functional, and when Chris opened the fridge it was filled with fresh vegetables and bottled water. Until recently mine had been stuffed with chocolate and oven chips, but I still hadn't reached this level of 'healthy', I'm not sure I ever could. I still wanted enjoyment from food, butter on my toast, sauce on my steak and the odd ice cream now and then, and if I exercised, I could have this.

Chris brought out a couple of large tubs of Greek yoghurt, several punnets of raspberries and the last of the season's peaches, soft and fragrant. I tasted a raspberry, jaw-achingly tart and yet sweet, as he put a pan on the stove. We chatted as he boiled the raspberries with a small amount of low-calorie sweetener then sieved them to get rid of the seeds. Then he mixed the pulp into the cool, creamy yoghurt and added some peach purée to another tub of yoghurt and put them in the freezer. This was a man used to looking after himself, he'd obviously been single for some time. While we waited for them to freeze we drank green tea and talked until it was time to taste the ice cream. He held out a spoonful to me and I couldn't believe how creamy and delicious it was.

'And a fraction of the calories,' he said.

I'd been highly sceptical about this and expected to be thoroughly underwhelmed by it, but I loved the frozen yoghurt and planned to make some for Ella to try for the cafe, everyone was looking for a healthier alternative these days. And for me this discovery was even more special because ice cream had always been a trigger food. But this was healthier and not only did it taste wonderful, I didn't feel like I'd blown my diet. This was a revelation.

'Thanks Chris,' I said as he walked me back to my flat along the beach late that night. It was after midnight, it was a bit of a hike, but I felt alive, and very much awake.

'Why are you thanking me?'

'Because you showed me tonight that there are alternatives, there are other roads to take.'

'In that case, thanks to you too – because last night you introduced me to the "Elvis is Dead Long Live the Peanut Butter Explosion" – and kale smoothies have never tasted as good as that,' he laughed. And we strolled along laughing together in the darkness – an uncomplicated friendship with no expectations. I'll always remember that night, walking side by side under the stars, I was happier than I'd been for a long time. My heart had always longed to return to Appledore, and finding a friend like Chris completed the picture, and made it even better.

I had thrown myself into my new life, working hard in the cafe and even harder in the gym. I made Chris's 'froyo' for Ella, who loved it and introduced it onto the cafe's ice cream menu, starting with raspberry, then strawberry, then peach. For me it was a lifesaver, and whenever I felt the need for ice cream I had a scoop of this delicious stuff and found I really enjoyed it – yes as much as salted caramel with hot fudge sauce – I know! As summer slowly moved on, slipping into early burnished autumn and the fresh fruits became scarcer, we used frozen and tinned fruits with the yoghurt.

I loved my job and I loved working with Chris – he got me, and not only did he now laugh at my humour, he often joined in. He said I was 'refreshing' and I made him laugh with my irreverent attitude to exercise and eating. Meanwhile he made me groan at his obsession with whole foods and calorie counting and stretching. Sometimes, in the middle of a really tough workout I'd swear at him by hurling names like McDonald's, Domino's, Burger King – and he'd flinch like it was garlic to a vampire. And doughnuts? He hated them with a passion; 'Toxic. No nutritional value whatsoever,' he'd say when I told him I was lusting after a Krispy Kreme.

'Who cares about nutrition? They are delicious and you get sugar all round your mouth, unless of course you go for a glazed one with sprinkles. I've learned to eat those and still keep my lipstick on,' I offered him a high five at this achievement, but, not surprisingly, he left me hanging.

'Doughnuts are the devil's work, Dani,' he'd tease and then make me do ten more lunges because I'd 'sworn' in the gym.

Chris and I were as different as two people could be, but I stuck to my part of the bargain and turned up at the gym and gave everything… most of the time.

'You'd better not let me down and bring shame to the doorstep of this establishment,' he'd say, if ever I slacked. 'My business and my future depends on you and your fat lazy butt.'

Where once I'd have been horrified at the word fat, I learned to laugh at it. Fat was not a dirty word, it was what happened when you ate a lot and didn't exercise. Only I had made myself fat, and only I could do something about it. I knew my good work would all disappear if I slipped up and found myself head first in a freezer, my face eating its way out of salted caramel ice cream, but for now it was good, not least because of Chris.

I was able to talk to him in a way I hadn't with anyone else, even Karla. I suppose the fact he had the time to devote to me helped, but it was more than that, we were drawn to each other as good friends are. We shared jokes, enjoyed the same music and I was even growing to *almost* like weight training. The physical effort was still tough and vaguely unpleasant, but this was outweighed by the rewards I felt as a result of the effort. It made me feel stronger, more able to cope emotionally and physically with what life threw at me. I was soon able to carry huge cartons of ice cream round the kitchen, help the delivery men with crates of fresh fruit, move the barrels containing soft drinks without getting out of breath. I felt more active, more vital.

Being able to be honest and open with someone who understood was soothing and healing. I talked to Chris about my mum and how she used to hurt me with her words. He reassured me that she probably hadn't meant to hurt me, that she was ill, had an addiction, but when you're little you don't understand this. And even now, at thirty-nine, I still didn't understand how my mother could say those things. I'd watch Karla with her children, considering their feelings, protecting them from everything from the common cold to nasty kids in the playground, but as a child, I lived with the nasty kid in the playground. I left the sanctuary of school and caring adults to go home to my mother's cruel remarks, her baiting, never knowing who she would be when I opened the door.

As well as comforting me, Chris liked to tease me, but when he did, it was affectionate. His words didn't define me, I was so much more than that, I was intelligent, funny, attractive. Karla had been telling me for years, but perhaps I needed to hear it from someone else? Someone like Chris. I appreciated his advice because it came from an objective, unbiased place, he wasn't my lover and he wasn't my best friend who'd known me for ever. Here was someone who I'd known a few weeks, yet he'd seen me in a completely new way. He didn't judge me for being overweight and hungry, he just said 'let me help you with that,' and I felt supported.

I still screamed at him sometimes to 'STOP!' which I often followed up with some abuse, but it was all in fun, and I became so much more positive to embracing movement. I didn't sit on the sofa dreading having to get up, I didn't order pizza because I couldn't be bothered to cook, I loved creating new healthy dishes and was slowly becoming the woman I'd always wanted to be. These days I actually looked forward to the exercise, because Chris made it fun. And if I had a tantrum or shouted, he didn't screech at me or call me names, he smiled calmly and allowed the storm to pass. I'd never been able to retaliate at home, I'd always been too scared, so shouting at Chris when he made me unhappy with his demands in the gym was surprisingly therapeutic. And I knew when I'd calmed down, he'd still be there for me, waiting, calm and ready to continue.

I felt like I'd been living under a cloud all my life. And the word 'fat' was a big dirty raindrop waiting inside the cloud to land on me. But not any more. So while keeping the rain at bay, I also began to listen to my body instead of swallowing my feelings down with food. I stood in front of the cake shop, the ice cream van, the cafe and the fridge and asked myself if I was really hungry, and sometimes I said no and moved on. If I really, really wanted the ice cream/éclair/chocolate bar, then I would have one, I wouldn't deny myself, because that's how I became fat in the first place. Denial leads to longing and longing leads to a binge, but not any more, I felt in control. This was real life, and the road to becoming slimmer and healthier wasn't going to be quick or easy, and as someone who'd used food all her life to stay sane it would always be part of me. I just needed to manage it and, like a recovering alcoholic, I had to learn to take each day at a time. And some of those days were hard and it wasn't all lettuce leaves and lunges – there were days when I ate a cream cake or a couple of scoops of a new ice cream in the name of 'testing' and 'research'. But I didn't eat so much I made myself feel sick, as I often had in the past. I tried not to hate myself afterwards too, which wasn't the easiest, as that had always been my default status.

I also faced the fact that I would never be eight stone, and even if I did I wouldn't be happy because that wouldn't be right for me. I would struggle to maintain a low weight. I loved food and wanted to live a full life and I'd seen those skinny girls at school, smelled the sick in the toilets, heard the retching and I didn't want to swap one addiction for another. I'd realised many years ago my mother's legacy would be with me for ever, and it was up to me to deny it. Abstinence, be it from food or drink or gambling, is easy for a little while, staying 'on the waggon' can last for weeks, even months, but I had to promise myself to stay on for a lifetime, because I'd seen what the alternative was. Mum would go for days sometimes without a drink, desperately trying to be sober, but denying herself the drink made her want it more, and when she fell off the waggon it seemed to be worse each time. Even the sober days, when life was filled with a strange calm, became tension-filled, just waiting for the inevitable and spectacular fall. I'd seen Mum come undone so many times, I knew that to deny myself totally wasn't the answer. And if I 'failed' I tried not to be too hard on myself. If sometimes I had an extra scoop, or a pouring of hot fudge, and felt guilty, I tried to get it into perspective. I hadn't hurt anyone, I'd just eaten something I liked, and often I'd just go for a long walk on the beach and work it off and out of my head.

In the early part of our training relationship Chris said part of my 'recovery' was to start being more honest and so I'd confessed about the two waffle cones and the chocolate bar I'd eaten that week. 'Oh and Wednesday we went to a curry house, so there was that…' I'd added. It was my father's birthday and it had brought the past back in quite a big wave and I'd weakened, this would happen and I knew it, but I tried not to let it take me over.

When I'd confessed I remember Chris looking at me, slowly shaking his head, he seemed sad, disappointed even, and I felt like I'd let my favourite teacher down. So for the next few days I ate like a supermodel, almost starving myself, eating only leaves and mineral water with the odd chicken leg and I lost three pounds and he seemed pleased, but I was so hungry I felt ill and had no energy. I didn't tell him.

'You need to find some equilibrium,' he said when we'd finished the workout, 'I know you're not eating properly, I can see it in your eyes… in your energy levels.'

'Yep I have come to bed eyes and come to bed energy levels,' I laughed.

He'd started to smile when I made a joke, but his face turned serious. 'What's wrong with you today, Dani?' he asked.

'I'm tired and fed up,' I admitted.

'That's my fault,' he said. 'I made you feel bad about eating and I started the cycle all over again. I'm sorry – I sometimes have to work out what works for each client, and with you it's about allowing you to make the choices.'

'I swing from one extreme to another, from a food high to a food low – and when I tell myself I can't have something I want it,' I said.

'That's okay that's human, there's nothing wrong with you, Dani,' he said. 'You seem to think you should be perfect, that if you're anything less than perfect then you're a bad person. But being human is about being flawed, we all make mistakes, bad judgements and that's all part of living… it makes us who we are, real people. I see lots of people at the gym who eat right, live right and look gorgeous, but it isn't everything – and it won't make you happy. You have to be happy first…'

'But how can I be happy when I'm overweight and worried about my health?'

'I can't answer that for you, it has to come from inside. Stop beating yourself up and thinking everyone else has all the answers. They don't, and you're not the only one struggling through.'

He was right, but he didn't know what I was struggling with. He didn't know what kept me awake at night and how the sound of the sea whispered my secret back to me again and again.

Chapter Eight

The Bacteria Diet

Diet Diary: December 2009; Fermented foods? Gut bugs? Please? Just thinking about this diet caused me to forget the man and mainline Snickers Bars. I gained 4lbs and a LOT of empty chocolate wrappers.

'What the hell?' Chris said one evening as I slaved over the rowing machine. I'd finally got the hang and the co-ordination – or so I thought – and was beating quite a rhythm.

'I know, I'm working up a sweat and I haven't complained once,' I said, pleased with my progress and taking a masochistic pleasure in my burning limbs.

'I'm not talking about your rowing, I'm reading all about you on the *North Devon News* website,' he said. I looked up and he wasn't even watching me, he was scrolling through his phone. 'Apparently you are, and I quote, "killing yourself with carbs", and you pop downstairs into the cafe each evening alone for a midnight feast of ice cream,' he was looking at me questioningly.

'Oh, the newspaper article… I wondered when that was being published. I've checked every week but was probably usurped by all the recent UFO sightings in North Devon, not to mention The Psychic Goat. Glad it's finally in but I'll admit in the absence of an extra-terrestrial or a goat with powers, I exaggerated my story. I told Rhonda that the doctor said I wouldn't see fifty… she's probably made a right meal of that, hasn't she? But it's annoying because I didn't say anything about eating at midnight.' Then I heard it in my head, Rhonda asking if I popped downstairs into the cafe to eat ice cream at night, in secret – and I'd said yes. Damn her! 'Oh well, I suppose that would make a good addition to the story, especially when I lose all the weight, I could say how disgusting and greedy I *used* to be.'

'Not sure that's quite the image we want for the gym,' he was saying, still reading.

'Mmm sorry about that, I was just being sociable, not quotable,' I said, 'and any publicity's good publicity, Chris. So… what are the photos like?' I was panting now, still going strong, but hurting everywhere and my lungs were at the point of explosion. 'Do I… look as delicious as the… ice cream?' I laughed, and wheezed, remembering the way lovely Rhonda fluffed up my hair and gently lowered my off-the-shoulder top. 'You have beautiful shoulders,' she'd said, 'show them off.'

'I haven't got to the photo yet, I'm still reading the article…'

'Let me see!'

I instinctively stood up, desperate to get off the rowing machine to see the article on his phone. In my haste I'd forgotten my feet were strapped in and lurched forward in a rather inelegant way, flailing my arms in the air and making a loud guttural sound as my feet brought me back to the machine with a bump.

'You can't get off the rowing machine until I say,' he smirked, then looked up and feigning surprise added; 'Oh you literally *can't* get off it.'

I was lying on the floor a twisted torso, my feet still strapped into the rowing machine. I was trying to be authoritative, demanding he show me his phone while attempting to release myself by crawling along the floor on my stomach. I hadn't seen any of the gorgeous gym bunnies do this particular move, especially while sweating, wheezing and shouting expletives, thank God Rhonda wasn't here with her photographer now.

'HELP ME, CHRIS… you can see I'm in some distress,' I said, reaching my arms out to him.

'No, you have to stay on… and on… and on.'

I was so exhausted I couldn't form a sentence so just shouted words loudly back at him; 'sanctimonious', 'gym-obsessed', 'muscular airhead' were just some of the insults but he laughed and said 'ooh that really hurt, save your energy for the machine, ice-cream obsessed, self-pitying food cheat,' and carried on scrolling through his phone. 'Dick… head' was all I could muster after that, and still he wouldn't unstrap me.

'It's like being in Guantanamo,' I yelled. 'You are cruel and insensitive and a bloody torturer.'

'Hey, have you read any of this?' he said.

'No… how could I, I'm incapacitated?'

'Apart from being a secret ice cream eater who's close to death, it says you ran away after your mother died and had a tragic love affair you haven't ever got over.'

'No I… God I can't believe she wrote that! Okay, okay yeah it was all a bit bloody tragic now you come to mention it. Let me see,' I was now staggering towards him. And when I got there I saw the headline and immediately felt sick; 'Ice Cream of Being Thin!'

'What the bloody hell…' I said, reading it out loud under my breath. *'Dani is hoping to be flabuless by her fortieth birthday. Dani Sheridan is a BIG lady with BIG ideas – she's planning to lose a LOT of weight by giving up Caprioni's famous ice cream.*

'Dani, 39, who works at Appledore's oldest ice cream cafe has returned to the village after a twenty-year stint in London. Her career involved buying and eating cakes for a living – and she says it certainly shows, but now she's struggling with ice cream. "I sometimes pop downstairs at midnight in secret and sample the delicious ice cream," she said. But having been told her weight will KILL her, Dani is now on a strict diet and exercise regime with Chris Taylor from the 'You work it out' gym in Appledore.

"'I was bullied at school, the other girls called me Piggylicious," tearful Dani explains. "I left Appledore when my boyfriend broke up with me because he said I was too fat," she told North Devon News. *"It broke my heart, and now I'm determined to cast off this weight, change my life and do my bit for charity," said the curvy ice cream queen.*

'We will be featuring Dani in our "Dani the Dieter's Special" pull-out later in the year when she's promised to run 10k in a bikini.'

I could feel my face glowing as Chris repeated the words, 'Curvy ice cream queen? Piggylicious?'

'Don't... don't... and it was actually *Piglicious*, she got her facts wrong.'

'Oh that's okay then.'

I ignored him, I was trying to compute the fact that some of the worst bits of my life had been laid bare before North Devon and the surrounding areas, while not having a heart attack. But my immediate concern was more pressing. 'and I *never* said I'd wear a bikini,' I sighed, disappointed that lovely Rhonda had revealed everything I'd told her, and turned in to a treacherous bitch the minute her digits hit the keyboard. 'I should have known she'd elaborate on the whole bloody thing.'

Chris smiled, taking the phone back from me; 'Well we've got our work cut out if you're running 10k by your birthday... in a bikini.'

'Walking. Fully clothed.'

'Running... it's a 10k *run* not a *walk*.' He continued to scroll as the photos slowly appeared. 'Dani... I hate to ask, but why are you naked on a bed of ice cream?'

'What?' I made another grab for the phone, but he was too quick for me and moved out of the way while still scrolling.

'You stripped for the *North Devon News*. It's not quite the image I had in mind for the ambassador of my new personal training venture,' he laughed.

'I did *not* strip – I'm not naked in the photo, it was an off-the-shoulder top and ...' I snatched his phone so I could see; 'Oh God, I look like I'm naked behind all that ice cream.'

'Exactly. I presume you knew this photo was being taken? I mean, no one in their right mind would agree to having their photo taken in *that* position?' He peered at the photo too closely pretending like he couldn't make it out.

'I agreed to everything, I was fully clothed, I just didn't think that the end… *product* would look like this.'

'Oh, it looks like after all that midnight ice cream eating you knocked yourself out with sugar and they "arranged" your body like that.'

'I *posed*,' I said, horrified at my unintentional page-3-style position splashed across the whole screen like an ad for some sex chatline. 'And before you ask how I got my leg up there, in that position, Rhonda helped me.'

'Oh no,' he laughed, 'Rhonda didn't help you. Rhonda helped *herself*, and turned you into some kind of ice cream porn pin-up.'

I was mortified, this wasn't the plan at all. I would now be an object of ridicule and online fetishists' dreams for eternity.

'And then there's the ex-boyfriend…' he started reading from the article; '"Singleton Dani hopes to reunite with her teenage sweetheart and recently watched him from behind a set of bins at the cafe; 'I think I may still have feelings,' she confessed. And here at the *North Devon News* we love a happy ending, so let's hope Dani can get slim and get her man"…' then he stopped reading. 'Did you know they'd written this?' he said, looking up at me, an expression of pure horror on his face.

'You mean about me bingeing on ice cream at midnight or stalking my teenage love behind the bins?' I asked horrified.

'The bunny-boiling behind the bins bit.' He was loving this, laughter dancing in his eyes, his lips twitching with a smile.

'Look, I just mentioned... that I happened to see him and... it was never meant to go in the paper, I thought Rhonda realised that.'

'She's a journalist, you were doing an interview, she's going to print it all, if she didn't she wouldn't be very good at her job.'

Oh God this was truly awful. I'd wanted to sweep into Appledore like the avenging angel, beautiful, successful, a changed woman in stilettos ready to stamp on the haters and the bullies. And there I was in the local paper seemingly naked behind an ice cream mountain, bingeing like a pig, and spying on my ex.

Chris could see I was angry and was trying to look serious now but his eyes were still laughing; 'Dani, you don't know when to stop talking. I thought you knew all about journalists.'

'I do... I just didn't know this one. Rhonda's a two-faced lying tabloid bitch.'

'*Lovely* Rhonda?' he said, laughing.

I just put my head in my hands. 'It's a media intrusion,' I muttered, which made him laugh out loud.

'It's not an intrusion if you tell them everything then lie down and let them photograph you,' he was shaking his head.

'I've been violated by the press, aren't there injunctions I can take out against this sort of thing?'

'Don't feel too bad, Dani. All publicity is good publicity,' Chris mocked, 'and in better news, they got a great shot of the gym.'

'You're welcome,' I muttered.

'Caprioni's will be pleased,' he continued, still scrolling through; 'they get name-checked several times – not to mention the money shot of "the curvy ice cream queen" on one of their tables, the ice cream porn gang will be turning up in their droves – good for the cafe business – not necessarily the gym business.'

'Oh Chris I'm sorry, I hope it doesn't do your business any harm, having "a curvy ice cream queen" representing your gym. I just wanted to help.'

'I know, I know and even if you've closed me down I'll still laugh at all this in years to come when I'm bankrupt and begging on the street.'

I covered my face, fresh embarrassment washing over me as I thought once more of the finer points in the article and the way bloody Rhonda had made me spew my life out while she 'innocently' chowed down on a Chockerbocker Glory.

'It's all fine,' he was saying, and he went to hug me, which was unexpected and awkward and I said 'Oh' like I was alarmed and he jerked slightly which caused us to bang heads. We both laughed and I slapped his arm like a stupid teenager.

After an extremely awkward departure, I grabbed my stuff from the changing rooms and ran all the way home. Then, I got into my car and drove straight to the local McDonald's. I needed sustenance and carbs to get me through this traumatic media intrusion. I sat in the drive-thru queue thinking about what Rhonda had written about me and Jude. I'd planned to walk back into Jude's life with my head held high and my body slimmed down at my fortieth birthday. I was going to sashay in, feigning surprise at his presence after twenty years and make him see what he'd lost. I needed my closure after all these years. But how could I do that now? Now I was ridiculous, the curvy ice cream queen lying naked behind a row of sundaes, then there was the stalking and declaring my undying love... and seemingly both admitting to stalking him and declaring my undying love. But that was just one of...

But that was just one of my problems as I was soon to discover... only minutes later.

'One Big Mac with a large strawberry shake and large fries please,' I called absently into the receiver, thinking how easily it slipped off my tongue. One burger wouldn't kill me, but it might prevent me from killing someone else, I felt so betrayed by Rhonda – I'd thought we were friends.

'Sorry, I can't hear you, can you say it louder please?' came the tinny response.

The last time this had happened I'd ended up with a salad instead of a burger because they hadn't heard me properly – it was horrific! So I leaned right out of the car window so they could hear me clearly.

'One Big Mac with a large strawberry shake and large fries please,' I repeated a little louder. They must have new people training, I thought, imagining biting down into that doughy, meaty heaven and sipping on that sweet shake. I was still highly stressed and when the voice asked me a third time to repeat myself, my patience was gone and I yelled my order crossly into the receiver. Loudly and clearly. 'ONE BIG MAC. ONE LARGE STRAWBERRY SHAKE. AND ONE LARGE FRIES PLEASE!'

I was wondering if I could buy up every copy of the *North Devon News*, then remembered that would be pointless because it was also online – for ever – thanks to bloody Rhonda and her bloodthirsty need for a story.

'Is it ALL for you, madam?'

I was shocked. This was no business of hers, but as always I went into nice girl, guilty mode and said; 'NO, I'm buying for a friend.' The lies came thick and fast, like a McDonald's shake. I was reverting to the woman I was before, how quickly we slip. One first-world drama around a local newspaper story and I was cheating and lying to the staff at McDonald's. Who knew where this would end? Yes I could drive off into the sunset and avoid the binge and the post-binge followed by self-hatred, loathing and weight gain – but the thought of those fries was holding me fast.

I pulled up to the first window and paid the sniggering member of staff. Pulling up to the second, I saw two servers holding the newspaper on the page where my picture was. I hadn't expected my story to feature so largely, my photo took up half a page – I looked HUGE.

In a millisecond, it dawned on me that these kids had iPhones and the last thing I needed was to be caught mid-burger and downloaded for the world to see. I could only imagine the You-Tube videos, 'Curvy Ice Cream Queen Staging Night Raid on MacDonald's'.

'Oh sod it,' I said too loudly as I put my foot down, revving noisily, and whizzed through the drive-thru at about 100 miles an hour and just kept going along the coast road like a fugitive.

I raced back to the cafe, saw a light on and ran inside, locking the door behind me. Sue, Ella, Gina and Roberta were all having a cup of tea.

'What the bloody hell?' Sue said.

'I'm famous,' I sighed, quickly scrolling through my phone to find the article and handed Sue the phone so they could read it for themselves, it was too painful for me to see again. They crowded round my phone as I rushed over to the counter and grabbed myself a cone. I'd just given up that wonderful feast from the golden arches – this would be my compensation.

'Oh love, I'm deviated for you,' Sue sighed, looking up from the phone.

Ella and her mum looked at me, concerned. 'Oh Dani,' Ella said, 'you're doing so well, don't let this stop all your good work, you've been so happy.' She tried not to let me see her looking at the huge cone in my hand, but I think we all knew what she was thinking.

'I saw this earlier,' Roberta was saying excitedly, delighted by the mentions of Caprioni's and how delicious the ice creams were.

'I just had a close call at McDonald's drive-thru,' I said, keen to share my pain. 'Some of the staff had a copy of the paper and I think they might have been planning to take a photo of me eating.'

'Oh love, as if it's not bad enough they'll already be Photoshopping the newspaper photo, they have their own now. Photoshopping is evil in the hands of teens – you should see what they did to that lovely photo of me and Delilah for our summer campaign. It was X-rated, no woman or dog should have to endure that…'

'Mum, I don't think you're helping Dani,' Ella said, tactfully.

'Sorry love, but on a positive note it's great publicity for the cafe…' Roberta added, looking up from her phone, 'we've already had a few tweets today asking is that where the fat girl works?' she said, like this would make me feel better.

'Oh great,' I said, standing at the counter, my eyes filling with tears.

They all got up and brought me to the table, arms around me, making cooing noises.

'I just feel a bit, exposed… you know?' I licked my ice cream, it felt good, soothing. Even in my devastation I'd considered the flavour options and gone for Sorrento Lemon, sweet and creamy and tart all at the same time, and for a few seconds every time I licked, I felt slightly better.

'It'll be a nine-day wonder. This time next week it'll be another story,' Ella smiled comfortingly.

'Unless the Japanese get hold of it,' Roberta added, 'they made a TV programme of one of our dramas, didn't they Ella – remember when that boy proposed to the girl and we lost the ring in the sand?'

'Yes, Mum, but I don't think Dani needs to hear about it now.'

'I was on all fours, they got a big shot of my backside, I said to Ella, "Is Japan ready for my bottom?" But I got fan mail, they like big bottoms in Japan, you'd go down a storm.'

Ella looked at me and apologised with her eyes.

I gave her an 'it's okay' nod back, after what I'd been through today being told I had a fat bum was nothing. 'I just feel betrayed, that reporter wrote everything down, everything I told her.'

'That Rhonda is a tough cookie... hashtag Rhonda the Rottweiler I call her. She did a complete hatchet job on our "Beyoncé Boosts".' Roberta sighed and then added matter-of-factly, 'And now she's dead to me. But don't you worry, my love, I know people, I'll have her run out of town.' I think she meant it.

'Roberta, if you're talking about the Italian chef at the hotel, he isn't Mafiosi, he's just saying that so he can get in your pants,' Sue giggled and nudged her and Roberta roared laughing.

'Don't listen, Delilah,' she squealed, covering the pretty little dog's ears with her hands. Delilah frantically tried to lick her, which caused her glittery eyepatch to fall slightly. She was a rescue dog who'd been badly treated by previous owners and had been left with one eye. She had all our hearts, and the sweetest little face, and given everything she must have gone through, her eager tail wagging was testament to being healed. And watching her twirl and bark with happiness and excitement made me feel ashamed for ever feeling sorry for myself.

'You're right about Rhonda, what a convivial bitch,' Sue was saying.

'It could have been worse,' I sighed. 'I'm just glad she didn't print my weight. At least that's one thing that can remain sacred.'

'You mean 13 stone 2 love?' Sue said, her head to one side, her voice oozing sympathy like being that weight was terminal.

'Oh... she printed it?' How had I missed that revelation?

'Yes – that's the beauty of online journalism, you can update it as you go along,' Roberta added, with an equally pitying smile, her head to the other side, they were facing me with the same expression, like bloody sympathetic bookends.

I couldn't believe I was in this situation. I'd always been a private person, I may have appeared to be loud and funny, an open book – but I wasn't. Having hoped to quietly step back into life in Appledore I was now being publicly humiliated. My dirty washing was everywhere – and the worst of it was – it was all plus size.

And what on earth would Jude think if he read this article? I'd wanted to return a strong woman and show him how I'd changed from the submissive girlfriend I used to be. I wanted him to see me at my party in a sparkly dress. I wanted him to want me, so I could say 'no' and for once I'd be 'the one that got away'. Instead I turn up in a double-page spread in the local newspaper, lying half-naked on a table full of ice cream, declaring war on fat.

How could I ever face Jude again? In all these years since, I'd kept my silence and my dignity – yes there was a little online stalking, the odd indiscreet silent phone call in the early days, but nothing more. I'd planned my revenge, it would be dignified and classy, as cold as clotted cream vanilla, not like an advert for bloody Weight Watchers.

He probably wouldn't even come to my party now, thinking I'd been leering at him in the dark behind the bloody bins. I bet Rhonda the Rottweiler was round at his now offering him all kinds of bribes to sing like a canary, and knowing him he would.

'Oh Sue, I don't know what to do. I have to go… I can't stay here in Appledore with all this, it's not fair on all of you,' I said.

'People taking pictures and everyone knowing everything about me, it's the worst thing.'

'Now you know how celebrities feel,' she said, 'paps everywhere, no place to hide. This is your life now, Dani – you're like… like… a fat Kardashian.'

'Thanks Sue,' I said, horrified anew. And she smiled and closed her eyes like a wise old tabby, in a 'you're welcome' kind of way.

I escaped the madness of the cafe and headed upstairs to my sanctuary. Just as I locked the door my phone pinged and gave me a start, it was Roberta kindly forwarding me a video of my earlier 'performance' at McDonald's. I was hanging out of the car screeching 'LARGE FRIES' at the top of my voice. 'You could have staged this at the cafe,' Roberta had added at the bottom.

I deleted it, knowing it would be hanging around in cyberspace for ever anyway.

I'd sent Karla the link to the article and given her a few minutes to read it before I called her. God love her she tried – she said it wasn't all that bad, they got my age right and my eye make-up looked lovely, but on further questioning admitted it was possibly the worst thing she'd ever known happen to another living creature. 'You're going to be prey on the streets, trolled online…' she started.

'Don't, oh Karla don't…'

'Oh and the McDonald's LARGE FRIES is trending on Twitter,' she said, with a giggle.

'Don't laugh, Karla.'

'But it's funny, you look totally crazy!' God, even my best friend found me hilarious, this wasn't good.

'And there's the stuff about me stalking Jude,' I said, trying not to cry, again. 'I feel such an idiot.'

'Damn, and I already sent the invitations to everyone, him included – with strict instructions that it was a surprise party and you know nothing.'

'Oh God.'

'Tell me Dani, what the hell were you even doing lurking behind the bins?'

'I wasn't… the reporter described it like that but… oh what's the point. I just didn't want to see him. I was in my gym gear, sweaty with no make-up on and after all these years… you know the plan. I really wanted to lure him in and have the deep satisfaction, the final closure of pushing him away.'

'You wanted him to want you so badly it hurt when you told him to bugger off?'

'Yes, you know I did.'

'So explain to me why you went to the papers, told them you'd been hiding behind the bins looking at him and then had your photo taken lounging naked across a table of ice cream.'

'I wasn't naked or lounging,' I looked again. 'Okay it *looks* like I'm naked and lounging. I look like a fat Roman emperor, don't I?'

'Yes, but they Photoshopped it, didn't they? No one would lie in that weird position and put their leg up like that… would they Dani?'

My silence spoke volumes.

'Oh well, you were never the most flexible, but you're rocking that peanut butter explosion.'

I couldn't speak, even my best friend, the voice of reason in my life was laughing at me.

'So, what do you want to do now – page 3 for *Ice Cream Monthly*, a porno shoot for the Freezer Fetishists channel on You-Tube?'

'Witness Protection…' I muttered. 'I'll get a new identity and leave for South America tonight.'

'Sounds like a plan, wish I could come with you, the kids are driving me bonkers. Archie's ruined a brand-new sports kit on its first outing, and Freddie's just puked up on the new carpet.'

'That sounds like bliss.' I sighed, thinking for the first and only time in my life that, given the choice, I'd probably rather clean Freddie's sick up than deal with the embarrassing aftermath of the curvy ice cream queen and the *North Devon News*.

Chapter Nine

The Zen Diet

Diet Diary: January 2010; Fell madly love with Marc who loved yoga and Buddha and joined him in his New Age vegan life doing sun salutations and eating only leaves. But he dumped me on the Summer Solstice, so I spiked his green tea with vodka and fled… to the nearest McDonald's. Gained 10lbs.

I went to bed feeling empty and a little scared, I hadn't considered the impact a single newspaper interview might have. This might seem stupid given that my career was in PR, but that was work, and this was personal. I'd assumed because I wasn't in the hustle and bustle of London media, it would be a kinder, more forgiving article. I didn't expect the photo to look like that, I didn't expect Rhonda to mention my weight or the fact that I had fled after a 'tragic' love affair.

Later that night I tiptoed downstairs into the cafe and made myself a hot chocolate with lashings of cream accompanied by a whole packet of digestives. I used to do this when I lived at home; after I'd put Mum to bed I'd go back downstairs and be comforted by a big mug of warmth. As much as I worried about her drinking, it was always a relief when she was so drunk she had to go to bed. The next morning I'd get up and go to school exhausted from a late night and wondering what I'd come home to. It could be a repeat performance, smiling Mum smelling vaguely of drink as I walked in the door, morphing into nasty Mum by the time *Coronation Street* came on, and positively vicious Mum by *News at Ten*. Then as Reggie Bosanquet said goodnight at 10.30, she was usually fast asleep in the chair, or on the floor, shattered from drink and bitterness. Sometimes she'd start early in the day, especially around anniversaries and birthdays, she'd get all the wedding photos out and steep herself in gin and memories and I'd come home from school to find her in a urine-soaked heap. I would be told how useless and fat and ridiculous I was for several hours, she'd blame me for my dad's departure then eventually sleep, wherever she landed. Sometimes I'd go to school the following day and she'd still be in the same position when I returned.

But sometimes she'd go on the waggon, and I'd glimpse the mother she might have been. I remember it in vague moments, kind words like faded newsprint. She once baked a cake that smelled of roses; she pushed me on a swing on a rare visit to the park. But these were isolated memories with nothing in between. I remember picking strawberries together one summer, the joy of being with her sober, happy, oh the jam we would make. But on the way home she stopped at a small off-licence, asking me if I'd like a bar of chocolate – of course I did, but I knew what it meant, so I said, 'No, Mum, let's go home and make jam instead.'

'We will, of course we will,' she said, climbing out of the car. She returned without any chocolate, but with a carrier bag containing a large bottle of cheap gin. I knew what it was because at ten years old I recognised the label through the plastic bag. I didn't say anything, and neither did she, but later that night when I suggested we make the jam, she told me I was a fat greedy kid who only thought of her stomach. Like many other nights, I cried myself to sleep, and the strawberries we'd picked were left in a bag in the car, rotting for days.

Thinking of these times was painful, and I tried to push them from my mind and make jokes and think funny thoughts, but what I *couldn't* get out of my head was the night she died. Rain lashing on windows, a storm turning the calm sea into a thunderous, roaring beast, and me, alone, watching from the beach, my mother alone in bed.

And as all this came flooding back to me now as I sat in the Ice Cream Cafe. I filled a long sundae glass with ice cream and sprinkles. I added chocolate flakes to make it beautiful and then swallowed it all down along with the memory. And then I had another one and ate until I couldn't eat any more.

The next morning, I turned on my phone and checked the newspaper online. There were more than a hundred comments, not all complimentary, but some supportive and even a few nice ones about my hair, and Caprioni's ice cream. Perhaps it wasn't going to be too bad after all and I tried to focus on all the lovely things that had happened to me since I'd been here. When that didn't work, I slathered a tonne of butter on two thick slices of toast and swallowed without tasting to ease the stress. It worked, temporarily, it always did, until afterwards when, filled with butter and self-loathing, I'd regret every mouthful. I tried to tell myself I needed energy from carbs, who knew what today might bring? When you're being trolled boy do you need carbs. I now had to think like Bear Grylls (or a fat Kardashian?) because I didn't know when or where I might be spotted or videoed – apparently #McDonaldsLARGEFries was still trending.

I ate another slice of toast and looked out of the window, watching the world wake up, the deliveries, the newsagent taking in his newspapers, workmen shouting from some new scaffolding at the hotel. Marco was wandering along the beach with Cocoa, his lovely chocolate Labrador; I heard he'd inherited the dog from his uncle. I could see where she got her name, she was so sweet and a delicious chocolate colour, romping down the beach. There was always something new, always someone to watch along the front, but today it had lost its magic. Even when Cocoa decided to chase a bike along the front and Marco was in hot pursuit, more animated than I'd ever seen him, I couldn't raise a smile. Everything I'd come here for, a new life, weight loss, closure on Jude and forgiveness from my mum seemed to be slipping through my fingers.

Then I saw Chris, running along the beach like his life depended on it, and I had this weird urge to run after him and join him. I told myself that would be silly, that I'd probably collapse before I even reached him, besides, imagine the picture that would make for any keen amateur paparazzi – the curvy ice cream queen trying to keep up with muscle man. So instead, I got dressed and headed for work, glad I could go down the back stairs and didn't need to 'be seen' out the front. You never knew who was watching, and call me paranoid, but it was the end of a long summer and now the kids were bored with Pokemon Go, I worried they might come for me.

By 6 p.m., when my shift finished there was still handful of what Sue called 'amateur pappardelles' hanging around. She was loving the drama and offered to help me 'escape' so I could go for my gym session, for which I was grateful. We left the cafe together and I hid behind her, under one of her diaphanous glittery shawls, while getting in my car, there was no way I was running to the gym today, I'd arrive with quite a posse. 'There's nothing to see here,' Sue suddenly yelled, causing a stir as they all immediately looked up, and headed blindly to where her voice was coming from. I felt like I was starring in a zombie horror movie and just put my head down and drove.

Arriving at the gym, I was horrified to see a gaggle of women waving banners saying 'NO to Body Shaming', 'Your Worth is not measured by the Size of your Waist!' 'Don't Diet Dani!' 'Don't Pander to Puppet Patriarchy!'

My innocent engagement with the local press about a dieting challenge had now caused feminist outrage. I knew I wasn't some patriarchal puppet, but clearly they thought I was because they'd made a lovely poster using the photo of me on the table of ice cream with Donald Trump's head superimposed on my body. I wasn't sure what they were trying to say, and having thought this could get any worse, it just had. I couldn't even walk in to the gym now, I couldn't strut past a naked Donald Trump and say 'I see ya sisters, but I don't hear ya, I'm just popping in here for an hour of body shaming.'

I called Chris from my car. 'I can't come to the session,' I said. 'The world is chasing me and there are women out here telling me I'm being exploited and now Donald Trump's involved and nobody wants that...'

'Not dramatic at all,' he monotoned.

'This is just so awkward, I can't walk past them.'

'It's all backfired,' he said, 'I feel responsible, I just wanted you to come on board to promote my personal training. And look what's happened.'

'It's not your fault, if anyone it's mine, I was naive and stupid going to the newspaper. I thought I knew what I was doing, but I walked right into that custard pie,' I said, thinking how delicious custard pies were then batting it away.

'I'm sure what you're going through is much worse, but everyone seems to think I'm some kind of "fat hater" who has no time for overweight people. Someone on Twitter said, "he's not a personal trainer, he's a personal tyrant!" There's even a #FreeDani campaign started up online because apparently I've bullied and body-shamed you into working out.'

'I'm so sorry, Chris.' It was one thing attacking me for my gluttony but it was another attacking the people I cared about, who were just trying to help.

'Oh it's fine,' he said. 'I've never been called a "fat fascist" before. Oh yes, and *The Sun* are running a story saying "Fatties Banned from Gym."'

I had to laugh, and so did he. 'Oh Chris we've caused a fat global outrage.'

'Yeah, it's not every day we get to do that,' he laughed.

'I was trying to give something back to you and Ella – you both had this belief in me and I was so touched. I didn't realise this would happen. Now I'm bloody paranoid, there are a few shifty guys hanging around who look like they might be press photographers.'

'Yeah, I reckon they've been waiting for you to arrive with a big ice cream, or to see me kicking a fat person out of the gym,' he laughed. At least Chris seemed to be taking it in his stride.

I half-smiled; talking to him always made me smile, even now when everything was so awful.

'Look I'll drive around a bit, go and get something to eat at Westward Ho, no one knows me there – yet – and hopefully they'll bugger off – and I'll come back later,' I said. I won't deny a big part of me just wanted to run away as I had in the past. I was sorely tempted to drive back and never return to the gym, but I was the one who got Chris into this and he was sticking with me so I couldn't walk out on him now. Besides, it would just be proving to those people who were abusing Chris that they were right. So more than anything now I was determined to carry on at the gym.

'Perhaps I should leave it until you've closed before I come back, do you mind staying on after ten?' I asked, knowing it was usually well after ten before he left.

'Could you make it a bit sooner, I'm busy later,' he said. 'About 9 p.m.?'

'Yeah… 9 p.m. is great… doing anything nice?' I asked. I know we'd only known each other a short time, but I felt like I could ask him this. He was always in the gym, rarely went out, didn't drink or smoke or even eat that much so it was unusual for him to close early and I was intrigued as to where he might be going. 'Hey have you got a hot date you haven't told me about?'

He laughed, and so did I, Chris didn't have time for dating, his life was his business, his gym. 'This is my girlfriend,' he'd always say looking around him, 'I just don't have room for a woman in my life.'

He wasn't offering to tell me where he was going, but he was a good-looking guy and I wouldn't be surprised if it was a date. But I *was* surprised at how this made me feel, and put it from my mind.

I arrived in Westward Ho half an hour later, to see a place utterly changed since I'd last visited as a younger woman. The 'Old British seaside' style of fish and chip shops and amusement arcades remained, but there were now high-rise holiday flats and a more continental feel to the place. It made me sad to think how we kept these images of the past in our minds, but revisiting them, the story was always different. It was the same with the people from our pasts. I'd remembered Caprioni's with Sophia at the helm, my mother in our old house (which I couldn't bear to even go and look at). Then there was Jude as a younger man, charming me with his smile. I wondered what his story might be since we last saw each other, and my stomach lurched as I thought about how I'd been so enslaved to him back then. And now my story was laid bare for the world to see and comment on.

In leaving London and taking on this personal challenge of losing weight, I'd seen myself as strong, gaining control of my life, my body and my future. But those protesting women outside the gym saw me differently. They viewed me as a puppet, believing I'd been influenced by the media, capitalism, patriarchy and Victoria's Secret. I understood where they were coming from, but for me that really wasn't the case. I'd been overweight most of my life and now I just wanted to be healthier, happier, and yes I probably was influenced by all those things, but the desire to change was coming from inside me. I'd had a slip-up but going to the gym and seeing the protestors made me want to prove I was no puppet – this was me doing this for me. And the difference between success and failure was to persevere, and that's exactly what I was going to do.

In the past I'd hidden things away, but now I was being honest with myself and it was thanks to Chris, because with him there was no place to hide. It freaked me out when he asked me about calories and workouts, but in pointing out when I was lying to myself about the distance I'd done on the treadmill and the number of calories I'd eaten it made me more honest with myself. I told Chris some of the stuff about Mum and he shared stories about his own family and how his brother, a barrister, had always seemed so much more successful than him. I'd asked him if he could be anything in the world what would he be, and he said 'a gym owner'. I pointed out that, to some people he was living the dream. 'Don't compare yourself and everything you do to your brother,' I'd said. 'I spent a long time competing in my career and even when I landed a big account, someone somewhere had always landed a bigger one. "Comparison is the thief of joy",' I quoted. It was something attributed to Theodore Roosevelt, I'd seen it on Facebook years before, but it was true. 'I never heard that before, but it's so true, I like it,' he'd said, 'sometimes I find it hard to see my life as worthwhile as my brother's putting murderers in jail.'

And while I offered titbits of advice with accompanying quotes from Facebook and dead presidents, he gave me the benefit of his BA in Sports Psychology training and an A level in nutrition.

'Did you ever learn how to deal with coping mechanisms around ice cream?' I joked.

'Yes, there was coursework on that very subject,' he said. 'Basically one covers one's eyes and runs through an ice cream cafe.'

'Mmm as I work there that might be a tricky,' I said. But I'd realised by now that I had my own coping mechanisms, I had a great incentive in my party, my new dress and the start of this new life. I told Chris about my birthday party and said if he was kind to me in the gym I'd invite him.

'Will there be ice cream and evil trans fats?' he'd asked.

'Yes, and much carb-loading sprinkled with a sugar topping.'

'Then count me in,' he'd said. Chris was turning out to be fun and not as serious and sensible as he'd seemed at first when he stood there in electric blue lecturing me on how many calories there were in a slice of pizza.

Walking through Westward Ho, I smelled the fish and chips and, I'll be honest, I toyed with going in and ordering myself a slap-up. But the more I thought about it the more I realised that it wasn't about hunger it was about self-destruction. I was a kamikaze dieter who never reached her goal because that's when life became real. When I'd lost weight in the past, a relationship usually followed, not because I was slimmer, but because I was more confident. As a slimmer woman I reached out, smiled at strangers, went on dating websites. But like in all relationships, there would be rocky patches, times when things weren't perfect – so I walked away, straight into the safety of my relationship with that juicy threesome: fats, sugar and good old carbs. Those guys never let me down, they didn't two-time me or criticise me or argue – they just kept on giving. I wondered if I would ever be able to open myself up to a real relationship one day. I might have to stick around for the difficult bits, the painful parts – and I didn't do pain, I hadn't done it since I left Appledore that night.

I came to the fish and chip shop, a waft of warm, savoury air hit me, like a friend beckoning me inside. But this wasn't my friend – what kind of fool starts to build themselves a house, then after a few weeks knocks it down? I'd been building on my fitness, improving my diet and though I'd never be an 'Alex' kind of girl, I could be the best version of Dani. I was doing this solely for me, and it was my definition of success, not Chris's or the protestors' or even my friends at the cafe. I wanted this, but I would have it on my terms, and it was time to forget the rest of the world, ignore their trolling and criticising, shut out my mother's voice and do it without the white noise of everyone else telling me what I should and shouldn't do. And the only person I wanted on this journey with me, was Chris… and a little bit of phone time with my girl Karla.

I walked along the beach, finally able to take stock and think about where I was and what I was doing. I didn't want my life plastered across Appledore. I'd left here to get away from the past, there were things I didn't want people to know, private stuff that I had to protect. I just hoped that was still possible.

At about 8.30, I decided to head back to the gym, I could be there by 9 and fully worked out by 10. It was funny because these days I didn't feel myself unless I'd exercised, which was something new and exciting for me.

Pulling up at the gym, I was a little late, the summer evening traffic coming out of Westward Ho had been busier than I'd expected, but I knew Chris would wait for me. The protestors had gone now and to my relief all was quiet outside the gym, which meant I could continue on with my quest. I was just about to get out of the car when my phone pinged, it was a voice message from Chris, the signal around here came and went and judging by what he was saying it must have been sent a little while before.

'Dani, I think perhaps we should hold off the sessions in the gym for a couple of days, the women are still outside and I wouldn't be surprised if there's a photographer around too. Look I'll call you and we'll sort something out as soon as this has blown over.'

I was disappointed, I'd been looking forward to the workout and to spending time with Chris. He'd obviously left the message earlier when the women were still here, so perhaps it would be okay to go in now? He'd be glad to see me, pleased at my commitment, so I turned off the engine and walked across the car park. Typical Chris, I thought, he was probably giving me the option of not coming – it might even be his way of testing me. 'There you go Dani, the first obstacle pops up and you abandon the gym.' But I wasn't going to quit this time, it was tough, but I was tough enough to handle it.

I could see there was a light on in the gym so I walked up to the double doors and pushed, but they were locked, so I knocked hard and waited, but no answer. This was unusual, Chris never locked up when he was inside the gym, he was always concerned about turning potential new customers away. I walked around to the other side of the gym where the treadmills were; they looked out across the car park – Chris said it helped to have a view when you were on a machine, people stayed on longer if they had something to look at. So I stood on my tiptoes and peered through the window, I could see someone inside but it was hard to make out at first. Then I saw them, Chris and beautiful Alex, both standing in the weights area where we did our sessions. He was standing against the wall, and she was leaning on a cross-trainer, they were chatting, but to me the body language was so much more, and within seconds I saw him touch her hair, run his hands through it. Every moment of this was agony for me as I watched, I wanted to turn away, but I couldn't, and as they both put their heads together and kissed, I felt like I'd been shot in the heart. I knew I'd been growing fond of Chris, I'll admit I had feelings for him, but because he was so good-looking and I had no confidence I'd never seen it as a possibility. But I couldn't help feeling hurt that he had fallen for someone else, and not just anyone, it was someone who was the antithesis to me – a totally gorgeous, skinny blonde. Looking at the two of them together now, I could see how perfectly matched they were. Both fair-haired, beautiful, fit and able to run for miles without wheezing, complaining or stopping for cake. In my world that made them soulmates.

I was in agony, surprised at how deeply this had struck me. At the same time, I accepted this with the same inevitability I'd grown to accept my dad not turning up on a Sunday, or Mum never appearing at the school gates to take me home. I was used to disappointment, but even so it surprised me how much the tableau of the two of them upset me. He'd never been mine, he never would be, we were just friends... and yet, I'd secretly harboured a hope that perhaps he was different. Looks like I was wrong... again.

I pulled away from the window and tried to take in what I'd seen, whether it had been going on for a while. As I'd sweated and panted and talked on and on while lifting weights and making stupid wise cracks, had Chris been looking at Alex and wishing I'd just shut up? They might have been looking at each other all the time, secret glimpses, deep longings, and I'd been so self-obsessed I'd totally missed it. I knew he was just a friend and would never look at me – but I never expected him to fall for someone so obviously beautiful, it was a cliché and I'd thought he was a little deeper than that. I'd believed that Chris had a sensitivity many men lacked. I'd imagined he might be one of the few guys who sees beyond the curvy figure and fuller frame at the woman underneath. But he was just like all the other men, he talked a good talk but when it came down to it, he wanted a beautiful blonde on his arm like everyone else. And who could blame him?

I drove home that evening fully prepared to stop off for a pizza on the way, I even slowed down as I passed the pizzeria, but I didn't. I couldn't understand why I felt so conflicted. I had to pull over to the side of the road and call Karla. 'We're friends, I've never ever thought of him in any other way,' I said, 'but I think I might have been lying to myself.'

'Of course you have,' Karla said. She was scary, like a mind reader, she knew me so well, and she was never afraid to say exactly what she thought. 'You feel something for him, it's as clear as the nose on your face.'

'Oh God why am I such an idiot…'

'You and every other red-blooded woman within a twenty-mile radius. Dani, you're not an idiot – if you hadn't ever thought about kissing him on the ellipticals there'd be something wrong with you,' she laughed.

I couldn't help it, even through my pain and hurt and disappointment, my best friend made me smile.

'He's gorgeous...' she continued, 'I've seen the photos, checked out the gym on Facebook and he's hot!'

'Okay, he's lovely to look at, but I'm not shallow, Karla, our friendship comes first. The very fact he's so handsome and gorgeous means it's never been something between us. So why do I feel like he reached in and took my heart out?'

'Ooh it's even worse than I thought. You got it bad and that isn't good, girl. Yep, you've fallen for him and you can dress it up as pretty as you like but you weren't in control of this one. Chris snuck up behind you when you didn't have your "boyfriend armour" on,' she said, reminding me of all the times I'd turned down a possible suitor because I didn't want to get hurt.

'And I'm in control of this too,' I lied. 'I might have a crush on him, but he's a friend, just a good friend.'

'So why have you called me at 9.30 at night from the side of the road to tell me you just saw your "good friend" kissing a beautiful woman?'

'Because... they were together, where we do our weights... and he'd called to cancel me... because he would rather be with her,' I blurted.

'And you're not jealous at all, are you?'

'No, I'm not.' I was. 'I just wish... he'd told me, I never expected him to do that to me.'

'Dani, he hasn't done anything to you,' she said, 'it's not his fault you've got a big crush...'

My friend, as usual, was right – I'd tried to shake it off, kid myself he was my mate, but all the time I'd been having little moments thinking about him, I missed him when he wasn't there and I loved his attention. I'd denied my feelings even to my-self because I needed to steer a steady boat on this ocean. I had weight to lose, a party to plan and a life to start. I didn't need a broken heart caused by unrequited love thrown into the mix – but it looked like that's what might have happened.

After speaking to Karla, I drove back to the cafe feeling numb. I needed to take a break from Chris and the gym, the intensity of the workouts and my burgeoning feelings might wreck every-thing and I had to stay on track for me. But as I walked into the cafe and breathed in the aroma of hot chocolate sauce I won-dered if it was already too late.

Chapter Ten

The Sleeping Beauty Diet

Diet Diary: June 2010; David was gentle, sensitive and gorgeous – the fairy tale! So I embarked on the diet of nine hours' beauty sleep followed (in the absence of a Prince's kiss) by a tonne of complex grains. I lost 5 pounds. Then David came out. I should have known, he had more hair products than me! I ditched the grains for sugary carbs in pure doughnut form – and gained back the 5 pounds.

I woke, opened the curtains, and the first thing I remembered was Chris and Alex together in the gym the night before. My stomach dropped like lead and I felt vaguely nauseous. I was annoyed with myself for turning something good into something that might destroy me. Relationships didn't work for me, I'd been out with several unsuitable men while living in London and they had only made me unhappy. I'd watched my friends get engaged and married and move through all the watersheds of life, but I felt like everyone else had an instruction manual and that I'd lost mine at the door. I was annoyed with myself even more now because I'd come to Appledore single with no intention of meeting anyone. I'd just wanted to live here happily without any complications. And now I'd got a massive crush on the first man who'd given me any attention – I always fell for the wrong one.

As if on cue, I gazed through the window and spotted Chris running along the beach, and my heart squeezed a little. Perhaps it was as well I wasn't going back to the gym, I couldn't work with him any more knowing I had these feelings, I'd just keep thinking about Alex and him together and feel like the third wheel. I'd liked the fact I was the only woman in his life, we were like a bickering couple, and I loved that we could laugh together and tease each other. But now he was with someone it changed all that, but then again had it ever been that simple or had I made it into something good in my head?

Falling in love for me was like catching a cold, inconvenient and spoiled my plans – not that this was actual love, it was just a silly, pointless crush on my personal trainer. At the same time, there was no bloody cure and in the past when I'd suffered from unrequited love or having my heart broken, I'd eat. I was determined not to get caught in the same trap this time though, so I wandered down to work with a heavy heart and empty stomach.

There's that saying about things coming in threes, and it's sometimes something nice, but given that the first surprise had been finding Chris with Alex, I knew there were two more 'delights' coming my way. I didn't have to wait long for the next!

As I was going to give myself a break from workouts with Chris, I'd decided to use the cafe as my gym that day. Marco was off and he usually carried in the deliveries when they arrived, but I made sure I was ready and waiting when the lorry came. Even in my heartache I derived mild pleasure from the fact that I could carry several crates up the cafe steps and into the back kitchens without flinching. I wasn't wheezing or panting, and I was fast too. This felt good, my firm thighs and stair skipping were enough to make me happy, I didn't need a man in my life – even if he was just a friend. 'You in training for that 10k?' Len the delivery driver asked.

'Oh you saw the newspaper,' I said, my heart sinking slightly wondering if Len was now imagining me naked behind all that ice cream.

'Were you…'

'I *wasn't* naked and I have no intention of running without any clothes on!' I said firmly. Bloody hell, there were all kinds of rumours growing from a simple (if treacherous) article.

'I wasn't going to say that you were…' he looked surprised at my slight outburst.

'Oh, sorry, it's just that the other day someone asked me if I was running the 10k naked while carrying an ice cream sundae,' I said. It wasn't helped when Roberta confirmed this to the local press because she knew it would be good for publicity.

'No, I was going to say, were you able to get back to see your mum before she died.'

This stopped me in my tracks. I felt like I'd been hit in the face.

'Yes,' I said, shocked he'd even ask.

'The wife said she had a hard time.'

'Oh?'

'Margaret, my wife… she was a friend of your mum's, said she died of a broken heart,' he added.

I felt my throat tighten. This was none of his business, but I was back in a small village and I knew this would happen. No one ever knew about Mum's drinking, it was a well-kept secret and would have devastated her if people knew. Even now I had to keep that secret, I don't know why, it had just been ingrained in me and as I felt so guilty about her death I felt I had to protect her even now.

'She'd sometimes come over to ours and be in tears,' he went on. I wanted him to stop, I didn't want to hear about Mum's unhappiness, I'd lived through it with her. I hated myself for everything that happened and was just beginning to work through it when clumsy Len starts poking around in the wound.

'Mum was depressed, she… never really got over Dad leaving and…'

'That must have been hard for both of you,' he said, piling the empty crates back in the van. 'I just remember her crying her eyes out and when we saw you in the paper, Margaret said "that poor girl – I hope she can forgive herself".'

I didn't know what to say. No I hadn't forgiven myself, but at the same time I'd foolishly hoped that people round here might have forgotten the circumstances of Mum's death. Len meant well, but I didn't want his or his wife's bloody pity or forgiveness, I wanted everyone to keep their noses out of my life. Mind you, putting myself in the local paper was hardly going to keep me and my past under the radar. But it seemed the damage had already been done.

I spent the rest of the morning in the back kitchens keen to avoid any more attention, and when I returned to the cafe I picked up my phone and saw that Chris had called. He'd left a voice message saying the protestors had left and the coast was clear for me to come back and do some work. He said all this in his usual cheeky, teasing tone – but for once it didn't make me smile or fill me with warmth, all I saw was that kiss. I wasn't ready to chat to him yet. I needed a little time to myself, just mixing ice cream. It was a soothing process, just churning and adding, folding fresh fruit purées into eggs and double cream was pure therapy, but the more upset I became as I thought back on Chris and Alex and my earlier conversation with Len, the stronger the urge was to find a bloody big spoon and dig in!

I kept telling myself that I wasn't the old Dani, I was the new improved version and I could resist this. I wouldn't go back to the gym for a couple of days, but I would take good long walks along the beach and eat well. I stirred the rich, creamy mixture and told myself I wouldn't binge on food that made me hate myself later.

I tried to concentrate on the mixing and detach myself from the delicious flavourings, the soft, pillowy comfort of cold vanilla creamy cafe latte, fresh peach and raspberry, but even that couldn't wipe away the sting in my stomach every time I thought of Chris.

'You should get Marco to help you with that,' Roberta said, once I'd finished and was lifting the huge cartons of mixes into the freezers, but I told her I was a big strong girl and quite capable.

'You're right, we don't need men do we, love?' she smiled.

'No, but I need to do my workouts wherever I can,' I said, refusing to even think about men, 'this is a weight-lifting exercise in itself.'

'Oh yes, you don't want to go back to a sedimentary lifestyle just because of a few saddos,' Sue commented from the coffee machine, looking out at the kids with their iPhones pressed against the window.

'Haven't they got the message?' I said, feeling angry. 'I'm hardly likely to start tucking into a big sundae in the window for them to snap. Perhaps they think I'm going to hurl myself into the ice cabinet and eat my way out,' I said, aware I was sounding like some irate Z-lister. 'It's not like I can't control myself around ice cream,' I huffed, 'because I can.'

Roberta gave me a questioning look.

'Roberta, I can. I'M NOT OUT OF CONTROL,' I shouted.

'I never said you were, luvvie, but when you're stressed you do like a nice big "Elvis is Dead Long Live the Peanut Butter Explosion".' She gave me a look and wandered off.

'Yes, but I'm not out of control… I'M NOT OUT OF CONTROL, I'M NOT OUT OF CONTROL!' I shouted after her, repeating this because she was a bit deaf and I wanted to make my point – but not to Jude, who was now standing in front of the counter looking straight at me. I felt like I'd been smacked in the face, this was the last thing I needed today, meeting Jude again after all this time was huge, and I'd wanted to be in a good place physically and mentally. I wasn't – and I also had raspberry sorbet down my front from the mixing. I had to take a deep breath; 'Oh it's you. I didn't know you were there,' I said.

'But you ARE in control, apparently,' he said with that cheeky grin. He was wearing a fabulous suit that looked incredibly expensive, his hair was shorter and he smelled vaguely of French aftershave. Apart from some grey hair at the temples and a few wrinkles, he looked exactly the same as he had when he used to come in here all those years ago asking for a strawberry sundae and two spoons. He'd always turn up just before my break, I'd hear the bell tinkle over the door and he'd waltz in, a wave to someone here, a nod there. Everyone knew Jude. He was a chancer who had left school before he should and worked for his dad at the local garage. He'd tinker with the cars for a few hours, then go off for a smoke, a read of the paper, a whistle at the girls wandering along the front in shorts. But that was before me, he said. He told me he never whistled at another girl after I'd agreed to go out with him, and the way he looked at me back then I'd stupidly believed him.

That first summer had been a revelation for me. I'd never had a boyfriend before, and even though I'd had admirers I'd never had the confidence to say yes. But Jude had enough confidence for both of us. On our first date at the cinema in Barnstaple he'd kissed me during *Sleepless in Seattle* and just took my breath away. I'd never been kissed before, and as Meg Ryan and Tom Hanks held hands on top of the Empire State Building, I felt his warm breath on my neck and his hand on my thigh. I remember thinking, this is it, it doesn't get any better than this.

Love was everywhere in those heady summer days, the sea whispered sweet nothings as it whooshed onto the shore. The songs in the charts were all about love and we'd play them on the jukebox in the cafe. I can't hear the Spice girls '2 Become 1' without thinking about that summer when I finally felt free. I began to loosen the chains from my mother and believed I could be anything I wanted to be. Johnny Depp and Winona Ryder were an item – and so were Jude Morris and Dani Sheridan. Now I got it. The thing I'd never really understood until that kiss, love and sex and life. Jude had given me a superpower I'd never realised existed, but at the same time he was dangerous, because what he gave, he could so easily take away... and he did.

I remember years later reading a quote from a thirty-something Winona Ryder about how she'd always have Johnny Depp in her heart. 'When I met Johnny, I was pure virgin,' she said. 'He was my first everything. My first real kiss. My first real boyfriend. My first fiancé. The first guy I had sex with. So he'll always be in my heart. For ever.'

And that's how I'd felt about Jude – he was my Johnny and whether I liked it or not, he'd always be in my heart. When it was all over and he was nothing but a bittersweet memory, I'd wonder why it still cut so deep. Your older self smiles at your naivety, but at seventeen you think it's for ever, and for ever takes some getting over. Looking at him now, thirty-nine years old, still handsome, still charming and still with that killer smile, I knew he had the potential to be as irresistible as double chocolate chip with salted caramel sauce. And my willpower that had recently become so strong, now felt under attack.

'I saw the article, and the photo,' he whistled under his breath, 'I guess you're not the girl you used to be?'

I just smiled, aware I was batting my eyelashes, amazed he still had an effect on me.

'If you're referring to the fact that in 1993, at the age of seventeen, I didn't strip off on our first date, then yes I've changed.' Things were different back then, some girls did – and of course it wasn't long before I joined them, but he said I wasn't like the girls he'd known before. He was so experienced, and apparently so were his girlfriends, in fact one of the reasons I finally gave in to his gentle persuasion was because he'd hinted that one of his old girlfriends wanted him back. In retrospect I should have let him go then.

'I… I'm glad you called in,' I said truthfully. I needed to address the whole newspaper thing, I couldn't leave it hanging there like a cloud between us. I asked Roberta if she'd mind if I took a break and I gestured to a corner seat – the one we always sat in together. He walked towards it and I followed, how easily we slip back, perhaps I hadn't changed as much as I'd thought? Then just before I sat down, he said; 'Haven't you forgotten something?'

I looked puzzled.

'Strawberry sundae – we always shared a sundae here.'

I was hesitant, I didn't want him to think I would just do his bidding, or that I was still in thrall to him and his strawberry sundae. But I nodded and asked Roberta if she'd make one and within no time she brought one over.

'Two spoons,' she said kindly, and with a smile at him and a wink at me she left us alone.

'You're looking good, Dani,' Jude said, his eyes on my breasts, his spoon pushing into the ice cream, firm but gentle. I remembered the way he used to kiss me as we'd lie by the sea wall at dusk, his hands under my top, up my skirt. His kisses had been eager, forceful, but his hands were gentle, his hips on mine, my thighs cold and naked, I had him inside me and no one could take him from me when he was there. The pleasure and pain of the first time would always be his, in spite of what happened later.

He offered me a spoonful, but I didn't accept. It felt like an intimate act that belonged in the past, and by taking the mouthful I was giving in to him again, handing my heart to him. But he took it anyway, placing a chunk of strawberry on top of his spoon and pushing it slowly into his mouth like he was consuming my heart.

'Delicious,' he said, not taking his eyes from me.

I could feel my blush rising up into my forehead. I didn't like to spoil the moment, but I also didn't want to be photographed sharing a sundae with Jude. Apart from the obvious, I didn't know his situation – an intimate chat over a sundae may not be a good thing.

'I have to warn you,' I said. 'I'm a marked woman and if I were to even dip my finger in that whipped cream we would be all over the internet,' I was exaggerating, but, I knew, I was also flirting.

'So you're back here in the cafe.'

'Yeah.'

'You haven't changed, Dani.'

'Just older and wiser,' I said, refusing to meet his eyes. I was filled with a toxic cocktail of attraction and resentment. I should hate him for the way he'd treated me all those years ago, but he was still smooth, still good-looking, still charming.

I asked if he lived around here and he described his home. I knew where he meant, it was a huge, stunning white house high up over Appledore.

'So you've done well for yourself? What happened to your dad's garage?'

'Oh we sold that a few years ago, I just dabble in bits of business here and there now. So I bet you're happy to be back here… with all the ice cream you can eat?'

I shifted a little, feeling uncomfortable. Did he think I was some kind of scoffing machine?

Karla always said I was my own worst enemy and offered men all kinds of reasons to talk down to me. I told them I had a weight problem, before they told me; I said I ate too much, before they pointed it out. And I always, always, announced to my dinner date in a defiant and some might say *challenging* way that I *would* be having dessert. And I often pointed this out before the starter had arrived.

Perhaps I'd done this with Jude and he was just picking it up again after all these years? But I wanted him to see that I'd changed, I'd lived a big life in London and I wasn't a Saturday girl at Caprioni's, I was the manager here now, well, when Ella was away. I was also in control of my weight and feeling good about myself and I wasn't going to let one catch-up with him turn me back into that weak teenager. I had to communicate this to Jude now and make him realise I wasn't the girl he'd once known, I was a woman now, a sensual, intelligent successful woman who didn't apologise for herself.

'I wanted to explain, the bit about watching my ex-boy-friend...'

'Me?'

I nodded, and shifted in my seat. 'Yeah... but...'

'Behind the bins?' he laughed.

'Mmm well that wasn't true... well not strictly.'

He stopped licking his spoon and gave me his full attention. 'Oh I'm disappointed, Dani... I hoped you might still be hot for me,' he was smiling, teasing me, but at the same time I knew he was testing the water. With the heads-up from the newspaper article and my batting lashes and blushing cheeks, he must have been aware of the effect he still had on me. I could almost see his smile of satisfaction as he picked up the spoon again.

I blushed furiously – I could never hide my feelings from Jude. 'You're an open book, Dani,' he used to say.

'I haven't forgiven you,' I started, desperate to get back on track.

'For what?' He was either completely clueless or playing the part because he didn't want to talk about it, Jude was always hard to read.

'What you did... all through our relationship, but especially that night...'

'Oh Dani... that was a long, long time ago, you can't hold it against me. We were just kids back then.'

'I suppose... but I felt the article implied you were the reason I left and the reason I came back... it isn't the case, the reporter just got carried away.'

'Rhonda? Yeah I *know* Rhonda.' He said this like he 'knew' her very well. This triggered something for me. Jude would often hint about other girls, suggesting there was more to his friendships with them, a whistle under his breath, the emphasis on a word. When I was younger I would be confused and upset by this, and would tearfully ask if he was two-timing me, or if he didn't love me any more and I'd weep and wail and behave like my life was ending. But in those days Jude was the only person who seemed to care about me, who really loved me, without him I was nothing, because at the tender age of nineteen, I'd been worn down by life. My need for love, comfort and someone to be with made me vulnerable to all kinds of manipulation.

'Oh Dani, you're so unsophisticated,' he'd say admonishing me for my gaucheness. 'I was only talking to her,' he'd say, when I complained about him whispering in a girl's ear at a party. He was so convincing I soon realised it was silly of me to get all wound up about him merely being friendly with another girl – until the next time. In the end he made me feel like it was me who had the problem, that I was possessive and unreasonable, but when I told him I liked the boy at the butchers he sulked for days. I accused him of being 'unsophisticated' as he had me so many times – and he finished with me. I was devastated but we were back together within two days, and it was enough to stop me challenging him ever again. I didn't have anyone to talk to about this back then, my friends were as clueless as I was, and my mother wasn't available. But as he said, he was a kid, and so was I – we both behaved differently then, we'd been through a lifetime since, but some things just couldn't be brushed under the carpet.

'So do you ever hear from Jane?' I asked, tentatively.

'Who?'

'My best friend, surely you remember *her?*' I felt angry, how could he forget her?

'Oh yeah… Jane. She went long ago, joined a band, ran off with the bass player, was somewhere in Australia last time I heard.'

I was glad for her, Australia was the right place for Jane, she needed a big space, somewhere with room to be herself, unfettered. She was too much for Appledore, it could never contain her crazy in its cobbled streets leading to the sea she loved. Whereas I saw this cosy village as my sanctuary, she saw it as somewhere pinning her down, the sea her only escape. I hoped she'd found another sea somewhere, and that she was happy and thought fondly of me as I did her. She'd always been there for me back then – until that night.

'So, Dani, let's stop talking about the past – when are you and I going to get it together?' Jude suddenly said, whisking me back from Australia and Jane.

He was looking directly at me, his eyes twinkling, his manicured hands tapping gently on the table.

Oh God, there was something about his voice that drew me in, confident, sure of himself, but gentle. Just hearing him say my name took me right back to where it all started. How easy it would be to lose myself in his eyes again, my rational mind knew it would be idiotic, especially as according to Facebook he was now a married man. It made me angry to think he was here flirting with me when he had a wife at home, he hadn't changed at all.

'Are you married?' I said, wanting to give him a jolt.

'Yes, I'm married.' He didn't flinch.

'Anyone I know?'

'You might, I think she was in your year. Kathy… she used to be Kathy Parkes.'

My heart thumped hard. Kathy Parkes, the pretty girl who was captain of the netball team, head school bully and someone who always seemed to find me so bloody amusing. 'I remember Kathy Parkes,' I said, without smiling. They deserved each other.

Then he added, 'But we're separated.' I doubted that.

'Oh I'm sorry about that. Do you have any children?' I asked.

'Yes… we have two boys, they're everything to me.'

I was vaguely moved by this, and I looked at him. Our eyes met and I thought wouldn't this be the ultimate revenge? A night in flagrante with Kathy Parkes's husband. Would this heal the hurt from all the times she'd pulled my hair, called me names, and laughed about my weight?

I watched Jude eat the sundae, gently lifting the cream first then digging deeper into the sweet, fruity interior. He was the original bad boy, and I hadn't slept with anyone for a long time, and though I was firmly in control, I had to steer this well, because I was in dangerous territory. He licked his spoon after each mouthful, savouring the thick, fruity purée drizzle on top, and underneath, the fresh strawberries and cream. My friends from yesteryear were right, you can tell a lot by the way a guy eats his ice cream.

'What brought you back here?' he said, between mouthfuls.

'I don't know, the call of the sea…?' I sighed.

'More like the call of the strawberry sundae if I know you,' he laughed.

I smiled through gritted teeth, wishing he'd stop referring to my bloody appetite. There was more to me than the love of a good sundae.

'I'm over that, I don't define myself by food,' I said.

'I don't believe you.'

I looked at him and imagined us twenty years before, the same table, the same ice cream. And I suddenly didn't want to be here with him any more – he had drawn me so easily back into the past. But the past wasn't a place I ever wanted to visit again.

'I don't think I ever really dealt with what happened here,' I said, changing the subject. 'You hurt me Jude,' I heard myself say. 'You played around and it was all a big joke to you, but you manipulated me until I wasn't myself. I couldn't make decisions, my judgement was impaired so I ran away…'

He looked straight ahead, but I could see the flicker at the side of his face as his jaw tensed. 'I wondered what had happened to you.'

'I thought you might have at least got in touch,' I said, this new, braver Dani saying what she felt, thinking more about her own feelings than offending Jude. Chris had taught me that – Karla had tried to, but she didn't have his blue eyes and his way with a 3kg medicine ball.

'Dani, I tried to contact you… I was distraught when you left like that.'

I looked at him; 'Really?'

'Yeah, I couldn't find you anywhere and no one knew where you'd gone.'

'Did you ask here at the cafe? They had a forwarding address for me.'

'Yeah, they refused to give it to me.'

'But why, everyone knew you were my boyfriend?' I said, challenging him, and I wasn't going to take it all in like I had done before.

I'd called Sophia when I landed in London, I told her if Jude came in to give him my new address. Even though I'd escaped his orbit, I was still under his spell and had he called or got in touch, I would have been straight back on the first train, but he hadn't.

'Who did you speak to?' I asked.

'Oh some Saturday person… some guy with an Italian name – he left years ago.'

It could have been anyone. 'Marco?' I suggested. He recently said how he'd done some shifts the same summer as me, but I'd left by the time Marco started.

'Yeah, that's right, Marco, he just wouldn't give me any details.'

'I can't think why. Funnily enough, Marco's back, in fact he's in later…' I would ask him if he remembered, I doubted everything Jude said.

'Look it doesn't matter… I told you, it's all in the past. I left here too for a while, it wasn't the same without you, Dani,' he said, and his fingers gently and discreetly reached out to touch mine.

I pulled away, I wasn't being sucked back into Jude's charm, his lies.

I barely had time to think about this, when I felt his fingers on mine once more, the smiles just for me, the way his eyes undressed me. I hadn't had this kind of attention for a long time. I kept reminding myself I mustn't fall for this. He was bad for me, he was married – but he'd said they were separated. Perhaps they were. Was he telling me the truth? I was different now, perhaps he was too?

'It's great to have you back, Dani, I needed a little excitement in my life,' he said, casting his eyes over my breasts. 'Perhaps we could get together?'

'I'm busy,' I said.

'Look, I'm free later tonight, we could go back to yours.'

'What about yours?' I said, testing him. I had no intention of going anywhere with Jude.

'It's difficult… Kathy's there…'

'Oh, yes your wife. But I thought you were separated?'

'We are, well, it's difficult, she's difficult, but you and me, we could have a laugh.'

'A laugh?' Whatever spell there might have been was well and truly broken. Was that all I was to him? Was it all I'd ever been?

'Yeah… you know, talk about old times and…'

'Have a laugh?' I looked at him with incredulity and he looked away. I wasn't looking for love, in fact I'd given up on it, but if ever I was in a relationship again, it would be for a lot more than 'a laugh'.

He seemed annoyed now; 'You're right, you've changed, you're more uptight than you used to be, and that's saying something.'

I felt the blood rise in my face, how vile he really was; how was I ever taken in by him?

'Just because I don't want to "have a laugh" with some married loser I knew two decades ago doesn't make me uptight. It makes me astute,' I spat, standing up. 'Have a nice life Jude.'

With that I moved away from the table, leaving him there, his mouth half-open, surprised that sweet, naive Dani had finally walked away. And it felt better than any ice cream sundae I'd ever had.

As strong as I felt as I walked through the cafe, away from Jude, the minute I arrived in the kitchens I wanted to collapse in tears. It had been one hell of a twenty-four hours and now memories were coming in on me again like the tide. Could I ever escape the relentless past? Had coming back here been the biggest mistake of my life, was I ready to run again?

I spent the next few hours working alone in the kitchens by myself and desperately trying to avoid temptation, comfort, some kind of release. And as the day wore on the seed grew, the voice in my head told me I needed comforting. Just one pizza, or perhaps a portion of chips, and later a little ice cream? I needed it, deserved it, couldn't live without it.

And so, when my shift was over and everyone assumed I was heading to the gym, I headed for the red-light district of food instead. I drove straight to the pizza place I'd discovered on my first week back here, pulled up outside, and thought about what I might have. I longed to melt my feelings into a large pepperoni, smother my hurt in cheese and then, just in case any feelings might emerge, I could push them back down with chocolate fudge cake. That thick fudgy icing was a poultice for the pain of everything that had gone before and everything that might get

me again, and back home there was a cafe filled with ice cream –
why stop at fudge cake?

It was after ten and dark when I reached the pizzeria, the light
from the shop was beckoning me in, and I wanted to wrap myself in soft, doughy garlic bread like a warm duvet. I walked up to
the window, there was a queue of people inside and I wondered
if I'd be recognised from the article, but I didn't care. I wasn't
going back to the gym, Chris didn't really want me there, he
would rather be surrounded by bouncy Alexes who flicked their
hair and flexed their muscles. He needed to be with someone like
him, someone who was calm and did their exercises and didn't
have to make a fool of herself trying to be the centre of attention
the way I did.

As I reached for the door, I saw someone I recognised, one of
the mean girls from Kathy Parkes's school crew who'd christened
me Piglicious. Apart from a few wrinkles, she didn't look much
different from the girl she used to be. And it occurred to me that
if she saw me now, late at night buying pizza to take home and eat
alone, then she might just have won. She didn't care though, did
she? She didn't care if I bought pizza or not… but suddenly I did,
because if I didn't care about that kid who was bullied at school
and bullied at home – no one else would. 'Funny Dani who can't
stop eating'; Dani who can't play netball, and Dani who, according to my mother, would never make anything of herself because
she's 'fat and lazy'. My parents and Jude had driven me in one
direction and I was damned if I was going back there. I'd always
been alone, I was the only person who really cared about me and
it was down to me to look after whatever I had left of Dani.

These past few weeks had taught me that I didn't have to rely on food for comfort. I could take pleasure in friendship and physical activity. Chris had made me work hard, he'd told me I could do stuff, and at first I hadn't believed him, because I hadn't believed in me. But now I was starting to believe in myself, that I could do things I'd never dreamed of. I'd swum ten lengths, it may not seem much to some, but it was an ocean to me. I ran, I lifted heavy crates, I didn't lie on the sofa watching weight-loss programmes and wishing it was me – I got off my bum and did it! In just a few weeks I was stronger than I ever thought I could be, and when I looked in a mirror, I actually liked what I saw. I'd never believed it possible – but Chris had and he was right, but now I had to stop relying on Chris, take what he'd given me and move on. As Roberta had said only that morning as I carried huge cartons of ice cream and delivery crates; 'we don't need men'.

And I still had my prize, my wonderful reward waiting – my *red sparkly* dress. Instead of buying the usual black jersey and covering up, I was going to shine, literally, at my birthday party in October. I couldn't wait to show everyone; I couldn't ruin that now.

All the ingredients were here in Appledore, I had a wonderful job with potential, I'd made some lovely new friends and now I just needed to be happy with me. I'd enjoyed feeling fitter, slimmer, stronger and I'd felt the flickering of a tiny flame igniting inside. But that flicker was never going to ignite into a flame if I stayed in that pizza shop, so I turned around and went back to the car.

And when I got back to my flat, I made a ham salad sandwich with whole-wheat bread and a cup of hot tea. It was the food of a winner, and tasted even better than a meaty feast pizza with cheese crust and garlic sauce.

Chapter Eleven

The Taco Cleanse

Diet Diary: November 2011; The guy in the local Mexican takeaway was cute and I needed an excuse to visit – on the hour! The diet involved eating as many tacos as I could eat – what was not to love? By Day three I'd lost 2 pounds and we were making eye contact over the quesadillas. Then he Face-Timed his girlfriend and I realised I had guacamole on my cheek.

'You are kidding me?' was Karla's response when I called to tell her the next day to say that Jude had turned up in the cafe. 'Well, he must have liked what he saw, because last night he texted yes in his RSVP to the invite to your "surprise" party.'

I felt a vague sense of satisfaction.

'So he wants another lick of the Dani ice cream?' I said, feeling pleased with myself and the way I'd walked away, as he had so many times. 'He didn't like it when I told him I will not be the hot fudge sauce on his ice cream sundae though!'

'You didn't actually say that did you?'

'No, but I wish I had. Anyway, I feel better and then here comes the best bit, afterwards I didn't buy a large accessorised meaty feast pizza and chow down like a beast.'

'That is a bonus. I'm so proud of you walking away from him… and the pizza, just a shame you didn't punch him in the face first.'

'Yeah, that would have been sweet, but it might have made a mess on the tables. And then there's always the prospect of Rhonda the Rottweiler hearing of it and turning it into a front-page lead.'

'I wish I could punch him… this guy almost ruined your life, he caused you so much pain that you ran away from the place you love most.'

'It wasn't his fault about what happened, it was mine – I was the one who just left.'

'Yes but he was the catalyst…'

'I know, but I can't blame him for what happened to Mum, that was my fault.'

'No it wasn't, Dani. You've done so well, you don't need this now.'

'I hear you, and I appreciate it, I really do. But it's over now.'

'Yes, but I'm just worried he's going to turn up at your birthday party and try to seduce you. I hope you have your armour ready, girl.'

'Of course, but I do think he had feelings for me back then. Turns out he'd left the area when I did because he couldn't bear to be here without me. And he says he did try to find me after I left, but Marco wouldn't give him my contact details.'

'Mmm I met Marco, there's a guy with issues.'

'Yeah, but I can't see him being protective of someone's phone number. He didn't even know me, I'd long gone.'

'So Jude lies again, big surprise,' she sighed. 'I think being with Chris has made you realise how good a relationship with the opposite sex can be... because it wasn't about sex. You said it yourself, you got to know each other as people, okay you then went one step further and fell for him, but that's because you were vulnerable.'

'I'm not vulnerable any more. And I've worked through the Chris thing.' I so hadn't.

'What in two days? I don't think so.'

'Yes... okay, not quite, but I'm getting there. Chris is my trainer and friend end of, I just needed to know that's all it is – and now it's been confirmed,' I said, still feeling a twinge of pain at the thought of him kissing Alex.

'Yeah, but just be careful if that creep Jude comes anywhere near you at your party... Archie NO!' she suddenly shouted, apparently her youngest was emptying a cereal packet all over the dog, so I said I'd call her later.

The following morning I woke and opened the curtains to a bright blue early September sky. I stood a while watching the morning open up, then I had a text from Chris asking if I wanted to do some training. I did, but I couldn't face the gym again – the idea of seeing him with Alex. I couldn't have borne their eyes meeting, an intimate, secret brush against each other as they passed, me talking away on the treadmill as he timed me and rolled his eyes at her. I knew the score, I just didn't want it rubbing in my face.

Then like clockwork, I saw Chris walking along the front, not running as usual, I saw him look into the window of the cafe, shielding his eyes and looking through the glass. He must be wondering where I was, and probably concerned about me. I'd been so selfish and overdramatic flouncing off like that and he had no idea I'd seen him with Alex. He probably assumed I was lying low.

He was looking up now at my window and I felt the soft thud of a pebble and lifted the net curtains. I rushed to open the window; 'What the hell are you doing?' I laughed, despite my stupid, irrational hurt feelings I was elated to see him.

'I'm Romeo to your Juliet… get down here now and start running!' he said, with a mock-stern face.

I was slightly hesitant at this, I didn't want to rely on him any more, I was okay to run alone and be alone. But then again I'd be cutting my nose off to spite my face because this was my friend and he wanted to support me.

'Hang on, I'm coming down,' I called back and quickly threw my trainers on and my huge jersey jogging trousers and black T-shirt that could home a family. I was rather pleased to see they were a bit baggy and I almost danced down the stairs into the cafe.

He was standing at the door smiling. I instinctively gave him a hug and we stood together for a few seconds in an embrace. I felt a rush of warmth and friendship (or was it lust) and when I let go I was aware he still had his arm around my waist. And yes, I actually had a waist now.

'Dani, where've you been? I've been texting you.'

'I'm sorry, it all got a bit much… the newspaper, then Jude, my ex, turned up.' I obviously didn't mention the main reason, that I'd seen him kissing the most beautiful girl in the world and realised I had a raging crush on him so had kept away.

'Yeah it must have been tough for you with all that going on. Are you okay now?" he asked, his eyes widening.

'I'm getting there, it made me want to push my face into a big pizza and eat my way out. Or put my mouth under an ice cream nozzle and press "fast". Or get a great big burger, lavish it with cheese, dressing, and…'

'I think I get the picture,' he smiled.

I stopped thinking about the burger – for now.

'Then there's the protestors and the local kids who seem to think it's fair game to try to take a photo of the fat lady from the ice cream cafe scoffing something tasty… but, breaking news, I've resisted all temptation.'

'Great,' he said, giving me a high five. 'I'm proud of you, Dani.'

I glowed like a little girl at this.

'I think the repercussions from the article are dying down now – finally,' he said.

'So you're not the gym-owning fat fascist any more?'

'Apparently not,' he laughed. 'But it's been a real test for you and you passed.'

'Yeah, the kids and their iPhones kind of escalated after Roberta attacked some who seemed to have their iPhones trained on me. They didn't, I was just paranoid, but Roberta is a bloodhound and one whiff and she was rolling around outside the cafe with one kid in a headlock... it wasn't her finest hour.'

'I'm trying to picture it, at the same time I'm trying not to.'

'Yes, I wish I could unsee it, especially when Sue got involved, fortunately we bribed them with ice cream to keep schtum. But the whole sordid incident seemed to start a vendetta and the lovely kids who come in for ice cream have suddenly become ruthless paparazzi.'

He was laughing at this and shaking his head, then he looked up and into my eyes. 'I'm just glad to see you,' he said, 'I missed you at the gym.'

'I missed the gym too,' I said, aware he was gazing at me but not allowing this to confuse my feelings this time. There was no ambivalence – just Chris being himself and doing his job – and it was his job to make clients feel good, like they were his favourite person on earth. And if a by-product of that was some of the more susceptible ones falling for him then that was our problem and we had to deal with it and not let it get in the way. I looked beyond him, out to the beach. 'Are you doing a run this morning?'

'Yeah... you coming with me?'

I nodded and before he could say anything else I set off. This was the first time we'd run properly together, I'd watched him do his morning run from my window, never imagining I'd join him one day. I was amazed at my energy, loving the feeling of racing along the beach with Chris behind me. He was a faster runner than me of course, but after hours pounding the treadmill I was holding my own. And then he ran past me laughing, and I tried to catch up, but fell by the wayside. I was fully expecting him to continue his morning run and leave me behind. But then, in the distance, I saw him turn around and begin to run back.

'Come on, Dani, don't give up, you can do it… think 10k,' he was calling as he approached me.

'No, no I'm not fast enough, I'll only slow you down… this isn't a training session, you don't have to be nice to me.'

And he stopped dead in his tracks; 'Why would you say that?'

'Well it's just that this is your morning run, you shouldn't have to feel obliged to run with me when it isn't my training hour.'

'I never feel obliged to do *anything* with you – I work with you because I like working with you.'

'But you've been so good already, you train me for nothing and…'

'No it hasn't been for nothing, I've seen you blossom in the past few weeks, and that's why I do this job. And it works both ways you know, you've given me your time and taught me stuff too.'

'Like what?' I laughed and looked doubtful.

'That working out doesn't have to be serious, if you fall flat on your face it's okay to laugh at yourself. And sometimes, you can let go a little and enjoy a drink, something nice to eat, or if you really want to throw caution to the wind you can have a few hours off in front of the TV with a *small* bag of sweets.'

'Stop right there, mister, or you'll go to hell,' I teased.

He laughed; 'We're coming from different places here – give me time to catch up and before you know it I'll be sitting on that couch all night with a regular bag.'

'Supersize it before you invite *me* round,' I joked.

'Yeah but only if you promise to enjoy it without hating yourself, Dani.'

'Oh how the tables have turned, Chris telling his student to eat without guilt.'

'Yeah, well you're doing great, but we still need to sort that head out.'

'I can't help it, I doubt you've ever hated yourself.'

'I've hated myself, sometimes I still do,' he said, a shadow crossing his face.

He sat down on the sand, beckoned me to join him and so I sat next to him. We were both facing the sea, a little ruffle of British summertime breeze ran through my hair reminding me that autumn was just around the corner. Chris was running sand through his fingers and we both sat in silence for a few minutes, him taking in the view, me getting my breath back.

'I know exactly how it feels to hate yourself you know,' he suddenly said into the silence. 'I've never told anyone this before…'

I turned to look at him.

'Well, not anyone in my adult life… but it doesn't go away, you have to manage it – I struggle every day.'

'With what?' I was so confused, what could this slim, attractive confident man possibly struggle with?

'Myself… I struggle with me – the way I am, the way I feel. As you know I'm not from round here so no one knew me as a kid, but I spent my childhood being fat, very fat.

'You? Fat?' I couldn't imagine this.

'Yes, I lived for food and I loved it, so I do understand when someone tells me they find it tough.' He went on to explain that he'd been born prematurely and gone on to be a sickly child, so his mother and grandmother made it their life's work to feed him up. 'The portions were huge and delicious and when I cleared my plate they would clap. I learned from an early age that an empty plate was something to be congratulated.'

'I still like that theory,' I smiled.

'Yes and I associated food with being home and being loved. Home was my sanctuary from a world that mocked me, I'd be beaten up in the showers after games, called horrible names – kids can be bloody brutal.'

'Oh Chris I had no idea.'

'I've never told anyone, but I think, as your trainer… and your friend, I should probably have been more honest. You probably think I've lived this charmed life and have all the answers, but I don't.'

'Yes I must say on bad days I've wanted to scream in your face that you should walk in my shoes.'

'So I should be honest with all my students?'

'If you feel ready to share it then yes.' I felt even closer to him knowing he'd gone through the same experiences as I had, and glad he felt he could share this with me. God knows it wasn't easy.

'You really should share this with your students,' I reiterated. 'You're a success story, a walking winner we can all look up to and be inspired by.'

'That's a nice way of putting it, I've always seen "revealing my former self" as a sign of failure, that I'm not what I seem, that I'm flawed.'

'Chris, we're all flawed, and I guessed there must be something about you that's not golden-skinned and firmly biceped. I sensed a vulnerability somewhere under that spectacular body,' I laughed. 'But that's what makes you special, you're sensitive and seem to understand, that's probably why, because you've been there.'

'Yes and I shouldn't really be saying this to you as you're a client – but having been fat felt like a dirty secret.'

'I know, I know, and you kept it hidden. That's the problem with being fat, or even slightly overweight, it's like your appetite is out there, like you might as well be wearing a T-shirt with "I'm messed up in the body and the head and I ate ten doughnuts for breakfast."'

He laughed at this, 'You didn't... did you?'

'Do I look like the kind of girl who eats ten doughnuts for breakfast?' I said, then thought about this. 'Don't answer that,' I laughed.

'That's what I mean about you... your whole demeanour around food, diets and eating is so refreshing. You've made me see that it isn't actually a terrible thing to eat ice cream, it won't kill me – yes eating it all day every day might...'

'I was doing that scientific experiment before you came along and saved me.'

He smiled; 'I think perhaps we've saved each other, Dani.' He said this with such sincerity and such meaning that it brought tears to my eyes. For me there was no doubt that he was one of the keys to me losing weight; I'd lost over a stone, but because of the exercise it looked more. His kindness and sensitivity along with his teasing had also helped me lose some of the other weight, the baggage I'd taken away from Appledore and carried around with me all my life.

'So how did you change from a fat kid into the embodiment of fitness with your own gym?' I asked.

'As someone who was once fat, I'm always a bag of crisps away from going back there. It's a cycle and one I've been dealing with for years. At eighteen, I joined a gym. But I went to the other extreme, I never socialised because I worried I might eat something "bad", I didn't drink, I only ate unprocessed foods. I was finally slim, and felt like I belonged, but inside I was still that fat little guy who got beaten up every day. I opted out, became a bit of a loner – I just lived to exercise. It gave me the safe haven that I used to find in eating. I didn't know how to *be* anyone's friend, because I'd never really had one. Then you came along and you weren't particularly impressed with me. You were unapologetic about who you were and how you behaved and I found that so refreshing.'

I was amazed at this revelation, in the gym Chris was the guy everyone high-fived, women fancied him, men wanted to be his friend. Yet thinking about it, he didn't seem to have any close friends. I'd never questioned this, assumed it was because he was building his business and didn't have time, but now I understood. And I was proud to be his friend.

'Wow, you make me sound amazing,' I smiled. 'I hope you can remember all that so I can record it.'

'I love the way you can always see the funny side of things, even when the whole village is hounding you – still you make jokes about it. Nothing is serious and anything is possible to you, isn't it?'

'Mmm within reason. You said it yourself, I make fun of stuff that scares me, I make jokes to hide what I really feel, but I am essentially me. I don't pretend to be anything I'm not.'

'At the same time there's this sadness in you… as a trainer, it makes me want to rescue you.'

I looked at him, surprised.

'Yeah, when we first met, my immediate feeling, apart from the fact that I knew you'd be fun to work with, was that you didn't like yourself. And I knew if I could just make you see how good it feels to have a body that moves… that you feel happy in, then you can realise your potential. In everything.'

'I think with your support I'll achieve that.' I already felt like a stronger woman, and as for not liking myself very much, I was getting there.

'It's a long journey, for both of us,' he said. 'We might never be exactly who or what we want to be, there'll always be that fat little kid somewhere inside, but that's why I think you and I hit it off. I think we've both had a positive impact on each other. People worry about getting the "right" trainer, but it works both ways, and I feel like I've got the "right" client with you.'

I was happy, it amazed me that he'd thought so deeply about our dynamic, that he'd even analysed how we both benefited from working together, but now I'd realised I had feelings for him I felt vulnerable in our working relationship. I'd always said I had to do this on my own terms to give myself the best chance.

'I want to stay working with you but I think being at the gym makes me look at myself too critically,' I said. 'I can't help but compare myself to all the slim, beautiful women who work out there and it has a negative effect on me.' I didn't mention the fact that I also felt too fragile to be in the vicinity of his love affair with a stunning gym bunny.

'I know there's no point in me telling you you're as lovely as anyone else, so I'll leave it for now and hope you find that out for yourself. Look, we don't have to be in the gym all the time, in fact I'd welcome a change of scene. We can run on the beach, and if the weather doesn't permit, you could come to my place... or I could come to yours?'

I wondered, given my recent feelings, if this would be wise. As much as I didn't want to watch his love life blossom under my nose with gorgeous Alex, I wasn't sure about the intimacy of each other's homes either. I didn't want to rub my face voluntarily into something I wanted but couldn't have so I knew I had to keep a slight distance if I was going to manage my feelings around Chris. To have him in my living room doing sit-ups and bicep curls would be easy on the eye, but not necessarily on the heart.

'Exercise at home? Perhaps...' I said, probably sounding doubtful.

'You're still motivated aren't you, Dani?'

'Absolutely,' I said, keen to make it clear that I still wanted this. 'I feel so much better, more agile, slim... well slimmer, I'll never be Alex…' I heard myself drop her name in and glanced at him quickly to see if this registered. What on earth was I doing?

'Enough, Dani, stop looking over your shoulder at how wonderful everyone else seems to be. They aren't.'

'Sorry,' I sighed, 'I know, I thought I'd moved on. Comparing myself unfavourably to the beautiful gym goddess was last season's Dani – I've grown enough not to do that any more.' I said this to myself as much as Chris.

'Hey, we both still have a way to go. Lots of work to be done…' he smiled, patting my back.

I groaned.

'But that doesn't mean it can't be fun too.'

'Oooh you mean we can have *three* whole organic raisins after our two-hour workout? You spoil me, Chris.'

He laughed; 'Actually, I was going to ask if you fancied an ice cream, the van's over there.'

'Yes,' I agreed immediately.

'But first we run to the end of the beach,' he said, jumping up quickly and holding out his hand to me. I reached up and took it we were sealing our friendship again and it was great to have him back on side, fighting my corner, and we began running together. As we dashed along the beach I expected him to drop my hand, but he didn't, and I held on to his, wondering what the hell I was doing to myself. And what the hell would Karla say if she saw me prancing down the beach hand in hand with him? I was in a dangerous place and just asking to have my heart stamped on.

Eventually we finished our run, after which I staggered around the beach disorientated, which can't have been a pretty sight. I then fell flat on my back, sweating and groaning and waggling my legs about because I couldn't actually feel them any more.

Chris stood over me like master of the bloody universe looking completely unruffled, not a bead of sweat in sight.

'I'm in agony!' I wailed.

'Lactic acid,' he said.

'Oh shut up,' I responded, then after a little while, still waggling, I said; 'You know what the cure for lactic acid is?'

'Let me guess… another run?'

'NO!' I yelled. 'ICE CREAM, I want my ice cream NOW!' And I banged my arms and legs on the sand like a toddler having a tantrum. Then I looked around quickly to check there were no wannabe paparazzi around – what a video that would make. Chris laughed as he fell to the ground, joining me on the sand and looking up at the sky.

'So what you're saying is you want another run before we stop for ice cream?' he teased.

I sat up and looked at him, shielding my eyes from the sun. 'I want an ice cream, but dare I?' I asked, seriously.

He looked puzzled.

'The thought of having an ice cream scares me… will it trigger an avalanche of sundaes? Should I be doing this, Chris – even in the presence of my trainer. I've been so good I shouldn't spoil everything.'

'As you often remind me, eating something nice more than once doesn't make you a serial killer,' he laughed.

'Okay,' I said, 'I don't need too much persuasion. I'll race you to the ice cream van and the last one there pays!' And we ran across the beach like two kids to where Ella was waiting. Naturally, Chris won so I was paying; he was so competitive he'd almost rugby-tackled me as we reached the van.

I ordered two raspberry frozen yoghurts and Ella leaned out of the van whispering under her breath; 'You sure you want to do this, there are kids around with iPhones.'

'I can cope,' I laughed. 'Let them take their photos, but they're not taking my cone – in fact if anyone tried to take it from me I would bury them in the sand, all the time holding up the cone so it wouldn't be harmed,' I announced. I was illustrating this by holding my cone high in the air, but Chris grabbed it and made to run up the beach. I moved swiftly, and grabbed his arm, pulling it towards me. Ella was laughing loudly and so were we.

'It's a good workout – he steals my ice cream and I run,' I said, sticking my tongue out at him.

'You two are like kids,' Ella laughed. 'Hey, talking of kids, there are some lads watching over there, and they've got their phones up,' Ella was saying.

'If they want to take a photo of me, then let them have it,' I said, feeling good, happy.

'That might be the answer – let them have their photo, it's what all the A-listers do.'

'I know, darling, and I'm just bored with being papped while I'm trying to eat my ice cream and drink my champagne,' I said, in my 'bored film star' voice.

Several kids followed Chris and I with their phones and I said, 'Come on let's give it to them.' I linked arms with Chris and we struck an over-the-top pose with our ice creams. The kids giggled and took pictures and at one point Chris put his arm around me and it felt nice. Too nice.

'I know I shouldn't be flattered, I can only imagine the bloody caption on those photos – but I've never had quite so much attention. I feel like a celebrity, we're the Posh and Becks of Appledore,' I laughed, licking my ice cream with gusto. It was delicious, sweet, yet refreshing and fruity, nestling in a treacly waffle cone.

'I reckon we're more Gwyneth and Chris…'

'Before the conscious uncoupling?' I said.

'Oh yes in their heyday, when love was in the air and birds were singing, and Apple was just a twinkle in Chris's eye.'

'You'd better not let Alex hear you say that,' I smiled, 'the goddess might be jealous of the fat girl – for the first time in her life.'

'Alex?'

'Yeah… beautiful Alex from the gym, I heard you two were an item?' Don't ask me why I had to introduce this note of darkness, we'd had such a lovely time I suspect the masochist in me wanted to really test our friendship.

'God you can't do anything in this village without everyone finding out, can you?' he said, and just at that moment a little girl appeared and asked if she could take my photo. I was relieved, even though I'd been the one to mention Alex I didn't want her in our friendship, she had the best of him, so I could surely have the rest of him?

I dragged Chris into the shot and we both posed and pouted – two Hollywood wannabees on a beach in Devon.

We finished our ice creams and I headed off for work. As soon as I walked into the cafe, I was busy making more ice cream, then working on the counter. But I felt good after our run, and better for spending time with Chris.

The cafe was, as usual, total madness, with Gina vaping in the doorway most of the day and Sue and Roberta on full throttle. The weather was so lovely it seemed that everyone in and around Appledore wanted ice cream; a little bit of late summer sunshine meant a lot of ice cream.

When we finally had a few minutes' break, I joined Gina in the doorway, breathing in her French vanilla as she held the vape pen in the air like Bette Davis. I told her all about the kids catching me on the beach with an ice cream, and how we'd posed and she smiled; 'Oh Dani you are fabulous, honey, you just don't let anything get to you, do you?' she said admiringly.

'I do, but I think I hide it well,' I said.

'Don't hide anything, sugar, you just let it all out. You might not be skinny, but you're sensual – I reckon you should model underwear with your figure, I did some of that in the States,' she smiled at the memory.

'Underwear modelling? So that's what they're calling it these days, is it?' Roberta piped up, as she walked out into the sunshine with her cup of tea.

'Oh ignore her, darling, she's just jealous – she'd love to be me, wouldn't you sweetie?'

'What, on the slag heap?' Roberta growled and Gina roared laughing. These two were constantly bickering, but I felt it was essentially good-hearted; I often heard them giggling together. Roberta was Gina's auntie, and poor Ella was often in the middle of their 'banter' and it was actually quite funny to watch her 'referee' the two women. But I wasn't a shy spectator as I'd often been in the past, they dragged you in unquestioningly into their 'family' and you couldn't help but become part of them.

When I finished work I wandered out through the back of the cafe to take the outside stairs up to my flat. I had to walk through the cafe courtyard and in the summery dusk I could see a small vehicle parked there. As I got closer I could see it was a beautiful little gelato cart. I'd been on holiday to Italy a few years before and fallen in love with the cute little ice cream trucks in the square, with their stripy awnings and little wheels.

I ran back into the cafe where Ella, Gina, Sue and Roberta were all crowded round one of their phones having a conversation.

'Whose is that lovely little gelato cart?' I asked as I walked over and joined them.

'Oh it's… just an old thing, we're going to send it for scrap,' Roberta said. I was amazed at this, it was beautiful and so Italian I thought she'd love it, but she was quite bonkers so I didn't really pay much attention.

'Oh no, don't send it for scrap, it's beautiful. Can't we keep it? We could use it for the frozen yoghurts?' I said. 'They've gone down so well this summer we need to really brand them and next summer we could put the gelato cart on the beach or outside the cafe, depending on the weather. I could give it a go and take it down on the beach this week. I could test it out for next year, I'd love the chance to take in the last little cracks of summer sunshine too,' I added. It was now September and the air was definitely cooler, the days shorter and I welcomed the opportunity for some last gasps of late summer. Pushing it along the beach, would also be a great workout, that's how I thought these days. 'You can't send it for scrap…'

'Erm… I'm not sure,' Ella suddenly said.

'Oh I'm sorry.' Had I talked over her and missed something?

'I'm sorry Dani, we can't, it's dangerous. We need to scrap it… I've arranged for it to go,' Ella said, looking at the other two.

'Oh it's fine…' I started, confused at her reaction. Ella was always positive and generous about everything, she'd even put me on commission on top of my salary for coming up with the frozen yoghurt idea, which I told her was Chris's. 'No it's yours,' she'd said, 'buy him a drink for it, but own it.' So now I was a little bewildered as they all glanced at each other. I also felt hurt, it reminded me of the mean girls at school who talked behind my back, Kathy Parkes laughing at me and pulling my hair, not allowing me onto her team. I thought all that was over, but it came quickly, like a breeze, the exclusion, the feeling that I wasn't part of something.

Ella must have seen the expression on my face because she stood up and put her arm around me. 'It's okay, Dani. It's a great idea, but we can't keep it.' I felt slightly soothed by this, the girls were my friends and I had to stop being paranoid. Just because I'd been hurt by people in the past didn't mean it was inevitable.

'Yeah it's not that we don't want you to use it… it's just that it's dangerous,' Roberta said. And Ella, Sue and Gina nodded eagerly, repeating the word. I didn't understand how the cart could be dangerous, but what did I know? They were all quite, quite bonkers, and I went home to my flat very confused, but when did those girls ever make any sense?

Chapter Twelve

The Cookie Diet

Diet Diary: February 2013; I wanted to be slim for my friend Karla's wedding, I was a bridesmaid and the best man was GORGEOUS! So I ate cookies all day for six weeks and had to have my dress made bigger. Oh, and the best man asked the other bridesmaid out.

The following morning I was up early and dressed, waiting outside the cafe for Chris to run by. I wanted to surprise him and as I hadn't been to the gym I had this need to move, I actually liked how exercise made me feel. Okay, I still liked how doughnuts and chocolate and ice cream made me feel – but the aftermath wasn't the high of exercise, it was more self-flagellating.

After half an hour, I realised he might not be running that day, which was unusual. I was disappointed, but I just set off on my own, I didn't have to rely on other people to do my run. I waved at Ella, who was already in the ice cream van on the beach serving up breakfast brioches and coffee. I ran on, and she stuck up two thumbs in an encouraging gesture and I heard Roberta shout 'you go girl!' which made me smile. I ran towards Instow, and didn't stop until the estuary water wouldn't let me go any further, and then I ran back. I arrived at the van and lay on the ground as I had the day before, only this time Roberta came out and 'rescued' me with a coffee and a brioche.

'Mum, Dani's on a diet,' Ella said. 'Don't tempt her with brioche.'

'Oh yes please – do tempt me with brioche,' I laughed. 'I've earned this. If I run and jump and move I can eat too – it's a revelation,' I said, between bites of the soft, sweet warm bread and creamy ice.

'Good for you, love,' Roberta smiled; she settled down on a deckchair by the van, Delilah her little Pomeranian sitting on her knee.

'Delilah looks cute today,' I said, taking a sip of hot coffee.

'Designer… French, I ordered if off the internet,' she smiled and Delilah's tail wagged, making the blue pompoms on her white dress dance. That dog had a better wardrobe than I did – and she rocked it. 'And here you are again on the newspaper website, licking Caprioni's ice cream,' she smiled, 'fantastic publicity.' Delighted, she held out her phone and I held my breath hoping there was nothing horrific on screen, frantically scrolling through several Delilah photos until I came to the ones of me and Chris taken the day before on the beach. In one photo I was holding a huge cone and so was Chris and we were laughing and I suddenly felt a little pang. There was even a non-hysterical caption that didn't mention my curves, and BIG wasn't written anywhere, let alone in capitals, which was refreshing. It read, 'Dani Sheridan, who's running 10k in the autumn, was enjoying an ice cream with her trainer on the beach.'

I was pleased, for once I looked quite good, and I wanted to call Chris and share this with him.

'So, we've got a happy ending,' Roberta said, taking back her phone and scrolling through with a smile. 'I've already shared the photos on all our platforms, you can't pay for ads like this, two good-looking young people in love, on the beach eating our ice cream.'

I was touched and shocked by this description, I'd never seen myself like that – and knowing how brutally honest Roberta could be, this was praise indeed, but it was her other comment that surprised me. 'Thanks Roberta,' I said. 'But we're not in love.'

'Really? Looks like that to me.'

'He has a girlfriend.'

'Well, he's with the wrong one. He should be with you, I mean you're not Miss Piglicious any more, are you? Hope that name doesn't stick, love.'

'Mum, it will if you keep saying it,' Ella rolled her eyes.

'I like saying Piglicious,' Roberta whispered rebelliously, and gave me a wink. I wasn't offended by Roberta, she made me smile; she was the kind of woman who wouldn't let what others say put her down, she'd own it. I could learn a lot from Roberta. I loved the dynamic between Ella and her mother, the way they switched roles, teased each other and irritated the hell out of each other – but ultimately had a mutual love and respect. How I wished I'd had that with my own mother, but it wasn't meant to be and I was lucky to have these ladies in my life, they made me feel so welcome in their world. And when Roberta referred to my weight it was far less destructive than the way my own mother had done. I was emerging from my chrysalis, but it was hard to break free sometimes.

I had to stop harking back to how things used to be for my own sanity. I had people around me who were all on my side. They were kind and supportive and wanted what I wanted for me, which is all that mattered. And I had discovered that the key to unlocking what I wanted was exercise, movement. I loved the pounding of my feet on sand, the sun on my face – and if I also lost a few pounds along the way then hurrah!

I wanted to be healthy and slimmer, of course, but a real achievement would be the day when I didn't hate myself for looking at a bloody doughnut. As Chris had said only a few days before when I'd asked him why I couldn't stop thinking about doughnuts; 'A soft, doughy bun filled with jam is made to be loved, it would be weird if you didn't like it.' And I realised I wasn't strange, we're all struggling with something on this journey – mine happened to be doughnuts and sundaes. But now I finally felt like I belonged and I was spending time with people who accepted me in a way I hadn't been accepted before.

After my delicious breakfast, I headed for the cafe. As I walked, I texted Chris to tell him we were in the paper and tease him that I ran that morning and where the hell was he?

My phone then started ringing and it was him. 'Sorry I didn't make the run this morning, Dani, I wasn't up in time and had loads to do here too. I've got more equipment arriving today.'

'Oh that's a shame, I wanted to impress you with my running.'

'You have. The fact you got up and did it on your own is impressive enough, without any badgering from me. But I'm surprised you made it…'

'Why? Oh ye of little faith…'

'No, no I have faith—'

'Do I detect a little spikiness in my trainer this morning?' I said. 'Is it because I haven't been to the gym… or are you pissed off because you haven't done a run and I have?' I teased.

'I'm sorry, I had a late night.'

And up popped an unwelcome image of him in flagrante with Alex, and my bubble was well and truly popped.

'I'm tired,' he continued, 'and… yes, you annoying woman, I wish I'd done my run, but now it's too late because the gym's opened.'

'Come down tomorrow morning?'

'Why, you're not planning another run are you? Three times in three days?'

'Yes – what's so strange about that? I'm a machine!'

He genuinely laughed at this, which amused me.

'It's not that funny,' I said in mock annoyance.

'Oh it is. I'll see you on the beach tomorrow morning at 7.30… I'll buy you breakfast, but you'd better have your running legs ready.'

I smiled as I turned off the phone. I missed not having him around every day. But I couldn't go back to the gym just yet. I didn't want to face the possibility of protesting women or beautiful women brushing against my trainer.

Later that day I was working with Marco. This was always hard-going because he was anti-social, and that's putting it kindly, but being me I didn't just leave him alone as he probably would have liked. I made it my mission to cheer him up and engage with him. It usually went something like this: 'Hey Marco, look at this new sundae I made, it's got salted peanuts and fudge sauce, a sort of sweet and salty treat.'

'Dani, you have once more amazed me. What a time to be alive,' would be a typical response, all said in an expressionless tone with no smile. He was actually hilarious, even if he didn't mean it and sometimes I just said things so I'd get a response like that. We all did. Gina was always teasing him about girlfriends and she and Roberta were planning to set him up on a blind date but he point-blank refused, saying; 'Two old women sending me on a blind date – it is the end of days.'

This particular afternoon he was on form, without even realising it. He'd managed to offend several customers and make some little kids cry, which he would see as a day well spent.

'Do you hate people, Marco?' I asked as we cleaned up after we'd closed.

'Not everyone, just most people – hell is other people,' he said this without humour, and one could easily mistake Marco for a serial killer-in-waiting. But he had a kind heart; I saw him some mornings on the beach hugging Cocoa his dog, and

I'd seen the way he played gently with Delilah. Marco's light-handed baking was also an indication of his heart in my book, and one day he'd make someone a lovely husband. I was just glad it wasn't me.

'There are some lovely people though – what about Ella and Roberta, they are lovely – and Gina and Sue… and I try to be nice too.'

'You try too hard.'

'Oh do you think so – but you like us all really?'

'Yes but if you tell the others I would have to kill you.'

'Fair enough,' I said, concentrating on removing some disgusting chewing gum some pig had put under a seat. 'Marco, do you know Jude… Jude Thomson?'

'Cocky? Full of himself?'

'Well, he used to be…'

'No, he still is.'

'Okay, so you know him. Do you ever remember him coming in here asking about me… about twenty years ago?'

'Oh yes, that's right he came in and I wrote his words down on a piece of paper and kept it in case one day you ever came back for your lost love…'

I wasn't sure if he was kidding; 'You didn't, did you?'

'No,' he looked at me with disdain.

'I just wondered that's all. He didn't ask you where he might contact me?'

'He's never spoken to me in his life and I haven't ever uttered a word to him.'

So, Jude had tried to play me again. Was anything that came out of his mouth the truth? The joy of this though was that I really didn't care any more – I was well and truly over Jude.

I left Marco and joined Roberta, Ella and Sue at the counter, they were giggling because Sue had joined an online dating agency.

'Do men expect you to do that textsexy thing,' Sue was asking Roberta, who was apparently the dating guru.

'Ooh nothing wrong with a bit of sexting,' Roberta said. 'I'm always sexting.'

'She's not,' Ella assured me, 'she just gets confused.'

Roberta was amazing for her age – she must have been in her late seventies, but she was always on her phone. She had Twitter, Instagram, Facebook and Snapchat and she wasn't afraid to use them. And despite what Ella said I wouldn't be surprised if Roberta did sext, in fact Sue told me she used to sext her local vicar, but I wasn't sure if that was true or Sue just being - Sue. Roberta was now handing me one of her business cards with a self-styled title 'Digital Marketing Manager/Singer, Caprioni's Ice Cream Cafe' emblazoned across along with a photo of her dressed as Beyoncé. There were no words.

She was offering/threatening to do at least two of her 'acts' for my party and was just enlightening me about her 'repertoire' when Gina appeared in the doorway, a mass of golden blonde hair, the light behind her making it look like a halo above her head. 'Dani, just wait till you see my Cher,' Roberta growled, making her hand like a tiger's paw, 'and my Rihanna makes them weep.'

'You can say that again,' Gina said, putting down shopping bags, climbing on a stool and starting to vape, sending blueberry and menthol notes into the air. She looked like she was sitting in the middle of dry ice and was about to emerge any second in a glittering dress and give the performance of a lifetime.

'Oh Gina, Roberta's helping me with my sextuals,' Sue gushed, clutching her crystal-encrusted phone with matching nails. 'I met this lovely man at The Beaver Inn, so romantic. We sat on the patio drinking white wine and watching the sun go down over the Pacific Ocean.'

'Atlantic Ocean…' Gina monotoned from her blueberry vape.

'Whatever,' she continued, ignoring this minor detail, 'anyway, I asked Roberta how I should play it and she's instructing me in the art of sextual flirting. What she doesn't know about carnival knowledge isn't worth knowing. She put me right on the Tinder, didn't you sweetheart?' she added with a satisfied smile.

Gina nodded, absently, at least I think that's what she was doing, I couldn't see behind the cloud.

She put down her vape pen and looked at us. 'Be very careful with the sexting, Sue,' she said, looking and sounding like a Mafia moll, her accent caught somewhere between Barnstaple and LA, all red lipstick, hair and heels lost in a cloud of blueberry vape, 'you meet someone on a dating website, you send a little flirtatious text, then a stranger turns up at your door, you have wild, unabandoned sex, the best orgasms of your life, next thing, he's sending you photos of his junk.'

'What's the name of this dating website… so I can avoid it?' Sue said, pen poised eagerly.

'I don't know what dating websites you've been on Gina, but they don't do that at "Grey and Gorgeous",' Roberta huffed. 'Frank only sent me a photo of his dog.'

'Is that a euphemism?' Gina asked.

'No,' she said, horrified. 'It was a Schnauzer.'

'I bet it was,' Gina smiled to herself.

Roberta ignored this; 'Anyway, forget about Frank's Schnauzer, there are pictures all over the net of our Dani naked, and covered in ice cream.'

'It wasn't quite like that…' I started for the millionth time that summer.

'Honey, I know, she's on every feeders' porn site this side of Seattle. Dani, you do know that, don't you?'

I didn't, and fortunately at that point a mum and child appeared at the counter to order ice cream which allowed me to make two scoops and a tub, process this and move on.

'So who was the lucky guy I saw you sitting with in here the other evening?' Gina asked as I returned to my seat. 'He had a snazzy suit on, you should have seen his car too, plenty of dollars there, babe, do we know him?'

'Oh that was Jude… he lives around here.'

'Oh yeah… I remember him. Jude. Cocky, full of himself? Are you two having a roll in the hay?' Gina said.

'No, I'd rather be on my own than with someone who just wants me for sex.'

'Ooh I'd rather just have sex,' she sighed. 'But my advice in a word? Diamonds. Get diamonds off of him and then it doesn't matter what happens or where he goes. And you won't feel used if you have a few k to your name after the event.'

I could only imagine the life Gina had led, having apparently run away from Appledore as a teenager like me, but while I went to London she took LA by storm. She'd recently shown me some old photos of her in LA, lying by swimming pools, curled up on a huge, circular Hollywood bed and at parties with film stars. 'Wow Gina, you have had such an exciting life,' I'd sighed, looking through them slowly, taking everything in.

'No,' she said, 'you have to look beyond the surface – nothing is what it seems, Dani. I chased a dream a long time ago, and when I arrived there it was nothing like I'd imagined... because what I'd imagined didn't exist. Don't make the same mistake I did and stick around waiting for it to become what you want it to be – it never will. However much you want it.'

Gina's words had made me think about all the things I'd ever wanted. I'd been waiting to be slim all my life, putting things off until I'd lost weight, hoping one day it would happen. It had been the same with Jude, despite leaving Appledore, I'd never really left him behind and had spent almost twenty years wondering what if? But now, for the first time I was living my life – I'd bought the sparkly dress, joined the gym, and almost forgotten Jude. I was taking Gina's advice, and wasn't waiting around in the hope that someone would turn into the person I'd hoped they would be.

The pinks and blues of summer moved on, segueing into the browns and golds of autumn, and life took on a comfortable rhythm. I wasn't the new girl any more, I was Dani from the cafe, and I ran along the beach each morning with Chris, shared my days with a crazy group of women and felt very much part of life here. It was now a week before my party, seven days left of my thirties, and the night I was hurled headlong into my fortieth year had to be very special. Karla was coming down a couple of days before to help me prepare and I couldn't wait to spend time with her, I'd missed her so much.

I'd met up with Chris most mornings for our run, sometimes on the beach, and when the tide was in we'd run along the front and each time he made me run a little further, a little faster. He was always challenging me. 'When you push hard and do stuff you never did before, that's when you grow,' he said, in his trainer-speak as I called it. But I liked it. I liked the way Chris made me feel about myself, that I could and I would, and the more he encouraged me, the more I could do. We would stop and have coffee or breakfast after the run, I still enjoyed good food, delicious ice cream and sweet stuff, but I didn't feel the need to stuff myself like I used to. On pleasant autumn days, when the weather was mild Chris and I would sit on the beach after our run, chatting about everything and anything, but I never mentioned Alex and neither did he. I didn't feel comfortable bringing up Chris's girlfriend. Despite becoming very close and talking about our lives and our pasts, I didn't want to hear about his relationship, and it seemed he didn't want to share it with me.

When we were training together, it was just us. I wanted our sessions to be that way, one on one, it helped me focus and I didn't want to be distracted thinking about the two of them naked and rampant. I suppose I was trying to pretend she didn't exist, not in a weird, bunny boiler way, but because my friendship with Chris was special to me.

My own love life was non-existent – I'd seen Jude briefly in the cafe when he popped in to tell me had to go away on business that week, but Karla told me he'd sent an RSVP to say he'd be back in time for my party.

Jude wandered into the cafe thinking he was still in with a chance, but I knew I'd moved on from him now. He was firmly just a memory from my past.

He'd caught my hand and looked straight into my eyes with such tenderness, I had to look away; 'Dani, you look good, you've lost loads of weight, I may have to go out with you again.'

'You really think you can just click your fingers, don't you?' I said, shaking my head and moving away, but he followed me around the cafe as I wiped each table. He'd never been this attentive when we were going out together, usually it was me following him, literally. But suddenly he was interested, and I couldn't help but feel this new-found interest in me was nothing to do with my new look, but only because I wasn't interested in him. I had suddenly become a challenge.

'Do you remember? You'd take off your shoes and we'd walk through the surf, and then we'd end up in the sea?' he said, leaning on a table, his arms folded.

I softened slightly at the memory and looked at him; 'Yeah and once we were nearly caught by a man walking his dog.' Even though things hadn't worked out, I had to smile at the madness of our youth.

'And you wanted to rush out of the sea and put your clothes back on.'

'Because I thought he might be a serial killer,' I laughed.

'You were always such a scaredy-cat, Dani.'

'I still am.'

'You need a big strong man to look after you.'

'Mmm shame there aren't any round here,' I said, continuing to wipe.

'I'd look after you, I've got plenty of money and a nice car,' he said. 'I bet you'd like a ride in my car.'

I looked at him incredulously.

'Go on, come for a ride in my new Audi?' he said, sounding nineteen again. He hadn't changed at all. I declined his offer, and he eventually wandered off into the night, probably looking for another woman to ride in his fancy car. I was horrified to think how once I'd been taken in by this man who had nothing to give. I'd been young, inexperienced and was the perfect target for someone like Jude because I never bit back, but not any more.

The following morning during my run with Chris, he asked when I would be going back to the gym. 'After my birthday party,' I said, 'the weather will turn cold and I'll be glad of a treadmill.' I also hoped I'd be able to handle the whole Alex thing and feel good enough about myself not to be intimidated by the body beautifuls.

'The protestors have gone now, haven't they?' I asked, wondering if I might need to run the gauntlet.

'Yeah they only stayed a couple of days, it wasn't even a nine-day wonder, more like nine hours.'

'Thank God. In the end it all worked out well, my initial intention was to get publicity for you and the cafe and apparently sales are up here.'

'Yes same with the gym, we definitely had a spike in new members.'

'And as for me, I am apparently flying high on niche sites for men who like the fuller figure… and their women covered in ice cream. So if things don't go well at the cafe, I have a big future in chilled goods online.'

'Well, I always said you were delicious,' he smiled, as we reached the end of the beach.

I was so out of breath I tried not to think about the fact I was blushing at his words. Damn, I hated it when Chris was nice to me, I wasn't used to a man teasing me like that and it made me think the impossible.

We both sat down on the sand to get our breath back. With Chris I could be myself, talk freely, no make-up, no pretence, after all he'd seen me at my worst in my gym gear. He'd had me shouting at him, crying in his face, he'd seen me shoot off the back of a treadmill, become embedded in a rowing machine and must have seen my bum wobbling on the cross-trainer as I tried, inelegantly, to co-ordinate my legs and arms. And still he was my friend.

'So,' he said, running sand through his fingers, 'what happened with your ex, Jude, are you back together yet?'

'No way,' I said, gazing beyond him, watching Marco throwing a ball for Cocoa in the distance.

He picked up a polystyrene cup that had been abandoned nearby and filling it with sand, he turned it over, patted it and lifted the cup; 'Voila! A castle,' he said, and I guessed he didn't want to talk about Jude any more. Neither did I.

'A mini castle,' I said.

'Ah yes, but a castle all the same – doesn't matter about the size, it's my castle and I like it.'

'You big kid,' I said, finding a tiny pebble and putting it on top. 'So what about your love life?' I said, trying to sound indifferent. I had to mention her, it would be rude not to now he'd asked me about Jude; 'You're still seeing Alex Gym Goddess?'

'Yeah, kind of.'

'I saw... the way you look at each other.'

'Really?'

I nodded; 'You make a gorgeous couple.'

He didn't say anything more and neither did I. What else was there to say?

'Are you happy?' he suddenly asked; he wasn't looking at me, he was staring out beyond the horizon, somewhere beyond the estuary to where the sea came in.

'Happy? Yes... are you?'

'I think so. I'm very happy now, here on this lovely beach talking to you and soaking up the autumn sun.'

He seemed to be avoiding the bigger question.

'And life generally? It's good for you?'

'Yeah. There are one or two things I'd like to fix, but on the whole…'

'What about Alex, does she make you happy?' I asked this because in my heart I wanted my friend to be happy. I could move on from my crush and be the friend he needed, and I was genuinely looking out for him, and I didn't want anyone to hurt Chris.

'Alex? Yeah, she's… we share a lot of the same goals, you know?'

'Goal sharing?' I said, suddenly amused by the phrase. 'Chris that's such a soundbite, you could be talking about a business partner… put some passion into it, mate.' I hoped that calling him 'mate' would make it clear there were no grey areas for me. I was his 'mate' and Alex was his 'girlfriend', and I wasn't labouring or bunny-boiling under any false misapprehensions.

He laughed; 'Yeah, you're right, I do need to inject some passion.'

I tried not to think about him injecting passion into Alex, but one thing was clear, they were together, and he obviously went for the total opposite of me. Apart from the physical differences between Alex and me (of which there were, sadly, many), she was quiet and sensible and calm and serene. She ran on the treadmill without swearing, sweating or screaming, and managed to lift weights without ending up in the back of an ambulance. Meanwhile I was too dramatic, too loud, too emotional – I wore my heart on my sleeve and even that wasn't as simple as it might sound, because just when someone got close, I hid it so they couldn't see, and I could keep it safe.

Chapter Thirteen

The Macrobiotic Diet

Diet Diary: August 2013; If it was good enough for Gwyneth it was good enough for me. I'd started seeing a fireman, a perfect physical specimen, but we were polar opposites. Macrobiotic millet, quinoa and spelt will, apparently, balance yin and yang, so I ate all this for twenty-four hours. I lost a pound. Two nights later he left to go out on a call to rescue a cat and moved in with its owner. So I dumped macrobiotics for doughnuts and ice cream. I gained back that pound within the hour.

Two days before my party, Karla arrived in Appledore. She parked up round the back of the cafe outside my flat, car roof down, sunglasses on, looking like a film star. I'd been waiting at the window and rushed down the steps; 'Hey, no one told me Halle Berry was coming to my party,' I yelled, taking the steps two at a time.

'And no one told me you were looking so HOT!' she shouted. 'Girl, you've lost tonnes of weight. You are looking so good!' She climbed out of her car and screamed, 'Partay!' and we ran to each other for a hug. 'God I've missed you SO much,' she was saying as she unloaded the car. Crates of wine, gifts for me, her suitcase filled with too many clothes, some even exploding through the zips of an overnight bag.

I'd taken the two days before my birthday off work so I could get ready for everything and now Karla was here she'd be able to help. And I just couldn't wait to spend quality time with my bestie.

'How are the kids?' I said once we'd taken everything upstairs into the flat, which now looked like a burglary had taken place there.

'The kids are infuriating. They pee everywhere, put mashed potato on the dog, push their toys down the toilet pretending they're submarines until the pipes are blocked and there's a flood. But they're adorable, the loves of my life and I wouldn't be without them.'

'And what about the other love of your life… your husband?' I said, putting the kettle on.

'Oh Dave? He is a nightmare, I work, cook, clean and wash for everyone and by the time I hit the sack I just sleep, but as usual he's complaining that I don't love him any more.'

'Why because you aren't sitting up in bed waiting for him in scarlet lingerie at the end of the day?'

'Something like that. He seems to think I don't care about him, about our marriage. But we never have time to ourselves, Dani – and at the end of a long day working with emotionally draining patients, I come home to two noisy, fractious kids… three if you count Dave. It's all just more of the same.'

I'd never envied married people with kids, and just hearing what Karla said convinced me that it wasn't a life I'd choose. 'You need time on your own,' I suggested.

'You're right, but I need someone to plan it for me and work out what to do with the kids so we can just be ourselves again.'

'I will come and look after the kids for a weekend and you two go off and do whatever you want to do.' It was Karla's fortieth a month after mine and I suggested they try to do something then, but I knew she'd never get around to organising anything, she was too busy and too chaotic.

'So tell me all about your love life,' she said. 'I'm an old married lady, I want to live vicariously through you.'

'Non-existent, as you know,' I said as I poured us each a glass of Diet Coke. 'Sure you don't want wine?' I asked.

'No, I'll stay sober with you.'

'Sorry I'm a bit of a bore when it comes to alcohol, aren't I?'

'It's understandable, Dani, after your mum. You once told me you sometimes hated the smell of it because it took you right back into the past and all her problems.'

'Yes – funny what triggers memories, isn't it? And it isn't just Mum and alcohol, I haven't been able to eat a chocolate sundae since I left here,' I sighed. 'After always eating them with my dad… too much hurt, too many memories and…'

I thought about how Dad had let me down and how Jude had also let me down in a similar way, deserting me and replacing me.

Karla could see I was perhaps thinking too much about the past.

'Let's try your new frozen yoghurt,' she said.

'It's okay, Karla, you don't have to change the subject, I can talk about the past now. You always wanted me to, you said it would help, but until now I've found it so hard. Being back here and feeling stronger has helped me face it; it will always hurt, but the pain is less keen now.

She did what therapists (and good friends) do and didn't comment, just listened as I made us two froyo sundaes with fresh fruit, a little syrup and a breath of whipped cream.

'All in moderation,' I smiled as we took them over to a table.

'Mmm and moderation in moderation too,' she winked.

We ate our yoghurt slowly, savouring the sweet and creamy flavours, the ribbons of fruit syrup, the soft, comforting clouds of cream. And as we ate I finally told her the truth of what happened that night twenty years before…

'That night, the night it all happened and I left here, was the night before my twentieth birthday, as you know. I'd been working in the cafe until about 8 o'clock,' I started. 'I'd been trying to call Jude at home all day and hadn't been able to get hold of him, it was long before mobile phones and I spoke to his mother who just told me he was out. I knew he'd probably be at his friend Pete's, tinkering with motorbikes in the drive, so obsessed with them he'd forgotten to call. Pete also happened to be Jane's brother and so I went over to their house; if Jude wasn't there Jane would be and I could hang out with her for a while – anything but go home. Mum had been particularly bad the past few days leading up to her wedding anniversary and I'd left her in bed, a bottle of gin by her side, the family photo albums on her lap.

'I knew Jane would understand if I turned up unannounced, even if Jude didn't. Jude always liked to arrange to see me, he said he didn't like it when I just popped in to "his" pub or called him too much, he said it wasn't "cool". So I went to Jane's and decided if he was put out I'd just say I was there to see her.'

'God what a dickhead,' Karla spat. 'He was so controlling.'

'I realise that now, but I was just a kid then... and I had no one else.'

She shook her head and I continued. 'Anyway, I went to Jane's to see if I could spot Jude and Pete in there working on the bike, but there was no one there. So I guessed they'd gone out and decided to call on Jane and see if she fancied hanging out for a while. It wouldn't be a hardship, having a girly time in with my best friend. I went round the front and knocked on her door, but there was no answer and as I was reluctant to go home I just kept knocking, thinking she'd have her music on. Eventually she answered and my first instinct was to laugh, because she looked dishevelled, her hair out of place, her eyeliner smudged. Her reaction to me standing on her doorstep was odd – where she'd usually just open the door and I'd walk in, she was standing there, blocking my entrance, standing on one foot and then the other. And then I heard Jude's voice from upstairs asking why she was taking so long.'

'Christ... he was sleeping with your best friend?'

I nodded. 'Yep, the girl who'd shared my lip gloss, my cigarettes, my secrets – had one of her own. When she tried to say something I just shook my head, I remember being aware of tears already rolling down my cheeks. I was shouting, "I don't want to know, I don't want to know," and holding up both hands, shielding myself from what she was trying to tell me. She looked guilty, but at the same time there was a sort of triumphant note in her voice.'

'Did she not apologise or at least try to seem sorry?'

'Yes, she kept saying "Dani… I'm so sorry… we couldn't help it. We've wanted to tell you for so long, but Jude kept putting it off, he didn't want to hurt you…" But that made it worse because I realised then this wasn't just a one-off, they'd been seeing each other. She tried to make out he'd pestered her into it, but I was walking away down the path and when I got to the gate I just said, "You could have told me, you could have said no to him. I'm your best friend Jane, we're like sisters… and you've thrown it all away for sex?" But then she hit me with the bombshell that it wasn't about sex they were in love.'

'And where was the little shit?' Karla was angry just hearing this.

'He never appeared, he must have realised what was happening and like the coward he is he stayed out of his own mess. But I didn't want to stick around and see him, I was too upset, so I just ran, I remember running along the beach trying to get away from the pain until I couldn't run any further.' I sat back in my seat, unable to eat any more, filled up with pain and memories as I remembered collapsing against the sea wall and crying helpless tears for the boy, the best friend and the life I'd lost. Without them I had nothing, I couldn't believe they'd betrayed me and I knew I'd never get over this.'

'So you left?'

'I had to. How could I ever walk through Appledore knowing I might bump into them – a loving couple – my boyfriend and my best friend.'

I was surprised to find I could still shed tears, and Karla comforted me, but I hadn't told her the rest of the story, how could I? How could I ever tell anyone what happened next?

Chapter Fourteen

The Five Bite Diet

Diet Diary: November 2014; Found this in a magazine at the doctor's surgery. I'd just had an abscess lanced by a beautiful doctor and was asked to return a week later for the romantic matter of packing the open wound. It wouldn't be pretty, but I might be if I followed this diet. Five. Bites. Was it physically possible to only eat five bites of a chocolate bar, I asked myself. It wasn't. I gained 3 pounds from eating chocolate and when I returned the hot doctor was nowhere to be seen. The nurse packed my wound, roughly!

I woke from a fitful sleep on the day before my birthday to Karla singing 'Happy almost Fortieth Birthday to youuuuuu' loudly in my ear. 'You're going be forty tomorrow, you're so old you can't get out of bed without help,' she laughed, trying to drag me from under the covers, before leaving me in a heap and skipping off to make 'birthday coffee'. I must have fallen back to sleep because it seemed like seconds later she was back.

'So are we excited about tomorrow?' she was saying, holding two steaming mugs of coffee and doing a little dance.

'Yes, but I hope you won't be dancing like that. I'll have to have you barred,' I joked.

'I hope you're going to bar that Jude, he sounds like such a tosser,' she said.

'Is that psycho-speak?'

'Yeah something like that. If I had to hazard a professional guess, from what you've told me I'd say he's all about control and keeping his women down so he looks better, and he worked on you during some very vulnerable years and pushed you into the ground.

'The irony is, it's all about his own self-esteem, I bet his father's a big brute of a man who controls him, and he feels the need…'

'Yes, that's exactly it. His father used to be his employer, he owned the business,' I said. 'Jude's sold it now, and looks like he made quite a killing judging by his lifestyle.'

Karla did a 'what did I tell you' shrug.

'You're good,' I smiled and we gave each other a high five.

'And you're strong. Don't let anyone let you think otherwise, you came back here to face the past, and that takes guts, Dani.'

Karla was right, I'd come back here a different person, and while being here I'd grown so much stronger. I'd been holding on to memories of Jude all this time. Now I could see him for the man he really was, I felt foolish for being taken in. But more than that, I felt angry on behalf of the young, impressionable, lonely girl I used to be and how he took advantage of her.

'I'm just glad you're here, Karla…' I said.

The sun was rising and I left Karla in the kitchen talking on the phone to her kids and headed for the beach where Chris was waiting. We didn't say much, just ran along the sand, in tune with each other. I liked that there were no complications. We ran for a long time that morning, I think he sensed my mood and we just kept going.

Chris and I stopped at the ice cream van, surprised to see Gina standing inside.

'I know, honey, I know,' she said before I could ask. 'It's not me is it…? I'm hardly *van* material,' she looked at Chris and gave him a wink, she was such a flirt. I imagined in her youth she'd eat men like Chris for breakfast. And he'd have let her – he clearly had a weakness for beautiful blondes.

We bought two coffees, I couldn't face anything to eat and Chris said he felt the same, and as we walked away Gina shouted, 'I prefer this one, Dani!'

I wasn't sure what she meant and looked at her puzzled.

'This guy here,' she said, cocking her head in Chris's direction. 'Much more you, honey… your other guy's a waste of space. Cocky… too full of himself.'

Chris and I both smiled at each other, knowing who she meant.

'Enough already, will you two get a room?' she said.

Now we laughed in embarrassment: 'Hey, you can't say that – this guy's not mine, this is Chris, he's my friend… and trainer,' I said.

'Oh that's a shame, you look so good together.'

'Ah she's too good for me, Gina,' he replied gallantly and I felt the familiar surge of feelings prickle my chest. Oh God, I didn't want to go there again.

'Ah she's sweet,' I said trying to cover my embarrassment as we walked away to drink our coffees on the bench on the front.

'Yeah – she's also just being nice, you'd never be with someone like me,' he said.

'No I wouldn't, you're right, I'm too good for you,' I said, with a smile. I didn't really believe I was too good for him, how could I? When I first saw him, I'd thought he was too good for me. But then I started to feel better about myself and I got to know him and discovered I wasn't the only kid in the playground who'd had troubles, and we had a connection. We also laughed a lot and I suddenly didn't feel like I wasn't good enough any more. In fact, I was beginning to finally feel 'good enough' for someone like Chris. And that was good enough for me.

After my run, I arrived back at the cafe and Karla was up and drinking coffee at a table with Sue and looking rather shell-shocked. Sue had that effect on you and even a trained psychologist couldn't keep up with her life stories of errant husbands and lost toyboy lovers.

'I mean I was in a monotonous relationship for a long time,' she was saying, 'one man, one woman and nothing in between.'

Karla looked up at me in relief. 'Never thought I'd see you running along a beach... and before breakfast too!' she said.

'Boy, you've changed, Dani… for the better.' This was a cry for help from Karla and I joined them at the table in the hope that I might rescue her, but Sue didn't stop talking until someone finally came in and ordered coffee.

'Ordinary or decapitated,' she asked, and I tried not to catch Karla's eye because I knew we'd both laugh. I'd told Karla all about Sue's malapropisms, and I was glad she was able to hear one for herself.

Over coffee, Karla asked me how I was feeling about the whole Jude thing.

'Oh I'm okay, I knew it would be hard to take on the past. He was – is a selfish, immature, self-obsessed dickhead and I knew that in my heart, but it was nice to have it confirmed in the flesh. He married the school bully, they deserve each other, I just wish he'd realise that I'm genuinely not interested in him. Honestly in all the years we went out, he never gave me so much attention, but now I keep brushing him off he's all over me.'

'He thinks you're still that naive girl begging him to walk all over you again.'

'Exactly, and I'm so not.'

'That's how much you've changed, Dani. Even up to a few months ago you might have been manipulated and fallen back in with him. I still can't believe you're the same person, morning runs, red sparkly dresses, evenings spent with your trainer at the gym…' she said.

'Yes. And I'll be straight round to the gym the day after my party, but it's been nice taking advantage of this autumn sunshine and exercising out of doors. Chris says it's good for producing vitamin D,' I said, smiling.

'Yes, being out in the sunshine is good for the soul too,' she said. 'And on the plus side, being outside is better for the ego – you don't have to look at the gym bunnies and constantly compare yourself to the supermodel he's going out with.'

'Okay, okay, I admit there's that,' I smiled; she knew me so well.

I ordered us more coffee, it was lovely sitting in the cafe together watching the world go by. Karla said all the characters I'd told her about were coming to life before her eyes and it felt like a window on my world.

Marco brought our coffees over and I introduced him to Karla. I knew he'd be monosyllabic and possibly rude, then again I'd have been disappointed if he hadn't.

'Marco's been here for years, haven't you?' I said.

'Yes but I'm not as old as you,' he said quickly.

I was delighted, if he'd been remotely pleasant then everything I'd told Karla about him would have sounded like an exaggeration.

'It's my birthday party tomorrow, you are coming aren't you, Marco? I know you like fun,' I gave Karla a wink.

'Yes, which is why I won't be here.'

'Oh Marco please… it won't be the same without you.'

'Sorry, I'm doing something else tomorrow night,' he said and unsmiling walked away.

'Isn't he hilarious?' I said to Karla, who had her mouth wide open in comedy shock.

Then Marco, who'd been walking back to the counter, turned round; 'That guy you asked me about, Jude or something?'

'Jude yes?'

'Cocky, full of himself?'

'Yes, that's him.' I raised weary eyebrows at Karla.

'He's married.'

'Separated actually.'

'Married.'

'Separated.'

'Married.'

'Hey,' Karla said, 'what are you trying to say, Marco?'

'That monsters are real, and they're walking among us. Some you might call your boyfriend,' he said this in his Halloween voice and I shuddered.

'He's not my boyfriend, he used to be.'

'I think he still thinks he is,' Marco said. 'I passed here the other night, he was in here, with you, alone.'

'Yes but nothing happened, he was just being a pain, and wanted me to take a ride in his new car.'

'His wife bought him that car.'

'Really?'

'Yes, her family's rich, they say that's why he married her.' Marco clearly kept quiet but listened, I had no idea he was such a mine of juicy gossip.

'You know a lot about all this, Marco.'

'Yes, I know Jude's wife, I know his girlfriend too.'

'You mean he's being unfaithful to his wife… to Kathy Parkes?'

'Oh yes,' he said, nodding slowly as he walked away.

'I bet he tells everyone they're "separated", except his wife,' Karla said, when Marco had sauntered off.

'Yeah and I bet he's doing what he always did, cheating on her with every woman in Appledore,' I sighed. He hadn't changed at all, and if I'd been the same girl that arrived here I might have been taken in and betrayed by him again. The more I discovered about Jude, the more I disliked him.

'You don't feel sorry for *her* do you?' Karla asked.

'Kathy bloody Parkes? No I don't. I was just thinking about fate and revenge and how by walking out on him and then Jane going, we left a fitting gift for Kathy,' I smiled. 'She picked on me, and made my life a misery – now Jude's making hers one.'

'What goes around comes around,' Karla said, shaking her head.

'Yeah,' I said, 'you know what? I'm texting him now to say don't even think about coming to my party.'

'But I thought you wanted to grind him into the dirt with your stilettos?'

'I did, but I'm not sure I've got the energy or the time, I'll be too busy enjoying the party.'

'Don't uninvite him – I think he should be there – I think it's time for closure and a delicious slice of ice cream cold revenge.'

'What do you mean?'

'I'm not sure yet, but we'll think of something; I'm a psychologist, I'm great at twisted mind games,' she said, with a wink. 'And if I can't think of anything, I'll just grind him into the ground with my stilettos on your behalf.'

'And that,' I said, 'is exactly why you're the best friend I ever had.'

Chapter Fifteen

The Victoria's Secret Angels Diet

Diet Diary: October 2015; If I ate egg-white omelettes, oatmeal and Japanese yams, plus did workouts involving heavy lifting, I would, apparently, look like a Victoria's Angel. I lost 5 pounds, still didn't look like an angel, so gave in and did my own workout – the heavy lifting of doughnuts. Gained 12lbs.

A birthday always makes you think of birthdays gone by, like what you were doing ten years before on the same day, or even the year before. On my fortieth, I couldn't help but think about my twentieth birthday, when everything changed. Telling Karla some of the story had brought it all back and I'd tried to forget about it, but the rest of that night just kept sweeping over me, refusing to go away.

That night, when I'd realised Jude had been cheating on me with my best friend I ran through Appledore, along the beach. I hadn't a clue where I was going, but I knew I was ready to leave this place, I just wasn't ready to go home and pack. As I ran along the beach, a heavy storm was threatening, the skies were black, rain spots were hitting my face. Distraught about Jude and my best friend, I headed to the place I'd always turned to – Caprioni's. It was late, and as everyone was home because of the storm, the cafe was empty and I guessed Sophia was about to close. But being Sophia, she'd welcomed me in out of the rain and the wind now curling up into the sea.

'Come in and have some ice cream,' she said, gently ushering me into warmth and light and safety, my only sanctuary from the storm outside and the storm at home. Most of the staff at the cafe were young, and we treated the place like home, wandering in after college or school and doing our homework there, most of us probably escaping something at home. 'My Ice Cream Orphans,' Sophia used to call us. Looking back, I think we were her children in Gina's absence.

She could see I'd been crying, but was discreet enough not to ask, besides, she knew Jude and probably guessed it had something to do with him. I wondered if anyone in the cafe knew about Jude and Jane, was I the only one who didn't?

'I know what you need,' she said, as the storm caught the string of outdoor lights, smashing them against the window. 'Your favourite – strawberry sundae with extra sprinkles,' and she got to work. This was the sundae I'd always eaten when I needed comfort, and Sophia was sensitive enough to know this.

She eventually brought the sundae to my table and while she kept busy cleaning the ice cream machine, and the storm raged, I ate and ate and ate. Until I couldn't feel any more.

'Brava ragazza,' Sophia said, clearing my plate. It meant 'good girl' in Italian, she used the phrase a lot, and she was of the old school who believed every problem, every emotional turmoil could be cured by a big plate of food.

After an hour, I knew I couldn't put it off any longer; I had to go home, there was nowhere else to go. Sophia offered to drive me, but her car wouldn't start so she called me a taxi and paid in advance.

I'd made my decision to leave Appledore, and hoped that by the time I returned home Mum would be out for the count and I could make a quiet exit and leave a note. It might have been the coward's way out but I didn't have the energy at this point to face my mother, especially as Jude had proven my mother's words right. I was a failure and would never amount to anything, and now I couldn't even keep my boyfriend.

Despite my hopes for a discreet departure, I arrived home to my private hell – and my mum was at the centre of it. Having been drinking all day, she was now roaring drunk, but more melancholy than usual, weeping, wringing her hands together.

Still devastated by the betrayal of the boy I loved and my best friend, I couldn't take this, not now, and for the first time I told her; 'You've never been a mother to me.' I remember my words so clearly; 'I'm going away from here and away from you,' I yelled in her face. For once she was more subdued and even in her alcoholic mist she seemed shocked that I would say this.

'Don't… don't leave me, Daniella,' she cried. 'I'll stop, I promise I'll stop if you'll just stay. I can't be on my own.'

'You'll be on your own because that's what you deserve, and I won't be here any more to mop you up. You're disgusting,' I shrieked, as I threw some clothes in a bag and emptied her purse of all she had.

'If you leave me I'll die,' she called as I ran down the hall to the front door and back into the torrential rain in the windswept night.

'GOOD!' I yelled back, and slammed the door. I'd finally taken control. I couldn't even feel the rain stinging my face, the wind whipping my hair as I headed for the railway station where I waited until morning for the next train out of there. I sat in the rain and the cold all through the night, and as bad as it was, it was still better than going home. And when daylight came and I climbed on that train I was euphoric, like a huge weight had been lifted from me and my life was starting again.

Little did I know that as I sat alone on the train, the world whizzing by, my mother was taking pills with her final drink.

It was only after I'd been in London a couple of days and phoned Sophia to tell her where I was that I found out.

'They found her this morning, the police have been trying to get hold of you. They think it was suicide,' she said.

I was devastated, I blamed myself and still do. For years I lay awake at night believing I'd killed my own mother. If I'd stayed that night she'd still be alive – and if I'd been a better daughter she may not even have become an alcoholic.

Fortunately, life seems to give us what we need, and meeting Karla by chance in a bar when I first arrived in London saved me. Finally someone was on my side and now, after all these years, I'd shared part of my story with her. I could begin to finally heal, but the scar would always be there, the hurt, the blame, the guilt… and my mother's final words, her warning; 'If you leave me I'll die.'

If I'd known how bad she was, or realised the impact of me leaving – I would have stayed, if only for a short time to try to help her, but I didn't, and I paid for it. I will forever regret not being able to help my mum, but I knew now this was something I had to live with, to wake up to each morning and to sleep with each night – it was part of me, but it didn't have to rule me. And I wasn't going to let it hold me back or stop me from living my life any longer.

The day of my birthday dawned and I was determined to make it a positive, happy time for me. This was the beginning of my new life, and I was going to look fabulous, feel good and have a wonderful time, for me, no one else. My best friend was here and all my lovely new friends would be at the party too.

I woke to a text from Chris asking me to meet for our usual run and I knew it was the best way to start my day, spending time on me. I dressed quietly, left Karla sleeping, and headed off for the beach where Chris was waiting.

'Here's the birthday girl,' he shouted as I ran towards him.

'Don't remind me, I'm still thirty-nine in my head; it hasn't sunk in yet,' I said, catching up to him as we jogged along the beach. It was the end of October, but the sun must have known it was my birthday – she was sitting in a blue sky dotted with little puffs of white ice cream clouds.

As we ran along, I waved to Ella in the van, and called to Roberta walking her little dog Delilah and I smiled at the friend running beside me. In that moment, the dark clouds lifted –

this was happiness. I was back in a place where I belonged with people who cared about me. I didn't need a high-flying career or a man to validate my life, I just had to be me and be happy. It sounds simple, but it had been tough getting here, especially with all the baggage from my past, but this was my happy place where the shadows were finally starting to fade.

'Come on,' said Chris as we ended our run. 'As it's your birthday I'll buy breakfast.' So we wandered over to the van where Ella produced a huge brioche that could probably serve about ten people. I couldn't wait to tuck in, and I know I sound like a smug gym bunny, but I promised myself an extra hard workout the next day to make up for it. On top of the giant brioche were forty candles, all lit, and as Ella started to sing 'Happy Birthday' I could hear a choir of voices – and out came all my friends from the cafe, walking along the beach towards me. Roberta leading the charge, voice at top volume, Delilah in a tutu and tiara, Gina dressed like she'd just walked off a catwalk, Sue in her usual leather, feathers and sequins. And at the back Marco as sullen as ever and clearly not enjoying himself but that's how he rolled. And when I spotted his lips moving, I couldn't make out whether he was singing happy birthday or blaspheming under his breath, but I was touched by all of them. And I couldn't help it, I cried, and Chris drew me to him and, putting his arm around me, whispered, 'Happy Birthday lovely lady' in my ear.

Everyone continued to sing and as I blew out my candles through tears, I thought – yes, I'm finally home.

'Close your eyes, we wanted you to have your present early,' Ella was saying, 'you might want to use it at the party.'

And with that, she ran behind the van and emerged round the other side pushing the beautiful Italian gelato cart.

'Oh… oh… I can't believe it. Is it mine?' I asked.

She nodded; 'Yes, you'd talked about visiting Italy and the wonderful gelato carts and when we heard about your birthday we searched for one.'

'I searched the bloody globe!' Roberta piped up.

'But it was supposed to be a surprise and then you spotted it before we'd had a chance to hide it,' Ella continued. 'It's filled with birthday-cake-flavoured ice cream.'

'So that's why you were all so weird about me wanting to keep it?' I said, hugging Gina, Ella and Roberta.

'Sue made the stripy awning, she's great with colour,' Roberta said, 'she's made a matching dress for Delilah and she's even put matching pompoms on.'

'Yes pompoms are all the rage on the catwalks of Milan,' Sue nodded knowingly, 'only the best for our Dani.'

This wasn't the first time I'd been referred to as 'our Dani' by the girls in the cafe, but each time it touched my heart. I really was meant to be here, and this was the family I'd never had.

'You're all wonderful,' I said, and Chris lifted his T-shirt to my face so I could wipe my eyes.

'The cart is a gift,' Ella was saying, 'but it's a bit more than that. I'd like you to use it to sell your lovely frozen yoghurts, and after costs, all the profit from the cart belongs to you.'

'Oh no… I couldn't,' I said.

'Oh yes you can. I was given the van when I came back to Appledore to get me started and I already feel like it's taken me

somewhere I never thought I could go. Everyone should have
a little start, so try it out and see where the gelato cart takes
you,' she had tears in her eyes as she hugged me. Then Gina,
Roberta, Sue and even Marco (grudgingly) gave me a hug and as
the weather was so lovely Ella brought out a large picnic blanket
and we sat on the beach sharing the brioche. I felt happy, healthy
and loved, like I finally belonged, I was part of a kind of family,
something so many people take for granted, but something I'd
longed for all my life.

Later, as we strung glass lanterns around the little courtyard garden at the back of the cafe, I thought about my journey to this
point. Now I was more honest about me and about the past, and
truthfully the painful part was that I'd wasted years of my life
feeling guilty. It was also difficult facing the fact that I'd saved
a little bit of my heart for a man who hadn't been worth it. I'd
always known Jude was a cheater, even before Jane, but a little
part of me had hoped he'd changed, and he hadn't. I felt rather
foolish for my younger self, but I'd learned my lesson and while
he may not have changed, I had.

Tonight I would face my past, my present and my future with
confidence, turning on my sparkliest smile for everyone. I was
finally me, the real Dani, a bubbly, attractive, confident forty-
year-old woman, who was living the life she wanted, the life she'd
dreamed of as a child, the one she longed for through years of
loneliness. I was single and happy and there was a certain free-

dom in realising you don't need another person to validate your-self, and my journey forward would be with my good friends.

The cafe had closed at 6 p.m., so we could decorate and pre-pare everything. Marco had offered to be the barman, much to everyone's surprise, but I took it as a huge compliment as he hadn't even planned on coming and hated parties, but apparently had said (albeit grudgingly) 'I'll do it for Dani.' Roberta was the DJ for the evening and against my better judgement I'd agreed to her performing 'a floor show' later. Ella had created amazing cocktail-flavoured ice creams, from mojitos to pina coladas and though I didn't drink, I would certainly enjoy those ice creams. Ella and Roberta were also providing a wonderful buffet, deli-cious canapés of pink prawns with pale green avocado and spiky lemon, big shiny green olives scattered around rustic platters of Italian meats and cheeses, and lots of vibrant salads filling two huge trestle tables. Gina and Sue were 'the party decorators', and while Sue rushed around like a mad hen wrapping herself in fairy lights and glitter, Gina took on an 'advisory role', sitting on a bar stool emanating sweet vapour and shouting the odd instruction. By the time we were ready, candles flickered like little suns in jars around the tables of the cafe, inside and out music played and everywhere there were fairy lights. It was a chilly evening, but Roberta had managed to get some patio heaters and it felt like summer, in so many ways.

'I'm so happy here,' I said to Karla as we stood and surveyed the beautiful scene. My little gelato cart had pride of place and Sue had even strung some fairy lights around it. I'd never owned a house, I leased my car so this cart was probably the only thing that belonged to me, and it felt good. I now had something to call mine in a place I called home, and that's more than I'd ever hoped possible.

After a minute taking all this in, the two of us rushed upstairs to my flat where I finished getting ready. Karla had home-dyed my hair that afternoon, transforming my dark brown locks to a swinging, shining deep auburn – and then came the dress.

'You really have transformed yourself, you even have worked-out arms,' Karla said, admiringly, as I pulled the sparkly scarlet over my head.

'I have a worked-out life too,' I smiled, as she gasped at the dress. Having not yet seen myself in it, I hoped it was a gasp of admiration and not horror.

'Dani, you are rocking that red, I'm so proud of you.'

I walked over to the full-length mirror for the final effect as they do in TV makeover shows. And just like they do on TV, I gasped at the difference. I'd been wearing big sweatpants and T-shirts for weeks and when I'd bought this dress I'd tried it on in the shop and been a few pounds heavier. But now, with my full make-up, new hair and firmer arms and tummy, even I had to admit I looked good.

'Wow,' Karla said, and whistled as I walked into the living room. 'Girl, you will knock them dead tonight. You show that guy just what he's missing,' she smiled.

'I doubt he'll even notice me in that way,' I sighed, 'he'll be gazing at his gorgeous gym-goddess girlfriend.'

'Who?' she looked puzzled.

'Alex, I told you Chris is now with girlfriend.'

'I wasn't talking about Chris, I was talking about Jude – remember him?'

I laughed, a little embarrassed at my mistake.

'How quickly we forget,' she said, with a knowing look as I flustered.

In truth, I'd forgotten about Jude long ago. I'd held his memory and the idea of revenge all these years but really he wasn't important to me. Chris was the first person I thought of when I woke and the last one I thought of as I fell asleep each night; I couldn't help how I felt, I just had to manage my feelings and make the best of it.

'Come on let's go and celebrate me getting old,' I said, as I grabbed my friend's hand.

We left the flat and walked through the little courtyard behind the cafe – it looked magical in the dark, smothered in fairy lights, music drifting through the air. I stood in the doorway of the kitchens, waiting to enter, feeling like I was about to go on stage. I wouldn't have been able to face this a few months before, all the people, the attention, but tonight, I couldn't wait.

Once inside I was mobbed by old friends and new and handed lots of lovely gifts and hugged more than I'd ever been in my life. Everyone told me how wonderful I looked and though I still found it hard to accept compliments, I did so graciously. But there was one person who wasn't there to pay me a compliment, Chris, and despite myself, I felt my heart drop. He was probably busy at the gym or, I couldn't help thinking, with Alex. I felt disappointed that he'd let me down but I wasn't going to let a man spoil my fortieth birthday like I had my twentieth. And after a little while, when a boy I knew from school asked me to dance, I did, with feeling. We danced like the couple in *Dirty Dancing*, and I ended on a flourish, banging straight into Jude.

'Hey, you're throwing yourself at me now,' he was laughing.

'Oh I wasn't sure you were still coming,' I muttered without smiling. I hadn't seen him all night and presumed he'd got the hint and wasn't going to come, so it was a bit of a jolt now to see him here. He'd clearly had a drink, and was right up in my face, breathing on me which made me feel very uncomfortable, but I couldn't move because the place was really filling up.

'I didn't bring the car, planned to get pissed,' he slurred.

'Lovely,' I sighed sarcastically.

I moved across the room, away from him, walking over to the buffet tables to thank Ella for everything but he followed behind me.

'Dani, I know it's your party and you have to circulate, but what about us meeting a bit later... on the beach?' I was about to remind him in no uncertain terms that he was married when Karla saved me.

'Can I steal her away a moment?' she said to Jude, who nodded, holding out his hands like he was helpless to stop her. 'Don't thump him, will you?' she giggled.

'I just want to tell him to leave – he's spoiling my party.'

'No he isn't, leave him to heaven,' she said and handed me a glass of pink lemonade, which was sweet and cold and bubbly and delicious.

The party was really busy, the cafe full of people, lots of them spilling out onto the pavement outside and the little courtyard behind.

'Anyway, forget that dipstick… guess who's here?' she said excitedly.

'Who?' I knew exactly who, but I needed a moment to compose myself.

She leaned in and hissed, 'Chris!' and did one of her strange little dances which I assume she usually did with the kids.

'Is he… with anyone? A beautiful blonde girl…'

'Don't know, I've only seen him on Facebook, but I think it was him – and he's even more gorgeous in the flesh,' she laughed, raising her eyebrows and grabbing my arm. 'Come on I think he's out here,' she was saying as she pulled me out into the back yard. 'Is that him?' she pointed to the far end of the courtyard where he was standing with a drink. He looked different out of his sweatshirt, and gorgeous in jeans and a thick, check shirt, his fair hair lighter, his whole manner easy and relaxed. I just wanted to go to him and give him a big hug; he seemed to be alone, but she could pop up from anywhere.

'Yeah, that's him… wonder where Alex is?' I said, but didn't wait for an answer, heading straight over to see him. I felt like a celebrity, everyone was grabbing me and trying to hug me and wish me happy birthday.

By the time I'd got through the crowd, I'd lost Karla and Chris had moved a little and was talking to someone. I saw the long blonde hair and my heart sank, but I decided to go over anyway, I was a grown-up. So someone I had a crush on now had a girlfriend – I just had to 'woman up'. But as I approached I saw the tell-tale sign of vapour curling up and around them. It looked pretty in the fairy lights and the smell was sweet and fruity.

'Oh honey, you're here,' Gina said, hugging me. 'And you look so hot, doesn't she look hot, Chris?'

He smiled and nodded; 'Gorgeous, you look gorgeous, Dani.'

I felt stupid, like Gina was forcing a compliment out of him, but he was smiling and might even have been looking into my face. Oh God, had I got ice cream on my cheek?

'Well, I'll leave you two alone,' Gina said pointedly and swept off into the fairy-lit night. I'd forgotten she was there, and that's saying something because Gina is quite a presence.

'Thanks so much for coming, where's Alex? I must say hello,' I started.

'She's… she's not coming…' he started to say, but before he could finish someone was circling their hand around my waist. For a moment I thought Gina had come back, but as the voice in my ear said; 'See you later… I got the message,' I realised it was bloody Jude. I wanted to say, 'Oh piss off,' but I couldn't do that in front of Chris, what would he think of me? The long-held desire to grind Jude into the ground with my stiletto had been metaphorical until now… but now I wanted to grind my stiletto literally into his balls. I managed to hold down this urge and instead smiled sweetly, and in the voice of a nice teacher speaking to a troublesome pupil, I said, 'I'm sorry, Jude, I'm busy right now…' and turned back to Chris. It was pointed and anyone with half a brain would have realised I was saying, 'go away', but not Mr Arrogant.

'It's okay Dani… you chat to your friends – see you later at our rendezvous,' and with that he winked and disappeared. Ugh, he was aching to be stilettoed (and yes it *is* a verb).

'So, looks like you've got a late-night date,' Chris smiled as he watched Jude leave.

I smiled back, I didn't even want to discuss this with Chris, Jude was such an embarrassment. Perhaps one day I'd share it as a friend, but Chris had heard enough of my woes over recent weeks and this was a time for celebration. Suddenly I heard a distant thumping noise coming from the cafe. 'I think Roberta's about to give us a show,' I said, at which point Sue's voice came on the mic and announced the 'surprise arrival, of the amazing singer, Urethra Franklin'.

Chapter Sixteen

The Dani Diet

Diet Diary: August 2017; No more cleanses/detoxes/starvations, or trying to torture myself to become something I'm not for someone who doesn't care. I'm learning to eat healthy food when I'm hungry, and still enjoy ice cream, cakes and chocolate when I feel like it, because a life without carbs, sugar and chocolate is no life. I'm also learning to run without collapsing in a heap after three steps and so far I've lost 2 stone 3 pounds. And I'm trying really hard not to be one of those smug bitches I used to hate (honestly!).

Chris and I headed inside to see the 'show', but once again I was caught up with everyone and eventually I lost him in the birthday madness. Meanwhile Roberta was quite amazing; she channelled Aretha Franklin, followed by Beyoncé then a little Whitney Houston finishing off with a rip-roaring version of Cher's, 'If I Could Turn Back Time', which brought the house down. I sang along, thinking how, even if I could turn back time, I wouldn't, because right now, this was everything and I wanted to be in this night for ever.

We live our lives through good and bad times, but often it's only afterwards we realise what those times meant to us. And now I wanted to stop everything and just look around me, and take it all in. It was a birthday of friends, fairy lights, sea and stardust and I'll never forget it as long as I live. I think we all have these dreams when we're younger about where we'd like to be on our landmark birthdays – and one's fortieth is always New York, a spa somewhere in the Indian Ocean, even a maternity ward. But I would always have chosen to celebrate here in Appledore, on the North Devon coast, eating ice cream at Caprioni's.

At the end of the evening, to much cheering, Ella and Sue wheeled out the biggest ice cream birthday cake I'd ever seen. It was exquisite, a towering confection of ice cream, fruit and sponge cake, topped with sparklers and strawberries. And as I blew out my candles, I made a wish – that everything would stay the same, and that the rest of my life would always be like this.

I cut into the cake and we passed it round, toasting with champagne and another rendition of 'Happy Birthday' – the second one that day – and I thought about how far I'd come. I'd been the poor child, suffering through her despairing mother, then the confused teen hurt by love who ran away, and the woman who lived each day with guilt and disappointment. Nothing had lived up to my expectations, including myself – until now, and here I was at forty finally a happy, fulfilled grown-up in charge of my life. I was perhaps the luckiest woman in the world.

After consuming cake and champagne, people started to say their goodbyes. Even now, after being here all night, there were people I hadn't managed to catch up with – and we made drunken promises to stay in touch. This caused a minor trauma because in the chaos of the evening, I'd mislaid my phone and couldn't swap phone numbers. I was with Gina outside when I realised and asked her to ring my number – thank goodness Karla answered.

'Yeah, you dropped it in the madness,' she laughed, 'don't worry, I've got it safe.'

I smiled, feeling warm and fuzzy inside, my best friend always had my back.

Gina and I wandered into the cafe and joined the few stragglers that were left, Ella and Roberta were tipsy, and so was Sue. They were funny and happy – there were no shadows here, just laughter, ice cream and the constantly curling, scented vape from Gina's pen.

I suddenly glanced around, there was one person missing. I couldn't see Chris but Karla was standing at the counter inside the cafe and I asked her if she'd seen him.

'No, he must have gone,' she said absently, too absorbed in her thorough testing of Ella's ice cream cocktails. My disappointment at Chris's absence was equalled only by my relief that Jude had left, but then I remembered something he'd said about meeting him later. Oh God, I hoped he didn't turn up again, that part of my life was over – Karla said I needed closure and I'd had it since I came back here. Even if there'd been the slightest residue of feeling he'd stamped it down with his immature arrogance and self-importance. Seeing him again after all these years had made me feel stupid for ever being taken in by him. I associated him with being hurt and betrayed, and I wasn't in the market for that any more. The fact he was still with his wife was just the cherry on top of the sundae for me, and after all this time I could finally walk away from Jude without looking back.

By 1 a.m. Karla and I were left in the cafe alone.

'Your party was AMAZING!' she said. 'But I think the best bit has to be the fact that Jude is sitting in a hotel room alone somewhere in Appledore.'

'What do you mean?'

'Oh didn't I mention that you'd texted him and told him you were dying to sleep with him but wanted discretion?'

'No you bloody didn't, Karla… oh… hang on was that what he'd meant when he said, "I got the message"?'

'Probably. Thing is you left your phone unattended on a table, and I just thought, this is fate, I am meant to intervene. He's not good for you, but then you know that – I just worried slightly that you might be sad about Chris being with someone and he might swoop in like the creep he is.'

'You know I never could.'

'Yeah but I just wanted to make sure… so I told him to pay for a nice room and wait for you there. I said not to text or call, just strip off and wait until you knocked and say the magic words "happy birthday".'

'But I've no intention of doing that.'

'I know. So I called room service and asked them to deliver a bottle of wine for my friend's birthday, knock and say happy birthday and then just go straight in.' She looked at her watch, 'That should be happening… around now.'

'You are so naughty, Karla,' I laughed. 'I'm sure as a respected psychologist you could be struck off for doing something like that.'

'It's nothing, and considering what he put you through it's a drop in the ocean, but it kept me amused.' She smiled at me, then her face turned serious. 'Dani, you've come such a long way – are you happy?'

'I am. And as happy as this new dress and better, healthier body has made me, I was happy tonight because of my friends. I loved the warmth and humour and fun of it all – and that would have happened for me at any weight. This is my time and I'm just going to grab life and not worry about how I look or what people think, because tonight I realised people like me for me… not my tight bum or my shiny hair. And for someone who's felt unloved and unliked most of her life that's really something.'

'I'm proud of you, Dani… just one little thing? Can I complete my masterplan now and message Jude's wife to tell her he's in a hotel room waiting for a woman?'

I laughed; 'No Karla. I'm sure she's suffered enough, and has lots more coming her way, let's leave them to it. I'm happy, I don't need to get a kick out of other people getting hurt.'

'You're right, you're a spoilsport, but you have morals I suppose.'

'Yes and being married to Jude is punishment enough. So no more negativity, I need to be positive if I'm going to set my sights on the 10k next month…'

'You're still going to go through with it?'

'Yeah, I want to do it for me.'

'And that's the right reason,' she said.

'The old Dani would find this hard to believe, but I love running. I love the feeling of the wind in my hair, the sun on my face, feet pounding along the beach – it's almost as good as… well, ice cream.'

'I find that very hard to believe.'

'Okay… I lied, nothing's as good as ice cream, but running's better than I ever thought it would be.'

'Is that because of the company you run with?'

'Chris, you mean?' Just the mention of his name made my heart drop. 'Yeah, he's lovely, but I'm not deluding myself any more about men, at the end of the day, they're all the same, they just want pretty.'

'Hey, don't go all cynical on me, Dani, there are some good guys out there, you know. You just have to look and I'm sure you'll realise when you find the one. Why don't we sit outside and enjoy the fairy lights, and a couple of last drinks? I don't want your party to end.'

'Yeah great idea,' I said as Karla leaned over the counter and handed me a chilled bottle of pink lemonade and two flutes.

'Take these and wait for me in the courtyard. I'll be out in five,' she said, 'but don't get too chilly, put this on, it's October after all.' She handed me a parcel wrapped in glittery paper and a big blue bow, and when I opened it there was a red, cashmere throw inside. It was quite beautiful, a deep, vibrant red, soft and delicate to touch, and wrapping it round my shoulders felt like a big hug. 'I thought it might be nice for evening strolls along the beach,' she smiled.

I loved it, and after a million thank yous and kisses, I wandered into the courtyard under the stars and fairy lights and sat at a little table to wait for her. It was so peaceful out here, everything glittered and sipping my lemonade I thought about Ella's pink lemonade and roses ice cream. She'd called it 'Summer Nights' and tomorrow I would add edible glitter and see if we could remarket it for now – 'The Last Sparkle of Summer', perhaps?

I was sipping at my drink, thinking how lucky I was to get paid for working with all these lovely people – and ice cream, when I heard something on the other side of the wall. Then the wrought-iron gate slowly opened and someone was walking through. I couldn't quite make them out in the semi-darkness but my immediate thought was – shit, it's Jude, he's come to find me. But as he walked through, in the darkness, I recognised the walk, and realised it was Chris.

'Hi there – you came back,' I said, unable to keep the smile from my face. 'Have you forgotten something?'

'Yes,' he said, walking to the table and sitting down. 'Is this for me?' he picked up Karla's empty glass.

'It can be for you, I'll get Karla another glass when she arrives.'

'Oh, she's joining us?' He was smiling at me as I poured.

'Yes.' I smiled back and we clinked glasses, our eyes meeting. 'Are you okay?' I asked. He seemed different, nervous even?

'Yes, I'm good. Er… I've been meaning to tell you, Alex and I… we decided… it wasn't working.'

I knew this meant nothing for me, but it did make me feel ridiculously happy. I put on a sad face and said, 'I'm sorry', while stopping myself from leaping in the air, banging my fist on the table and shouting, 'YESS, even the gorgeous skinny girls get dumped!'

'Oh it wasn't a big deal. She's okay.'

'But are *you* okay?' I said.

'I'm more than okay, I'm here with you.'

I wasn't completely sure what he was saying, and I didn't want to start out on that unrequited love train again, so I just smiled and nodded and sipped. This was nice, just me and Chris together drinking pink lemonade under fairy lights.

'So do you want to talk about it?' Chris said, lifting his hand onto the table and placing it on top of mine. My immediate instinct was to pull my hand away, it was the kind of thing Chris might do to tease me and I'd swear at him and pretend I was horrified. But something in his eyes told me this wasn't the usual horseplay and I left my hand under his, it felt like all the sparkles from my dress were there.

'Talk about what?' I asked, trying not to sound too weird.

'You and me.'

'What about you and me?'

'I think it's worth a go, if you do.'

'Worth a go?' This wasn't real; it was like I'd written the script. Here was Chris, the man I really felt something for, but who could never feel the same about me, saying potential boyfriend stuff.

'What are you saying?' I asked, hoping to get some idea what was happening here.

'I'm saying yes to you. I… I've had feelings for you for some time.'

'Me? You mean… when you say feelings, do you mean as friends?'

He shook his head and I thought my heart would explode.

'Oh… in a man and woman way?' I asked. I had to nail this down, it was too good to be true and if I'd got this wrong I was in danger of making a total arse of myself.

'I'm saying I feel the same as you do. I'm saying yes… let's give this a go, I really like you, in a man and woman way,' he laughed. 'I just wish you'd said something sooner…'

'Mmmm,' I took another gulp. 'Said something sooner?'

'Yeah, when I read your text I couldn't believe my luck. I want you in my life, Dani.'

I took another large gulp. Text? And then it hit me, Karla had my phone all evening and like a magic little fairy psychologist she'd used it to rearrange my life. She'd sent Jude off to a hotel room by himself, and once she knew he was out of the way, she must have texted Chris from my phone declaring undying love. Oh God how could she do this? I had no idea what the text said – I would kill her when she turned up, but then I looked into his eyes and thought I might just hug her instead.

Chris then moved around the table and sat next to me, his arm around the back of my chair; 'I know you're shy… I get it now, but I honestly never thought you were interested in me that way.'

'Why?' I asked.

'Because you don't take anything seriously, you were always saying you were happy single… and then there was all that with your ex in the newspaper and I thought you were still holding a torch for him, so I gave up. I decided to settle for friendship instead.'

I laughed, 'Oh that newspaper stuff was just me imagining a past that never was – and Rhonda taking a story and running with it.'

'I'm so relieved, he didn't seem like your type at all when I met him tonight – a bit cocky…'

'Yeah and full of himself,' I added, having heard this so many times about Jude. 'Now, I'm almost embarrassed that I went out with him, but as a teenager I just fell for the first person who showed me any interest at all.'

'That's so sad, I know you had a hard time with your mother…'

'Yes, and she had a hard time with me, but coming back here I'm finally facing up to the mother she was and the daughter I was. I think we loved each other – we just didn't know how.'

'Is that the shadow, that sadness that's been there, because you seem different tonight, more… composed.'

'Yeah, I'm more comfortable with me, I just had to work through some stuff. My mum destroyed herself with regrets, and I won't do that – there's no point. It's destructive and knocks things down rather than builds them. I just took a long time getting over her death and feeling responsible for it.'

'Why would you feel that?'

I hadn't told anyone, but now I felt ready to tell Chris.

'She overdosed the night I left Appledore, the verdict was accidental death, but I know she killed herself. I said some terrible things that night.'

He reached out and squeezed my hand. 'From what you've told me your mum said some horrible things too, and perhaps her guilt was even greater than yours?'

'Perhaps?'

'When she sobered up she probably remembered some of the things she'd said and felt bad. She may have been searching for some answers, a kind of peace – a happier place, and that night, she found it.'

This was a kinder way of looking at Mum's death, and one I could perhaps cope with better. The guilt had begun to fade, but I would never get over what happened, it made me the person I was. If Mum's death taught me one thing it was to live your life and not be dragged down by bitterness and regret.

'I feel like Mum wasted her life, and until now, so have I,' I said. 'I've had awful relationships, I've never settled anywhere, but this is different.'

'You could see it as a waste, or you could think it was all leading to this, to Appledore and tonight and these fairy lights and this fine vintage lemonade,' he lifted his glass and I mine and we clinked them.

'Thank you for being my friend,' I said.

'I hope you might be able to see me as more than that,' he leaned in, and without the need for words, we kissed. And after my heart almost stopped, it danced around the courtyard, swooping in and out of the fairy lights. The kiss was soft and warm, and somehow, even then I just knew our first kiss held a promise of things to come.

'You hungry?' I asked, pulling away.

He looked puzzled; 'I could eat something… as long as it's low fat low carb… you know the story,' he laughed.

I shook my head. 'Sorry, but this is going to be the worst and the best thing you've ever eaten,' I smiled, standing up and taking his hand in mine. It felt like an act of trust for both of us, we'd both made do with friendship, when we had wanted more, and this was our chance to see how it fit. I picked up the candle from our table and we walked together into the cafe, now dark and empty. I placed the candle on the counter and went behind to where the ice cream lay under glass and, lit only by candlelight, I made a chocolate ice cream sundae exactly like Sophia used to make for me and my dad. Now it was time to taste it again, because I might just have found someone who could care about me, and hold my hand through all the memories. I wasn't completely healed yet, it would take time. But tonight we had all the time in the world.

I brought the chocolate sundae to the table with the candle and two spoons and together we shared the cold, creamy ice, the rich chocolate sauce and the warm, gloopy fudge. It was bittersweet, each mouthful held a memory, some happy, some sad, holding my dad's hand as we walked along the beach, the anticipation of going to the cafe. Excitement swirling around sadness, knowing we'd have to say goodbye too soon. Waving to him from the doorstep, the taste of chocolate and love still in my mouth, like a ghost of what might have been. But in spite of the memories, the lightness of whipped cream was now grounded by the crunch of the flakes and sprinkles, a perfect combination, on a perfect night, with the perfect man.

'I never thought you'd be interested in someone like me,' he said.

'Why?' I gasped.

'Because I'm boring, you said it yourself when we first met, "I bet you eat mung beans and rise before dawn," you said.'

I laughed; 'Was I really so negative about being healthy?' I took a mouthful of chocolate ice cream, the past still flooding my mind, but slowly fading, like chocolate sauce folded into vanilla ice cream. What happened would always be with me, but it would fade and one day become merely a shadow now and then over the colour of my days.

'You had a point,' Chris smiled. 'I had nothing else in my life and ironically it was you saying how boring I was that made me think you weren't interested and I should pursue Alex, who was.'

'Really? I thought she was simply irresistible and you saw me as the fat-girl client.'

'I know this sounds corny, but you've always looked lovely to me. Even when I first met you with your love handles and chubby arms I thought you were beautiful, you light up a room, Dani, and that's sexy. I've been out with so-called beautiful girls and when they're not worrying about breaking their diets they're stressed about breaking a nail, they're no fun,' he said, blobbing ice cream on my nose with his spoon. 'I want someone I can cover in ice cream, talk to and laugh with and just be me.'

'That's what I want too,' I said, 'though not necessarily the ice cream bit... then again.' I reached into the sundae with my finger and put a small blob of chocolate ice cream on his nose, then my arms around his neck, and I kissed him again.

Perhaps this was who Karla had told me to wait for – the for ever man who loved me whatever I weighed, however I looked, someone who believed in me. I didn't think it was possible, things like this never happened to girls like me – or perhaps I'd just never looked hard enough? Of course we all know nothing's perfect, and who knew what storm-tossed seas might be waiting for us? But for now, in the cafe, by candlelight, Chris and I would gaze into each other's eyes, eat ice cream, and let our love story begin.

And later, when the sundae glass was empty on a table, and Karla was probably fast asleep in bed, he took my hand and we walked along the beach, lit only by stars. We'd stop and kiss every now and then and he'd point out the different planets in the enormous midnight blue sky.

The sea was quiet and calm, no more whispering, no more taunting, just soothing, lapping waves slowly moving onto the beach and back again, everything in its place. Eventually we reached his home, and we walked in to the little fisherman's cottage. It was dark inside and he took my hand softly as we climbed the stairs together. Opening his bedroom door, the floorboards creaked beneath us, like they were welcoming me home. And we lay on his bed all night, getting to know each other all over again as lovers, until dawn rose over the sea. And when we made love, I never had any doubt, I trusted him completely, with every part of me.

I'd been yearning for this all my life, to be in someone's arms and loved as perfectly and completely as this. As he kissed my neck and moved down my chest, over my belly I felt like I'd swallowed the stars, and my body, my beautiful body, danced. I was so comfortable with him and with me, I wrapped my legs around him and begged for more. I felt sunshine on my face, and the warm breeze in my hair, and when it was over we lay together, and I cried, because things like this didn't happen to girls like me.

In the new morning we walked together along the beach, the white ice cream clouds scudded by and the gulls squawked above. Summer was over but Ella's van was still sitting on the blowy blue horizon, Roberta was walking Delilah in her new designer outfit, and in the distance was Marco throwing a ball for Cocoa. I looked back from the beach to see the pink and peppermint cafe, sitting on the front, watching us all, and waiting for our next chapters. I breathed in the sweet, salty air and looked at my blue-eyed companion and glimpsed sprinkles of happiness on my ice cream horizon. Who knew where this love might lead us? It might last for ever or be over tomorrow, but I wasn't scared, because whatever happened, being here with him now was what mattered. And it made me happier than a whole summer of chocolate ice cream.

Epilogue

I watch the sea through my window, waves charging against the sea wall, throwing foamy spray high into the greyness and back again. I love the relentlessness, the rugged beauty of the landscape during these cold, unpredictable winter months. I pull my red cashmere throw around my shoulders, luxuriating in the warmth.

Sitting here in the cafe at the end of the day, clutching my mug of hot chocolate, I think about the summer that's gone. It was the best summer of my life, where I achieved the impossible, and things finally worked out. I'm not skinny, I'm no gym goddess – nor will I ever be, because that's not who I am. I am slimmer than when I started this, but I still have curves, and you will never see me doing the downward dog or chowing down on a kale salad. Most mornings I would rather stay in bed under a warm duvet, and eat doughnuts and ice cream all day – and sometimes I do just that, but most mornings I get out of bed and set off along that beach, and run and run and run. The difference is that now I'm stronger, it's me who's in control, not the doughnut, the duvet or the ice cream – I'm still a curvy, happy girl and here in Appledore, I found my Dani-shaped hole, where I'm loved for being me. And just when I thought it couldn't get any better, at the age of forty I ran for my life. I'd never been healthier, my weight and blood pressure were down and my doctor gave me the okay to train and take part in the 10k charity run through North Devon. I arrived in Bideford at the starting point, not naked carrying a Caprioni's sundae, or sporting a bikini, but in tight, pink Lycra – an achievement as amazing as the 10k itself (I told Karla, if I should die during the 10k to bury me in the Lycra). I posed for photos with the *North Devon News* and even managed a short interview with Rhonda, but didn't overshare this time.

I started gently, waving to my friends at the starting point, hearing them cheering me on. 'Go for it, Dani,' Roberta was yelling. 'You can do it, girl,' Sue screamed as the gun fired and we were off. I pulled away, feeling confident, strong, remembering what Chris had said about technique and breathing. I'd trained hard for this, but nothing could have prepared me for the reality. The pain and elation of powering along flat beaches, through towns and villages teeming with life and memories, was physically and emotionally overwhelming.

By 5k I was exhausted and wanted to collapse. I pushed on through into 6k but felt done for. I almost stopped, but then I heard a familiar voice cheering me on – it was Karla driving alongside and shouting from her car. I didn't even know she'd be there, it was a lovely surprise.

'Come on, girl, you can do it!' she cried, as she beeped the horn and cheerleaded me on as she always has. I started to cry with exhaustion and happiness, I was so touched, she'd left her busy life to be here for me again, just when I needed her.

So I kept on, the weather was closing in and rain stung my face just like the night I'd run away. But this time, I wasn't running away, I was running towards everything I'd ever dreamed of. This was something that only a few months before I'd have considered impossible, but now I was taking on this huge challenge – and I wasn't going to fail. All the training, sweating, screaming, swearing and crying (oh yes, that won't ever change) had pushed me on, and each step amazed me even more.

Despite my euphoria, at 8k the pain in my legs was almost unbearable, spreading through my whole body. It was a throbbing, shrieking pain like I'd never felt before, my muscles screaming for me to stop, my feet refusing to do what they were told. And by 9k I was stumbling and staggering down the road as runners swerved past me onto the finish line. I started to cry again; with less than one kilometre left, all I wanted was to collapse, sweat in my eyes and hair, my feet throbbing in agony. I was nearly there, so near and yet so far, but my body wouldn't let me do this and I would fall at the final hurdle. But then I thought of that red sparkly dress, the way I alone had changed my blood pressure, my weight, my fitness and my life – and I kept going. And as I ran on through the spiking rain, the cold air and the cheering hordes I could see Chris emerging from the crowd, shouting louder than anyone else and running towards me. My vision was blurred, I could see nothing but pain, until I felt him next to me. 'You can do it, Dani,' he was saying as the wind and rain lashed our faces. The final kilometre was agony, but with Chris by my side I knew I could do it, and when we were almost at the finish line together, he slowed down.

'Go on Dani, it's all yours... take it,' he said. And in that moment I knew this was the love of my life, my soulmate, who stood with me, supported me, and loved me enough to sometimes let me go and be me.

I took those final few metres, hurling myself on and over the finish line, and he was there to catch me.

My long run through the rain is over – I am finally home.

Dani's Raspberry Frozen Yoghurt

This is the easiest, most delicious thing you will ever make, and you don't have to run 10k after eating it – even if you *have* to have several bowls!

Ingredients

Serves 4 (or one greedy person)

250g (10 oz) raspberries

2 tbsps seedless raspberry jam

250g (10 oz) Greek-style yoghurt

fresh mint leaves and raspberries to garnish

Only 100 calories per portion!

Method

1. Warm the raspberries and jam in a saucepan over a low heat for about 5 minutes or until the raspberries are pulpy. Stir occasionally.

2. Press the raspberries and their juice through a nylon sieve into a bowl, discarding the pips in the sieve. Now whisk in the yoghurt until smoothly blended and it's turned into a delicious bright pink.

3. Pour the mixture straight into a large freezer-proof container and freeze for 1 hour until the mixture is set round the edges. Take out the container and beat until the mixture is smooth, then return to the freezer. Freeze for another 30 minutes, then beat again. Repeat the freezing and beating several times more until the frozen yoghurt has a smooth consistency, then leave it to freeze for at least 1 hour.

4. If storing in the freezer for longer than 1 hour, transfer the frozen yoghurt to the fridge 20 minutes before serving, to soften slightly.

Chris says: 'Greek-style yogurt is just 17 kcal per level tbsp, with no trans fats, while double cream is 69 kcal for the same amount. Remember raspberries are high in fibre and full of vitamin C, whether fresh or frozen. DO NOT add any sugar… ugh!'

Dani says: 'It tastes fab, it's easy to make and the joy of it is that you can eat the lot without feeling guilty. So do it!'

A Letter from Sue

I have *loved* writing this delicious, calorific book! If I'm honest, Dani is one of the characters in my novels who is probably most like me. We don't take life too seriously and both of us have mega struggles with our weight, which isn't helped by a passionate obsession for trans fats and warm carbs and anything covered in hot fudge sauce. I agree with Dani, that a life without ice cream is no life, and despite dieting for many years it's those midnight ice cream trysts by the fridge that have come between me and my bikini. Yes, I'm aware of healthy eating, exercising and something called fruit – but there are days (and nights) when only salted caramel ice cream with hot fudge sauce will do. And I hope, for you, this book has been the calorie-free equivalent of a chocolate fudge sundae – without the guilt, and that you'll come back soon for another helping.

If you'd like to know when my next food-filled calorie-free book is released, you can sign up by clicking the link at the bottom of the page and I'll let you know. I promise I won't share your email address with anyone, and I'll only send you an email when I have a new book out.

If you want to taste a little of Dani's famous frozen yoghurt – try her easy froyo recipe, it's only 100 calories per portion, so even if I don't manage it, you can squeeze into that bikini this summer!

www.suewatsonbooks.com/

Sue-Watson-Books/201121939909514

Twitter @suewatsonwriter

Acknowledgements

Thanks as always to Oliver Rhodes, Claire Bord and the wonderful team at Bookouture who are all fantastic, keeping this ice cream truck on the road, guiding it over all those bumps and avoiding any wrong turns!

Huge thanks to Jessie Botterill for her guidance, enthusiasm and shared love of ice cream. Thanks and lots of gin to Kim Nash for her marketing genius, power breakfasts, friendship and sheer 'awesomeness'. Big thank you as always to Emily Ruston for taking my melted ice cream, shaping it and turning my hot mess into a delicious ice cream sundae. Big ice cream scoops also to Jade Craddock, for taking that sundae, adding clouds of cream and cherries and making it even lovelier. And a special sundae for the wonderful Alex Crow, marketing genius and computer mastermind who clears up all my website drama with a smile.

A special thanks to my dear friend Bruno Caproni, whose family once owned a restaurant by the sea, and who inspired this story in so many ways. I look forward very much to the day we can get together and laugh about old times with the wonderful Julian Evans over grande gelati in a square somewhere in Italy.

Another friend who's far away but also very much in my heart is Sharon Beswick, fellow Northerner, Amazon-ranking checker, good friend and wise counsel. Thank you for always being there, even though you're many miles away under a much hotter sun.

Having written two books in a very short time, I'd like to thank my family and friends, who haven't seen much of me this year and have all been so understanding. Thanks for not deserting me even if it seems, at times, like I'm deserting you for my laptop, ice cream and Appledore.

I'll be back soon, I promise…

CONTENTS

FORMOR

THE

SHEE CLETTI

CAHI

GLEN MAAM

GLEN SCÁL

An Stuthán

INISÓG

ARDÁN MOUNTAINS

SHEE NENTA

TIR

To Doreen
Who did everything else

Chapter 1: The Ghost

SOMETHING STRANGE WAS GOING TO HAPPEN. The seaweed at Greystones gave Niamh and Daire Durkan their first warning. On the Wednesday before Easter their mother had taken them to the beach immediately after lunch. There had been unusually high tides all that week. On Monday night gale force winds had lashed the coast, driving huge waves onto the rocks below Bray Head and flinging angry raindrops like showers of stones against the windows of the children's home at the foot of the Little Sugarloaf Mountain. But now all was quiet, the storm was over.

Niamh and Daire were walking along the beach between Greystones Harbour and Bray Head hunting for 'surprises' – their word for the strange objects they often found washed up after rough weather. Daire had already found an old tennis ball and Niamh had picked up a well-salted flower bulb. Then she noticed something glistening, half-buried in the sand. It looked like a coin.

She was reaching out to pick it up when she heard a horrible gurgling noise right beside her. She looked around. There was nothing strange to be seen, only the rocks and tide-pools and clumps of seaweed everywhere. When she turned back, her coin had vanished.

'That's strange,' she said.

'What's strange?' asked Daire.

'I saw a coin in the sand and now it's gone!'

'Where was it?'

'Just there, where that seaweed is now.'

'How could you see a coin there if there's a clump of seaweed on top of it?' objected Daire.

'The seaweed must have moved,' she said.

'Don't be silly. Seaweed doesn't move on its own,' said Daire and he reached out to lift it up.

7

'Don't touch it!' cried Niamh sharply.

Daire jumped. 'Why not?'

'It's bad. I can feel it. There's something wrong with it. When it moved I heard an awful gurgling sound.'

Daire looked at his sister's pale serious face and then at the seaweed.

'Oh, all right then,' he said. 'I won't touch it. I don't think I want to anyway. It smells terrible. We could move it with a stick though. That wouldn't be the same as touching it.'

'All right,' said Niamh, but she looked doubtful.

Daire found a stick among the rocks and pressed it into the slimy seaweed. Then he tried to push the clump over. Immediately he heard a horrible sucking noise but the clump didn't move. He tried to lift the stick free, but long brown tentacles had somehow coiled themselves around it. He pulled harder, twisting the stick back and forward. The sucking and gurgling grew louder and the awful smell grew stronger. He couldn't get the stick free.

'Oh, let's leave it alone,' urged Niamh. 'I don't like it.'

The slimy tentacles were now half-way up the stick. Daire let go and stepped backwards.

'That's very strange,' he panted.

'Let's go back,' said Niamh.

A chilling breeze began to blow off the sea. Great slippery masses of seaweed struggled out of the water onto the beach. The children ran as fast as they could towards the harbour where their mother was sitting quietly knitting.

* * *

The captain and crew of the Sealink Car Ferry, the *Saint Columba*, were very glad the stormy weather was over. Their sailings had all been delayed and at the height of the storm they had been unable to put to sea at all. Now with the water foaming softly under the ship's huge prow and a swirling cloud of seagulls overhead, they were moving out of Holyhead under a calm sky.

Rónán Connolly – a cousin of Daire and Niamh – and his mother and father were standing on deck watching the coast of Wales grow smaller behind them. It had been a long journey from Euston Station in London to Holyhead and they were glad to be out in the fresh air and sunshine again. At last the mountains of Wales could no longer be seen, so they all went down to the restaurant for a meal. It would be three hours before they would reach the coast of Ireland and dock at Dún Laoire.

Rónán had been in Ireland only once before when he was three years old and he could scarcely remember his cousins or his uncle and aunt. Now he was eleven, the same age as Daire, and one year younger than Niamh and he felt as if he was going to Ireland for the very first time.

* * *

'Shall we tell Rónán about Glasán?' said Niamh.

They were sitting on the gate of the Scarecrow Field looking across the valley to where the Great Sugarloaf Mountain raised its pointed rocky peak into the late afternoon sky. Rusk, their little terrier, was lying in the grass at their feet. At the mention of Glasán he raised his head and barked happily.

'Good old Rusk!' cried Niamh, getting down off the gate and stroking the dog's head gently. 'You still miss him, don't you?'

Almost a year ago, the three of them had been involved in an extraordinary adventure. It began in this very field on May Eve – the Celtic feast of Bealtaine. That evening the ancient magic came singing in the wind around the shoulder of the Little Sugarloaf Mountain and breathed on the field and awakened their scarecrow. His name was Glasán and he had been called from the Land of Dreaming to fight against the evil power of Scarnán, son of the Morrigan, the dreaded witch of a thousand shapes. Glasán and the children became firm friends and together they had many thrilling adventures ending in the great battle fought on the slopes of the mountain below Giltspur Wood. After the battle, Glasán returned to the Land of Dreaming but the children lived in hope of seeing him again.

They often talked about their adventure among themselves but they had never felt able to tell anyone else.

'Well, what do you think?' insisted Niamh when her brother did not reply.

Daire climbed down off the gate and stood beside her.

'I don't think he'd believe us,' he said.

'But it's going to be impossible to have him staying with us, walking through the fields, going up onto the mountain, without ever saying anything about it,' protested Niamh. 'He'd hardly think we'd invent something as extraordinary as that.'

Daire looked doubtful. 'You know it's true but it would seem different to him. If he told *us* a story like that would we believe him?'

'I suppose not,' sighed Niamh, looking disappointed. 'It's so hard to be still keeping it to ourselves after all this time. I wish we could share it with even one other person.'

'I know,' said Daire. 'Look. Let's wait and see what he's like. Then we can decide.'

They climbed over the gate again and walked up the laneway towards their house.

* * *

'There won't be room for both of you in the car along with Rónán and his parents and their luggage,' said Bill Durkan. 'We'll have a guessing game to see who'll come with me.'

'All right,' said Daire. 'What's the question?'

'What time is the boat due to dock at Dún Laoire? Niamh first.'

'Half past five.'

'Now Daire.'

'I'd say six o'clock.'

'It'll be in at a quarter past six. You're the nearest Daire so you can come. Sorry Niamh.'

'It's all right,'Niamh murmured, 'but I'd like to win sometimes. Daire always wins.'

'That's because you always think you're going to lose,' said Daire cheerfully as he followed his father out to the car.

Strangely enough, it was because Niamh was unlucky that she had the first of the many strange adventures the children were going to have that Easter.

When Daire and his father left to meet the boat Niamh felt restless. She wandered aimlessly about the house for a while. Mrs Durkan was preparing one of her special dinners for the guests. Niamh offered to help, but her mother was too busy to want anyone else around.

She wandered into the farmyard hoping Rusk would be there but he was nowhere to be seen. The late evening sunlight was beginning to fade and the shadow of the Great Sugarloaf was slowly creeping across the valley. Niamh felt lonely. She wished, not for the first time, that she had a sister. Another girl in the house would be able to share her thoughts. She would enjoy the pretty things she had gathered in her room. She would share the little games that Niamh now played on her own. Most of all, a sister might understand her moments of unexpected loneliness.

She told herself she was being silly and that once her father and Daire returned with the visitors she would be swept along in all the excitement and fun. But she couldn't shake off her feeling of sadness. She thought of going down to the Scarecrow Field but she felt that her memories of the good times they'd had with Glasán would only make her feel worse. Besides, the Scarecrow Field was in shadow and the air would be chilly.

She turned right and headed for a wooden gate that led into a field where sheep and lambs were quietly grazing. She had to tread carefully for the ground was soft after all the rain and she knew she'd get into trouble if she muddied her best shoes just before the visitors arrived.

Beyond the Sheep Field was a wide steep stretch of rough pasture. A grove of mountain ash grew on the far side almost surrounding a rocky mound that the children called the Cairn. The slender trees cast long evening shadows over the short grass. Niamh felt as if the grove had been waiting for her. There was one large grey rock at the centre of the Cairn. She climbed up and sat with her back against it. From here she could look out across the valley towards the majestic Sugarloaf and the richly wooded Glen of the Downs. The sun was almost gone and the quiet of the April evening lay over all the countryside.

This was Niamh's dreaming place. She imagined she could fly off the hill, out over the fields and trees and away, away beyond the misty mountains into the golden seas in the western sky.

She had been daydreaming for quite some time before she noticed a sound like wind rushing through the trees. But the evening was perfectly calm and not a leaf stirred on the branches over her head. The sound grew louder. Soon it was the howl of a gale blowing over an open lonely place. Niamh shivered. Then she heard a crashing pounding sound, as if all the loose rocks on the summit of the Small Sugarloaf were thundering down the mountainside on top of her. She leaped up in alarm and looked behind her. The top of the mountain glowed quietly in the last of the evening light. Still the wind sound whistled around her and the crashing and thudding grew louder and louder.

Niamh felt afraid. She began to hurry down from the grove but as she did she heard the crying of a voice above the wind. She stopped and listened. A cold feeling crept over her skin. There was someone or something behind her.

She turned her head slowly and looked. Close to where she had been sitting stood a ghostly figure. Even as Niamh gazed at it, it faded, flickered, then grew clear again. It looked like a very tall man. Though the air was perfectly still, his silver hair, beard and long robes were constantly blown as if he was standing in a gale. The figure faded once more, then as it grew clear again the man raised his arms towards Niamh and stared intently at her.

She turned, and without looking back, raced downhill. Even as she ran she thought she could hear his voice calling to her. Her heart was thumping and she was gasping for breath when at last she reached the gate that led into the farmyard. She stopped and looked back. The trees and the Cairn stood calmly in the dusk. She could hear nothing but the bleat of lambs and the occasional twitter of a bird settling down for the night. She paused to get her breath back, then she went across the farmyard and into the house by the back door.

There was no one in the kitchen but she could see a line of light under the dining-room door. There was a lot of talking and laughing and clinking of knives on plates going on inside.

'Oh no!' she whispered. 'I'm late!'

She turned the handle, opened the door and stepped into the light. At once the room grew quieter. A row of faces turned and looked at her. Her uncle and aunt and her cousin Rónán were there along with her mother and father and Daire. She stood holding the door open with one hand, not knowing what to do. Her father gave her a puzzled look but her mother's face meant trouble.

'Where on earth have you been?' she demanded.

'I – I was up at the Cairn,' replied Niamh.

'What were you doing up there at this hour?'

Niamh suddenly realised she could hardly tell her adventure to everyone just like this.

'I went for a walk,' she whispered. 'I didn't think it was so late.'

'Oh come in and close the door,' snapped her mother, giving her a look that said that her dinner was ruined and that she'd let the family down in front of the visitors. But when Niamh came to the table there was more trouble.

'Just look at the state of you!' said her mother. 'Your shoes are a disgrace and you've scraped your legs and dirtied your dress.'

'Looks like you've had an exciting time,' her father said quietly, looking straight into her eyes. 'Why don't you go and clean up, then you can have your dinner.'

When Niamh eventually sat down, Rónán gave her a look that said 'I know what it feels like. I've often been in the same position'. Daire looked sharply at her and muttered, 'What happened? You look as if you've seen a ghost.'

'I have,' whispered Niamh.

Then her mother placed the dinner in front of her – it *was* ruined – and her uncle began to ask her if she liked hiking and did she know much about the different trees and the animals that lived in the forests. Soon everyone was planning long walks and trips to the mountains and picnics. But Daire kept glancing at Niamh and wondering what it was she had seen. As soon as they had finished dessert he asked if they might 'leave the table, please'.

The grown-ups were glad of the chance to have a chat on their own, so Daire, Niamh and Rónán were allowed to go.

'You can bring Rónán's bags up to the bedroom,' said Mrs Durkan as they left the room.

As soon as they were outside the door Daire caught hold of Niamh's arm and said, 'What's all this about a ghost?'

'Wait till we're upstairs,' she replied.

They brought the case and a bag of books and toys up to Daire's bedroom which Rónán was going to share. Then while they sat on the beds, Niamh told them everything that had happened at the Cairn. Somehow the man seemed less frightening now. She remembered his face as being gentle and sad as if he was asking her for something he needed very badly.

They talked about it until it was time for bed.

'Do you really think she saw a ghost?' said Rónán, when Niamh had gone to her own room.

'She might have,' replied Daire.

'Girls are always making things up,' objected Rónán. 'You said she wanted to come with you in the car this afternoon. Couldn't she just have invented the story to make it seem like it was you who missed all the fun?'

'That wouldn't be like Niamh,' replied Daire. 'Anyway, that Cairn is very old. A chieftain is buried under it.'

Rónán raised his eyebrows. 'If there's a chieftain under it then why hasn't someone dug him up? You don't really know what's under it.'

'I suppose you're right,' sighed Daire. 'We don't really know.'

* * *

A full bright moon shone from the clear sky and its cold light glistened on the grass and trees. All was silent. Niamh was standing in the Sheep Field. She felt very lonely. She heard a whisper like the hiss of surf on a deserted beach. 'Niamh! Niamh!' it breathed.

'Yes! Yes! I'm coming!' she cried and she began running uphill, stumbling in the darkness. The voice called louder. 'Help me! Help me!' The wind began to howl. The shadowy trees frantically tossed their branches. Niamh ran onto the hillside below the Cairn. There she stopped, breathless and amazed. The ground was completely covered with seaweed – gurgling, sucking, slithering seaweed that glistened blue and silver in the moonlight. In the middle of it all, on top of the Cairn stone, stood a tall pale man with flowing white hair and beard. He stretched his hands out to her, appealing, while long tentacles crawled up along the rock, reaching out to wrap themselves around his feet.

'I'm coming!' gasped Niamh rushing forward, leaping over the seaweed. But the long sticky strands clung to her, holding her back. She struggled, but she couldn't move her legs properly. A long brown tentacle caught her by the neck and she fell screaming into the gurgling mass.

She opened her eyes. She was lying on the floor beside the bed with her legs entangled in the sheets. Her pyjamas were damp with sweat. A bird chirped outside and the pale light of dawn peeped in at the window.

Chapter 2: Beyond Giltspur

'LET'S GO UP AND SEE THIS CAIRN THING,' said Rónán. 'Niamh can show us where she saw the ghost.'

It was a fine bright morning. A light breeze was pushing great white clouds across a fresh blue sky. The children, dressed in anoraks and jeans, were standing in the farmyard.

'I don't think he was a ghost,' said Niamh. 'I think he was *real.*'

'But you said he appeared and disappeared before your eyes,' objected Daire. 'He can't be real.'

'If you ask me,' Rónán said with a superior look on his face, 'your imagination is running away with you. That dream of yours is completely crazy.'

'Anyone can dream,' replied Daire, who didn't like the self-important way Rónán was talking.

'Yes,' said Rónán, 'but we don't go around pretending it's real when we waken up.'

'Oh stop arguing!' shouted Niamh, who was beginning to wish she hadn't mentioned her adventure to anyone. 'If you want to see the Cairn then we might as well get it over with.'

They set off through the Sheep Field and up the slope towards the grove. The great grey Cairn-stone shone brightly in the morning sunshine, while dark cloud-shadows drifted over the grass and away across the hillside below Giltspur Wood. An air of quiet mystery hung over the grove, as if the trees were holding their breath.

Daire looked at Niamh. 'Do you think he'll be here?' he said quietly.

'Oh come on!' protested Rónán in a voice that sounded too loud. 'Don't start talking rubbish.' And he began walking quickly up the slope.

The others followed him and Daire felt a little ashamed of having shown he was afraid. They walked around the Cairn

examining the stones.

'I've often wondered how they managed to place that great slab of rock on top of the mound,' said Niamh.

'They probably used ropes and pulleys,' said Rónán.

'I don't know if they had pulleys in those days,' Daire said.

'Maybe Niamh's ghost lifted it up with his bare hands and set it on the top,' replied Rónán, with a smile that wasn't altogether pleasant.

A sudden cool gust of wind shook the grove. Niamh shivered.

'I'm going round to the sunny side,' she said. When she'd found a warm place she sat down. There were plenty of daisies in the grass and she began to pluck them, admiring the little pink tips on the petals. She could hear the boys on the far side of the trees. Rónán was talking about King Arthur and Camelot.

'They built massive castles in those days,' he said, 'far more interesting than these old Cairn things.'

'I don't think I'm going to like Rónán very much,' Niamh murmured. The breeze ruffled the grass again but this time it felt surprisingly warm. Niamh heard a crackling sound. She looked up. There was a line of fire all along the hillside below her. She leaped up and ran back towards the Cairn. The boys came running round from the other side.

'The hill is on fire!' cried Daire.

'I know,' Niamh said. 'It's burning on this side too.'

'We're completely surrounded,' gasped Rónán. 'We can't get out!'

The flames had grown higher, as tall as the children themselves and the heat was growing stronger every moment. Suddenly a second ring of fire appeared inside the first one. The children retreated onto the Cairn, standing right in front of the stone.

'Maybe they'll see the smoke down at the house and come and save us,' said Rónán, his voice trembling with fear.

'There isn't any smoke,' said Daire quietly.

With that a third ring of fire sprang up from under the ground. Hungry tongues of flame licked along the grass a few paces from the children. The heat was intense.

Daire was remarkably calm. 'This isn't real fire,' he said, looking steadily at Niamh. But Niamh was staring at something else.

'Look!' she whispered, pointing.

Beyond the outer ring of fire stood a tall pale figure with flowing white hair and beard. Even as they looked at him he faded so that they could see right through him to the fields beyond. Then his image grew clearer again.

'Is that your ghost?' asked Daire.

'Yes,' replied Niamh.

'He's coming this way!' cried Rónán.

They watched in fear and wonder as the figure drifted towards them. He moved through the fire as if it wasn't there, keeping his eyes fixed on them. As he drew nearer he seemed to grow larger and more powerful. The children huddled together, clinging to each other.

Suddenly the nearest ring of fire rushed forward towards the Cairn. The children leaped back against the great stone. There was a blinding flash of light. A thunderclap shook the earth and air. The Cairn seemed to swing upside-down and the children were falling, spinning dizzily through blackness while circles of fire flickered all around them. After a time they began to fall more slowly. The fires grew blurred, then melted away. At last they felt something beneath their feet, though even then they didn't feel sure that they weren't still falling. They stood, breathing heavily, holding on to each other, not daring to move.

'What happened?' whispered Rónán.

'We must have fallen off the earth or through the sky,' replied Daire.

They listened. There was no sound.

'I wonder where we are?' said Niamh. 'There's grass here and lots of stones too.'

It was quite dark but far off they could see a glimmer of pale light. As they watched it grew brighter. Now they could see the dark outline of distant hills, then some odd shapes nearer to them. The light grew brighter still. Somewhere a bird chirped. A long ray of light flickered across the countryside from the bottom of the sky and a bright sun peeped silently over the rim of the world.

The children looked around them. They were standing on a low hill. The odd shapes they had noticed earlier were the ruins of hundreds of buildings. Beyond the ruins a wide grassy plain stretched for miles to a line of misty blue hills on the horizon.

Directly behind the children there was an enormous white dolmen. The paved area where they were standing was surrounded by three circles of standing stones. Four wide avenues ran out from the dolmen to the east, west, north and south. Along the eastern avenue a tall man in flowing robes was walking towards them with powerful strides.

'It's the ghost!' whispered Daire.

He no longer looked shadowy or grey. His hair and beard were golden and he looked strong and solid. His long robes glistened with a thousand colours reflected from the sunlight. He strode right up to the edge of the inner circle. Then he stopped, bowed courteously and said, 'You are welcome to Tír Danann, though I must apologise for the way in which you were brought here.' His voice was strong and rich with a peculiar attractive accent as if he were used to speaking a different language. 'I had to be sure you would come,' he continued. 'If I'd spoken to you in your own world you might not have trusted me as I believe we look rather ghostly when we show ourselves in other worlds.'

The children looked at each other.

'Have we been kidnapped?' asked Rónán.

'Oh no! Perhaps you could say that I borrowed you, but you may return to your own world anytime you want to.'

'I think you should tell us who you are and why you have brought us here,' said Niamh.

The stranger smiled at her. 'Of course,' he said. 'I shall explain everything if you will follow me.'

He turned and began to walk back along the eastern avenue. The children followed a little distance behind him. The sun was now higher, its clear light brightening the empty streets of the ruined city. The tall stranger walked so quickly that the children found it difficult to keep up with him.

'If he disappears among these ruins we'll be stuck here forever,' muttered Daire as they hurried over the cracked paving stones and pieces of fallen pillars and arches. This had clearly been a great city a long time ago.

At last they stopped outside a magnificent building. Though it had now fallen into decay, they could see that the outer walls had once been completely covered with beautiful carvings of flowers, birds and animals. A flight of marble steps led up to two huge bronze doors covered with ornate writing that the children could not understand. There had once been a great arch over the doorway supported by two pillars, but this had fallen and the enormous stone blocks lay scattered over the top of the steps.

'Wait here,' said the stranger. He went up the steps to the huge closed doors. Then he slowly raised his arms, keeping his fingers fully spread and his palms turned downwards. He stood like this for a moment. Then he spoke one word in a sharp whisper. 'Oscail!'

For a second nothing happened. Then the children noticed a deep rumbling sound that grew louder and louder, until with a sharp creak and a harsh scraping of metal on stone, the great doors began to move slowly inwards. A shower of dust and small stones fell from above the doorway. Then a large block came away from the wall and landed with a thud at the stranger's feet, splitting itself in two. He stood quietly as if he had not noticed the danger. Then he slowly lowered his arms, bowed his head and gave a great sigh as if he was very tired.

When the dust settled and all was quiet he turned and beckoned the children forward. They climbed the steps and stood beside him. Niamh thought he looked older somehow and a little sad.

'We must make as little noise as possible,' he said. 'The building is not quite safe.'

The bronze doors had opened wide enough to let one person through at a time. The stranger stepped inside and the children followed. It was an extraordinary place. The room was completely circular. Daylight streamed down to every part of it from a round opening high in the dome of the ceiling. When the children looked up they could see the blue sky outside. The floor of blue and white slabs was a huge picture of waves on the ocean. Around the walls there were statues of strange-looking people on pedestals and between the statues the walls were covered with amazing pictures.

The stranger stood in the middle of the floor and turned to the children who were gazing around them in wonder.

'Now I shall tell you everything you need to know and show you why it was necessary for me to bring you here,' he said. His words echoed around the vast hall, like a voice that belonged to a time long past. 'You are in Tír Danann – the land of the People of Danann. This was the city of Shee Alman and this the Hall of the High Council of Danann three thousand years ago.'

'You mean this place is three thousand years old?' whispered Rónán.

'Yes,' replied the stranger.

Niamh and Daire glanced at each other and saw a look of wonder on each other's faces.

'Is this the country that is also known as the Land of Dreaming?' Niamh asked.

'Yes indeed,' replied the stranger.

'Are *you* one of the People of Danann?' asked Daire.

'I am Foras Mac Arda, of the High Council of Danann,' he said, looking intently at the children's faces.

There was a moment of silence.

'We once met one of your people in our world,' said Daire. 'His name was Glasán.'

'So I was right!' exclaimed Foras. 'You must be Niamh and Daire, the heroes of The Battle Below Giltspur! But who is your companion?'

'My name is Rónán, and since you all seem to know each other, perhaps somebody could tell me what's going on.' He was feeling left out and was angry about it.

Foras looked surprised.

'Rónán doesn't know about our adventures with Glasán,' explained Daire. 'But *we* don't really know what's going on either, or why you have brought us here.'

As he spoke they heard a distant rumbling sound and felt the floor tremble beneath their feet.

'That is a long story,' replied Foras, 'but I shall tell it to you as briefly as I can. The People of Danann once lived in the land of Ireland, though even then it was not a time of peace. The Fir Bolg claimed the land for their own, but we defeated them in battle at Moytura. Then the Formorian Giants invaded Ireland under their hated leader Balor of the Evil Eye. We routed them also on Moytura's plains.

'Time passed and the young world grew older. Your ancestors, the Sons of Míl, came to Ireland. There were many battles and many lives were lost. In the end a settlement was arranged by Manannán Mac Lir.'

As the name of Manannán echoed in that ancient hall a thrill of excitement ran through the children's bodies. Rónán, who knew very little of the old stories of Ireland, thought he could hear the crying of seabirds on a salt breeze above dizzy cliffs and the hiss of surf on a beach. Niamh and Daire suddenly recalled a chariot pulled by two white horses racing over a glistening sea and they saw again the stern joyful face of Manannán Mac Lir. Then they became aware of the face of Foras and his eyes looking keenly at them.

'I heard something about the battles of Moytura at school,' said Niamh, 'though I never heard what happened after that.'

'Come,' said Foras. 'I will show it to you.'

He strode across the floor to the first of the extraordinary pictures on the wall just to the right of the doorway. The children followed him. What they saw was like a huge map but it was as if they could really see each mountain and plain. The grass seemed to stir in the breeze, the rivers appeared to flow from the hills, waterfalls tumbled over cliffs, and the sea sparkled.

'Manannán said that the time had come for us to leave the land of Ireland. He brought us out of the old world into Tír Danann which he granted to us as our homeland forever. The land to the north of the mountains he gave to the Fir Bolg and he granted the Formorians their island homes as well.

'On the first day of our first spring in Tír Danann, Manannán came to us bringing water from the Well of Youth on Inis Óg. We had a great feast – the first Feast of Age. He told us to hold this celebration on the first day of spring every year and to bring water from the Well of Youth and drink it at the feast. If we did this we would never grow old. Then he left us and returned to his own land.

'All was settled and everyone was content. We built our cities – Shee Clettig, Shee Nenta and Shee Alman our capital – and for a thousand years we lived in peace.

'But the Fir Bolg had never forgiven us for defeating them at Moytura and even after so long a time they vowed to avenge themselves. They came streaming out of Tír Bolg just as the thousandth Feast of Age was being celebrated. There was fierce fighting here at Shee Alman. The battle lasted for forty days. Then Sreng, the leader of the Fir Bolg, was slain by my brother Lann who pierced his heart with a sword on the steps of this very hall. When they saw their leader dead the Fir Bolg panicked and fled back to their own land again.

'We had won the battle but at a heavy cost. Not only were many dead or wounded, but a great deal of the water of the Well of Youth had been lost. As a result, many of the People of

Danann aged suddenly and died.

'After this, the High Council decided to leave Shee Alman and build a city that would be more easily defended. They wanted to be sure that the Feast of Age would never again be interrupted. So Shee Alman was abandoned and all its glory fell to ruin. The new city was built on the River Bradán, just there.'

He pointed to the map and the children saw a shining white city set in the middle of a sparkling lake surrounded by dense forests.

'We called the new city Cahershee. It is there that the High Council sits now and from there that I was sent to call you into Tír Danann.'

He turned once more to the children. This time Niamh was sure his face looked older. There were lines across his skin that hadn't been there when he began telling his story. Daire noticed it too.

'Has the Feast of Age been interrupted again?' he asked.

Foras looked at him with serious kindly eyes. 'You have the gift of quick understanding,' he said. 'Yes. After two thousand years of peace in Cahershee, the Feast has once more been threatened.'

Chapter 3: A Cry for Help

HE LED THE CHILDREN to the next picture. This was another 'map'.

'Here you can see the Northern Mountains. It was through these that the Fir Bolg came to attack us at Shee Alman. After that, Manannán closed the mountain passes with snow to prevent them from ever coming that way again. That is what we call the Snowfields.'

To the children it was like looking at a film taken from the air. The mountains seemed to lie far below them On the northern side there was a great belt of glistening snow stretching right across the map. There were mountains and valleys of snow, frozen lakes and cliffs of ice. It made them feel cold even to look at it.

'North of the Snowfields lies Balbolg, the city of the Fir Bolg,' said Foras. The children could see a city built of dark brown stone. It had a high wall around it. A river flowed in at one end and out at the other through an opening in the wall that was covered with bars. It was a gloomy sort of place.

'Now look to the west,' continued Foras. 'Those are the islands of Formor, the Kingdom of the Formorians. The greater part of them lies below the sea and the Formorians live in caves underneath the islands. They are giants and terrible to look at.'

The children could see surging waves foaming white around the dark rocks of Formor.

'A month ago,' said Foras, 'three of our people went to get the water for the Feast of Age. But when they came to the shore of the Western Sea they could not cross over to Inis Óg for the sea had vanished beneath a horrible carpet of crawling, stinging seaweed. One of them was swept off the rocks by a sudden storm. He became entangled in the seaweed and was swallowed up along with the boat. Enchantments, charms and spells have failed to scatter this menace. The Feast of Age has not been celebrated and all the people of Shee Nenta and Shee Clettig have had to crowd into Cahershee under the protection of the power of the High Council.'

'Are they all growing old?' asked Niamh.

'Not yet,' replied Foras. 'The power of the assembled Council has been able to protect everyone in Cahershee. But the effort to maintain the protection is a great drain on their strength and it cannot be kept up forever.'

'I'm not sure if I understand all this,' said Rónán.

As he spoke they heard a deep rumbling coming towards them. The floor trembled beneath their feet and plaster and grit fell from the ceiling.

'We must leave!' said Foras. 'Follow me.'

He strode swiftly towards the door and the children followed him. The ground trembled again and a piece of the wonderful map fell from the wall and shattered on the floor. They stepped out into bright sunlight. Foras led them along the eastern avenue back to the great white dolmen. He moved so quickly that the children were out of breath when he finally turned and waited for them.

'The fall of Shee Alman is almost complete,' he said sadly, looking over their heads at the ruined city. They heard another rumble and the remains of a tall building quite near them crumpled in a cloud of dust.

'I shall explain further,' said Foras. 'The plague of seaweed is an enchantment brought about by the Formorians to prevent us celebrating the Feast of Age. Once the Danann are weakened enough the Giants will leave their islands and attack us. The Fir Bolg are clearly in league with them. Already groups of them have been sighted south of the mountains. As soon as they feel strong enough they also will attack.'

'But how could the Fir Bolg get past the Snowfields?' asked Daire.

'The only possible way is by sea, through the islands of Formor. That is why we are sure they have the help of the Formorian Giants.'

'So while your enemies are preparing to attack all you can do is sit here in Cahershee?' said Rónán. 'Can't you attack them first?'

'Any of the Danann who leave Cahershee now will begin to age rapidly. A few days journey could cost more than one hundred years. We would either be dead or too weak to fight by the time we reached Tír Bolg or Formor.'

'But *you* left Cahershee,' said Niamh quietly.

'Yes,' replied Foras. 'I did.'

Now the children saw that his face had grown even older and more tired and the gold of his hair had faded since that morning.

'That is why it is important that you give me your answer quickly,' went on Foras.

'What answer?' asked Rónán.

'Will you stay here and help us?' said Foras.

There was a moment's silence. The wind shook Foras's long robes and blew his hair back from his serious ageing face. The ground shook and cracks ran across the paving stones beneath the dolmen.

'What would we have to do?' asked Niamh in a small voice.

'Find a way to get the water from the Well of Youth and bring it to Cahershee or find Manannán Mac Lir and get him to save us.'

The children looked at each other.

'When did Manannán Mac Lir last come here?' asked Rónán.

'At the making of the Snowfields, almost two thousand years ago.'

'Do you really expect us to go looking for someone who hasn't been seen for two thousand years?' exclaimed Rónán. 'Anyway, we're only children. How could we fight against the Fir Bolg or the Giants of Formor?'

'There is much you can do – more than you realise,' replied Foras. 'You will not be relying entirely on your own strength. Power and knowledge will be given to you in Cahershee. All that can be explained later. But are you *willing*?'

'Of course we –' began Niamh, but Rónán interrupted her.

'Supposing we refuse?' he said.

Foras looked straight at him with grave eyes. 'Then I will return you immediately to your own world and I will go back if I can to Cahershee and await the end.'

'But we would be safe,' said Rónán.

'For the moment, yes,' replied Foras, 'but our worlds are not unconnected. If the powers of evil triumph here, it will not be long before they reach out to your world as well.'

'Could we have a few minutes on our own to talk about

this?' asked Niamh.

'Of course,' replied Foras and he turned and walked to the west side of the dolmen.

'I don't see what all this has to do with us,' began Rónán. 'I think we should get back home as quickly as possible before this place falls down on top of us.'

'But he said the evil could spread into Ireland as well,' objected Daire.

'He just said that to frighten us into staying,' replied Rónán.

'No he didn't,' declared Niamh. 'What he said is true. In fact it has already begun to happen.'

'How?' asked Daire.

'The seaweed at Greystones!' said Niamh. 'Can't you see? It's the same as the enchantment the Formorians have placed along the Western Sea.'

Daire looked shocked. 'I never thought of that,' he gasped.

'What are you two talking about?' demanded Rónán. 'I really wish somebody would tell me what's going on around here!'

Niamh quickly told him of their trip to Greystones beach and the seaweed they saw there. 'Anyway,' went on Niamh, 'even if the evil power of Formor couldn't reach us at home, I still think we can't just go off and leave a whole country full of people to be killed or turned into slaves. We would remember it for the rest of our lives and we'd never be really happy again.'

Rónán stared at her, then he looked at Daire.

'She's right,' said Daire in a slow serious voice, 'and there's something else. Glasán must be in danger too. Niamh and I *have* to stay. You can go back if you like.'

'There you go again!' cried Rónán angrily. 'Who *is* this Glasán?'

'I'm sorry, Rónán,' said Niamh. 'There just wasn't time to tell it all to you before we were brought here. Anyway, you probably wouldn't have believed us if we had.'

The ground shook again. Rónán had to step aside to avoid a deep crack that opened at his feet. There followed an even louder, deeper rumbling. The children looked up at the city. The great dome of the Hall of the High Council rippled for a moment above the ruined walls, then it suddenly crumpled inwards with a great roar and a huge cloud of dust rose like smoke into the air.

'I don't think we're going to have time to tell you about it right now either,' said Daire. 'Are you going to stay or not?'

Rónán sighed heavily and looked around him. Foras was walking back towards them.

'I think you're both mad and we'll probably all be killed,' replied Rónán, 'but I'll stay with you.'

They turned to face Foras.

'Have you reached a decision?' he asked.

'Yes,' answered Niamh. 'We are going to stay.'

'That is a brave and noble choice,' said Foras.

'One thing puzzles me,' said Daire. 'Why did the High Council not send Glasán to ask us to come? He wouldn't have had to "kidnap" us.'

Foras looked anxiously from Niamh to Daire. There was something in his face that made the children afraid. He sighed heavily and reached out placing his hands on their shoulders.

'I have dreaded this moment from the time the High Council chose me to do this task,' he said. 'Glasán was one of those who set out for Inis Óg. He was the one who was dragged under the seaweed. He did not return.'

A gust of chill wind sent dead leaves scurrying across the cracked pavement and tossed the children's hair. Niamh and Daire stood open-mouthed as if they had been turned to stone. Niamh tried to speak but no words would come out.

'I can feel the depth of your pain,' murmured Foras sadly.

At last Niamh whispered, 'Do you mean he's dead?'

'We fear that he is,' said Foras.

'But did anyone actually *see* him die?' said Daire. His voice sounded dry and he had to force the words out.

'No,' replied Foras, 'but it must be said that he is unlikely to have survived.'

Niamh felt a huge lump harden in her throat. Tears welled up in her eyes and dripped down her cheeks. 'It *can't* be true!' she sobbed. 'It *can't* be!'

Rónán reached over and squeezed her hand. 'If no one saw him die then he may still be alive,' he said.

'We will go and search for him, whether you need the water of Inis Óg or not!' declared Daire.

'You both loved him dearly,' said Foras.

Niamh and Daire nodded.

'Come then. It is not safe to remain here any longer.'

Chapter 4: The Battle Above the Falls

FORAS LED THE CHILDREN through the ruins of the western avenue to a huge gateway in a high wall. The gates themselves had long since fallen among the rocks and dust. They passed through the gateway and there below them lay the land of Tír Danann.

The path wound down into a thick oak forest covering the hillside below them. Far beyond that they could see wide plains with fields, woods and the gleam of distant rivers. Further off again, misty blue mountains lay piled against the sky.

'How far is it to Cahershee?' asked Rónán.

'Almost two days riding,' replied Foras.

'Riding?' said Rónán. 'Have you brought horses?'

'Yes,' said Foras. 'Here they come. Gasta the chestnut, Taca the black stallion and Cróga the dapple-grey.'

From the edge of the forest three fine horses, each with a white star on its forehead, came cantering towards them. They went straight to Foras and nuzzled his face with great fondness. He spoke rapidly in a low voice to them. The children could not make out what he was saying but it was clear that the horses understood him. They turned their heads and regarded the children out of large intelligent eyes. Then they whinnied in reply to Foras.

He turned and said, 'I've explained who you are and they're delighted to carry you. Are you able to ride?'

'Niamh and I had some riding lessons,' said Daire.

'I've never been on a horse in my life,' murmured Rónán.

'In that case,' said Foras, 'Niamh and Daire may ride Gasta and Taca. Rónán can ride with me on Cróga.'

The horses had beautifully decorated saddles and bridles trimmed with silver. They carried full saddle-bags and weapons. Foras gave a shield and a short sword with sheath and belt to Niamh and Daire. To Rónán he gave a shield and a spear with a blade that gleamed in the sunlight.

They mounted their horses and Foras led the way with Rónán sitting behind him. Niamh and Daire followed down the slope into the forest. Sunlight fell softly through the pale green leaves onto the path as it wound steadily downwards. There was no sound except the tread of the horses or the occasional cry of a crow high above them.

They rode in silence for some time, then as Daire and Niamh drew level with Foras he suddenly said, 'Speak your mind, Rónán!'

'Pardon?' said Rónán, looking surprised and embarrassed.

'Speak your thoughts,' repeated Foras. 'I can feel the storm of doubt whirling through your mind. Do not be afraid. You are right to wonder and worry. Ask what you wish and I shall answer as well as I can.'

Rónán glanced at Niamh and Daire. 'Well,' he began uncertainly, 'I was wondering why you brought us from our world to Shee Alman instead of bringing us direct to Cahershee. It would have saved a long journey.'

'Indeed it would,' replied Foras, 'and it would have been a lot safer. But the divide between the worlds is enormous. It is very difficult to cross from one side to the other. There are only a few places where your world and ours touch, places that are almost in both worlds. One of those places is at the Great Dolmen of Shee Alman.'

'How did you get across?' asked Daire.

'I didn't really cross to your world at all' answered Foras. 'I was in Shee Alman all the time. I just made sure you could see me. Had you hesitated any longer I would have failed and you would have been left on the hillside thinking you had seen a ghost. That is why I used such a dramatic way of bringing you here.'

'Are you a magician?' Rónán asked.

Foras laughed. 'Some people would call me that. The People of Danann have developed powers that most others have not yet learned to use. Everyone is a magician. Magic is the power of your mind. You could make these trees dance if you thought it strongly enough.'

'Can you make things appear and disappear?' Rónán asked eagerly.

'Yes I can,' replied Foras.

'I'd love to be able to do that!' sighed Rónán. 'can you conjure up gold or weapons or a horse?'

'It's not quite as simple as that,' Foras said smiling. 'Every act of magic uses up the magician's energies. The greater the magic the more effort is needed. If I were to conjure up a horse I would be completely exhausted and it would take me several days to recover. So it's not something we do unless we really have to. Serious over-use of the power can lead to death.'

The children could hear the sound of rushing water growing louder and nearer. It wasn't long before they rode out of the trees onto a bright grassy place beside a river that raced and foamed over huge grey boulders. Foras reined in his horse.

'This will be a good place to rest,' he said.

'I wish someone would magic up a meal,' said Daire. 'I'm starving.'

'We can provide that without using magic,' replied Foras as he helped Rónán to dismount. He took a bag of fine goatskin from one of his saddle bags. Then he spoke to the horses and they wandered off contentedly to graze on the fresh spring grass.

Foras seated himself on the ground and opened his bag. He had brought bread and cheese, a cake full of very plump fruit and apples that smelled and tasted as if they had been drenched with honey.

Everyone ate hungrily and as they ate they began to feel more cheerful and confident. The warmth of the sun and the steady rush of the river gave the children a comfortable, excited sort of feeling.

'How long would it take to learn to use these magic powers you say we all have?' asked Rónán.

'It takes long years of training to do the simplest things,' replied Foras. 'That is why so few people manage to do it. In Tír Danann, a hundred years of practice is only the start of a magician's learning.'

Suddenly Gasta, Taca and Cróga whinnied loudly and throwing up their heads they came cantering over to where Foras was sitting. He rose quickly and spoke to the horses and they answered him. Then he turned to the children.

'There's someone coming through the woods. We had better move along. Keep your eyes and ears alert and your weapons at the ready.'

They gathered up the remains of their meal and were soon riding through the trees again. The path followed the course of the river, winding ever downwards. No one spoke. Their ears strained to catch every sound. Their eyes searched the light and shade between the trees for any sign of movement. So they travelled for a long time and the day grew warmer and the air heavier.

When the danger seemed to have passed they began to relax. They talked more and watched less carefully. Niamh and Daire told Rónán the story of their adventures with Glasán, including their meeting with Manannán Mac Lir in his own wonderful country.

When they had finished their tale Rónán looked thoughtful. 'You were right,' he said. 'I wouldn't have believed you if you had told me all this before. Now it is different.'

Foras had listened with great interest, especially to their description of Manannán's Country.

'Manannán has honoured you greatly,' he said, 'and Glasán often sang your praises in Cahershee. You will find the Lords of Danann hold you in high honour.'

'What is Cahershee like?' said Niamh.

'It is a beautiful place, built to delight the eye and refresh the mind.'

'It must have been very difficult to build it in the middle of a lake,' said Daire.

'Our architects and engineers have had many years experience of that. The High Council placed power in the stones and enchantments in the forests around the lake. No enemy can pass through that forest safely.'

All this time they had moved through deep green shadows and splashes of golden sunlight. The sound of the rushing river was always in their ears. Niamh felt as if she was riding through a beautiful painting.

Soon the light grew brighter and the sound of the water grew louder till the air was filled with a quivering excitement. Suddenly they came out of the forest onto a wide ledge high above the Plain of Danann. To left and right huge cliffs plunged steeply down to the level lands below. The river, with a roar of joy, flung itself over the cliff-edge, thundering dizzily down over foam-drenched crags into a wide boiling pool at the base of the cliff. The noise of its falling filled all the air and white spray rose up like steam, dampening the rocks and grass all around. A steep path twisted and turned down the face of the cliff to the pool below the waterfall. From there the river flowed on, winding out over the wide green plain, glistening in the late afternoon sunlight below a pure blue sky.

'It's beautiful,' sighed Niamh, gazing out over miles of open countryside and little clumps of woodland to where tall blue mountains faded along the horizon.

'Is that the Enchanted Forest?' asked Daire, pointing to a larger patch of dark green far off in the centre of the plain.

'Yes,' replied Foras. 'If your eyes are keen you may see the tops of the shining towers of Cahershee in the centre of the forest.'

He had no sooner spoken when they heard a dreadful screaming. They turned quickly and saw a line of dark warriors with swords, shields and helmets, rushing out of the trees behind them.

'Fir Bolg!' cried Foras.

The Fir Bolg were only a little taller than the children themselves, but their bodies were broad and their limbs thick, and strong. They moved with surprising speed.

Foras's sword made a flashing circle from its sheath onto the head of the first of the Fir Bolg, slicing his black helmet in two.

Niamh didn't have time to draw her sword. Rough brown hands gripped her hair and dragged her off Gasta's back so that she fell heavily on the ground. The force of her fall drove all the breath from her body and she lay helpless, unable to raise her sword or shield. For a second she saw above her a pair of fierce brown eyes in a dark sweaty face with a black beard. A raised sword swung down towards her. Then Gasta's hind leg shot out with the force of a sledge hammer striking her attacker on the jaw. There was a loud crack and he fell with a thud on the grass beside her.

Niamh struggled to her feet. The horses had moved away towards the path at the cliff edge. Foras was driving two of the Fir Bolg back into the forest with a blazing ball of fire which had appeared at the point of his sword. Daire was raining blows with his sword on a very surprised-looking warrior as if he had been fighting battles all his life. The clanging of their swords and shields echoed from the rocks and trees and sparks flew as metal crashed upon metal. Then with a sudden rush the Fear Bolg leaped forward, driving his black shield with all his weight into Daire's face and chest. The force of the attack sent Daire staggering backwards to the ground. The dark warrior snarled and raised his sword to strike. Niamh leaped forward and swung her sword wildly. The blade caught the Fear Bolg across the back of the hand. He screamed in pain. Blood spurted between his fingers and his sword flew spinning through the air. Then he turned and fled into the forest, roaring as he ran.

'Look to Rónán!' cried Foras.

The children spun around. Rónán had been driven onto the rocks at the edge of the river. He had lost his shield and blood was flowing down his face from a cut on his forehead. He was jabbing at a Fear Bolg with his spear, but the Fear Bolg was blocking the spear with his shield and lashing out with his sword, trying to force Rónán into the river.

As Niamh and Daire rushed forward, Rónán drove his spear towards the Fear Bolg's chest. The dark warrior dropped his shield and stepping quickly to one side, he gripped the spear-shaft and pushed with all his strength. Rónán unbalanced, lost his footing on the wet rock and fell backwards with a cry into the raging waters.

As a shock of cold water struck his body, Rónán heard Niamh scream his name. Then he was swept away in a confusion of foam, bubbles and roaring water. He had no time to think or be afraid. His eyes were blinded by water. Water poured into his mouth and up his nose. A huge watery strength threw him against a rock but he was too confused to feel the pain. He was spun around and swept backwards towards a great watery roaring. Then, quite suddenly, he stopped moving. Torrents of water still poured over him. He seemed to be breathing water. Something was pounding inside him. He felt an unbearable pain across his chest. Then through the pain and noise he heard a voice inside his head. It was clear and commanding. 'Hold on to the spear! Do not let go!'

He wanted to obey. But where was the spear? And where were his hands? He could feel nothing but cold, a heavy dragging chill. An icy darkness rushed up from below him. He was falling, falling into the darkness.

When Niamh screamed the Fear Bolg turned and raised his sword, but Daire dealt him a heavy blow to the side of the

head and he fell to the ground and did not move again. Both children turned to look for Rónán.

Foras was already on the rocks at the side of the river. They saw Rónán's head reappear for a moment above the water as he was flung against a boulder. He was still gripping his spear with both his hands. The force of the current swept him backwards to the edge of the waterfall and there the spear stuck fast, wedged between two rocks.

Foras stretched out his arms. He called up all that remained of his strength and sent it across the raging water to where Rónán was weakening on the edge of the falls. His thoughts forced their way through all the pain and cold, commanding him not to let go. In his mind he gripped the spear, taking its weight and Rónán's. He drew it against the force of the river away from the waterfall, through the currents and foam and noise, ever nearer to the bank of the river.

Niamh and Daire watched amazed. When Rónán was within reach they gripped his sodden clothes and dragged him from the water. He lay on his back without moving, his hands still gripping the spear. His face was deadly pale.

'Is he dead?' asked Niamh.

Foras knelt beside him and opened the top of Rónán's anorak. He felt his neck carefully.

'He is not dead,' he replied, 'but he lacks breath.'

He opened Rónán's mouth, tilting his head gently backwards. He closed Rónán's nose between his finger and thumb and placing his own mouth over Rónán's he breathed steadily into him. Then he lifted his head away. Rónán lay still and pale as before. Again Foras breathed into him. This time Rónán's chest rose and when Foras lifted his head a strange rattling breath came from Rónán's throat. Then Rónán took a short jerky breath, then another. He coughed and gasped, then he moaned and opened his eyes.

Foras placed his hand on Rónán's forehead. 'Codladh sláinte chugat,' he whispered. Instantly Rónán's eyes closed again. His breathing became slow and steady and a little colour crept into his cheeks. Foras took the spear from his fingers and gently turned him on his side.

'He will be all right,' he said wearily, 'but we must keep him warm.'

Niamh heard something moving behind her and turning she saw that Gasta, Taca and Cróga had come back from the cliff path. On Foras's instructions she found dry blankets in Taca's saddle-bags. Having removed Rónán's wet clothes they wrapped him in the blankets.

'It is not safe to remain here,' said Foras, glancing towards the woods. 'There is a better place below the cliff.'

He stood up, but he staggered and only saved himself from falling by gripping Taca's saddle. The horse turned its head to its master and whinnied.

'Are you all right, sir?' Daire asked anxiously.

Foras turned to him and only then did the children realise what the battle and the rescue of Rónán had done to him. His hair had grown grey and thin. His face had become deeply lined and his skin had taken on a transparent look. His eyes, set in dark circles, had sunk deeper into his face, though they still shone with a fierce determined light. He clung to the saddle, breathing carefully for a moment.

'Do not worry about me,' he murmured. 'We must attend to Rónán first.'

They carried Rónán to Cróga and set him in front of Foras who rode with his arms around him. Niamh and Daire followed on Gasta and Taca. Foras led them carefully down the cliff path, winding their way among great smooth boulders and the occasional oak or ash tree. The sun was now low in the western sky, sending long golden beams across the Plain of Danann and glistening on the endless, restless curtain of white water cascading down the cliff on their left. The evening had an air of sad beauty that filled Niamh with a great longing and loneliness. She remembered Manannán's country and the green grassy place above the glistening sea, the tinkling of silver leaves on the tree of the golden apples and the scent and softness of apple blossom falling on her face and her bare feet.

Gasta neighed, tossing his head, and Niamh awoke from her daydream to find they were beside the thundering pool at the base of the cliff. Showers of fine spray were drifting across the grass making small rainbows in the evening light.

Foras had turned away from the waterfall and was moving below the cliff face to the right. They soon came to a place where the cliff curved inwards. A small overhang provided a shallow roof while to left and right the rocky arms of the cliff enclosed the space and sheltered it. The light of the setting sun shone directly in, warming the air. Daisies peeped from the grass and young ash and hazel trees grew on the grassy ledges around it. As they rode in, the sound of the waterfall grew hushed and a feeling of quietness descended on them.

'We can rest here,' said Foras.

They laid Rónán gently on a blanket on the ground, and then they unsaddled the horses and left them to graze. Foras attended to the gash on Rónán's forehead which was still oozing blood, while Niamh and Daire gathered sticks for the fire. By the time they had a good pile of twigs set in a circle of flat stones Rónán's forehead was almost completely healed.

Foras was exhausted. He sat beside Rónán with his back against the rock face while Daire brought him the saddle-bags. From one of them he took a small green box and gave it to Daire telling him to open it. Inside Daire saw what looked like fine green sand.

'Sprinkle a little of it slowly on the twigs,' said Foras in a feeble voice. Daire did so. The sand glistened as it fell. The twigs crackled, red sparks shot out and a little smoke curled up and vanished. Then clear smokeless flames began to lick up from the pile. Before long a warm fire was burning cheerfully.

They arranged Rónán's clothes around the fire to dry. Then they took a frying pan and a long, very cold metal box from one of the saddle-bags. The box contained strips of meat wrapped in herb leaves. When the fire had settled down to a steady hot glow, they put the meat in the pan and set it on the flat stones. Soon the scent of herbs and meat cooking filled the children's nostrils, making their mouths water. While the meat was cooking, Daire went carefully to the pool below the waterfall and filled two bottles with water. He returned quickly, keeping one hand on his sword. He was glad when he was beside the fire again.

The sun had now set, filling all the western sky with a gold-red glow. Niamh turned the meat in the pan while Daire took bread, cake and apples from the goatskin bag. Foras poured some water into a silver cup. He placed the tip of one finger on the surface of the water and said, 'Bí mar deoch na sláinte dó!' He placed his hand on Rónán's forehead. Rónán opened his eyes. He looked around him with a puzzled expression on his face.

'Do not speak,' said Foras gently. 'Drink this.'

He held the cup to Rónán's lips. Rónán swallowed a few

drops. Then he took a larger drink. He sighed and lay still for a moment. Then his eyes brightened, his face cleared and he tried to sit up.

'Ouch!' he cried. 'My side hurts.'

'Your side was bruised against the rocks when the river swept you away,' said Foras.

'How did I get down here?' asked Rónán. 'The last thing I remember is hanging over the edge of the waterfall.'

'Foras saved you,' said Daire eagerly. 'He drew you out of the river using the power of his mind and then . . . . '

'Say no more!' commanded Foras, raising his hand. 'What was done had to be done. Now we are all hungry and the meat is ready. Let us eat and restore our strength.'

The children had never felt so hungry in all their lives nor had they eaten meat as juicy and tasty as this. Foras ate little. He was silent, as if deep in thought and his eyes strayed out beyond the glowing fire to where the darkness was stealing over the Plain of Danann.

When the meal was over the children sat in the comfortable heat of the fire and discussed all that had happened to them that day. It seemed a long time since morning and they found it strangely difficult to remember where they had been before Foras called them into Tír Danann. It was Rónán who finally recalled climbing up to the Cairn below the Little Sugarloaf. When he mentioned it, Niamh and Daire looked at each other in a puzzled sort of way and said, 'Oh yes!' as if they were recalling an almost forgotten dream.

'Oh goodness! cried Niamh suddenly, her eyes wide in alarm. 'We've been away all day. Daddy and Mammy will be looking for us. They'll be sick with worry.'

'Do not fear,' said Foras in a calming voice. 'The time you spend in this world is not taken from the time you spend in your own. If you were to return to Ireland now, you would be back at exactly the same moment that you left the hillside below Giltspur. So no one will be looking for you and no one will be worried.'

'Thank goodness for that,' said Niamh.

They talked on into the night. Foras told them tales of the early days in Tír Danann and the building of Shee Alman, Shee Clettig and Shee Nenta. He described the great rejoicing at the annual Feast of Age when water was brought from Inis Óg and the feasting lasted all night long, with music, dancing, poetry, displays of fireworks and magical wonders. His words wove a spell of happiness and delight and as the shadow of fear melted from the children's minds, their bodies grew heavy with the need for sleep.

Rónán dozed off quietly and Foras placed an extra blanket over him to keep him warm. Daire was gazing into the glowing embers of the fire, dreaming to himself, when he became aware that all the talk had stopped. He turned to Niamh but her eyes were already closed. Foras got up, walked unsteadily to the fire and put a few more twigs on it. He had become very thin and bent. As the twigs caught fire he looked out beyond the circle of firelight into the night. Far off in the darkness something howled mournfully. He sighed heavily, turned and saw Daire watching him.

'Are you ready for sleep?' said Foras.

'I was thinking that I ought to keep watch and let you sleep,' replied Daire.

Foras shuffled over and sat down beside him.

'Mine is a tiredness that rest cannot cure,' he said. 'I shall not sleep tonight. It was kind of you to offer to keep watch. More than that, it was brave, for you are afraid – afraid of what might come upon us out of the night! Remember this: being brave does not mean that you feel no fear. Being brave is being afraid but not giving in to it. You will feel fear many times before your task in Tír Danann is completed. But you are brave, Daire, strong oak wood. Remember that you are brave and you will not be overcome.'

He placed his bony hand on Daire's shoulder and squeezed him encouragingly. Then he gave Daire a blanket to put over Niamh and one for himself.

'Sleep now,' he said, 'and fear not. I shall keep watch and no evil shall pass me this night. Codladh sámh.'

Daire covered Niamh. Then he rolled himself in his blanket and immediately fell into a deep, dreamless sleep.

Chapter 5: Good-bye to Friends

NIAMH BECAME AWARE of voices talking quietly nearby. Then she heard a thrush making silver music. She was lying on something hard. Suddenly she realised she wasn't in bed. She opened her eyes and struggled up onto her elbow.

It was early morning. The sky overhead was pale blue but away in the west stars still winked above the Plain of Danann. Their camp at the foot of the cliff lay in chilly shadow but the fire was glowing brightly and Niamh could feel its warmth on her face and arms. Small round loaves had been placed on the stones around the fire and the scent of warm bread drifted invitingly towards her.

Beyond the fire at the entrance to the camp, Foras and Rónán were talking together in low steady voices. Niamh immediately realised that it was a very private conversation and that she should not interrupt.

Beside her Daire stirred, yawned and stretched. Then he sat up and looked around. Niamh nodded towards Foras and Rónán.

'What's going on?' whispered Daire.

'I'm not sure,' replied Niamh, 'but I think if someone had saved my life I would want to say something special to them – something more than I know how to say.'

Rónán turned and walked slowly towards them. He looked very serious, as if he had just understood something very important that had to be done and was determined to do it properly. As he reached the fire Niamh and Daire stood up and folded their blankets.

'Foras says we should have breakfast,' said Rónán.

'Is he not going to join us?' asked Niamh.

'I don't think so,' replied Rónán, looking back to where Foras had walked further out and sat down upon a rock.

Breakfast was warm bread, cheese and fruit with water

from the pool below the waterfall. Rónán said nothing further about his talk with Foras so the children ate in an uneasy silence. At last Daire said, 'Is anything wrong?'

Rónán looked at his cousins for a moment. 'Foras wants to tell us something when we're finished eating,' he said.

Gasta, Taca and Cróga had been grazing further out from the cliff where the grass was thicker. Now they came back to where Foras sat and he patted their heads and talked to them.

As the children tidied up the breakfast things Foras stood up and struggled back towards the camp followed by the horses. He walked very stiffly, leaning on Rónán's spear. When he reached the fire he tried to straighten himself a little.

'Good morning,' he said, breathlessly. 'I hope you slept well. Was the breakfast to your liking?'

'Oh yes, thank you,' replied Niamh.

'Good,' said Foras, as he eased himself down onto the grass and rested his back against the cliff-side.

Niamh and Daire were startled to see how much he had aged during the night. His hair and beard had turned white as snow. His cheeks had sunk so far in that he could scarcely be recognised as the same person who had set out with them from Shee Alman. His neck was thin and wrinkled. The bones and veins of his hands showed clearly through his transparent skin. He struggled for breath for a moment, then he gestured to the children to gather round him.

'Do not be distressed by what you see,' he said, looking up at them with eyes full of concern. 'After all, I am more than three thousand years old! My body was a lot younger when I left Cahershee. I had hoped my energy would last until I brought you safely there. Now, that cannot be.'

He closed his eyes, breathing deeply to gather his failing strength. Then he continued.

'I no longer have the power to return you to your own world. You will have to go on to Cahershee alone. Listen carefully. The river that flows from the falls is called An Corrán. Follow the Green Road by the river. On no account must you leave that road. Once you reach the Enchanted Forest, Gasta, Taca and Cróga will guide you safely through. There is food in the saddle-bags. Rónán?'

He looked from one to the other as if he was unsure if Rónán was still there.

'I am here,' said Rónán, kneeling beside him.

'Good,' breathed Foras. 'You must take my sword. It has power you may need to call upon before you reach safety and friends.'

Then he looked up at Niamh and Daire.

'I am glad I have met you, the chosen ones of Manannán. Remember you are special. Do not lose courage. Keep to the Green Road. I am going now. If you find my son alive, tell him that I was glad in the end.'

He closed his eyes and his head sank back against the rock. Then he gave a long deep sigh and lay still.

Rónán stood up. 'He's dead,' he said.

For a long time they stood in silence, not knowing what to say or do.

'What did he mean by "If we find his son alive"?' said Daire at last.

'He was talking about Glasán,' replied Rónán. 'He was Glasán's father.'

Niamh felt a hot breath on her cheek and turning she found Gasta beside her. She put her arm around his neck and pressed her face into the horse's warm golden mane. Her mind was sinking in a dark pool of sorrow. Foras was dead. Glasán was missing, probably dead. She was lost, with Daire and Rónán in a strange world with terrifying enemies ready to attack at any moment. Everything seemed hopeless. Then she heard Daire's voice.

'Look!' he cried. 'Foras is changing!'

She raised her head and looked. His face and his long white robe were bathed in a shimmering silvery light. As the light grew brighter he became transparent, but what they could see through him was not grass and rock but something like sunshine on fast flowing water. A delicious scent of apple-blossom filled the air and for a moment Niamh felt an unexpected thrill of joy. Then the silver light faded, the flowing water disappeared and nothing was left but a trace of the delicious scent and Foras's robe lying on the grass. Foras was no longer there.

'What happened to him?' whispered Daire.

'I don't know,' Niamh replied, 'but I think it was something good.'

'What should we do with his robe?' asked Rónán.

'We should bury it beneath a pile of stones to mark the place of his death,' said Daire.

Everyone agreed and soon they'd heaped a fair-sized cairn of rocks on the spot. Rónán took his spear and set it upright into the cairn. Then he took Foras's sword belt from where he had left it near the fire and tied it around his waist. He drew the sword slowly from its sheath. It felt so heavy he could scarcely hold it. He gripped the hilt in both his hands and tried to raise the weapon above the cairn as a last salute to the person who had saved his life. Suddenly the sword began to rise by itself, drawing his arms up after it. The long blade flashed in the air above his head and he saw a word written in letters of fire along the shining steel. Briefly the letters flickered and flamed, then they vanished. Rónán drew the sword down again and slid it carefully into its sheath.

'Do the letters T-I-N-E mean anything to you?' he said.

'Tine. It's Gaelic for Fire,' replied Daire. 'What put that into your head?'

'I saw it written on the blade of the sword. It lasted only for a moment but the letters were flames!'

'That must be the name of the sword!' said Niamh. 'The High Council must have placed magical power in it. I wonder what it can do?'

'It can raise itself in the air,' replied Rónán. 'I couldn't have lifted it. Perhaps it will do other things. I'm really glad we have it. We may need it before we get to Cahershee.'

They gathered up their blankets and breakfast things and stored them in the saddle-bags. Rónán stamped out any twigs that were still glowing in the fire while Niamh and Daire saddled the horses. Then they took a last quiet look at Foras's cairn, mounted the horses and set off.

They headed left, joining An Corrán where it flowed out from the pool below the waterfall. The Green Road was a fairly smooth grassy track that followed the course of the river down to the plain. Rónán felt nervous riding Cróga on his own, so they moved at an easy pace.

The sun was now well up. Away in the west great heaps of creamy-white cloud glowed against the bright blue of the sky. A soft breeze with the scent of springtime was blowing towards the children as they rode. Larks twittered happily in the sunny air and there was no sign of enemies.

After an hour they reached the level plain. They paused on a grassy bank to allow the horses to drink and to stretch their own legs. Rónán in particular felt stiff from sitting on the horse. Looking back the way they had come the cliffs seemed misty and much taller. The waterfall was a silent white line scarcely moving over grey rock.

'I wonder why the Fir Bolg didn't follow us down the cliff?' said Niamh.

'Maybe they were afraid,' replied Daire. 'We put up quite a fight.'

'They might gather more of their friends now they know we're here,' said Rónán. 'They're sure to know where we're going as well.'

'In that case we'd better get a move on,' said Daire. 'We'll be able to make better speed now we're on smoother ground.'

They set off at a canter. The plain was less level than it had looked from the cliff. It was really a series of gentle slopes and small hills dotted with groves of oak and hazel trees. The road kept in sight of the river which was quieter here, flowing with steady strength. It turned in gentle curves leaving wide spaces of soft damp turf or tall green reeds where water-hens nested. Willows grew along by the water's edge, trailing their thin branches in the damp grass.

They rode steadily until early afternoon, when they came upon the first house they had seen since leaving Shee Alman. It was set on a small green hill and surrounded by a white stone wall. The land around it had been tilled and there was a large orchard on the southern slope of the hill. A paved pathway led up to the house from the road.

The children reined in their horses.

'Shall we go up to it?' said Daire.

'No,' replied Niamh. 'They're bound to be suspicious of oddly dressed strangers. I think we should go on.'

'There's probably no one there' said Rónán. 'If we can get inside, it would be a great place to have lunch out of sight of the road.'

'That seems like a good idea,' said Daire. 'Let's go up.'

He turned Taca's head and led the way up the path. Niamh reluctantly followed behind the boys.

They rode to the left around the white wall towards the orchard. At the southern end of the wall they came upon a tall black-barred gate. Through this they could see into the garden. It was beautifully laid out with smooth green lawns where daffodils nodded below graceful flowering trees. A path of many-coloured stones led up to a two-storeyed house

of beautifully-cut granite. It had tall windows and a door of polished bronze.

Daire dismounted and tried the gate. It was not locked.

'Shall we go in?' he asked.

'I don't think we should,' said Niamh. 'It's obviously a very private place.'

'Oh come on!' said Rónán impatiently. 'We can at least knock on the door. If there's no one at home there's no harm done and we can do what we like.'

'Supposing there *is* someone there?' murmured Niamh, but Rónán had already dismounted and he didn't hear her.

They tethered the horses to the gate and walked up the path. Just before the door the path divided into two to encircle a pond. At the far side of this a broad jet of water curved gracefully down from the mouth of a bronze fish set on top of a rock. A strange stillness lay over everything.

Rónán paused before the door. There was a bell hanging from the wall with a chain that reached almost to the ground. 'Shall I ring it?' he said. He seemed less sure of himself now they were here.

'You might as well,' replied Niamh sullenly.

Rónán pulled the chain. A sweet ringing filled the garden, echoing around the encircling walls. The strength of it surprised the children and it kept on humming long after Rónán had let go of the chain.

'If there's anyone here they'll have heard that!' declared Daire.

'If there's anyone within a kilometre of here they'll have heard it,' muttered Niamh.

They waited. No footsteps sounded inside and the door remained closed.

'Let's have a look in through the windows,' said Daire.

To their surprise the windows showed multi-coloured reflections of themselves and the sky, but they couldn't see in.

'It's probably a special glass that allows them to see out while no one can see in,' Rónán said. 'Anyway, there doesn't seem to be anyone here.'

They turned away from the house and looked down the garden towards the gate where the horses were patiently cropping the grass. From the door of the house they could see out over the garden wall to where the river wound its way westwards.

'The road ahead looks easy enough,' said Rónán. 'We might reach Cahershee this evening if we make good speed.'

'Let's have lunch in here,' said Daire.

'We can't,' said Niamh. 'We've got to let the horses graze and we can't leave them wandering outside.'

'Can't they graze in the garden?' said Daire.

'They'll destroy the lawns and eat the flowers,' replied Niamh.

'Oh they won't do that much harm,' said Daire. 'Sure there's no one here.'

'That doesn't make it right,' answered Niamh.

'Why are you making such a fuss?' said Rónán. 'This is an ideal place. We have fresh water and it's sheltered.'

'I'm not making a fuss!' declared Niamh. 'Anyway, I don't like those windows.'

'Isn't that just like a girl,' said Rónán, turning to Daire. 'She won't have lunch in a beautiful garden because she doesn't like the windows.'

'Oh don't be so stupid!' cried Niamh.

'Wait a moment,' said Rónán. 'Will you please tell us what's wrong with the windows?' It was clear that he thought Niamh was behaving like a little spoiled girl, but that *he* was being very grown-up and patient with her.

'I'll tell you what's wrong with them!' shouted Niamh. 'We can't see *in* through them and that means that at this very moment, someone could be standing in there looking *out* at us without our knowing it! You can have your lunch here if you like. I'm going out to have mine in the orchard.'

She turned away and stormed off down the path to the gate. Daire and Rónán looked at each other. The idea of an unseen watcher was not pleasant.

'Come on,' sighed Daire, and they followed Niamh down the path and out of the garden.

Chapter 6: Beauty or Beast?

THE HORSES WERE UNSADDLED and allowed to graze in the orchard. The children sat with their backs against the tree trunks. It was a pleasant place to be. The sun poured down through blossom-covered branches making delightful patterns of light and shade on the grass. Robins, finches and blue-tits chirped and fluttered overhead. But the children felt uneasy and nobody spoke while they ate.

'Well this *is* a pretty scene – a picnic below the plum-trees!'

Though the voice was light and musical, the children were so startled by it that they leaped to their feet, turning to where they thought the speaker should be. But they could see no one. Then they heard a merry laugh, like a peal of little silver bells. They turned back and saw her, standing below the flowering trees with the sunlight and shadows falling upon her as if she was a part of the orchard that had suddenly come to life. She moved lightly towards them over the grass, smiling as if she was delighted by their confusion and amazement.

Rónán's hand moved onto the hilt of his sword. The horses neighed loudly and Niamh saw them bolting through the trees towards the garden gate.

But Daire could see nothing but the young lady, for she was the most beautiful girl he had ever seen or imagined. She was tall and slender and her every movement was a graceful act of beauty. Her long hair was a deep chestnut colour that glowed red-gold where the sunlight played upon it. Her laughing eyes were the colour of bluebells in the woods in May and her smiling red lips parted to show teeth of perfect whiteness. Her slender body was clothed in a long green-blue gown, covered with patterns of leaves and flowers. Her arms were bare and her golden skin was smooth and moist and tinged with the slightest pink.

Daire stood with staring eyes and open mouth. The lady, seeing the effect she had on him, smiled all the more. Her eyes twinkled merrily as she fixed them on Daire's face, ignoring Niamh and Rónán.

'Well my fine young man,' she said in a soft coaxing voice. 'Who might you be?'

'I'm Daire.' He heard his voice answering as if it did not belong to him.

'Daire,' she repeated slowly as if she was tasting his name. 'What a fine manly name! And why is Daire having a meal in my orchard?'

All the time she spoke she kept her eyes on Daire's face and he found he could not look away from her. A faint doubt flickered in his mind. Why could he not move his eyes? She smiled at him again. She was so beautiful her face seemed to shine like a star.

'We are on our way to Cahershee,' he replied. Then he heard another voice saying, 'Who are you?' The lady's eyes turned from him and he saw her looking at Rónán.

'Who is this?' she asked sweetly.

'My name is Rónán and I'd like to know who you are.'

'You do not trust me!' exclaimed the lady.

'I do not mean to be unfriendly,' returned Rónán, 'but we are travelling in a strange land and it is hard for us to tell a friend from an enemy.'

'Very wise,' murmured the lady to herself as she looked away from Rónán and turned her attention to Niamh. 'We don't see many attractive young ladies travelling in these parts.'

Niamh had been feeling left out of the conversation, for the lady had seemed to ignore her. Now she was glad to have a chance to speak.

'I'm Niamh,' she said. 'We didn't know it was your orchard. You see we came here to help the People of Danann to get the water from the Well of Youth. Foras was bringing us to Cahershee.'

The lady was very interested now. 'Where is Foras?' she asked, looking around as if she expected him to appear from behind a tree.

'Foras is dead,' said Niamh. 'He grew older as we went along and after . . . . '

'Oh I see!' said the lady quickly. Her lovely face showed no sadness or surprise. Only her eyebrows flickered a little. She looked quickly at each of the children. 'So you are travelling alone. I'm afraid you will find it impossible to reach Cahershee by the Green Road. There are many Fir Bolg watching the way. Wolves have come out of the north and have been seen on the bridge at Cúl Glas and there are rumours of strange things moving over the land by night. You are in very great danger!'

'What are we to do?' said Daire in dismay.

The lady looked at him again. Her face was serious. Then she suddenly smiled like a burst of sunlight from behind dark clouds.

'Do not be afraid. There is another way to the north of the Green Road. It is difficult to find and more difficult to follow, but I shall lead you there and bring you safely to Cahershee.'

Niamh and Daire heard a sudden ringing sound and something bright flashed in the sunlight. Rónán had drawn his sword.

'No!' he cried, stepping swiftly forward. 'Most definitely no!' His face was frowning and his mouth was set in a stubborn line. He was holding Tine with both hands so that it pointed at the lady as if he expected her to attack him. 'Foras told us on no account to leave the Green Road,' he went on. 'He knew all the dangers. He wouldn't have told us to do what was wrong for us.'

There was a moment of stunned silence. Niamh and Daire looked at the lady to see if she was angry. She stared solemnly at Rónán for a moment. Then suddenly the orchard was filled with her lovely bell-like laughter. Her eyes sparkled. She seemed delighted with Rónán's display of strength.

'Oh!' she laughed, pressing the palms of her hands together. 'What a strong, young protector you have! It must be fine to have such a brave intelligent leader.'

As she said this she looked straight at Daire, examining his face, looking deeply into his eyes. Rónán stood scowling at her. He wasn't sure how, but he felt she was making fun of him. Daire began to feel ashamed. She obviously thought he was weak and unable to look after himself.

'He – He's not our leader,' he muttered.

'Oh!' said the lady in mock surprise. 'Are you the leader then?'

Rónán and Daire looked at each other. Their look was a

question, but Niamh noticed that it soon became a challenge. Oh no, she thought, they're going to start a fight in front of the lady.

'We have no leader,' she said, stepping between the boys. 'We never even thought about it until you mentioned it.'

A flicker of disappointment passed across the lady's face, but she smiled again quickly. 'I see you are intelligent as well as beautiful,' she said. 'Will you follow Rónán and refuse to follow me or will you make up your own mind?'

Though Niamh couldn't understand why, she felt an overpowering urge to disagree with Rónán, to show that she could decide for herself. Why had he spoken out so definitely as if her opinion did not matter? And yet, there was something about this meeting and all that had been said, that made her uneasy.

'Of course I can make up my own mind!' she declared. 'We certainly won't be able to deal with the Fir Bolg and the wolves on our own. What you suggest seems reasonable.'

'Of course it's reasonable,' purred the lady. 'I'm only trying to help.'

Daire wasn't sure what they ought to do. He very much wanted to stay with this beautiful lady but Rónán's words had reminded him of Foras's noble face and the brightness in his eyes as he told them to stay on the Green Road.

'One thing puzzles me,' he said. 'If you live here, why didn't Foras tell us about you? He knew we would be passing by your house.'

'Perhaps he forgot,' replied the lady sweetly. 'After all, he was growing very old. Old people often forget things.'

Daire looked steadily at her. The way she had answered cleared his mind. Now he knew what they should do, though saying the words took an enormous effort. 'I – I agree with Rónán,' he said at last. 'I think we should do what Foras told us.'

The lady looked at him coldly. He knew she did not like him any more, but he felt strangely relieved.

'Will you also refuse me?' the lady said to Niamh.

Niamh looked at Daire and Rónán. They were staring at her with pale serious faces. She turned back to the lady. 'Could you not come with us along the Green Road?' she said.

'No,' replied the lady. 'If you want my help you must be willing to follow me.'

'I'm sorry,' said Niamh. 'I'm willing to go with you but I can't leave the others.'

A shadow of anger flickered over the lady's face. She looked at each of them in silence. Then she brightened again.

'Very well,' she said lightly. 'When trouble comes, remember that I offered to help you and that you refused my help.'

She turned back to Niamh. 'You, I think, wanted to trust me. I like you. You are unusual, for you have both intelligence and beauty. Such beauty deserves to be adorned.'

She opened a purse that hung from her belt and drew from it a fine silver chain on which hung a silver medallion. In the centre of the medallion there was a circle of precious stones. They were deep blue with one black stone set in the middle, so that it looked like a twinkling eye.

'This will remind you of me and it may protect you from our enemies,' she said and she hung the medallion around Niamh's neck.

As she did so, Daire saw something that he hadn't noticed before. An eye looked out from each of the leaves that decorated the lady's gown. He decided that he didn't like the design.

But Niamh was delighted. No one had ever told her she was beautiful before. No one had ever given her anything as lovely and precious as this. She lifted the medallion in her fingers, feeling its weight, admiring the shining silver and the sparkling blue stones.

'Farewell to you,' said the lady. 'I am sorry you did not trust me. I hope you get to Cahershee safely, but I fear you will not.'

She stepped away from them, passing below the flowering trees, blending once more into the sunlight and shadows of the orchard. As she vanished a startled magpie flapped noisily up through the leaves overhead and flew off westwards, calling with a hard rattling voice. Then all was silence.

Niamh fingered the beautiful medallion that glittered on her breast. She felt different but she liked the new feeling. She was strong now, sure of herself. She turned to the boys. They were pale and unhappy-looking. Rónán still held Tine in front of him and Niamh thought he looked ridiculous.

'Why don't you put that silly sword away?' she said

sharply.

'Look who's talking about being silly!' replied Rónán. 'You're the one who told her everything.'

'And what was wrong with that?' demanded Niamh in a haughty voice. 'She was offering to help us.'

'But you don't even know who she was!' protested Rónán. 'Didn't you notice she avoided answering when I asked for her name?'

'The way you asked her I can't say that I blame her,' retorted Niamh.

'Look,' said Daire, 'we've made a decision. Now we've got to get to Cahershee. Let's not waste time arguing.' He turned and walked up towards the garden wall where the horses were waiting.

'Some decision,' muttered Niamh as she followed him up the slope.

Rónán sheathed his sword. 'We're only following Foras's instructions,' he said. 'He told us very clearly that *on no account* were we to leave the Green Road.'

'Foras can't have known everything that was going to happen,' argued Niamh. 'The situation has changed. Didn't you hear the lady say there were Fir Bolg watching the road and wolves waiting at the bridge?'

'The question is whether you trust Foras or her,' said Rónán.

'It's not so long ago since you were the one who didn't trust Foras,' snapped Niamh.

Rónán stopped and looked at her. 'I have the best of reasons for trusting him now,' he said, with a quiet sadness in his voice.

The look on his face made Niamh feel uneasy. She turned away and walked on up to the horses.

From the moment the lady had placed the medallion on Niamh's neck, her feelings had begun to change. She became more aware of herself with every minute that passed. She was aware of the sheen of her long dark hair and how it curved in against her shoulders. She became conscious of her face, the smoothness of her skin, the shapeliness of her nose. When she looked at the boys she felt the brightness of her eyes and knew their colour and their dark depths. When she spoke she was aware of the redness of her lips and the whiteness of her teeth. As she moved she felt the shape of her body and knew her own gracefulness. She was worth looking at. Anyone who didn't notice her was either dull of brain or being deliberately rude or jealous. She was due everyone's attention.

Daire had saddled Taca. Niamh walked to where Gasta was waiting, but as she approached his head the horse shied away from her. She frowned in irritation. She had always been good with horses. She moved again towards Gasta's head, reaching out to pat his long brown neck, but once again the horse snorted and turned away.

'What's the matter with this silly horse?' she muttered angrily.

'Perhaps he doesn't like your new eye,' said Rónán.

Niamh glared at him but she said nothing. In the end, Rónán held Gasta's head while Daire saddled the horse.

'Rónán could be right, you know,' Daire said, as he looked over the horse's back at his sister's sullen face. 'Why don't you take the medallion off?'

'It's my protection!' snapped Niamh. 'I'm not taking it off for anyone. And I'm surprised at you turning against the lady. You could look at nothing else when you saw her first. If you'd agreed with me we could have been half-way to Cahershee by now.'

'She was beautiful, all right,' sighed Daire, 'but I saw something else in the end.'

'What?' demanded Niamh.

'I saw that she didn't really care about Foras. She wasn't at all upset when you told her he was dead.'

Niamh was taken aback by this. She searched her mind for an answer. 'Maybe she didn't know Foras,' she suggested. 'Tír Danann is a pretty big place. You can't expect everyone to know everyone else.'

'But she wasn't even interested,' insisted Daire. 'You *must* have noticed that!'

'The trouble with Niamh is that she doesn't want to know the truth,' said Rónán.

'And you're too dim to see it!' shouted Niamh.

She hoisted herself quickly into the saddle. Gasta shifted unhappily and shook his head violently up and down so that Daire and Rónán stepped back quickly. But Niamh gripped the horse with her knees and tightened her hold on the reins. 'If we're going to get ourselves killed we might as well get on with it!' she said, and turning Gasta sharply, she galloped off in the direction of the road.

'I don't know what's got into her,' sighed Daire, as he helped Rónán onto Cróga's back and settled himself on Taca. 'She's like a different person.'

'I know,' said Rónán. 'There's been something wrong with all of us since we left the Green Road. Niamh didn't want to come up here. It's a pity we didn't follow her advice.'

'We'd better get after her or she'll be so far ahead we'll never catch her,' said Daire.

They urged their horses forward to the path and descended quickly to the Green Road.

Chapter 7:
In the Teeth of Wolves

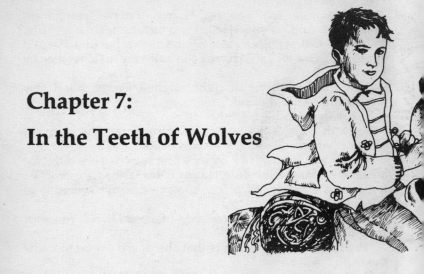

THEY RODE AS IF THEY WERE IN A RACE. Niamh led the way at full gallop with her hair streaming out behind her. The boys chased after her, with Rónán holding on to Cróga for dear life and hoping he wouldn't fall off. A strengthening wind blew in their faces. Clouds rolled up from beyond the western hills and swallowed up the sun. They passed woods and low hills and they saw two more houses to the north of the road but they did not stop.

By mid-afternoon both horses and riders were growing tired. They slowed their pace and the boys eventually caught up with Niamh. On their left the river had grown wider and slower. A flock of wild duck rose up in a flurry of alarm and flapped noisily away southwards but the children didn't see what had disturbed them. Away to the north they saw a grey and yellow dog hurrying across the countryside. It didn't seem to notice them and eventually it vanished among a grove of trees.

After a time they came to a small wood that grew between them and the river. A stream flowed through the wood, gurgling noisily over smooth rocks before it joined An Corrán. There was a grassy place on either side of the stream. They decided to stop for a rest and let the horses graze, but they did

not unsaddle them.

Daire and Rónán filled their bottles from the stream and took a good drink of the clear cold water. Niamh sat apart from them. She hadn't spoken at all during their ride.

The wind was blowing strongly through the trees, tossing their branches and filling the woods with strange creaking sounds.

'I've been wondering why that lady didn't stay in Caher-shee with the rest of the Danann,' said Rónán. 'Won't she grow old the way Foras did?'

'Maybe she isn't one of the People of Danann at all,' suggested Daire.

'In that case,' Rónán said, looking at Niamh, 'what is she?'

Niamh said nothing. She got up and walked away from them through the trees to where the stream entered the river. She stood there with her back to the boys, gazing out over the dark swirling water, the green countryside and the grey clouds scurrying above it.

The horses had wandered up towards the road to graze the long grass at its edge. From somewhere above their heads the boys heard a sound, not unlike a football rattle. Rónán looked up. A huge glossy magpie with a vicious beak and glinting

eyes was staring keenly at him.

'One for sorrow, two for joy,' said Rónán.

The magpie shuffled sideways and called out its rattling cry again. Daire looked up. 'If that's the case,' he said, 'what's twenty or thirty for?'

Rónán looked again. All the branches were alive with enormous magpies. 'There's something wrong here!' he cried, leaping up.

Suddenly all the magpies began to call out together, filling the wood with a dreadful racket. As Rónán and Daire scrambled up the bank from the stream the air was filled with a storm of black and white bodies. Daire was almost knocked to the ground by the force of the attack. The birds landed on his head, shoulders and arms. He felt their claws piercing his skin. Sharp hard beaks stabbed viciously at his face. Blood began to trickle down his forehead and across his cheeks. Then the dreadful truth dawned on him: they were trying to peck out his eyes! He screamed in fear, trying to protect his face with his hands but the weight of the birds made his arms almost impossible to move. He threw himself on his knees, pressing his face between his legs.

When the first magpies landed on Rónán's head he got such a fright that he lost his footing and slithered down the bank to the stream. When he stood up again, Tine was in his hand. He hadn't time to wonder how it got there, for the birds were upon him immediately. He swung the sword above his head. Its long blade glowed like a flame as it flashed through the flying bodies of his attackers. Showers of feathers and sparks fell on his face. Soon the ground around him was covered with the torn bodies of birds. More and still more darted and dived at him till his hands streamed with blood, his arms ached and his head was dizzy. Still the sword fought on.

Niamh heard the uproar in the wood and turning quickly she saw Daire and Rónán vanishing under a blizzard of black and white birds. It was clear that in a few moments they would be hacked to pieces. She drew her sword and raced along the bank to the rescue.

When she reached the place where Daire was crouching she raised her sword to strike, but the medallion at her breast gave a jump, tugging sharply on the silver chain about her neck. There was a dazzling flash of blue light. At once, all the birds flew away towards the road.

Niamh was still standing with her sword in the air when Daire raised his head. The sight of his face gave her a shock. His forehead and cheeks were gashed and scratched. Blood was flowing down his face and dripping off his chin. He looked about him wildly, expecting to be attacked again.

'The horses!' cried Rónán. 'They've got the horses!'

The magpies had descended on Gasta, Taca and Cróga, stabbing with cruel beaks all along their bodies. The horses neighed loudly and reared up, kicking and snapping at their tormentors but they were no match for the birds. After a brief struggle they took flight, galloping in terror along the Green Road with a cloud of magpies swirling above them like a swarm of giant bees. The children watched helplessly as their horses vanished westwards. The wood grew silent again.

Rónán struggled wearily up from the stream. Niamh turned and glared at him.

'Now we're really in a mess!' she fumed. 'We've no horses, no food, no blankets and our shields are gone as well.'

'I know what you're going to say,' he sighed. 'we should have gone with the lady.'

'Well it's true!' shouted Niamh impatiently. 'If you'd listened to me none of this would have happened. If it wasn't for my medallion we'd all have been pecked to death or blinded by now.'

'I know,' murmured Daire, 'and thanks for saving me.' He suddenly sank to his knees. Behind the lines of dried blood his face had turned sickly pale.

'I think he's going to faint,' said Rónán, moving quickly to Daire and putting his arm around him. He looked up at Niamh. She was staring at them as if they were strangers.

'Oh, do pull yourself together!' cried Rónán. 'Take the bottle and get some water.'

As Niamh went down to the stream an unhappy doubt stirred in a corner of her mind. She knew there was something wrong with her. When Rónán had looked up at her she hadn't been worried about Daire at all. She had been thinking how queenly she must look to these two blood-stained frightened boys. What was happening to her?

She bent over, reaching into the stream to fill the bottle. The medallion hung out from her neck, swinging back and forth, glistening prettily. She closed her fingers around it. Her doubts vanished. She felt better again.

Daire drank some water and they washed the blood from his face. As soon as he felt well enough, they set off walking along the Green Road. There was nothing else they could do, though they knew there was very little hope of their ever reaching Cahershee.

They walked and walked and saw nothing and heard nothing but the lonely sighing of the wind in the trees. The land ahead of them began to slope steadily upwards and their legs and feet were soon aching. Nobody spoke, but as the evening light began to weaken, each of them grew more fearful. At every turn in the road they expected to find their way blocked by the Fir Bolg. At every wood they watched fearfully for the magpies. And each of them knew the darkest dread: the fear of the unknown things that might come drifting over the land once darkness fell.

Another hour passed. They were hungry and cold and they knew they wouldn't be able to walk much further. Away in the west the cloud began to break and a pale gold light lit up the horizon. Their road had come to the top of a hill. On the right stood a tall pine wood, its trees black against the evening sky. Below on the left the river flowed darkly. Straight ahead the land sloped gently to where an old stone bridge carried the road across a stream.

'This must be Cúl Glas,' said Daire, 'and there's no one on the bridge.'

Just then, something rose from the grass and stepped onto the road about halfway between them and the bridge.

'That's the dog we saw earlier,' said Rónán. 'It looks like a skinny alsatian.'

'That's not a dog,' Daire replied slowly. 'It's a wolf!'

As he was speaking, five more wolves crept out of the grass and joined their leader. They formed a line across the road blocking the way.

The children stood perfectly still, staring at the row of sharp ears, mean yellow eyes and hungry red mouths. Suddenly the wolves began to run towards them.

'We've killed bigger wolves than these!' declared Daire as both he and Niamh drew their swords.

'I've never even seen a wolf before,' said Rónán, 'but I'll bet this sword has.'

Tine came singing out of its sheath. Glowing lines of red and gold flickered along the blade and the word *Tine* shone clearly above the hilt. 'Tine!' cried Rónán in a loud voice, holding the sword on high.

The wolves halted when they saw the sword. They were so near, the children could hear them panting and see their red wet tongues hanging out between their sharp yellow teeth. The leader threw back his head and gave a long ghostly howl that made the children's skin shiver. It echoed across the river and through the woods. From behind them the children heard an answering chorus of howls. They turned quickly. The road behind them was filled with wolves.

The wolf leader charged.

'Quickly!' cried Daire. 'To the woods! Get up into the trees!'

They ran for their lives, their hearts thumping in panic and their legs weak with fright. Even as they reached the wood they realised it was useless. More wolves were waiting for them among the trees. In an instant the pack sprang upon them from all sides.

Rónán swung Tine in a frenzy of rage and fear. Wolf bodies soon covered the ground around him. Where Tine's blade struck fire leaped up. Wolves with burning fur ran howling through the woods. For a moment the wolves drew back from the terrible sword.

Rónán turned and saw Daire's sword fall from his hand as a huge grey wolf caught him by the wrist. Niamh was being dragged along the ground by two wolves that had gripped her by the ankles.

Then the wolves rushed at Rónán again. Once more Tine burned and cut but the wolves were coming too quickly now. He felt a stab of pain at the back of his leg and suddenly he was falling. He swung the sword blindly, then he was swallowed in a nightmare of snapping teeth and snarling mouths.

I'm really going to die, he thought as he fell.

Then everything stopped. The horror was over. The wolves had disappeared. He was lying on his back. Above him gold-tinged clouds drifted against a glowing blue sky. A sweet steady ringing sound vibrated in the air. Rónán wondered if this was what it was like to be dead.

He tried to sit up but a dart of pain in his left leg made him lie still again. He decided he wasn't dead. But what had happened? Slowly he turned onto his side. He saw Daire lying face down in the grass near the trees. Then he heard voices. He raised his head and saw Niamh sitting up. She was

drinking from a small silver cup and she was talking to the lady with the chestnut-coloured hair.

Rónán sat up carefully. Blood was trickling from the marks of the wolf-teeth in his left hand. It had begun to ache and he couldn't move his fingers. The left leg of his trousers was torn and blood was seeping through the cloth just below his knee. All around him the grass was trampled and spattered with blood. Wolf-bodies lay where they had fallen, their faces frozen in deathly snarls. Tine was on the ground beside him. As the fingers of his right hand closed around the familiar hilt he thought of Foras and felt comforted.

'I see you did some damage before you fell,' said the musical voice of the lady.

He hadn't noticed her coming towards him, but now she stood over him smiling sweetly. She poured a few drops of clear liquid from a small glass bottle into the silver cup.

'Drink this,' she commanded.

Rónán took the cup. 'What is it?' he said.

The lady looked steadily at him. 'Can it be that you still don't trust me?' she said.

'I suppose you must have saved my life,' replied Rónán, looking around him as if he expected to see the wolves returning. 'How did you do it?'

The lady smiled. In the light of the evening sun her face was even more beautiful than he had remembered it.

"I knew you would not get past the bridge,' she said, 'though you did not believe me when I told you so before. When I saw the wolves gathering towards the road I followed them.'

'Weren't you afraid?' asked Rónán.

The lady laughed her silver laugh. 'Oh no! I have dealt with the wolves before. They do not like my little bell.' From inside the breast of her gown she drew out a tiny bell on a fine silver chain.

'So that's what I heard!' said Rónán.

'Now will you trust me enough to take the drink?' she said.

'I suppose so,' replied Rónán, looking closely at it. It was a clear liquid but tinged with pink. He put it to his lips and sipped. The fragrance of it filled his head like a summer's day in a garden of lilacs. His mouth and throat tingled as he swallowed it and he felt his body glowing as it went into his stomach. A delightful warm feeling spread along his arms and legs, driving out all pain and tiredness. He drained the cup and handed it back to the lady. She was smiling delightedly showing all her teeth.

'You liked that,' she purred.

Rónán stood up and slid Tine back into its sheath. 'Yes,' he replied, 'but I'd still like to know what it is.'

Niamh had come over to them. Rónán was amazed by the change in her. Her eyes sparkled, her skin shone and she looked fresh and lively. There was not a scratch or bruise on her, as if the wolf-attack had not taken place. She was beaming with delight and the medallion on her breast flashed dazzlingly. 'I was right!' she declared in a voice full of triumph.

Daire groaned.

'I think your companion is in need of my attention,' said the lady sweetly.

Rónán realised with a shock that from the moment the lady had spoken to him he had not thought of Daire at all. As they walked to where Daire was lying he noticed that the pain in his leg had gone. He looked at his hand. The prints of the wolf-teeth had vanished. There was no bruising and he could move his fingers freely.

The lady bent over Daire. He had suffered the most in the attack. All the wounds that the magpies had inflicted on his face had reopened and blood was trickling into his eyes and down his cheeks. Both his hands had been bitten by the wolves. His trousers were torn and there were many gashes on his legs. His breathing was uneven and he seemed to be barely conscious.

Rónán supported him from behind while the lady poured a few drops of the liquid into his mouth. Almost immediately his breathing quietened and his eyes opened. Rónán watched fascinated as the gashes on Daire's face slowly began to close. Soon there were only thin red lines where the wounds had been. The red lines turned pink, then grew paler and finally vanished completely.

'What happened?' asked Daire, looking around him. 'Where are all the wolves?'

'The lady saved us,' Niamh announced proudly.

Daire stood up. 'Whoever you are,' he said, 'I owe my life to you.'

'Indeed you do,' replied the lady.

The tone of her voice made Rónán look sharply at her. For an instant he saw a greedy eager look in her eyes, then the moment passed. Neither Niamh nor Daire seemed to have noticed. Daire's sword was lying in the grass a little way off. Rónán picked it up and gave it to him.

'If being brave was enough to make victory certain, then you would surely make it to Cahershee alone,' said the lady as she watched Daire sheath his sword. 'But there are greater dangers here than you realise. You *must* come with me. I will bring you safely beyond our enemies.'

She began to move away towards the wood. Niamh and Daire followed her but Rónán hung behind. The lady stopped and looked back at him.

'Are you not coming with us?' she asked.

Rónán was standing alone. He felt terrible. Obviously both Daire and Niamh had accepted the lady. He had to admit that she had saved their lives and healed their wounds. Yet deep down inside he knew there was something wrong about it all. He kept recalling Foras's face and hearing his last words.

'I know you have done much for us,' he replied, 'but Foras did warn us not to leave the Green Road.'

'Oh really, Rónán!' cried Niamh. 'You're being absolutely stupid!'

'This lady has just saved your life,' added Daire.

'I know, I know,' replied Rónán unhappily.

The lady walked back to him. She fixed her lovely eyes on his and spoke to him in a voice full of concern. 'You cannot go by the Green Road. You have already been attacked twice. What more proof do you want? Are you going to go on alone?'

Rónán knew he was defeated. 'Of course not,' he said. 'I'll come with you. I just don't know why you bothered to come back to save us.'

The lady smiled at him and putting her arm around his shoulders she squeezed him playfully. 'Oh, I couldn't let such fine young bodies go to waste among the wolves,' she purred, as she drew him along towards the woods.

Once they were walking among the trees she took her hand away. The touch of her fingers had sent a chill through Rónán's body and what she had said did nothing to make him feel easy with her.

'It's almost as if we were pieces of meat in a butcher's shop,' he muttered to himself.

Chapter 8:
Dance of the Midnight Fire

THEY WALKED DOWNHILL through the pine trees and out onto
an open grassy place. From here they could see over a wide
stretch of countryside to the north. The land was flat and
boggy. Great tufts of spiky green reeds stood up between
pools of water that reflected the blue and pink of the evening
sky. On their left a brilliant sun hung just above the horizon,
flooding all the countryside with a glowing golden light and
sending long shadows creeping across the bogland.

'That is Altán Amplach,' said the lady, pointing north-
wards. 'That is where we must go.'

The children saw a low wooded hill standing above the
bogland like an island in a sea of reeds.

'It looks very far away,' murmured Daire.

'I'm afraid it is,' sighed the lady, 'and you must be feeling
hungry already.' She looked at them, running the tip of her
tongue along her red lips.

Of course they were hungry! They hadn't noticed it until
now, but once the lady had spoken the word they felt a
longing for food that made it hard to think of anything else.
She eyed them mischievously.

'We shall have plenty to eat when we reach the safety of
Altán Amplach,' she said. Then she turned back towards the
wood and called out 'Anfa!' in a clear ringing voice. An

answering whinny came from the wood and out of the trees emerged a beautiful coal-black horse. It was small and slender of leg but its coat was glossy and its movement smooth and sure. Its saddle and harness were of black leather, ornamented with silver leaves and eyes.

'What a beautiful horse!' cried Niamh.

'You may ride with me,' said the lady. 'I'm sure our gallant warriors won't mind allowing their lady to rest her legs.'

She smiled to herself again. Then with a quick light movement she mounted the horse and having settled Niamh in front of her she set off downhill. Daire and Rónán followed on foot.

Soon they were travelling out across the bog, winding their way between clumps of tall reeds and dark slimy pools. The path was a little higher than the bogland. It was mostly dry but rather uneven and the boys found it hard to keep up with the horse.

The lady and Niamh were chattering in low voices. Every now and then they burst out laughing, but the boys could not hear what was being said.

'That woman laughs too much,' said Rónán grumpily. He was growing tired and he felt so hungry he thought he wouldn't be able to bear it.

'What's wrong with laughing?' said Daire.

'There's nothing wrong with laughing,' replied Rónán, 'but she does too much of it to be – to be – *real*!' That's the word I've been looking for. She's not *real*!'

'Don't be ridiculous!' protested Daire. 'She was real enough to rescue us from the wolves. If she hadn't come along the three of us would have been eaten alive. Think of that.'

'I *am* thinking of it,' Rónán said, frowning, 'but there are things that don't fit in.'

'What doesn't fit in?' said Daire.

'She didn't ask us how we lost the horses,' replied Rónán.

Daire stopped and looked Rónán in the eye. 'You sound as if you were going out of your way to find reasons not to trust her. Here's a lady who saves our lives and you're complaining that she didn't ask about the horses.'

'Listen,' said Rónán desperately. 'She didn't ask because she already knew. She said we'd been attacked *twice* already. That means she knew about the magpies. Why didn't she save us then?'

'Probably because she knew that the medallion would do it on its own. Don't forget she gave it to Niamh as a protection. As for knowing about the first attack, Niamh could have told her.'

Rónán didn't reply. They had fallen so far behind that the lady had stopped and was looking back at them.

'I know she's rather strange,' continued Daire. 'I didn't trust her myself until now. But I think you'll just have to admit that Niamh was right and we were wrong. We should have gone with the lady in the first place.'

He turned away and began walking after the horse. Rónán trudged along behind him.

The sun was now half-set. The bogland was more in shadow than light but ahead of them, Altán Amplach was still bathed in brightness as if it belonged to another world. On and on they walked. The path made sudden sharp turns to left and right so that an unwary traveller would easily have ended up at the bottom of one of the deep slimy pools. Rónán wondered with a shudder, how many unfortunate bodies lay below the dark bog water.

The sun slipped below the horizon, leaving a rosy afterglow in the sky. At last they reached the dry grassy ground in front of Altán Amplach. It was a large circular mound. Its high curving banks were set with white rocks. Along its outer rim a double circle of birch trees stretched their bony fingers at the sky.

Daire and Rónán followed the horse along a narrow path up the bank and into the trees. In the centre of the mound there was a wide flat grassy space and in the middle of this a huge block of granite lay on its side, like an altar. Near the stone there was a pile of twigs and above this a small black cauldron hung on a hook from an iron frame.

The lady dismounted and helped Niamh off the horse. 'No one will disturb us here,' she said. She seemed very pleased with herself. 'I shall prepare a meal for you but I shall need more firewood. Daire and Rónán will gather twigs for us while Niamh attends to Anfa.'

By the time the boys had gathered two good armfuls of dry twigs the lady already had a crackling fire blazing below the cauldron. Stars were winking above the circle of trees and the air had grown chilly. The fire was a cheerful sight.

'Gather some more!' commanded the lady. 'The nights are

cold here and we shall need a good warm fire.'

It wasn't easy to find more twigs in the failing light. The boys were so weak with tiredness and hunger that their legs were trembling, but they did as they were told. The aroma of the cooking drifted among the trees and made them feel faint.

'If I don't get something to eat,' said Daire, 'I'll bite the bark off one of those trees!'

A deep darkness had covered all the bogland around the mound when Daire and Rónán returned to the fire. The lady was sprinkling red dust into the cauldron and stirring it in with a black rod. In the yellow flickering light her face looked strange. She wasn't smiling but her eyes were intense, almost wild. She was talking to herself in a low voice.

Niamh was kneeling on the ground beside the lady. She looked as if she was dreaming of something far away. The medallion on her breast was a blaze of light.

There was now a large pile of firewood beside the granite block and the lady seemed satisfied. Rónán and Daire sank to their knees in front of the fire and watched as she ladled out the contents of the cauldron into three round black bowls that had a handle on either side of them. The air was heavy with the sweet warm scent of the cooking. It made them feel madly hungry and weak-limbed.

She handed the first bowl to Niamh, who immediately raised it to her lips and began to drink. Then the lady carried two bowls to the boys. 'Drink this and you will feel no more *hunger*!' she commanded. She said the word *hunger* as if she wanted to burn it into their minds.

Rónán jerked his head upright and was suddenly aware that he'd almost fallen asleep. The sound of the lady's voice had startled him and his right hand had gripped the hilt of his sword. The sword was tingling. It seemed to press out of its sheath into his hand. Hunger! The word was being repeated inside his head, but who was saying it? A black bowl appeared before his face. 'Take this!' said a sharp whispering voice. His left hand obeyed. He took the bowl and held it to his lips. It contained a dark black soup. A sweet drowsy steam rose from it into his nostrils. His head began to swim. He turned his face away from the bowl and saw Daire gulping the hot liquid. A black dribble was trickling down his chin. Then Daire began to fade as if Rónán was looking at him through a mist.

'You are hungry, so hungry. Drink it. Drink it,' urged the voice. He could resist no longer. He put the bowl to his mouth. The steam warmed his face and stung his eyes. The soup tasted very sweet and heavy, like hot, over-ripe bananas.

Something was pressing hard against his right hand. He thought of Tine. He tried to look at his sword but he could only see the inside of the black bowl. Black water was swirling before his eyes, roaring in his ears. He was sinking into darkness. A face came through the water: an old lined face with white hair. The face was talking. 'Hold on to your sword!' it said. 'Hold with both your hands!' He dropped the bowl and groped for Tine's sheath with his left hand. He couldn't see properly. Everything was wavy and blurred. He thought he could see a fire and a gown covered with eyes –

real eyes, bloodshot and blinking. The lady's face floated up to his. Her eyes were wild and staring and she was laughing. He heard his own voice saying 'She laughs too much'. Then his head grew too heavy and he fell over sideways into a deep dizzy blackness.

* * *

The thin cold moon was a slice of bone high above the dead grey trees. Rónán knew the mound was full of bones, years and years of bones. The bones were dreaming. They wanted to get out. They were pushing against the white stones. A large white boulder was moving. A skeleton hand squeezed out around it. Then another bony hand appeared and another. They rolled the boulder away from the side of the mound. Out of the dark tomb they came, a dreadful white army of the dead. They crept up the mound on all sides, slowly dancing among the moonlit trees. Rónán could hear their bones rattling as they danced and chanted, circling the granite altar.

> 'Beware, beware!
> She'll swallow your soul.
> Give us our souls.
> Beware, beware!'

They set their bony hands on the fire and held them up as burning torches. Then they turned to him with their hollow eyes and their long cold teeth chanting:

> 'Set us free from the pain,
> The long cold pain.
> Save us! Save us!
> Set us free! Set us free!'

Someone was trying to tug Rónán's sword from him but he held on with both his hands. Burning fingers of bone reached for his face. He could feel the heat as the flames neared his eyes. He heard himself scream . . . .

He was sitting upright with his eyes open. Sweat was pouring down his face and back. He could see no skeletons but he could still hear the bones rattling. A huge fire was roaring in front of him sending red and yellow tongues of flame leaping and licking into the air. Showers of glowing sparks soared into the dark circle of sky above the trees. A harsh rattling sound was coming from overhead. Red eyes glowed in pairs along the branches. The trees were alive with magpies!

Rónán looked around. Daire was no longer beside him but the black bowls still lay on the grass. In the darkness beyond the tree-trunks row upon row of yellow eyes peered wickedly at him. The mound was surrounded by wolves!

'I knew it was a trap! I knew it!' he cried, leaping up. But his head swam and his legs were weak and he stumbled to his knees. He closed his eyes for a moment, breathing heavily, trying to recover his strength. Then he heard a dreadful, blood-chilling scream.

'Don't, don't! You can't Niamh! It's me, Daire! Please, oh please!'

Horror twisted through Rónán's body at the terror in the voice. He struggled to his feet and drew Tine from its sheath, gripping the hilt with both hands. The blade flashed in the blazing firelight and strength flowed from it into his body. Holding the sword in front of him he ran around the fire towards the stone altar. What he saw there made him stop dead.

Daire was lying helpless on the altar. His hands and feet were firmly tied by cords that passed through metal rings at either end of the stone. Niamh was standing at the far side of the altar. Her face was pale and her eyes wild and staring as if she was sleep-walking through a dreadful nightmare. Her arms were stretched out over Daire's body and the fingers of both her hands were tightly gripped around the hilt of a long black knife. The blade of the knife was pointing at Daire's chest.

The lady was standing beside Niamh. Her face was filled with greedy delight. Her arms also were stretched out over Daire's body. She had no knife, but her eyes were fixed on the knife in Niamh's hands. The lady leaned over the altar. Niamh leaned forward as well. Slowly the lady raised her arms above her head. Niamh's arms moved at the same time, holding the deadly knife above her. The medallion swung out from her neck, shining with dazzling brilliance.

Rónán's legs were trembling. He thought he was going to faint. But Tine was glowing as if it was red hot and power was flowing from the blade into his arms. He raised it above his head and the sword hummed as it moved through the air.

'Now!' cried the lady. 'Kill! Kill!'

She jerked her arms swiftly down. Daire screamed, the wolves howled and the magpies chattered. Rónán, with a cry of horror, leaped forward and swung his sword at Niamh's neck. The blade left a circle of light in the air as it passed below Niamh's outstretched arms and sliced through the silver chain about her neck. The medallion spun above the altar for a moment, then it exploded in a shower of tiny blue flames.

Niamh felt a light tug at her neck and something falling away from her. Then she saw Daire's terrified face. Why was he tied to this rock? She was holding a dreadful knife above her head. Someone was screaming 'Kill him! Kill him!' Why had she to kill him? She looked to see who was screaming. There was a woman of extraordinary beauty beside her. The woman's arms were pointing at Daire's chest.

'Kill him!' she hissed. 'Kill him now!'

'No, no!' screamed Daire. 'In Manannán's name!'

'Kill!' screeched the woman.

For a second of dreadful agony, Niamh stood with the knife above her head. Then with all her strength she swung it down, driving the blade deeply into the woman's right arm. There was a moment of incredible silence. The woman looked at her arm with eyes full of horror and amazement. Then from deep in her throat there came a low animal growling. As the growling grew louder she began to change. The chestnut colour drained from her hair, leaving her grey and ragged. Deep wrinkles ran across the smooth skin of her face. Her white teeth grew into long yellow fangs. Her beautiful eyes became bloodshot, glowing red in the dark.

She grasped the handle of the knife in her left hand and wrenched it from her arm. As her dark blood dripped onto the altar, she threw back her head and uttered a dreadful shriek. Instantly a storm of cackling magpies whirled through the air. The yellow-eyed wolves charged howling across the grass. The fire swirled up into the sky showering the mound with burning embers. With an ear-splitting crack the stone altar fell apart flinging Daire to the ground. The circle of leafless trees raged and twisted, lashing the children with their long, grey arms. The mound spun madly and the children were flung through a dizzy confusion of fire and bones, howling wolves, savage birds and dreadful withering faces. One last shriek hurt their ears. There was a blinding flash of light, a clap of thunder, then all was darkness.

When the spinning stopped the children felt dizzy and confused and they could see nothing.

'Daire? Are you still there?' whispered Niamh.

'Yes,' Daire replied, 'but I can't see you.'

'I'm sitting on something prickly,' said Rónán.

'It's damp here,' said Daire as he stood up and took a few steps in the direction of the other voices. 'I think – '

They heard a splash.

'Damn!' cried Daire's voice. 'I've stepped into a pool of water. We must be in the middle of the bog.'

'We've got to keep together,' said Rónán. 'If we drift apart we won't be able to find each other again and we could fall into one of those deep pools and drown. You keep talking Niamh and we'll move towards your voice.'

They had to crawl very carefully on their hands and knees and they were soon soaking wet and covered with mud. They kept putting their hands into cold slimy messes that didn't smell very nice. Once Daire caught hold of something that wriggled in his hand. He flung it away with a shudder.

'Why is it so dark?' said Niamh. 'There was a moon and stars out earlier. Maybe *she* has thrown a blackness over everything so we can't escape. She might be out there watching us, waiting to – '

She stopped suddenly.

'What's wrong?' asked Rónán. 'Why did you stop?'

'You – you don't think she could have blinded us?' stammered Niamh.

There was a long moment of dreadful silence. Then Niamh and Daire heard the familiar sound of Rónán's sword sliding from its sheath and there in the darkness they saw Tine, glowing brightly quite near them.

'Oh well done Rónán!' cried Niamh in relief. 'Hold it up and we'll move towards you.'

Daire reached him first. Niamh wasn't far behind. Daire reached out, found her arm and guided her onto the clump of reeds where he was standing.

'Thank goodness we're together again,' panted Niamh. She suddenly threw her arms around him and burst into tears. Then all three of them wept.

'Take it easy,' whispered Daire. 'We're all right now.'

'I'm sorry,' sobbed Niamh. 'I'm sorry for everything. I just don't know why I did it.'

'Well I do,' replied Daire. 'You were under an enchantment. It wasn't really you that behaved like that.'

'But I was going to kill you!'

'Yes, but you didn't.'

'It was as much our fault as yours,' said Rónán. 'If we'd listened to you and stayed on the Green Road we wouldn't have met the lady and none of this would have happened.'

'What are we going to do now?' said Daire.

'We'll just have to wait here until morning and then try to find our way out of the bog,' replied Rónán.

They sat together on the clump of reeds and gazed into the darkness. It wasn't very comfortable but at least it was dry. Rónán laid Tine across his knees. The gold-red glow of the sword was a comfort to them in the long cold hours where every plop, splash and hiss made them imagine strange slippery creatures and unseen ghostly dangers.

Slowly the night passed. In spite of their anxiety they dozed uneasily and awoke each time with sudden jerks of fear, not knowing how long they had slept. At last, when they thought they could bear the waiting no longer, they felt a light breeze in their faces and far away on their left they saw the first pale light of dawn. The blackness around them grew thinner. After a while they could see the outline of hills against the soft pink sky. The light grew brighter. Veils of white mist drifted above the brown bogland. Then the tip of a brilliant sun sent a long golden ray of light across the countryside and every dewdrop on the bog sparkled like a diamond. The night was over.

Chapter 9: The Enchanted Forest

'Now all we have to do is find a way out of here and walk to Cahershee,' said Daire, with a grim smile.

The children stood up stiffly. They were cold and damp and very hungry. Rónán slid Tine back into its sheath.

'That's strange,' said Niamh. 'I can't see the mound.'

They looked about them. The sun was now fully risen. Far away to the south they could see the dark wooded hill from which they had set out the evening before. But Altán Amplach had vanished and so had the path by which the lady had led them through the bog.

'She must have taken it back to wherever she came from,' said Rónán. 'Come on. We'll have to find our own way out.'

They set off across the bog treading carefully on the soggy peat, leaping from one clump of reeds to another and often sinking to their ankles in mud and water. Their progress was maddeningly slow. Time and again they had to turn back and seek a new way through the maze of dark green pools. It was close to midday when at last they struggled onto the firm green slope of the hill above Cúl Glas.

They climbed the hill, walking through the dark pine wood and out once more onto the Green Road. Below them lay the bridge. All seemed quiet, but the memory of savage magpies and vicious wolves made them keep their hands on their swords as they descended towards the river.

Under the mossy stone arch of the bridge the water gurgled and splashed. Quickly the children crossed over. Then they climbed down to the river's edge where they gulped down the clear cold water and bathed their faces.

Feeling refreshed but still ravenously hungry, they faced the Green Road again. As they walked the sky cleared and the day grew warm. At first they talked about the adventures they had come through. Then they wondered about what lay ahead of them in Cahershee. But soon they were too hot and tired to talk, so they trudged in silence past woods and fields, over gentle hills and around the base of steep ones. They walked till the sun shone in their faces from the west and their legs were numb with tiredness.

At last, as they came to the top of a gentle rise, they saw the road ahead vanishing into a thick forest of oak, ash and birch that stretched as far as they could see.

'The Enchanted Forest!' breathed Niamh.

A great feeling of relief surged within them at the thought of being near the end of their journey, yet they also felt anxious about entering a place so full of unknown enchantments.

'No enemy can pass through the Enchanted Forest safely,' murmured Daire. 'That's what Foras said. Let's hope the trees know we're friends.'

Niamh led the way down the slope. Soon they were passing under graceful spreading branches. It was like walking into an enormous airy cathedral. Massive grey tree trunks, as tall as church spires, towered above them. The ceiling of young green leaves was so high up it was like a pale green sky. Between the widely spaced trees the forest floor was richly carpeted with grass. A bright green light streamed down from above and the whole forest glowed with a delightful clearness. Everything was perfectly still.

'It's magnificent!' whispered Daire, as the children stole across the grass. Niamh and Rónán did not reply, it seemed disrespectful to break the majestic silence of the trees. This indeed was the Land of Dreaming: a quiet airy place where your mind could wander. Surely it was impossible that such a beautiful woodland could be a threat to anyone.

They walked through the vast quietness, passing deeper and deeper into the forest. It was a long time before they realised that their path had vanished and they no longer knew which way to go. At the same moment they noticed that the silence had changed. It was now a whispering. Leafy voices ran from tree to tree, hurrying ahead of them, passing on the news of their arrival. The trees bowed and nodded, touching each other with their long feeling branches.

'I'm afraid we've awakened the enchantment,' murmured Rónán uneasily.

'My legs are growing very heavy,' whispered Niamh.

In fact all three of them had been finding it increasingly difficult to walk. It was as though their legs didn't want to leave the ground. Soon they were scarcely moving at all until finally they stopped altogether. They stood rooted to the ground like three small statues while the whispering grew louder and wilder.

The stronger the whispering grew, the heavier the children felt, till to their horror, they began to sink into the earth. In vain they cried out and struggled to free themselves. Slowly, and steadily their legs entered the ground till they were buried up to their waists. Then the whispering grew calmer and the sinking stopped. They wriggled and twisted and groaned but the soil closed tightly around them, holding them fast.

'What happens now?' gasped Rónán.

His question was answered by a new sound. A loud pounding shook the earth. Something large and heavy was moving towards them. They tried to draw their swords but only Rónán succeeded. The other weapons remained trapped in the earth.

The pounding grew louder still. They could feel the vibrations along the ground.

'Look! Oh look!' cried Niamh, pointing to their left.

Galloping at full speed towards them they saw Gasta, Taca and Cróga. Gasta came directly to Niamh and stretched out his handsome chestnut face to her. She reached up her hands to him, stroking his head and kissing him delightedly.

A rush of whispering ran across the leafy forest ceiling. Gasta raised his head and neighed loudly. Taca and Cróga stamped the ground impatiently with their strong hind legs. The whispering died away and the children felt the grip of the earth loosen around their waists. Before long they were able to scramble out onto the solid forest floor and embrace their rescuers with great joy.

Soon they were riding swiftly through the forest. The horses knew exactly where to go so the children made no attempt to control them. They had been riding for almost fifteen minutes when they saw a great thickness of trees ahead of them. As they drew nearer to it, they realised they were approaching a wall of living tree-trunks with not enough space between them for even a bird to pass through. But the horses kept up their steady gallop. In vain the children pulled on the reins. Gasta, Taca and Cróga could not be stopped. A second before they struck the wall the children shut their eyes and braced themselves for the bone-crushing collision, but none came. The horses moved steadily onwards. Opening their eyes the children saw grey trees passing like ghosts through the horses and their own bodies. After a time the ghost trees vanished and they were riding through the bright green forest again.

'Good old Gasta,' whispered Niamh. 'I should have trusted you.'

It wasn't long before her trust was tried again, for now they were heading towards a blackness. As they approached it the air grew chilly, but the horses sped on as if they could not see the danger. Suddenly they were swallowed up in a darkness so deep that they could see neither trees nor ground nor the horses beneath them.

'We might as well be galloping through a black sky!' called Rónán as he clung tightly to Cróga. Now the fears and frights began. Strange twisted faces with wild hair and staring eyes loomed out of the darkness and flew along beside them. Long fingers reached out to feel their hair and touch their necks. Chilly breath blew on their skin while echoing voices whispered and laughed.

Niamh kept repeating, 'Good old Gasta. Good old Gasta,' for her heart was beating wildly with fright. It seemed a long time before the phantoms faded and they at last saw a greyness ahead. They began to see the outline of trees. The greyness changed to pale yellow, then green and suddenly they were careering through the delightful evening forest once more.

Gradually the horses slowed down. Overhead, patches of blue sky could be seen between the leaves. Splashes of light dappled the forest floor and bluebells covered the ground like a perfumed mist. Further off beyond the trees the children could see a great silvery brightness. At last they came out of the forest onto a wide green lawn that slanted gently down to an enormous shining lake. In the middle of the lake stood the wonderful city of Cahershee.

Niamh, Daire and Rónán sat very quietly and gazed in wonder. Under the golden light of the evening sun the white walls of Cahershee rose high out of the brimming lake. Beyond the walls polished towers and domes mirrored the brightness of the sky. All around and above the city the air glistened and twinkled with an unearthly light and the lake shimmered with rippling reflections of the gleaming walls. Directly in front of them stood a magnificent golden gate and from towers on either side of this, pennants of blue and gold fluttered gently.

Silently the children dismounted and walked across the grass to the edge of the lake. As they approached the water they saw a movement on the top of the towers. Sentries appeared along the battlements. The children stood close together, suddenly feeling very small and rather lonely.

'Won't they be surprised to see us!' murmured Rónán.

'I hope they aren't expecting anything spectacular,' added Niamh. 'Just look at the state of us.'

They looked at each other. They were covered with mud and dried blood. Their faces were pale from hunger and exhaustion and their clothes were in rags.

'I wish Glasán was here,' sighed Daire.

Suddenly horns and trumpets gleamed along the walls and a proud fanfare echoed out across the water. At the same moment the lake began to swirl and foam. From below the gurgling water a paved roadway emerged which soon ran dry. When the road was in place the fanfare stopped.

'I think we're meant to walk across,' said Daire, nervously. He led the way and Niamh and Rónán joined him on either side. The horses followed behind them.

'I suppose this road could sink as easily as it came up,' muttered Rónán.

'We'll just have to trust them,' said Niamh.

As they approached Cahershee the great gates began to open, sliding away to left and right. Beyond the gateway they saw a courtyard bounded on three sides by high walls. Directly in front of them there was a tall rounded archway leading into the city. Crowds of people were streaming through the arch into the courtyard. They did not rush or jostle each other but moved with a steady sureness.

Wide stone steps led up from the lake to the paved area before the gateway. Into this area strode two lines of men in short blue tunics. Each of them carried a long yellow staff. They formed a guard to left and right. As soon as the guard was in place the fanfare sounded again and all movement in the courtyard ceased.

The children climbed the steps, then they halted, unsure what to do next. Two tall figures in white robes bordered with gold approached them from the gateway. One was a lady with long golden hair. Her face shone with strength and beauty. The other was a man with white hair and beard, though his face was not old. The eyes of these people were kind, but they had a searching, testing look that made the children feel they were in the presence of great intelligence and understanding. The man glanced at the lady. She nodded. Then he turned to the children and spoke.

'Have I the honour of speaking to the Children of Giltspur?'

Daire, who was standing slightly in front of Niamh and Rónán, suddenly knew it was his task to answer for the others. Up to this, he had no idea what he would say to these extraordinary people. But the name Giltspur called up the memory of brave battles fought against evil enemies. He recalled the friendship of Glasán. He felt once more the power of Manannán Mac Lir. He straightened his tired body to its full height, and said in a strong voice, 'I am Daire. This is my sister Niamh and my cousin Rónán. We are the children Foras was sent to find. We have come here at his request from the slopes of Giltspur.'

A murmur ran through the crowd in the courtyard at this speech. The tall man bowed to the children. Then he turned to his companion. She looked kindly at Daire and said, 'You are welcome to Cahershee. We have awaited your coming with anxious hope.' She looked from Daire to Niamh and then to Rónán. 'We can feel great courage beating in your hearts, but you also bear a burden of untold sorrows. Our brother Foras has not returned with you.'

'We have suffered much on our journey,' replied Daire. 'Foras spent his strength for our protection. He aged and – '

Suddenly Niamh uttered a long groaning sound and before anyone realised what was happening, her legs bent below her and she crumpled to the ground. Instantly attendants hurried to her.

'I beg your pardon!' cried the white-haired man. 'We have kept you talking on the steps of our city without thought for your weariness or the sufferings of your journey. Come, you shall rest and be refreshed. There will be time enough for talk later.'

Niamh was placed on a stretcher and covered with a rug.

On a signal from the man, the guard lined up on either side of them. A trumpet sounded and the crowd in the courtyard parted. As they moved through the gateway the people bowed respectfully.

In this way they entered Cahershee.

Chapter 10: Cahershee

NIAMH AWOKE WITH A DELIGHTFUL feeling of refreshment. Early morning sunlight was slanting through a large open window on her left. White lace curtains billowed in the soft breeze and a delicious scent of flowers drifted in from outside. She could hear the snip-snip of a garden shears. Someone spoke and the gardener answered cheerfully. Then the snip-snip began again.

The bed in which she lay was covered with a white bedspread and there was a huge white pillow under her head. The walls of the room were white, the gently arched ceiling a very pale blue, like a summer sky.

The night before was only a vague memory. She recalled being carried on something soft along corridors among many people. Then she had been lifted onto a bed in a softly lit room. A cup had been set to her lips and a warm liquid had filled her mouth and slipped down her throat. She had felt relaxed and closed her eyes. Now it was morning.

A door softly opened in the wall on her right. A girl came in. She had blue eyes and golden hair drawn back from her face to form a pony-tail held by a golden ring. She was taller than Niamh and she wore a white tunic gathered at the waist by a blue cord. The girl smiled.

'Good morning Niamh,' she said. 'Did you sleep well?'

'Very well, thank you,' replied Niamh. 'Where am I?'

'You are in the house of my parents, Córtas and Órga. It was they who greeted you at the gates of Cahershee last night. My name is Amra. Would you like some breakfast?'

'Yes please!' Niamh answered hungrily.

The girl smiled at Niamh's enthusiasm. She bowed politely and quietly left the room. Niamh pushed herself up in the bed. She had just realised that she had not eaten properly since their picnic in the orchard two days before. Now as she sat in this comfortable quiet place, all the horrors and dangers of those days seemed like a bad dream from which she had just awakened.

Amra returned carrying a tray of breakfast. She set it on a table beside the bed and handed Niamh a bowl of warm water into which a fragrant oil had been sprinkled. When Niamh had washed her hands Amra gave her a towel.

'Where are Daire and Rónán?' Niamh asked.

'They have rooms nearby,' replied Amra. 'I have already brought them their breakfast.'

Amra left Niamh to enjoy the meal at her ease. The tray was generously laden. Pears, plums, cherries and grapes were piled high in a silver bowl. There was a dish of roasted grain, a jug of the creamiest milk, a pot of honey that smelt like a garden of daffodils, crisp rolls of bread still hot from the ovens, butter and jam with whole strawberries in it.

Niamh ate well and when she was fully satisfied she lay back and examined the room more carefully. There was another door just opposite the end of her bed. On either side of this the wall was adorned with polished copper images of waves and fish and a tall man in a chariot riding over the sea, with birds flying above him. She knew this must be Mannanán Mac Lir. Seeing his image there made her feel as if she had safely returned to a place where she belonged.

She heard a gentle knock on the door and Amra entered.

'Did you have enough to eat?' she asked.

'Oh yes, thank you,' replied Niamh. 'It was lovely.'

Amra took the tray. 'If you'd like to bathe, the bathroom is through there,' she said, pointing to the door at the end of the bed.

'Thank you,' said Niamh, suddenly remembering how ragged and soiled her clothes were. 'I really look awful.'

'Don't worry,' smiled Amra. 'There are fresh garments there too. Once you are ready I shall take you to see the city.'

The bathroom was large and round. The floor and walls were tiled in blue and green. Sunlight filtered down through a high ceiling of frosted glass. The bath was a circular pool sunk in the floor with steps leading down into it.

'It's really a small swimming-pool,' thought Niamh as she shed her clothes and stepped into the warm comfort of the water that continually bubbled up from below. At the edge of the pool there was a glass shelf with bottles of bath-oils and

liquid soaps. Niamh soaped herself well, then she let herself
float luxuriously, soaking her hair, rinsing away all the grime
of her long difficult journey.

She dried herself with huge soft towels that hung on a warm
rail by the wall and there also she found fresh clothing,
including a white tunic embroidered about the neck, sleeves
and hem with flowers of purple, green and blue. She admired
herself in the huge mirror by the door and laughed happily at
her own prettiness.

Amra was waiting for her and she brought her out into a
wide hallway. Sunlight poured in through the open doorway.
On the steps outside, Daire and Rónán were admiring the
view of the city. Niamh was surprised when she saw them, for
they were both dressed in green tunics gathered at the waist
by leather belts on which hung short daggers in cleverly
decorated sheaths. Rónán still wore Tine at his side. They
looked like young warriors from an ancient Celtic tale.

'If I hear any remarks about skirts or legs, I'll drop you in the
nearest fountain,' joked Rónán.

'Don't worry,' replied Niamh. 'You look fine – really.'

'So do you,' Daire said. 'Are you all right now?'

'I feel great,' said Niamh and she meant it.

Two young men in the blue tunics of the Guard arrived at
the bottom of the steps. They bowed respectfully and the taller
one said, 'Greetings to the children of Giltspur from the High
Council of Danann. The President of the Council requests you
to honour the People of Danann by attending a special
meeting at the Great Hall at noon today.'

'We shall be happy to come,' replied Niamh.

'The President requests that you accept Amra, daughter of
Córtas as your guide to the Great Hall,' added the messenger.

'We gladly accept,' said Daire.

'We shall bring news of your acceptance to the President,'
replied the messenger. The young men bowed again and left.

'The People of Danann consider it a great honour to be
invited to join a meeting of the High Council,' said Amra.

'What will we have to do?' asked Rónán.

'You will probably be asked about your journey here,'
replied Amra, 'and the Council will want to consider what to
do next. I shall show you the way and you can see the city as
we go.'

She led them down the steps and through the streets of

Cahershee. Most of the houses were white-walled and roofed with red tiles though the main public buildings were of skilfully cut granite and had roofs of polished copper. All had window-boxes and hanging baskets of red, blue and yellow flowers that nodded in the soft morning breeze.

The children passed under archways and across delightful little bridges above canals of perfectly clear water where brightly-coloured fish flickered and glided. Wide tree-lined streets opened onto wider squares where orchards bloomed and fountains made tinkling rainbows in the morning sunlight.

Everywhere they met people going calmly about their business and everyone greeted them with a smile and a bow in the quiet manner of the Danann.

'They look remarkably contented for a people under threat from such dreadful enemies,' remarked Rónán.

'The people of Danann never panic,' explained Amra. 'We know the threat and have set our minds on overcoming our enemies. While Cahershee is protected by the High Council we remain safe. Now that news of your arrival has spread through the city, everyone feels more sure of victory.'

Daire wished he could feel as confident of success as Amra seemed to be, though he thought it better not to speak of his fears. But Amra suddenly turned to him and said, 'Of course we realise that victory is not certain. But we know you have been to Manannán's country and have been granted the gift of the golden apples. Only those who have greatness of spirit are entrusted with that gift. That is why we are confident.'

Daire looked at Amra's eager face. Her bright blue eyes were looking straight into his. 'You knew what I was think-ing!' he said. 'Can *all* the Danann read people's minds?'

Amra laughed. 'I just sensed the way you were feeling. I didn't really read your mind. Only the greatest masters of thought can do that and it takes years of practice. Imbas, the President of the High Council, can read thoughts at a distance and speak to you with his mind.'

'Foras did that when he rescued me,' added Rónán, quietly.

'Glasán used to do it too,' murmured Niamh.

'They were both important members of the High Council,' said Amra sadly.

They passed along a stately street of libraries and art galleries. Amra showed them the Concert Hall and a building she called the Hall of Celebrations. Then they came to a bridge above a wide canal. Beyond the bridge their pathway turned gently through a pleasant green parkland towards a wood.

'We are almost at the centre of Cahershee,' said Amra. 'The Great Hall is within the wood.'

'What a wonderful idea!' said Daire, as they walked below the trees. 'A real natural wood in the middle of a city.'

Sunlight dappled the ground, birds fluttered busily among the hazel trees and holly bushes and the warm air was filled with wood scents.

After a short while they came out of the trees onto a green lawn above a wide shining lake.

'That is the Great Hall,' said Amra.

On an island in the centre of the lake stood a tall round building, its white stone walls glistening in the sunlight. The high polished dome was a mirror where small clouds drifted across the blue curve of the sky. All the lake shimmered with the moving reflections of the beautiful building and the air above it sparkled. A wide stone bridge spanned the lake to the enormous closed doors of the Hall. The children stood silent for a moment.

'This is almost like coming out of the Enchanted Forest and seeing Cahershee for the first time,' said Niamh.

'It is the city within the city,' replied Amra, 'the heart of Cahershee.'

'What exactly does the Council do to protect the people?' asked Rónán.

'They gather here early every morning and stay in session until noon. All the greatest masters of thought from Shee Clettig and Shee Nenta as well as Cahershee are gathered there now. Every member directs their power to thinking one thought perfectly clearly – preventing the ageing of the people of Cahershee. The combined power of the Council reaches out to everyone in the city, awakening each person's strength to resist the enemy.'

'Do you mean that they think that one thought for hours on end?' asked Daire.

'Yes. Their minds never wander. That is why they are so powerful.'

Just then they became aware of a soft musical sound coming from the building. It was as if a great choir had begun to sing a single chord of perfect harmony. It slowly grew stronger and more beautiful, filling the children with a feeling of delight and refreshment. As it reached its climax, the massive doors of the Hall began to open inwards.

'The session is over,' said Amra, leading them down to the bridge. 'They will send for you now.'

A company of the Blue Guard had emerged from the Hall and lined up on either side of the doorway. Already the two messengers the children had spoken to that morning were crossing the bridge towards them.

'I must leave you now,' said Amra. 'Do not be nervous. The members of the High Council hold you in great honour.'

'Thank you,' said Niamh, as Amra bowed and turned back towards the wood.

The messengers escorted the children across the bridge to the great bronze doors. Here they were received by Córtas and Órga who were delighted to see that Niamh was fully recovered. Then, with the Blue Guard on either side of them, they passed through the massive doorway.

They walked along a high well-lit passage where the walls were covered with wonderful carvings of birds, flowers and forest animals. To left and right wide archways led into many interesting rooms. There were rooms full of maps and pictures, libraries with books from floor to ceiling, rooms that looked like chemists shops and laboratories full of scientific instruments.

Soon they ascended a broad marble stairway until they came to high golden doors that swung open before them. The Blue Guard halted on either side as the children entered the chamber of the High Council of Danann.

It was like stepping onto the stage of a huge circular theatre. Row on row of white-robed members of the High Council sat, each one slightly higher than the other so that they all had a clear view of where the President was sitting at a round table of polished oak. Sunlight shone from the high dome into every corner of the room. The dome was supported by tall marble pillars and the curving walls glistened with restless silver.

As Niamh, Daire and Rónán crossed the floor, the thousand men and women of the High Council rose respectfully and a rustle of expectation ran through the assembly. The President came forward to greet them. He was a tall man with white hair and beard and startlingly bushy eyebrows. His face was deeply lined but his eyes were as bright and sharp as an eagle's. The children could feel energy radiating from him. He bowed, smiling kindly, and said, 'I am Imbas, President of the High Council. You are most welcome.' He guided them to the table where three chairs, like small thrones of carved oak, had been placed for them. He sat facing them, with Órga on his right and Córtas on his left. When everyone in the Hall was settled quietly, Imbas spoke again.

'The High Council of Danann thanks you for passing between the worlds and placing yourselves in great danger for our sake. We now request that you relate to us all that has taken place from the time of your first encounter with our brother Foras.'

A great silence fell on the Hall. Imbas's eyes looked from Daire to Rónán and then came to rest on Niamh. She knew she would have to speak first. She stood up, took a deep breath and began.

As she spoke she felt the complete attention of every member of the Council reaching out to her mind. Their intense desire to understand what she said made her memory sharp and brought words to her lips. As she spoke of the seaweed at Greystones, she felt the minds of the Council leap in understanding that the evil in Tír Danann had passed between the worlds. She felt a ripple of disapproval of the way they had been drawn into Shee Alman. A mental wave of applause reached her when she related how they had agreed to stay and help the People of Danann.

Then she felt that Rónán needed to speak. She turned to him and he knew she understood what he wanted to do. He rose to his feet as Niamh sat down.

'I would have to say, that at that time I thought it unwise to attempt to rescue you,' Rónán confessed. He felt the calm minds of the Council understanding why he had argued against staying. He told of their ride to the waterfall and described the attack by the Fir Bolg in which he had been driven into the river. The anger of the Council reached him without a word being spoken. As he described how Foras had rescued him, the Great Hall grew tense, as if they already knew what must come next. Rónán stopped. How could he tell them that Foras had died? He looked around at the thousand intense faces gazing at him and his courage failed him.

'Speak on,' urged the soft voice of Imbas. 'It is important

that we hear every detail.'

Rónán felt strength reaching out to him, willing him to continue. He told how Foras had aged and died. A surge of deep sorrow swept over him as he spoke, but as he told how Foras's body had marvellously vanished the sorrow ebbed away and a feeling of fierce joy and confidence filled the Great Hall.

'He entrusted his sword to me before he died,' continued Rónán and he stepped forward and presented the sheathed sword to Imbas, who accepted it gravely. 'I understand now that he gave his life to save me.'

'Understanding that will continue to be a great strength to you,' said Imbas.

Rónán sat down.

It was Daire's turn to speak. He told of their ride to the strange house within the walled garden and how the lady had come to them in the orchard. As he described her beauty and the way she had spoken to them, a rustle of unease ran through the Council. Everyone straightened in their seats and glanced at each other. When he told them how the lady had hung the medallion about Niamh's neck, there was a gasp of amazement. Imbas's eyes flashed and he gazed at Niamh as if he wanted to search her soul.

'Did you know who this lady was?' he asked.

'No,' replied Daire. 'We thought at the time that she might be one of the People of Danann.'

Imbas nodded. Then Daire told of the attack by the magpies, the ambush by the wolves and how the lady had reappeared and saved them. The Council were looking at him with great curiosity, as if he had said something beyond their ability to believe. When he began to describe their journey to Altán Amplach and the lighting of the fire by the stone altar, the tension in the Hall became so intense that his voice trembled. He stumbled over his words and at last he was unable to continue.

Niamh had been dreading this moment. With every word that Daire had spoken her horror and shame had increased. She knew what she had to do.

Chapter 11: The Lir-Stone

'I THINK THAT I SHALL HAVE TO tell this part of the story,' Niamh said, as she rose and faced the thousand members of the High Council. Everyone was looking at her as if they could scarcely believe that she was really there at all.

Forcing herself to speak the truth, Niamh told how, when the lady had drugged both Daire and Rónán, she had helped to tie her brother to the stone altar and how she had almost murdered him at the lady's command. The silence into which her words fell was almost unbearable. She could not understand the feelings flowing to her from the Council. But when she described how she had driven the knife into the lady's arm, there was uproar in the Hall. Everyone began talking at once and such a storm of feelings swirled around her that Niamh was overcome by the confusion and tears filled her eyes. Realising her need for support, Daire and Rónán rose from their seats and stood beside her.

Imbas raised his hand and silenced the Council. Then he turned to Niamh. 'How do you feel now about what you did?' he asked.

Niamh looked for a moment into Imbas's searching eyes and saw calmness and kindness there. She took a deep breath.

'I can offer no excuse for the way I behaved,' she said. 'The lady found the evil hidden in me and used it against me. I never realised before that I could become such an evil person.

I feel ashamed and shocked at myself.'

In the immense silence of the Hall, all eyes were on Niamh, but she knew they were not blaming her.

'Now I understand why Manannán chose you,' declared Imbas. 'You have understood the Morrigan's power exactly.'

'The Morrigan?' gasped Niamh.

'Yes. The witch of battle slaughter. She uses many disguises. The medallion she placed upon you is called the Balor Eye. It draws together every evil urge in the person who wears it. The longer it is worn the more powerful it becomes, so that its victim cannot tell evil from good. But the Balor Eye was only part of the enchantment. Even with the Eye destroyed, all the power of evil in you was still working. You resisted it at your moment of greatest weakness. You overcame not only the Morrigan but yourself. This is the true magic – the power within you to resist evil and do good.'

Then he turned to Daire. 'Have you forgiven your sister?'

'I never really blamed her,' replied Daire. 'We were all deceived by the lady's enchantment and I argued in favour of trusting her as much as Niamh. Rónán tried to warn me but I didn't believe him.'

Imbas looked at Rónán. 'Do you still blame your companions?'

'Not now,' answered Rónán. 'I was never convinced by the lady but I felt her power working in me. It was the memory of Foras's death and the strength of his sword that saved me, not any goodness in myself.'

'That was honestly spoken,' said Imbas. Then he turned to Niamh. 'What happened after you stabbed her?'

Niamh described the screams and confusion that followed her attack on the Morrigan, how they had survived the night in the darkness of the bog and how Gasta, Taca and Cróga had brought them safely through the Enchanted Forest to Cahershee.

'Altán Amplach does not exist in Tír Danann,' said Imbas. 'While you were there you were in the Morrigan's country. The blow you dealt her and especially your strength in resisting her will have weakened her power and given us more time to act. Had you sacrificed your brother she would have sucked the life from both of you, feeding on your youthful energies. That is why she rescued you from the wolves. She needed you to give her the gift of the dark side of yourself. Thankfully the goodness in you was deeper and stronger than she realised.'

Imbas paused then, lost in thought. Then he looked at each of the children in turn and said, 'You have suffered much on your journey here. Now that you realise the dangerous forces of evil that will resist you, are you still willing to travel to the Western Sea and seek the water from the Well of Youth on Inis Óg?'

'I am willing, for the sake of all your people,' declared Niamh 'but especially in the hope of finding my dear friend Glasán. Can you tell if he is still alive?'

The High Council grew very quiet again. Niamh could feel her sadness shared by everyone in the Great Hall. Imbas sat with his eyes closed for so long that Niamh thought he was not going to reply to her at all. When at last he opened his eyes he regarded her with a steady, serious face.

'There is something strange there,' he said softly. 'Neither life nor death. All I can say is that I have not felt his passing from Tír Danann. He may yet live, but how I do not know. Your feelings for him are deep and true. If he lives I am sure you will find him.'

'Thank you,' whispered Niamh.

'I am willing to go as well,' said Daire.

'So am I,' added Rónán, 'but I am worried about our chances of success. People more powerful than us have failed to overcome the seaweed. What more can we do when we reach the Western Sea?'

'That is a reasonable question,' replied Imbas. He signalled with his hand and two members of the Council stepped forward. On the table beside Tine they placed two sheathed swords, a small phial of bright red liquid and a rolled-up map of finest calfskin.

'This phial,' said Imbas, holding up the small bottle, 'contains a liquid we have named Folnamara. It is made from the juice of many herbs, roots and berries. A full month's enchantment by the High Council has also been placed in it. We believe it will cause the seaweed to shrivel away. The amount in this bottle will be enough to clear all the sea between the coast and Inis Óg.'

He handed the bottle to Daire. 'Take great care of it. All our lives may depend on that liquid.'

Then he lifted the swords. 'It is two thousand years since the people of Danann were last at war. We have not invented

new weapons of destruction as men have done in your world.
Instead we have developed the power of our minds. Some of
this power we have placed in these ancient weapons. Since
Foras has entrusted Tine to Rónán we think it right that he
should keep that sword. These others – Solas and Lasair – we
now give to Niamh and Daire. All three were used at the Battle
of Shee Alman. They will serve you well.'

Then Imbas unrolled the map. To the children's surprise, it
was as alive as the wall-maps of Shee Alman. They could see
Tír Danann from Cahershee to the Western Sea, as if they
were flying above it on a sunny day. Far below them, Cahershee glistened white in its dark blue lake from which An
Bradán flowed on to the south. Westwards the green
countryside rose gradually towards the massive heights of the
Ardán Mountains where long lakes peeped out from deep
shadowy valleys. Beyond the mountains the sea surged green
and glistening all along the rocky coast.

'That is Inis Óg,' said Imbas, pointing to a small bright
island surrounded by white-capped waves. 'The map shows
only what was known when our geographers drew it. It does
not show what is happening there now. The shortest route is
through Glen Scál and from there down to the coast. There is
another more difficult way across the mountains. It is too
steep for horses and the path is dangerous from rock falls and
hidden enemies. That way is better avoided.'

'Besides the Fir Bolg and the Morrigan, who are we likely to
meet on the way?' asked Daire.

'Since we have been confined to Cahershee many beings of
darkness may have crept into Tír Danann who otherwise
would not dare to cross our borders. As the Morrigan has
already shown herself, her sons Scarnán and Lofach may well
be about, though in what shape we cannot tell. Near the coast
the Giants of Formor may come ashore. Enchenn, the bird-
headed one, has been seen in the forests below Ardán. There
may be others.'

'That lot will be quite enough,' murmured Niamh with a
shudder.

'By the President's leave!' called a clear voice. Everyone
looked up. A strong-bodied young-faced member of the
Council had risen in his place.

'What is it, Donnán?' asked Imbas.

'I cannot see how we can, in all honour, send these children to face such dangers while we sit safely in Cahershee,' declared Donnán. 'I, for one, am willing to accompany them into whatever perils they may have to face.'

Murmurs of agreement arose from some parts of the Hall.

'By crossing between the worlds,' replied Imbas, 'these children have moved outside of Time. They will not age in Tír Danann. But for you, such a journey would mean rapid ageing and certain death.'

'I am willing to face that,' said Donnán.

'That is a courageous offer,' replied Imbas, 'but I cannot accept it. You all know how difficult it has been to maintain the protection of Cahershee since Glasán and Foras left. If even one of you leaves, the whole People of Danann will begin to age, the High Council's power will weaken further, our enemies will overrun Tír Danann and even these brave children will be swept away by the disaster.'

Donnán sat down again looking unhappy. There was a feeling of great uneasiness in the Hall. Órga caught Imbas's eye. He nodded to her and she rose gracefully to her feet. A respectful hush descended on the Council.

'Niamh, Daire and Rónán have come through great dangers to help us,' she said in a calm clear voice. 'The fate of Tír Danann depends on the success of their journey. As none of us can go with them, I propose that we give them the Lir-Stone.'

A loud gasp of astonishment greeted her words and everyone began talking at once. Órga sat down. Imbas waited calmly, allowing the Council to talk.

Rónán turned to Niamh. 'Whatever this Lir-Stone is,' he whispered, 'it must be very important.'

The air fairly crackled with feelings of excitement and anxiety. Snatches of conversation drifted down to the children . . . Our greatest treasure . . . It's only right . . . If the enemy capture it . . . the Balor Eye . . . They bear the mark of Manannán . . . never before . . . .

Gradually the voices quietened. 'Level your minds to our purpose,' called Imbas. The High Council sat in perfect stillness with their eyes closed. While the children could not understand the thoughts that were swirling around them, they could feel them in their own minds, like a tangled ball of wool that was steadily unravelling. Gradually a feeling of great calmness and certainty grew within them. When the

Council opened their eyes, the Great Hall seemed brighter as if a cloud had passed, allowing the sunlight to stream down from the dome high above them.

'It is decided then,' said Imbas, rising with Córtas and Órga. 'Please come with us.'

He led the way across the Great Hall to an archway covered with a curtain of glistening beads that parted of its own accord to allow them to pass through. Beyond the curtain a flight of steps descended into the very heart of the earth. The bare rock walls were hung with masks of silver, copper and bronze that lit up as they approached and grew dark again as they passed on. Each mask had a different expression: incredible delight, unbearable sorrow, fierce anger, great unselfish love. It seemed as if all the feelings that had ever been known in Tír Danann were shown there.

At last they came to a level floor before a wall of solid black rock. Two huge golden masks hung together on the wall. They showed faces full of frowning strength that stared a challenge at everyone who approached them. Niamh felt quite sure that they would do something dreadful to anyone who had no right to be there.

Imbas stepped forward and called out in a voice of piercing authority, 'Doras slán idir dhá aghaidh!'

For a moment nothing happened. Then the children heard a deep rumbling sound. The ground trembled beneath their feet. The wall of solid rock split between the masks and slowly moved apart.

Through the widening gap they saw an immense dimly-lit cavern. Wonderful blue-green pillars had been carved from the rock all around the rim of the hall.

Imbas led the children forward, pausing between two of the pillars while the rest of the High Council filed in to left and right forming a complete circle. The floor of the cavern was inlaid with two circles of gold between which were strange magical signs and images of fantastic animals. Lines of gold ran out from the middle of the circle like the rays of the sun. At the very centre there was a low pillar with a wide flat top and on this rested a beautiful golden box encrusted with precious stones of red, green and blue. The box shone with a light of its own and the energy that flooded from it tingled and crackled in the air of the cavern.

When everyone was in their place, Imbas raised his head

and sang out a long rich note. Everyone began to chant in a deep harmony that throbbed with power and though the children could not understand the words, they felt they knew the meaning deep inside them. This was the place of deepest enchantment in Cahershee. Anyone who had entered this room without right would not have been able to cross the enchanted floor in safety. As the chant rose and fell, Niamh, Daire and Rónán felt as if they were floating on waves of sound.

The chant rose higher, growing faster and more urgent. A door in the golden box began to slide open and a beautiful white light, tinged with rainbow rays, poured out into the cavern, covering the ceiling, pillars and floor with glistening liquid colours. The beauty of it filled the children with a thrill of great joy and as the chant of the High Council echoed triumphantly, Niamh, Daire and Rónán realised that they too were singing, a song that seemed to flow from inside their very hearts and they knew that that song had always been in them, waiting to be sung out with full joyful voice.

At last, with a long magnificent chord, the song ended.

Imbas turned to the children. 'Come with me,' he said in a low voice.

They followed him to the centre of the room. Every nerve in their bodies was tingling with excitement. He reached into the golden box. When he drew out his hands it was as if he was holding a living star, for rays of light shone through his fingers and danced on the children's faces and hair.

Imbas smiled with fierce gladness and holding his arms on high he cried, 'Behold, oh Lords of Danann, how the Lir-Stone shines its approval of what we do this day!'

Then he lowered his hands and opening his fingers he held the Lir-Stone towards the children so they could see it. They saw an oval-shaped crystal of light hung on a golden chain. It was almost as large as Imbas's hand. Its brightness did not dazzle their eyes but flowed into their bodies filling them with delight. As they gazed into the crystal's depths it began to change. Living mists swirled inside it, now glowing white, now fiery red, clearing to show the vivid blue of a summer sky and once again glowing white and mysterious.

'This is the Lir-Stone,' said Imbas. 'It was given to us by Manannán Mac Lir on the day he placed the Snowfields between Tír Danann and Tír Bolg.'

'It's so beautiful,' whispered Niamh, her eyes sparkling in the wonderful light.

'What does it do?' asked Rónán.

'It does whatever Manannán wants it to do,' Imbas replied. 'Its powers cannot be explained. It may warn you against enemies, drive off attackers, overcome evil enchantments. It may tell if Manannán is nearby. It is very dangerous to carry it if you are set on doing evil. If you are of good will it can raise your spirits and fill you with courage. It is our greatest treasure and responsibility. It must never fall into the hands of our enemies.'

As Imbas was speaking, the brilliant rays had quietened to a steady glow. The mists in the stone began to clear and the children saw a flock of white birds flying through a gentle rain of pink and white apple-blossom on a green hill above a shining sea.

'Oh!' cried Niamh, as a great longing surged up inside her. 'It's Manannán's country!'

The scene grew blurred as the mists swirled again. When Niamh looked up she saw Imbas gazing at her with a look of great respect in his eyes.

'That country is shown only to the chosen ones,' he said. 'In your moments of greatest darkness it will be a comfort to you.'

Órga stepped forward. From her pocket she took a purse of golden thread and gave it to Imbas. He placed the Lir-Stone in the purse and pulled the string tight.

'The one who wears this, wears courage and goodness that will not fail,' said Imbas. 'Which of you will bear it?'

The three children gazed for a moment at the golden purse. Each one longed to have it. Then Daire said, 'Niamh has endured the Balor Eye and overcome its evil power. She should be the one to wear the Lir-Stone.'

'I agree with that,' added Rónán.

'That was nobly spoken,' declared Imbas. Then he looked at Niamh and said, 'Do you accept this gift and the responsibility that goes with it?'

'I do,' replied Niamh, with a thrill of both fear and joy.

Imbas leaned forward and hung the Lir-Stone about her neck. Niamh was surprised by the weight of it and for a moment she doubted if she could bear the burden of carrying it through all the adventures that lay before her. Then she felt a sudden surge of happiness breaking over her like a wave from the sea and as the thrill of it ebbed away she noticed that the Lir-Stone had grown lighter and a great calmness had settled on her mind.

Suddenly everyone began singing again, a song of strength and hope. Niamh, Daire and Rónán joined in the song.

* * *

A great feast was held in honour of the children that evening. All the People of Danann dressed themselves in multicoloured tunics and cloaks and wore their most beautiful jewellery. They sang, danced and feasted in the Hall of Celebration and the streets around it. There was delicious food and delightful drink. They took up flutes, harps and pipes and played tunes as happy as daffodils nodding below the trees of springtime, as sprightly as scampering squirrels in a nut-filled autumn, as clear and lonely as sparkling snow on the Plain of Danann beneath the winter stars.

The beauty of the music brought Niamh and Daire back to the May evening below Giltspur Wood when they had first seen Glasán in the Scarecrow Field and he had played magic music on Niamh's tin whistle.

'You'll never forget Glasán's music,' murmured Rónán to himself.

'Oh yes,' sighed Niamh. Then she suddenly sat upright and stared at Rónán. Daire quickly put down his goblet of drink.

'How did you know?' said Niamh and Daire together.

'I – I could see it!' whispered Rónán excitedly. 'I could see you and Rusk and Glasán. He was blowing cuckoo flowers onto Rusk's head. He borrowed your tin whistle and played it without putting it into his mouth!'

They looked at each other in silence for a moment.

'What have you discovered?' asked Imbas.

'I think Manannán has given us another gift,' said Daire. 'Niamh and I were remembering the same scene at the same moment and Rónán could see it too even though he wasn't there when it happened.'

Imbas chuckled with pleasure. 'Truly Manannán has made you Children of Danann! That power will grow if you use it well, especially when all three of you feel something very deeply.'

The evening passed in beauty and enjoyment. Dusk came softly on and the moon rose glimmering on the waters around Cahershee. Stars sparkled in the dark overhead while the city lamps glowed along the streets below. At last the music ended and it was time for sleep.

Chapter 12: The Road to Danger

THE FOLLOWING MORNING the streets of Cahershee were lined with cheering people as Niamh, Daire and Rónán, accompanied by the full High Council made their way to the Western Gate. They wore long green cloaks over their tunics and their swords hung by their sides. Niamh wore the Lir-Stone in its golden purse about her neck, while from Daire's belt the precious phial of Folnamara hung on a leather thong. Rónán carried the map that was to guide them to Inis Óg.

Imbas stepped forward and a great hush fell on the crowd. From a richly decorated bag he took a silver flask. All the surface of the flask was covered with beautiful carvings of fruit-trees, birds and fish. The eyes of all the creatures were set with tiny precious stones. Imbas presented the flask and its bag to Rónán.

'Water from Inis Óg has been carried in this flask for three thousand years,' he said. 'It will hold enough for all the People of Danann for the water of the Well of Youth must be mixed with normal drinking water before being taken. If you succeed in returning with this flaskful, you will have saved everyone.'

'We look forward to that day,' Rónán replied, bowing respectfully.

Inside the Western Gate, Donnán was waiting with Gasta, Taca and Cróga. The horses were laden with full saddle-bags containing food, drink and blankets. Shields, bearing the image of Manannán's white birds were strapped to the saddles.

The children went to their horses' heads and stroked their foreheads. They could sense warm feelings of fondness flowing from the animals into them. 'It'll be like having old friends on the journey with us,' said Niamh, running her fingers through Gasta's mane.

'Farewell Children of Giltspur,' said Imbas. 'You carry with you the hopes and fears of all the People of Danann. The Lir-Stone and Folnamara will serve you well, but guard them from the enemy for they will stop at nothing to snatch these treasures from you. We have given Donnán permission to guide you through the Enchanted Forest. Once you are safely beyond its power, he must return to Cahershee.'

'Thank you,' replied Daire. 'We shall do our best.'

Horns and trumpets sang out their fanfare from the ramparts high above them. The great gates of Cahershee rolled open and there lay the lake shining under the early morning sun. Beyond the water, wisps of light mist curled around the trees of the forest. The fanfare sang out again. The waters of the lake swirled and bubbled and once more the roadway rose from below the lake like the wet back of a giant water-beast.

As the echoes of the fanfare died away the children mounted their horses. Then they waved farewell to their friends. Niamh saw Amra standing with her parents beside Imbas. Suddenly the girl rushed forward and handed a bright red flower to each of the children. She did not speak but there were tears in her eyes as she turned away.

Donnán mounted his horse and led the way along the roadway through the lake. When they reached the grassy bank below the Forest they turned and looked back. Cahershee shone brightly while its flags and pennants fluttered in the breeze and the waters of the lake reflected its beauty to the sky. The fanfare sounded again, the roadway sank and the lake swirled over it. The children raised their hands in final farewell, then they faced the Enchanted Forest once more.

As they passed below the magnificent trees Donnán started to chant in his clear rich voice. Far above them the branches began to stir. The young leaves rustled as a secret whisper ran across the forest ceiling. Then all was quiet.

'As of now this forest is your friend,' smiled Donnán, 'but I shall ride with you until you find the Green Road to the west.'

They rode side by side through the beauty of the morning. Birds fluttered and twittered, squirrels scampered along trembling branches and shafts of sunlight lit up patches of bluebells on the forest floor.

Donnán was a cheerful companion and they talked easily about life in Tír Danann compared to life in modern Ireland.

'What I don't understand,' said Rónán, 'is why, after all these years you have not invented as many machines as we have. You still use horses and chariots and you defend yourselves with swords.'

Donnán smiled broadly as if the question gave him great cause for happiness. 'If you had known two thousand years of peace, I doubt if your people would have wasted their time and wealth on the terrible weapons of destruction that the great nations of the earth now hold. If it seems strange to you that we have few weapons, it appears even stranger to us that your world has so many. You have more now than can ever be used.'

'But what about ordinary useful machines?' persisted Rónán.

'Of course we use machines,' replied Donnán, 'but most of your machines are for people in a hurry. While we have the water of the Well of Youth we do not grow old, so we have plenty of time. Besides, we long ago discovered that to develop the power of our minds – what your people would call magic – was a much more useful and far deeper kind of progress than just improving machines. For example, some of the People of Danann do nothing else but study plant growth. They can hear the throb of life within a plant. They can feel the juices flowing from the roots along the stem and into the leaves. They can share the excitement of the bud as it gently opens to release its flower petals into the sunlit air. In this way we have increased crop yields by touching and talking to plants.'

'That's amazing!' declared Rónán.

'The same applies to animals,' continued Donnán. 'We no longer force them to serve us. These horses carry us by their agreement. We have learned to speak to all creatures and we live in peace with most of them.'

'And I suppose you just think away your sicknesses too!' laughed Niamh.

'Almost,' smiled Donnán. 'Many illnesses can be prevented or cured by the power of your mind if you know how to use it. More serious illnesses are dealt with by groups of healers using their minds together. Herbs and chemicals are useful of course, but we rarely need them. Understanding people is the greatest skill of all. We have learned to sense each other's feelings so we have much fewer misunderstandings or disputes.'

'This must be a wonderful place to live,' sighed Daire. 'It's a pity our world hasn't developed the same way.'

'We weren't always so wise,' replied Donnán. 'When we lived in Ireland we were as warlike and selfish as everyone else. We have changed since then.'

'And *we* haven't,' added Rónán grimly.

'That's because most of the greatest minds in your world have concentrated on changing *things* instead of people. But do not be too hard on them. We have thousands of years in which to learn wisdom. Your people rarely live to be one hundred. Even here there is much still to be learned. We are not all healers or gardeners or gifted with understanding. Very few of us have achieved greatness in all these skills. Imbas is one of the few. Glasán was one of our greatest. I hope you find him alive.'

The mention of Glasán's name brought the children's minds back to the extraordinary task that lay before them, and looking ahead they were surprised to see the open plain beyond the trees. They had come to the end of the Enchanted Forest.

'This is where I must leave you,' said Donnán. 'The Green Road will guide you to Glen Scál. From there it is a short ride down to the coast. May we soon be together again in Cahershee.'

The children said their farewells and at last rode out from the trees onto the Green Road. Donnán waited at the edge of the Forest until a turn of the road hid the children from his view. Then he turned and rode sadly back to Cahershee.

But the children had the sun on their backs and a soft breeze on their faces and in spite of their anxiety, they felt a thrill of excitement as they set up a smart pace along the road. The land about them was level and fertile. It had clearly been farmed until recently. Fields of neat furrows lined the road on both sides but the fine dark soil was already being overgrown with greedy weeds. Orchards, now bravely in bloom, were knee-deep in coarse grass. Abandoned farmhouses looked silently out over the empty countryside.

Soon the Enchanted Forest was only a dark green patch in the landscape behind them. Far off in the west, the Ardán Mountains loomed misty blue and mysterious with a hint of white cloud above them. Faster and faster still galloped the gallant horses so that their hooves scarcely touched the ground and the children felt as if they were flying. The sun rose higher and the day grew warmer. They crossed a bridge over An Sruthán. The land began to rise, gently at first, then more steeply so that the horses had to work harder, though they did not slacken their pace.

The countryside about them changed as well. The tilled fields were left behind. Now it was open grazing where sheep quietly cropped the grass or sheltered beside the occasional granite boulder.

About noon they came to a place where a shallow stream chattered noisily across their path. On the far side of the stream a huge boulder stood to the right of the road. Behind this three tall pine trees grew, their limbs twisted and bent by years of westerly winds.

The children forded the stream and dismounted. They had lunch sitting with their backs to the boulder while the horses grazed the soft spring grass along the edge of the water. Rónán unrolled the map. It showed the road ahead twisting its way over the hilly landscape, entering the forest of Glen Maam then running along the bottom of Glen Scál beside a rocky stream.

'Seeing it on the map makes it look easy,' said Daire.

'Almost too easy,' murmured Rónán as he rolled up the map again. 'There's something very lonely about this place.'

They looked carefully around them. The Ardán Mountains looked a lot nearer. The shadows cast by drifting heaped-up clouds moved silently over their rocky slopes and were swallowed up in deeply shaded valleys. Away to the south and east the Plain of Danann lay open and flooded with light. Nothing stirred on the ground and no bird flew in the bright air.

Suddenly there was a flurry of flapping behind them as two enormous hooded crows rose from the pine trees. The children leaped to their feet. The large black and grey birds circled overhead on wide ragged wings, regarding them severely from hard unfriendly eyes. Then they flew off into the west, their loud caw-cawing echoing like mocking laughter.

'I don't like the look of that,' muttered Rónán.

'They might just be birds,' said Niamh.

'Normal birds don't laugh at you!' Daire declared.

As they remounted their horses, Niamh slipped the Lir-Stone inside her white tunic and drew her long green cloak carefully about her. Daire and Rónán adjusted their sheaths on their belts, making sure the hilts of their swords were close to their hands.

They rode swiftly through the afternoon. The road grew less green and more stony. It crossed small bridges over noisy streams and twisted its way round low boulder-strewn hills. Gradually the sun moved round to the south-west, casting a warm light across the road and bathing the high places of the mountains in gold.

The children had begun to consider where they might stop for the night when they came over the top of a low hill and saw before them a forest of tall pine trees cradled in a deep valley between two outstretched arms of the mountains.

'This must be the forest of Glen Maam,' Rónán said. 'The road runs through the forest, then swings to the south-west through the gap of Maam Ard into Glen Scál.'

'If we can get to Glen Scál before dark we could reach the sea in the morning,' said Niamh.

'It's a wonder we've been able to get this far without anyone trying to stop us,' murmured Daire, looking uneasily in all directions.

They rode downhill towards the forest at a cautious pace. The low evening sun cast long tree-shadows across the road ahead.

'If we are going to have trouble this might well be the place where it could start,' said Rónán.

As if to prove him right, the two hooded crows flapped up from the trees. They circled overhead watching, while their mocking caw-caw announced the arrival of the children to the whole forest. Niamh shivered. Even Gasta, Taca and Cróga seemed nervous as they passed below the towering pines. Patches of sunlight brightened the road ahead, but the deep forest on both sides was full of threatening darkness.

'Look there!' cried Niamh suddenly.

'What is it?' whispered Daire as they pulled the horses up short.

'I'm certain I saw people moving through the trees. There were lots of them, moving quickly.'

They stared into the dim light among the tree trunks.

'I can't see anything,' said Rónán. 'They might have been

shadows. When you're moving quickly you sometimes think that things you pass are moving too.'

'You're probably right,' Niamh replied, but she pulled her cloak tightly about her and pressed her hand against the Lir-Stone inside her tunic. It gave her comfort just to know it was there.

Daire and Rónán slipped their shields onto their left arms and urged their horses forward. As if feeling the threat of the dark woods the horses set off at a swift pace with the children leaning forward, eyes alert for danger.

The hooded crows followed overhead.

Chapter 13:
Hunt of the Dripping Shadows

TIME AND AGAIN DURING THAT RIDE Niamh thought she saw troops of shadowy people flitting through the forest on both sides of her. They seemed to move at exactly the same speed as the horses and they always vanished when she turned her head to see them more clearly. She decided not to tell Daire or Rónán. If they stopped again the shadow people would vanish. Anyway, she still wasn't certain that it wasn't a trick of the light or her imagination.

After a time the valley grew narrower as the massive mountains closed in from left and right. The road turned to the south-west climbing towards a high gap below heavily forested slopes.

'This will be Maam Ard,' said Rónán, as they entered the pass.

Even here the trees grew densely right up to the edge of the road. Their twisted limbs interlocked overhead so that the children were riding through a tunnel of ancient branches and the ground was littered with enormous cones.

Soon the roadway dipped steeply, winding in and out among sturdy pine roots that gripped the hillside like gigantic gnarled claws.

'This place is creepy,' whispered Daire, as they descended carefully from the pass.

'We can camp by the river once we get clear of the forest,' replied Rónán.

'And have something to eat,' added Niamh. 'My stomach is rumbling with hunger.'

They soon reached more level ground. Niamh had moved to the front, peering forward through the trees.

'There's a brightness of some kind ahead,' she announced.

At last they rode out of the forest. Then they stopped in

surprise. Directly in front of them lay a wide shimmering lake. At the far end of the valley a brilliant sun hung below a mass of clouds ribbed with red and gold. All the lake shone with the glory of the evening and the quiet reflections of the mountains that towered all around. It was a magnificent sight but not what the children were expecting.

'This is all wrong!' cried Rónán. 'There's no lake in Glen Scál!'

They dismounted. Rónán pulled the map from his saddle bag.

'Look!' he cried. 'There it is. The road runs straight through. There's a rocky stream but *no lake*!'

'Maybe this isn't Glen Scál,' said Daire. 'We might have gone astray.'

Niamh carefully examined the map. Then she looked up at the mountains on either side of the valley. On her right the forest curved around the lake below a high rocky top that glowed in the evening light. On the left the forest ended halfway round where a sheer cliff fell into the lake from a mountain whose summit was hidden in cloud. A pale yellow track led through the trees, then zig-zagged dizzily across the mountainside towards the cliffs above the lake.

'It's Glen Scál all right,' she said quietly. 'Everything else is exactly the same as it is on the map. It's Glen Scál with a lake added in.

'You're right, of course,' Rónán admitted. 'Look ahead. Our road runs directly into the lake!'

They gazed in silence. The sun grew lower. Every ripple on the lake showed as a dark line on the golden water.

'What's that?' said Niamh, pointing.

The boys shaded their eyes against the light and peered anxiously at a small black object that was moving towards them across the lake.

'It's a boat,' said Daire. 'Someone's rowing it.'

The boat grew larger and clearer. The oars dipped and rose with a steady rhythm.

'I'm afraid that *no one* is rowing it!' murmured Rónán, as he hurriedly put the map away and gripped the hilt of his sword.

Niamh felt her stomach knot with dread as she watched the dark boat draw nearer. The rhythm of the rowing grew slower, then stopped. Bright droplets dripped from the raised oars, making circular ripples on the water. The boat drifted a short way from the shore. It was quite empty.

'Would you like a trip in my boat?' whispered a hoarse voice behind them.

The children jumped with fright and spun round. A tall black shape in cloak and hood was standing at the edge of the trees. The air had suddenly grown colder making the children shiver.

'Who are you?' asked Rónán in a tense voice.

'Does the brave boy feel fear?' whispered the shape, mockingly. 'Does his little heart thump inside his tunic?'

'Can you answer questions as well as ask them?' replied Rónán, stung by the jeering tone of the voice. 'Who are you? Why don't you show yourself?'

The figure stepped forward. A vague blackness hung about it in the air and on the ground. Its face remained hidden in the darkness of its hood.

'I am the Ferryman,' whispered the shape. 'I can take you across the lake but you must pay a price for my services.'

Fear flowed from its throaty voice chilling the children's bodies, weakening their limbs.

'What price?' asked Rónán as he struggled to smother a rising feeling of panic.

The black cloak stirred and a long hard finger with a claw-like nail pointed at Daire. When the voice spoke again it had a greedy edge to it.

'He has a pretty bottle on his belt. Give it to me and you may cross the lake.'

Daire's legs trembled beneath him as he felt the unseen stare fixed on him.

'I can't do that,' he said, forcing the words out against his fear. 'Anyway, there is no reason why we should trust you to keep your word.'

The black hood shook angrily and the children heard a sharp hiss.

'Foolish, foolish, foolish,' growled the voice, as if it was grinding its teeth in frustration. Then its tone changed. 'Perhaps we can make an exchange. Give me your horses and you may take my boat.'

'Oh no!' cried Niamh. 'We couldn't do that.'

The figure turned sharply towards her and her heart thumped as she saw two tiny specks of red light peering at her from the blackness of the hood.

'Ah!' breathed the voice. 'The pretty face can speak. Why can't she give me the horses?'

'Because they don't belong to us,' replied Niamh, trying to keep the quiver of fear out of her voice.

The dark figure took a step towards her and leaned forward as if to examine her more closely.

'She has a secret!' it hissed. 'I can feel it. What is it?'

Niamh felt a cold evil mind trying to search her own. She knew she must not think of the Lir-stone, but fear was weakening her self-control. Images of faces and echoes of voices came whirling through her mind. She could see Imbas leading them down the steps from the Great Hall to where the frowning masks of gold guarded the secret cavern. The fierce faces on the masks rose up to challenge her. They softened and changed. They became Daire and Rónán. She could hear their voices clearly saying 'Resist! Resist!' With a surge of relief she realised that their minds had united with hers to help her. Making an enormous effort she shook herself and opened her eyes. She was standing between the lake and the trees once more. Daire and Rónán were staring at her and she could feel strength flowing from them to her.

The hooded figure must have felt it too, for it stepped back sharply and straightened itself to its full height.

'Never mind,' it breathed. 'Never mind.' It paused then as if to recover itself. When it spoke again its voice was icy. 'The horses may not be yours, but are they more important to you than the life of Glasán or the fate of Cahershee?'

'How did you know who we were searching for?' demanded Daire, concern for Glasán driving out his fear.

The dark hood shook and the voice hissed. Whether it was laughing or angry they couldn't tell.

'I know many things,' it croaked. Then a note of triumph sounded in its voice. 'I know that if you do not take my boat you will have to go by the mountain path and leave the horses anyway. So I shall have them in the end.'

Gasta, Taca and Cróga neighed loudly denying the black shape's claim to them.

'Why are you so interested in our horses?' Rónán asked.

The tall black figure leaned back and gave a dreadful croaking laugh.

'Why? To eat them of course!'

The black hood fell back and the children saw a giant bird-head, with the cruel curved beak and fierce staring eyes of a hawk. For a second they stood open-mouthed with shock. Then before they realised what was happening their swords came singing out of their sheaths and they had raised them above their heads. The blades flashed red in the sunlight.

Bird-Head laughed again. 'Keep your little swords for later. You will be needing them.' It drew its hood over its dreadful head, stepped back among the trees and melted into the darkness.

'What on earth was that?' gasped Niamh.

Before anyone could reply, a resounding crack made them jump with fright. They whirled around towards the lake. One of the beams on the black boat had snapped in two and the splintered ends of it were dangling in the water. As the children stood frowning at this latest surprise, another beam began to bend and twist till it also cracked in two. Now the whole boat was breaking up as if a pair of invisible giant hands were tearing it apart. The children watched in horrified fascination. Soon there was nothing left but shattered wood drifting across the surface of the water.

'I'm glad we weren't in the middle of the lake in that,' Daire said.

'What are we going to do now?' asked Niamh as they sheathed their swords.

'We can't ride through the lake,' replied Rónán, 'so the only way forward is by the cliff path. While I hate to admit it, Bird-Head was right. We'll have to let the horses go.'

'What if Bird-Head catches them?' objected Niamh.

'I doubt if it would really eat them,' replied Rónán. 'I think it said that just to horrify us. It uses fear to drain your strength.'

'I hope you're right,' murmured Niamh, putting her arm around Gasta's neck. 'I'm sorry,' she whispered to the horse. 'There's nothing else we can do.' Gasta turned his head and rubbed his warm face along Niamh's cheek. She could feel his strong horse mind understanding her and unafraid of the journey back to Cahershee.

'We could camp here until morning,' she suggested. 'The horses are tired and so am I.'

'And I don't fancy tackling that mountain path in the failing light,' added Daire.

'That's a sensible idea,' agreed Rónán. 'We're as safe here

as anywhere else.'

'As long as old Bird-Head doesn't join us for supper,' muttered Daire as he turned to Taca and began to open his saddle-bag.

Niamh glanced nervously towards the woods. She didn't want to even imagine what unseen horrors might be lurking in there at that very moment. Then she heard a gurgling sound, followed by a loud splash. She glanced over her shoulder.

'Look!' she cried. 'Look at the lake!'

Daire and Rónán turned from their horses. The water along the shore was heaving and swirling like a boiling cauldron. From below the surface of the lake, dark shapes began to rise twisting and changing as they came. Heads and arms sprouted, melted away and grew again. Dripping dogs splashed about growing and losing legs and tails. Watery horses arose and riders grew out of their backs. Two-headed wolves shook themselves dry, then grew into men with antlers on their heads. The nightmare army of Dripping Shadows waded towards the shore.

'Ride for your life!' screamed Daire.

They threw themselves onto their horses and raced off towards the mountain track. Yellow dust rose in clouds around the horses' hooves as they entered the forest and began the long steep climb onto the mountain. At first they thought they had got clean away, but as the road began to twist and turn Daire glanced backwards and saw the Shadows behind them.

'They're coming through the forest!' cried Niamh.

On both sides of the track they could see the Shadows passing like ghosts through the trees, growing and changing as they sped along. The road grew steeper but the horses didn't slow down. As the terrified children urged them on to even greater speed they heard the Shadows calling to each other in shivery whispers.

'What have they got?'

'Something hidden.'

'Where are they going, so fast, so fast?'

'To their deaths, for sure.'

'We'll meet you in the mountains.'

'We'll come to you in lonely places.'

'We'll walk with you in darkness and lie by you if you sleep.'

'Strangle them softly from behind!'

'Aye, the quick tight grip at the throat!'

Then they raised a chorus of ghostly laughter that chilled the children to the bone.

At last the horses broke free of the trees, veering to the right through gorse and heather high above the gleaming lake. The children leaned forward in their saddles, their green cloaks flying out behind them as they sped higher and higher. Rónán looked behind him. The Dripping Shadows had fallen behind but they were spreading out. Dozens of them were drifting along the edge of the forest far below. Others were crossing the heather, passing up along the cliffs and crags towards the summit of the mountain. The rest were following steadily behind the horses.

Before long the children came to the edge of a vast cliff. From here on the path was just a ledge twisting across the mountainside above a sheer drop to the lake below. The first part of the ledge was so narrow that bringing the horses any further was clearly out of the question.

A mocking 'caw-caw' made them look up. The hooded crows were circling overhead.

'I'll bet that pair of spies are enjoying this,' muttered Daire angrily.

As soon as the children dismounted, Gasta, Taca and Cróga neighed one farewell, then turned and charged at full gallop into the oncoming Shadows. The ghostly shapes scattered to left and right as the horses passed among them, then they reformed and ignoring the animals they sped up the slope after the children.

'Come on!' cried Rónán.

They turned and faced the cliff path above Glen Scál.

Chapter 14: The Bravest Act

RÓNÁN LED THE WAY, keeping well in against the cold rock of the cliff face. Niamh followed slowly, keeping her eyes on the back of Rónán's green cloak and her thoughts on the Lir-Stone.

When Daire faced the path his stomach turned over inside him and his head reeled. The cliff face above him seemed to lean outwards as if it wanted to push him off the ledge and send him screaming down to the cold lake below. He tried to step onto the ledge but his legs wouldn't move. Rónán and Niamh were getting further ahead. Behind him, the Shadows were drawing nearer. He could hear their ghostly whispers as they called to him. He shut his eyes and took a deep breath.

'All right,' he said to himself. 'I'm afraid of falling. But that doesn't mean I'm going to fall. I'm not going to let the fear stop me, so here goes!'

He opened his eyes and stepped forward.

At that moment he heard the swish of wings in the air. As he turned his head he caught a glimpse of a black and grey blurr hurtling towards him. The crow stabbed at his belt where the precious phial of Folnamara hung on its leather thong. Daire jerked his shield across his body. The hard beak

struck the shield with a loud *clunk* and the force of the blow
threw the bird to the ground. It scrambled and flapped in the
dust like a bewildered hen. Finally it uprighted itself and flew
off across the valley with an unsteady lurching flight.

'Pity you didn't break your neck!' Daire shouted angrily.
Then he turned and followed Niamh and Rónán.

After a short distance the path grew wider and Daire
quickly caught up with the others. Soon the three of them
were half-running, half-scrambling along the ledge as it
twisted and turned across the face of the cliff, climbing ever
higher above Glen Scál. Far below them the valley had fallen
into shadow, though the lake still shone with a pale reflected
light. Dark clouds had begun to gather overhead while in the
west the setting sun still brightened the cliffs and peaks with
gold.

They were so high up now that they could see beyond the
mountains at the far end of the valley to where rocky
headlands jutted out into a shining sea.

'Look!' panted Daire. 'We can't be all that far from the
coast.'

'Maybe,' gasped Niamh, 'but I can't keep going like this.'
Her throat was sore from breathlessness and she had a stitch
in her side.

Rónán's legs were trembling with weakness and his heart
was thumping so hard it hurt him. He looked back along the
ledge. The Shadows were still following them. 'I'll bet that lot
don't grow tired,' he sighed, as he leaned his back against the
cliff.

They forced themselves to struggle on but they were
growing weaker and the Shadows were slowly catching up on
them. After a time they became aware of a strange sharp smell.

'There's something lying on the path ahead of us,' said
Rónán.

At first it was too far ahead for them to see clearly. It seemed
to be constantly moving and changing colour. They were
almost on top of it before they realised what it was.

'Seaweed!' exclaimed Daire. 'But we're miles from the sea!'

'I'll bet it's the magic seaweed the Formorians have put
along the coast,' said Rónán. 'They've blocked the road
through Glen Scál with a lake and now they've closed the
mountain path with this stuff.'

Niamh said nothing. She was staring at the horrible

seaweed. It wriggled and slithered about like a nest of snakes. It hung out over the edge of the cliff, curling and dangling, looking for something else to cling to. It crawled up the trunk of an old pine tree that grew out from the rocks just above the ledge and it hung twisting and waving from the branches. It hissed and slurped as it wriggled and the smell of its rottenness made the children feel sick.

'Look out behind!' cried Daire.

Niamh and Rónán turned. A pack of red-eyed Shadow Dogs were yelping towards them along the path.

'Quickly!' urged Rónán, gripping Daire's arm. 'Use the Folnamara. It'll destroy the seaweed.'

'Of course!' said Daire, reaching for the bottle on his belt.

'No!' shouted Niamh. 'It's a trick. They want you to waste the Folnamara here so you won't be able to use it at the coast.'

'But we can't just stand here!' protested Daire.

Niamh didn't reply. Instead, she turned and walked quickly into the middle of the seaweed. Daire and Rónán were astonished. Niamh turned to face them. Long tentacles of seaweed curled around her legs. A long shiny brown tongue slid across her neck. She raised her hands to the boys.

'Come on!' she cried. 'It's not real. Don't believe what you see. Don't heed what you feel. The real danger is behind you.'

'She sounds just like Glasán,' said Rónán.

Daire looked at him in surprise, then both boys rushed into the seaweed after Niamh. The salty stench of it filled their nostrils and the sticky slime chilled their legs. But they found they could walk right through it without difficulty. Once they reached the other side the three of them ran like the wind, while the Shadow Dogs howled their annoyance and melted together and grew into tall women with snakes on their heads instead of hair.

After a time, the children were surprised to find that they were pulling further and further ahead of the Shadows. It was almost as if the dark shapes did not want to come too close to them.

'How did you know the seaweed wasn't real?' panted Daire, as they slowed down once more and tried to recover their breath.

'I think the Lir-Stone told me,' replied Niamh. 'I suddenly saw Glasán clearly in my mind.'

'So did I,' said Daire, 'and so did Rónán!'

'I feel as if I almost know him personally,' said Rónán.

As the sun slipped below the horizon the night wind began to blow across the mountain, piling dark curling clouds overhead. The children had come to a place where the mountain was deeply cut by a narrow ravine. Their path swung sharply left and passed under a huge rock that leaned out above the ledge. Beyond the rock the path ended at the ruins of a stone wall. From here they could see a torrent of white water rushing down the cliff face and thundering on black battered rocks far, far below. The noise of the water and the suddenness of the drop made them feel dizzy. A short stone bridge spanned the ravine to a ledge on the far side. It was very old and many stones had fallen from it leaving gaping holes.

'I don't like the look of that,' murmured Daire.

The slopes above the ravine were covered with enormous boulders. Here and there ancient pine trees clung desperately to the stony soil. The rising wind hissed through the heather and made the gnarled pine branches creak. The children's cloaks flapped nervously about their shoulders.

'I wonder why those Shadows aren't trying to catch up with us?' said Rónán, looking around uneasily.

Daire turned to answer him but his reply died on his lips. He pointed to the mountainside directly above them. 'Perhaps *that's* the reason!' he said.

Dark shadows were drifting among the rocks and trees, drawing ever closer together as if they were being sucked inwards by an unseen power. Gradually they melted together into one tall black Shape. The Shape pointed at the children. Suddenly a huge boulder turned over and came bounding down the slope towards the path.

'Take cover!' cried Rónán.

All three crouched in against the base of the overhanging rock and held their shields above their heads. The boulder crashed onto the ledge in front of them showering them with stony splinters, then it careered through the wall and hurtled down into the ravine.

The children heard a low rumble overhead. The rock trembled against their backs. Then the whole hillside seemed to rush down upon them as soil, trees and rocks roared onto the path. Dust and dirt showered over them making them cough while flying stones stung their arms and legs.

At last the landslide ceased and the dust-clouds blew away. The children struggled out over heaps of clay and stones. All the mountainside above them had been gouged out leaving an ugly confusion of roots, ploughed-up turf and dead trees. Worse still, the rock fall had demolished the bridge. Only a sad stump of it remained clinging to the far side of the ravine. The rest lay scattered in the foaming waters far below. A tall skinny pine tree had been carried down onto the ledge and left balancing ridiculously on its head with its torn roots in the air. It looked as if it might topple over at any moment and follow the bridge down onto the crags. There was no sign of the black Shape.

'So that's why the Shadows kept well back from us,' said Niamh. 'Now they have us trapped.'

'Perhaps it's time to see if these swords have any effect on Shadow People,' said Daire, looking back along the path.

Overhead a hooded crow cawed its amusement at that idea.

'Maybe we're not completely trapped,' suggested Rónán. 'That upside-down tree might be long enough to reach across the ravine. Let's see if we can move it.'

It was more difficult to topple the pine tree than they had expected. Only after Daire and Rónán hacked off some branches and the three children pushed together did it begin to move. It leaned out from the ledge, hesitated for a second, then suddenly plunged downwards with a great *whoosh*. The remaining branches shot up around the children's heads dealing Rónán a painful blow on the cheek. The tree did not quite reach the path on the far side of the ravine, but the roots wedged against the cliff, slightly to the right of the stump of the old bridge, a short distance below the ledge.

An eerie wailing, echoing round the cliffs, told the children that the Shadow People were drawing nearer. The sound reminded Niamh of lonely deaths and burial ceremonies.

'Now all we have to do is walk across,' said Daire.

Rónán scrambled through the branches and the others followed. Lying across the ravine, the trunk of the tree looked a lot thinner than before. The wind had been steadily rising. Now it swirled around the ravine, tugging at the children's cloaks. Far below, the torrent roared its watery warning over the waiting rocks.

'I hope this tree is well stuck at the far side,' muttered Rónán, nervously. 'We'd better go one at a time, just in case.'

He looked at Niamh and Daire. 'I suppose I'd better get on with it,' he added.

With beating heart and dry mouth, he stepped out along the trunk. After five steps he became alarmingly aware of how high up he was. A wave of panic swept through him. He stopped. He knew he was going to fall.

'Don't look down! Look ahead!'

Niamh's voice sounded clearly inside his mind. He looked straight ahead. He could see the roots wedged against the cliff.

'I'm going to walk right over there,' he said to himself. He took one step, then another, carefully avoiding the short stumps of broken branches that threatened to trip him. He was half-way across. The tree wobbled slightly under his weight. Again he hesitated.

'You're almost there,' urged Niamh's voice. 'Go on!'

He almost ran the last six steps to the roots. He leaped from there at the ledge, scrambling onto it on his hands and knees. He was dizzy with relief and his legs were trembling so violently that he couldn't stand up. From this side of the

ravine he could dimly make out the shape of the approaching Shadows.

'The Shadows are almost here,' he called. 'Come quickly!'

Niamh stepped onto the tree. She drew the Lir-Stone from inside her tunic and gripped it in her right hand. 'Now,' she breathed. 'I'm going to walk straight across. I'm not going to fall.' She began to walk steadily, keeping her eyes on Rónán. The wind blew her hair across her face and tangled her cloak against her legs. From the corner of her eye she saw a dark Shape moving high on the slope above Rónán's head. She heard the Shape cry out in a voice that struck her like a stone and set her teeth on edge. Her legs trembled. 'I'm *not* going to fall,' she breathed, gripping the Lir-Stone even tighter. She walked swiftly and steadily, refusing to be afraid. Then, unbelievably, she was at the clump of peat-covered roots and Rónán was reaching down to help her up.

'Oh, thank goodness!' she gasped as she scrambled onto the ledge beside him.

It was Daire's turn to cross. The light was fading. Overhead great black clouds swirled in the wind. When he stepped onto the trunk his throat tightened and his stomach heaved. How could he ever walk across this slender tree without falling off?

'Hurry! cried Rónán's voice. 'They're coming!'

Daire glanced back at the path. The Shadow People were streaming round the corner. He saw red burning eyes floating in strange black shapes. Their howling and wailing filled him with dread. He took a deep breath and began to walk steadily out above the ravine. He tried to keep his eyes fixed on Niamh and Rónán, but in spite of himself he could see the cliff at the far side falling down, down, to where the mountain stream foamed and swirled, tumbling down to Glen Scál. His heart was pounding painfully. His whole body was so tense that he didn't dare to breathe.

He was almost half-way over when the hooded crow swooped on him from behind. He saw the movement out of the corner of his right eye and just had time to raise his arm to protect his head. The force of the attack knocked him forward onto his knees. The pine-trunk shook violently. Stones and peat fell away from the roots and suddenly the tree slid downwards. Daire screamed in terror. Niamh and Rónán clung to each other in alarm. But the roots wedged again against the cliff face and the tree fell no further. Daire remained crouched on his hands and knees, too terrified to move. A dreadful laugh echoed around the ravine from the Shape above the children's heads.

'Look down at your doom!' jeered the voice. 'Look down where you will fall, spinning and screaming to the rocks where your skull will smash!'

A wild mocking chorus answered from the Shadows.

'I know that voice!' gasped Niamh. 'It's Scarnán – the Son of the Morrigan!'

If Daire was afraid before he heard the voice, he was totally panic-stricken now. His head swam as if he was going to faint. He felt as if the tree was turning under him and he was already falling. He dug his nails into the pine-wood till drops of blood oozed out of the tops of his fingers.

'Come on Daire. You can do it,' urged Niamh, but his mind was too filled with fear to hear her. Scarnán's voice was screaming inside his head, 'Fall! Fall!' Sweat streamed down his face and dripped off his nose. His stomach felt sick. His hands were so numb that he could no longer feel if he was holding on to the tree-trunk.

'You're letting go! You're falling!' jeered the dreadful voice.

'It's no use!' cried Niamh. 'I can't reach him. Scarnán has filled his mind with panic.'

She sat down on the path and swung her feet out over the edge.

'What are you doing?' asked Rónán.

'I'm going back to get him,' answered Niamh.

'You'll be killed!' protested Rónán. 'The tree is shaking as it is. It won't take both your weights.'

'Daire will be killed if I don't,' replied Niamh.

The tree had slipped too far down for her to reach. Rónán lay down, gripped her by the wrists and slowly lowered her to where the roots rested against the rock. Once her feet were on the tree Niamh let go of Rónán's hands, expecting to feel the clump of roots give way beneath her, but they held firm. She stepped out onto the trunk.

At that very moment the hooded crow struck again, stabbing viciously at the phial of Folnamara that hung from Daire's belt. Daire felt the jabbing beak and in spite of his panic he realised what was happening. Making an immense effort to overcome his fear he struck out at the bird with his hand. With a last savage snap the crow's beak sliced through the leather thong on which the phial hung. Then the bird flapped upwards, with the phial dangling from its beak. But the Folnamara was heavier than the crow had expected. As it tried to get a better hold on the leather thong, it lost its grip and dropped the phial.

The children watched in dismay as their precious Folnamara fell spinning into the ravine. For a second the beautiful glass phial glistened in the darkening air, then it struck the rocks and exploded in a thousand slivers. The priceless liquid splattered over the stones and was quickly washed away by the raging stream.

The Shadow People danced and jeered. Shrieks of grisly laughter from Scarnán's mouth made the children's skin creep. Niamh saw Bird-Head appear on the ledge behind Daire. The Shadow People swirled and melted and grew into one long black snake that began to crawl out along the tree-trunk.

Tears of anger stung Niamh's eyes. 'You may have destroyed the Folnamara, but you're not getting my brother!' she cried, and gripping the Lir-Stone tightly, she strode out above the ravine.

Everything grew silent. Scarnán's laughter died away. Bird-Head stood motionless. The Shadow Snake froze as it was. Daire looked up. Niamh was walking towards him as calmly and steadily as if she was walking on the ground. For a second he wondered if what he was seeing was a trick of his imagination. Then Niamh was right in front of him. Balancing on the narrow pine-trunk, far out above the dizzy ravine, she took off the Lir-Stone and hung it around his neck.

A wave of warm comfort surged through Daire's body. He saw a flock of beautiful white birds wheeling all about him. A soft rain of pink and white apple-blossom floated down, settling on the children's hair and clothes. A delicious scent drifted in the air.

'Come on,' whispered Niamh.

Daire rose to his feet and followed her. The white birds flew up and vanished into the clouds. The apple-blossom ceased falling. They reached the tangle of roots below the ledge. Rónán stretched down and helped pull both of them up.

Daire turned to Niamh. He took off the Lir-Stone and replaced it on her neck.

'That was the bravest act I'll ever see in my life,' he said.

Chapter 15:
Deepest Sorrow, Deepest Joy

THE STUNNED SILENCE WAS SHATTERED by an enraged screech from Scarnán. The Snake slithered across the tree, sprouting legs and horns as it came. Bird-Head followed quickly behind. The three children raced along the ledge. They turned sharply left out of the ravine and fled across the mountain path. It was almost dark. A line of red light glowed along the horizon of the distant sea.

Scarnán was running across the top of the mountain, screaming and waving his arms at the sky. The power of his words made the wind howl and rage so that the children could hardly move against it and they had to cling to the rock face to avoid being blown off the path. Gigantic black clouds rushed to him from all corners of the sky, swirling and boiling above his evil head. Lightning forked and flashed, brightening all the mountainside before plunging it into sudden darkness again. Thunder shook the ground. Again and again the lightning flashed. It struck the path right in front of the dazzled children, scorching the rock and setting fire to thorn bushes and twisted trees. Showers of sparks whirled around the children, singeing their hair and scorching their skin. Smoke from the fires stung their eyes and made them cough. Still they struggled against the howling wind, darting forward when the way was clear, crouching against the cliff when the lightning struck close by them.

It began to rain, suddenly and heavily. Great grey curtains of water swept down from the mountain-top, pelting the children till they were drenched to the skin. Small waterfalls splashed down over the rocks and the ledge ran like the bed of a stream.

Niamh slipped and was almost carried over the cliff-edge, but Daire caught her arm and pulled her to safety.

'It's no use,' she panted. 'We'll have to find shelter.'

'There's no shelter here!' shouted Rónán, trying to make himself heard above the wind. 'Anyway look who's behind us!'

Bird-Head was closing in on them. It was floating above the path like a ghost with its arms outstretched. Behind it the Shadow Army wailed and howled.

Forcing themselves forward against the wind and rain, the children turned a corner and saw two things in one instant. The first was the dark mouth of a cave on their left. The second was a monstrous person, twice as tall as a man, standing in the middle of the path. The rain lashed down upon him and the lightning sizzled in the air about his head. His face was broad, with very wide nostrils and huge fishy eyes. He had gill-slits on his neck behind his flattened-back ears. His long black hair hung down to his waist. He looked enormously strong. Most of his body was covered by a suit of mail that looked like giant fish-scales. His hands and feet were twice too large and the fingers and toes were webbed. He was holding a long two-pronged spear above his head. All the path around and behind him crawled with seaweed.

'A Formorian!' gasped Daire.

The children stepped back.

'Let's make Shadows of them!' hissed an icy voice behind them.

They whirled round. Bird-Head reached out to grasp them in its claw-like hands. There was nowhere else to go. They turned and fled into the cave.

They were quickly swallowed up in a darkness so thick that it was impossible for them to go on. Looking back they saw the mouth of the cave lit by repeated flashes of lightning. Fearfully they watched to see if their hunters would follow them in. Nothing happened for a while. The cave was calm and dry. Outside, the thunder boomed and lightning flickered through the pelting rain. A dark figure appeared in the mouth of the cave. Behind it they could see Bird-Head and the Formorian.

'Good-bye!' sneered the dreadful voice of Scarnán. 'Enjoy your tomb. It will be a slow death.'

He burst out into such blood-chilling savage laughter, that the children had to cling to each other to avoid falling down from the horror of it. Then he raised his arms and uttered a command that sounded like the snarl of a tortured animal. The floor of the cave trembled. Pebbles and grit fell from the ceiling. There was an ear-splitting crack and with a deafening roar the mouth of the cave collapsed, completely blocking the entrance with tonnes of solid rock.

After the rock fall there was a deathly silence. It was as if the outside of the mountain did not exist. There was nothing but total blackness.

'We've failed,' said Rónán, in a voice heavy with defeat. 'We've lost the Folnamara. Even if we could have reached the sea we'd have been powerless against the seaweed. They hunted us up here deliberately. Now we're trapped – buried alive.'

'There might be another way out,' suggested Daire, doubtfully.

'Even if there is,' sighed Niamh, 'I'm far too tired to go looking for it. I just want to lie down and go to sleep.'

'I'd rest easier if I was sure we were the only ones in this cave,' said Daire. 'If you uncover the Lir-Stone it might light the place up for us.'

'I should have thought of that,' muttered Niamh in a puzzled voice, as she lifted the golden chain over her head, loosened the top of the purse and carefully drew out the Lir-Stone.

They hadn't looked upon the crystal since Imbas had held it before them in Cahershee. It appeared different now, glowing quietly with a soft white light. As Niamh gazed into its depths she thought she saw a line of green light flickering in the very centre, but when she tried to make it out her eyes grew tired and it faded again.

She held the crystal up by the golden chain. Its pure light lit up a high curving roof of dark grey stone. The cave grew wider as it went further into the mountain and it was so deep that the light didn't reach the other end. Niamh led the way, holding the Lir-Stone in front of her. The floor was uneven but not rough. Massive boulders lay in groups in corners, as if they had crawled in there to go to sleep. The children had been walking for almost twenty minutes when the cave curved to the right and began to narrow. Soon it had become a long dark tunnel.

'I can't walk any further,' groaned Niamh. 'My legs are shaking.'

'So are mine,' said Daire. 'I think we should take a rest.'

'Let's go back' Rónán suggested. 'This place is too narrow for comfort. At least we know that the cave is empty whatever lies at the end of the tunnel.'

They found a corner where a number of low boulders formed what Niamh called a 'little camp'. They sat with their shields beside them and their backs to the boulders and Niamh placed the Lir-Stone on a flat rock in the centre. They talked for a while in low tired voices of the adventures of the day. It seemed a long time since they'd left Cahershee in high spirits and full of hope. Now they were trapped inside the mountain and the precious Folnamara was lost. Exhaustion and sadness made them sleepy. Niamh dozed off first. Rónán said he would keep watch in case something crawled out of the tunnel while they slept, so Daire wrapped himself in his cloak and fell into a deep sleep.

Rónán sat alone, trying not to imagine what dark horrors might be lurking in the depths of the mountain. He stared at the Lir-Stone. It was throbbing softly. He imagined he saw a green shape forming in its centre. Was it a tree or an animal?

Then he knew what it was. It had become a field bordered by chestnut trees. Swallows were sweeping along the field, flying low, then soaring and turning. They landed on a broad-brimmed hat worn by a friendly-faced scarecrow. The scarecrow blinked and smiled at him. Rain began to fall like large tears running down the inside of the Lir-Stone. The picture blurred and faded. Rónán's eyes closed and he was instantly asleep.

* * *

The cave grew colder. Rónán could feel it in his legs. Something cold was creeping along his body. He tried to sit up but he couldn't move. Now it was on his neck and closing over his face. It was water! He struggled and gasped. Someone was calling to him, telling him to hold on to his spear. He kicked his legs and his head broke through the surface of the water. Daire was lying on a rock in front of him. Niamh was bending over the rock with a shining star on her breast and a black knife in her hand. 'Don't! Don't!' screamed Rónán. Niamh turned to him with a sad pale face. She gripped him by the shoulders and shook him.

'Wake up Rónán!' she called. 'Wake up!'

He looked around him. There was no water. Niamh was standing over him. She was wearing the Lir-Stone around her neck and her face shone in its brilliant light. Daire was standing beside her.

'You were crying out in your sleep,' Niamh said.

'I was dreaming,' replied Rónán. 'Have I been asleep for long?'

'I don't know,' Daire said. 'We've only been awake for a few minutes.'

'I'm sorry,' yawned Rónán. 'I was supposed to be keeping watch.'

'It wasn't your fault,' said Niamh. 'We were all exhausted and anyway, nothing happened.'

'It's a pity we lost all our food,' Daire said. 'I'm starving.'

'Perhaps that's what Scarnán meant by a "slow death",' Rónán said grimly.

'We're not dead yet,' declared Daire. 'We've still to explore the tunnel. Let's be ready for whatever we meet.'

He drew Lasair from its sheath. Niamh and Rónán drew

Solas and Tine. All three blades flashed in the light of the Lir-Stone. They settled their shields on their left arms, then Niamh led the way into the darkness.

The narrowness of the tunnel was unpleasant after the openness of the cave. It twisted to the right, then to the left, slanting steadily downwards. The light from the Lir-Stone grew gradually brighter and all three children could see the green light throbbing clearly at the centre of the crystal. An hour went by and another hour. They grew tired again and weak from hunger. Niamh was about to suggest taking a rest when they turned a sharp bend and found their way blocked by a row of huge yellow fangs. It was like walking into the mouth of a gigantic wolf. The children stood quite still. Then ᴅaire stepped carefully forward holding his shield in front of him and keeping his sword at the ready. Once he got close to the teeth he lowered his shield and gave a sigh of relief.

'They're only stalactites and stalagmites,' he said. 'You know those rock shapes that grow when water trickles down through the roofs of caves.'

Niamh and Rónán came forward. The shiny yellow teeth had grown down from the ceiling and joined with the set on the floor to form thin pillars. The gaps between the pillars were too narrow for the children to squeeze through, but they could see their tunnel continuing into the darkness beyond.

'Now what are we to do?' asked Niamh.

'We'll have to break a way through,' Daire replied. 'Stand back a bit till I see if Lasair can deal with stone.'

He set his shield on the ground and holding his sword with both his hands he swung it with all his strength at the narrowest pillar. Sparks flew from the blade as Lasair passed cleanly through the stone. He swung the sword again. This time a large part of the middle of the pillar fell out and rolled across the floor. Then Rónán stepped forward and between them the boys made a gap large enough for them to pass through one at a time.

Beyond the 'teeth' the passage turned quickly to the right. After a few steps they came out of the tunnel into a magnificent airy cave. It was like entering a huge church. Enormous stalactites hung from the ceiling far above them. On the floor, stalagmites of all shapes and sizes had grown like gigantic half-melted candles.

The Lir-Stone began to shine with a clear powerful light as

if something in the cave had released its energy. Its rays sent glistening rainbows rippling over marvellous shapes of shiny yellow and grey stone. There were walls of stone organ pipes, and frozen yellow waterfalls, rivers of melted rock winding through spiky stone forests. The children's imaginations soon found new wonders.

'That looks just like an eagle,' said Rónán, pointing to a shape on the roof that seemed to have outstretched wings.

'There's a rabbit with a fox just behind!' exclaimed Daire.

'That one looks like a horse lying down,' said Niamh.

On and on they wandered through a wonderland of fantastic shapes. Water dripped from the roof, plopping musically into small pools on the floor. They tried the water in one of the pools and found it fresh and sweet. While they were drinking Rónán looked up.

'Look there!' he gasped, his voice full of admiration. 'That one looks just like a man!'

Niamh and Daire turned to see. The figure was standing by another pool a little further on. It appeared to be bending forward slightly, as if it was looking down at something interesting.

'That's amazing!' whispered Daire.

Niamh did not speak. There was something about the figure that sent a chilly shiver through her. She glanced at Daire. They began to walk towards the shape. Rónán followed them.

Seen up close, this figure was more like a statue. It was wearing a long-sleeved tunic and had sandals on its feet. One arm was slightly bent at its side, the other had begun to reach out with the fingers of the hand open. The head was perfectly formed. It had shoulder-length hair held back by a headband. The face had a kind, yet slightly sad expression.

The three children gazed in silence. Daire examined the face and trembled. He did not want to believe what he knew in his heart. It was a different face of course. This was a noble Lord of Danann, not a scarecrow. But the expression was the same. A lump of pain hardened in Daire's throat and a silent tear trickled down his cheek.

Rónán was puzzled. Niamh and Daire seemed to have fallen into a trance. Then he felt a twinge of alarm that quickly grew into a rush of such overwhelming sorrow that he gasped out loud. Now he realised the truth.

Tears were streaming down Niamh's face. Great sobs shook her body. This was more sorrow than she could bear. 'Glasán!' she wailed. 'Oh my dear lovely Glasán!' A ghostly echo of her voice answered 'Glasán' from the vast emptiness of the cave, then died away in the darkness. She stepped forward and throwing her arms around him she kissed the cold stone face. After a time she stepped back. 'It's no use now,' she sobbed. 'It's all no use!'

She lifted the golden chain over her head and stared blankly at the Lir-Stone. Then she looked up hopelessly at the face of

Glasán. 'I won't need this now,' she whispered. 'You can have it.' She reached up and hung the glowing crystal around his neck. Then she sank to her knees and crumpled up in despair at his feet. A deep well of loss and loneliness was overflowing inside her. She was drowning in it, drowning for ever.

A long bleak time passed. Then Niamh heard a voice calling her name over and over again. It seemed very far away. Who was it? She listened. It was Daire. His voice sounded very strange.

'Look!' he was calling. 'Look at Glasán!'

Wearily she raised her tear-stained face. Brilliant rays of green and white light were streaming from the Lir-Stone. The figure of Glasán had begun to glow as the light flooded into it. The surface of the stone was changing to fine dust and the pulsing light was blowing the dust away. The tunic grew green and soft. The sandals glistened gold. The frozen hair loosened and grew fair and fine. The skin of the face became soft and warm. The eyes grew moist and clear. The eyelids blinked. The mouth softened and spread into a friendly smile. Now the whole figure was alive, stretching itself to its full height and looking with surprise at the three entranced children.

'Niamh and Daire!' he exclaimed, throwing his arms out wide. 'What wonder is this?'

Niamh and Daire flung themselves upon him in wild delight and he hugged them in his strong arms while tears of joy poured down their cheeks.

'There now, young Beauty,' whispered Glasán, looking fondly at Niamh. 'There'll be no more tears.' Then he smiled at Daire. 'My Strong Oak Wood, Hero of Giltspur! How glad I am to see you!'

Rónán stood back shyly, overcome with wonder. Glasán looked up and saw him.

'But who is this brave companion?' he said.

Rónán saw deep kindly eyes regarding him with an expression so powerful that he trembled inside with joy and fear.

'I am Rónán,' he murmured.

'Rónán,' repeated Glasán. 'Rónán! Of course – the Little Seal! You must be a great swimmer.'

'I'm afraid I cannot swim at all,' answered Rónán, feeling awkward and afraid of disappointing this wonderful person.

Glasán gazed at him for a moment. Then he looked at

Niamh and Daire. Suddenly he began to laugh. He laughed till the cave echoed with his voice. He laughed till he had to sit down to catch his breath and wipe his eyes.

'Well I never,' he chuckled when he had recovered himself. 'How like Manannán Mac Lir to send me a seal that cannot swim. He always had an odd sense of humour.'

He chuckled softly again and his eyes sparkled with the same mischievous delight that Niamh and Daire knew so well. The sight of his cheerful face and the sound of his happy voice had already begun to heal the anxiety and pain they had suffered.

Glasán looked down at the Lir-Stone. He took it in his hand. Then he looked thoughtfully at the children and his face grew serious.

'I can see that your courage and goodness have been deeply tested. You have known intense fear and deep sorrow. Yet you have brought the Lir-Stone from Cahershee and have rescued me from a deep enchantment. You have a tale that needs telling. How did you come to pass from Ireland into Tír Danann?'

The children told him their story, from the beach at Greystones to the death of Foras. 'He gave us a message for you,' said Niamh. 'He said to tell you he was glad in the end.'

Glasán reached out and squeezed Niamh's hand. 'That message heals all,' he said.

Then they told him everything that had happened on their way to Cahershee, their stay in the city and the trials of the journey that led them to him.

'We were afraid we would be too late,' said Daire, 'and that you would have aged before we found you. We didn't expect to find you changed into a statue.'

'As for growing old,' Glasán replied, with a twinkle in his eye, 'the Formorians saved me.'

'The Formorians!' gasped the children.

'Yes,' chuckled Glasán. 'Of course they didn't intend to save me. My becoming "a statue" is part of the same story. Come I will show you.'

He stood up. Then he paused and lifting off the Lir-Stone, he hung it around Niamh's neck once more.

'The protection of the Lir-Stone and the honour of bearing it have been given to you. You have shown yourself worthy of it,' he said solemnly. 'Now, let me show you our secret.'

Chapter 16: The Well of Youth

GLASÁN LED THEM PAST MANY STRANGE SHAPES, through forests of stalagmites and curtains of stalactites, till at last they came to the very end of the cave. Here they saw a wide brimming pool that constantly heaved and rippled with a life of its own.

'My companions and I came to the coast, intending to cross to Inis Óg,' said Glasán. 'When the seaweed swallowed up our boat we tried to scatter it by chanting spells, but the Formorian Giants raised a sudden violent storm so that the sea rose up and swept me off the rocks. I became entangled in that dreadful stinging seaweed, but the sheer force of the storm freed me from it and carried me to the sea-bed at the foot of the cliffs. I saw the entrance to a cave, swam in and surfaced in this pool. When I struggled out of the water I felt weak and incredibly thirsty. I didn't realise that the sting of the seaweed carried a stone-enchantment. My limbs began to grow heavy. In the end I hardened up just where you found me. I couldn't move, but I couldn't change either – so I haven't aged, yet.'

'But you could begin to age now,' Rónán said anxiously.

'That is why we must act quickly,' replied Glasán. 'Neither the Morrigan nor Scarnán realise that this pool leads to the sea. The Formorian seaweed floats at the surface, so if we dive to the bottom of the pool we can come out below it.'

'But since we've lost the Folnamara we won't be able to destroy it,' objected Daire. 'We could hardly swim out all the way below the surface.'

'And don't forget that I can't swim at all,' murmured Rónán.

'The seaweed stretches only part of the way to Inis Óg,' replied Glasán. 'There may be a way to get beyond it. The Lir-Stone does whatever Manannán wants it to do. I believe that we can draw on its power, especially if the three of you direct the energy of your minds along with mine.'

'Do you mean that we could perform magic?' asked Rónán.

'Of course,' answered Glasán earnestly. 'You are a seal by name. Become a seal by nature. Think *seal*.'

The children looked at each other. Did he really mean that they could turn themselves into seals?

'Show us what to do,' said Niamh.

On Glasán's instructions they left their shields aside, but kept their swords carefully locked in their sheaths. Then he made them stand in a line at the edge of the pool. The dark swirling waters looked deep and mysterious.

'Hold hands,' he commanded. 'When the moment is right we must all jump together. Now, fix your eyes on the Lir-Stone. Let its energy pour into you. Think this thought clearly: once you touch the water you will become a seal.'

The Lir-Stone blazed like a sun on Niamh's breast. As the children gazed into it they felt its light flooding their bodies and their minds until they were swallowed up in its glory. A thrill of great happiness surged through them. They were lighter than air, made of joy. They could do anything. They could become anything. They would become seals as they touched the water.

'Now!' cried Glasán.

They jumped together. There was a sudden confusion of flashing light and chilly water. Bubbles gurgled in their eyes and ears. Then they were speeding downwards, head first while Glasán's voice echoed in their minds, 'Seals, seals, seals'. They could see the yellow-green rock rising around them as they descended into the darkness below. The speed at which they were diving surprised and thrilled them. The darkness soon gave way to a pale blue light. They reached the bottom of the pool and swam under a smooth stone arch into bright water. With a shiver of delight they realised they were entering the sea.

Rónán glanced to his left. Two small grey seals were thrusting confidently through the water beside him. On his right a larger seal was driving forward powerfully. Rónán felt a shock of joy and fear run through him as he propelled himself through the salt water. 'We did it! We did it!' he told himself. 'I am a seal!' He flicked his tail and felt the rush of his own speed as he darted forward over the shell-studded rocks. High above him the tangled mass of Formorian seaweed wriggled on the surface. Here and there beams of bright sunlight slanted down to the sea-bed. Silver-bodied fish flickered in and out of the light. Rónán felt an urge to chase them and catch them in his mouth.

'Swim straight and low,' said Glasán's voice in his mind.

Grey flat fish skimmed along the bottom raising clouds of silt and mud. One took fright and wriggled itself into the sand to hide from the seals. The sea grew deeper and darker. Rónán could no longer see the bottom. He felt the water pushing him towards the right so that he almost collided with Glasán.

'Lean against the current,' urged Glasán's voice.

Rónán thrust himself against the force of the water. He felt strong and sure of himself. Every movement of his seal-body brought a satisfying leap forward through the water. After a while he saw a brightness ahead. The sea-bed was rising below him like the foot of a hill. Pale sand glistened between smooth rocks. Green and purple sea-plants waved gracefully to and fro while blue and red striped fish darted by in shoals. A silver ceiling of light shimmered above him.

'We've done it!' announced Glasán's voice. 'We're out beyond the seaweed. Keep close together. Once your head enters the air you will return to your own shape.'

The children felt a growing urge to breathe the air again. They swam upwards towards the light. Their heads broke through the surface in a flurry, gurgling bubbles. Sunlight dazzled their eyes while they gasped in deep breaths of fresh sea air. They looked at each other's wet faces and grinned happily.

'You were magnificent!' panted Glasán. 'Look where we are.'

They saw beside them a tall green island gleaming beneath a pure blue sky. They were treading water in a sheltered cove where the sea was breaking quietly on a golden strand.

'That is Inis Óg,' said Glasán.

They swam towards the beach. It felt strangely awkward to be using their arms and legs again and they wished they could have kept the swimming power of the seals. Only when they were wading ashore did it occur to Rónán that he had been swimming normally without realising it.

The morning sun shone warmly on their wet tunics as they trudged over the sand towards the base of a low cliff. Here they sat down to recover their breath. Looking back at Tír

Danann they could see the Ardán Mountains towering misty brown and pale purple above the sparkling sea.

'I know I should be thinking of more important things,' said Daire, 'but I'm starving.'

'And I'm dying of thirst,' admitted Niamh.

Beside the rocks where they were resting the beach was littered with large white shells. Glasán picked up one of them.

'Thirst we can cure,' he said. He brought them to a place where a small stream came splashing down the cliff face onto the sand. He rinsed out the shell, then filled it. Everyone drank until they were satisfied. Then he filled the shell again.

'Follow me now,' he said, and carrying the shell with him, he led them up a narrow pathway to the top of the cliff. Niamh thought he had grown rather silent and serious. He was moving slowly with his head down.

The path brought them across an open grassy place. A soft breeze blew across the island. Seabirds drifted overhead on wide white wings, calling loudly to each other. To the north they could see the dim outline of the dark islands of Formor.

They hadn't gone far when they came to a small grove of hazel trees. Here Glasán paused. He was out of breath. When he had recovered himself, he pointed to two tall pillars of white rock standing close together a little further on.

'That is the gateway to Slí na nÓg – the Way of the Young,' he said. 'The path will lead you directly to the Well of Youth.'

He spoke quietly and slowly. The children looked at him in alarm. He smiled gently at them. 'I have been too long out of Cahershee,' he said. 'Our seal-change has drained my energy.'

'Shall I give you the Lir-Stone?' asked Niamh anxiously.

'No,' replied Glasán. 'You must have its protection on your way to the well. Do not worry. When you bring the water I shall be restored, but do not delay too long.'

He sat stiffly down on the grass and rested his back against one of the trees. He looked very tired. 'One thing before you go,' he murmured. 'Do not drink the water yourselves. If you do it will not save anyone else from ageing. While you are here you are living outside of time. Its effect on you might not be what you desire.'

'We will bring it safely to you,' promised Daire.

The three children hurried on to where the two white pillars gleamed in the morning light. The surface of the pillars was beautifully carved with spiralling designs that suggested springs of living water and fresh winds from the sea. They stepped between the pillars and instantly stood still in wonder. It was as if they had walked into another world. All the island was suddenly covered with beautiful white flowers that were almost as tall as the children themselves. They were like magnificent pink-tinged daisies with long silken petals and they filled all the air with a delicious fragrance. Niamh's eyes sparkled with joy as she stroked the flowers with the tips of her fingers murmuring, 'The Flowers of Youth' in a dreamy voice.

Rónán glanced back towards the pillars. Beyond them he could see the grassy island they had just left and Glasán sitting quietly with the shell between his hands. 'I think we'd better get on to the well,' he suggested. 'Glasán is waiting.'

They made their way through the sea of delightful blossoms. Flocks of small birds fluttered up from the flowers, flashing feathers of blue and green and making a music that sang of the joy of early mornings in summertime and the happiness of lively youthful things.

Soon they came to a wide circle of standing stones, each one decorated with carvings of the Feast of Age. There were scenes of young people wearing flowers in their hair, drinking, dancing and making music on harps and horns. Inside the circle there was a wide area paved with green stone. At the centre of this lay a large pond covered with glowing water-lilies. Wide stepping stones led to the middle of the pond where sparkling water was cascading over the rim of a gigantic shell.

'This must be the place,' whispered Daire.

Rónán unhooked the silver container from his belt and removed the lid. Then the three children stepped solemnly out towards the shell. They looked over the rim and gasped in astonishment. It was as if they could see right down through the island and the sea-bed below it and further on to the sky of another world. Living water continually bubbled up from the endless depths where blue-green shadows rippled in ever-changing patterns of light.

Rónán dipped the silver container in the water and filled it to the brim. 'There!' he said, holding it up. 'The Water of the Well of Youth!'

'Why don't you have a drink?' said a gentle musical voice.

The children spun around. An astonishingly beautiful boy was standing at the edge of the pond. His laughing eyes were as blue as a summer sky. His soft curling hair glistened gold. His face shone with a light that came from within him and when he smiled his teeth flashed like sunshine on snow. He wore a short white tunic trimmed with golden rings and gathered at the waist by a golden cord. His feet were bare.

'This water gives the gift of youth,' he said. 'Why don't you drink it?'

'We were told – ' began Niamh, but her voice died away. A great longing suddenly filled all three children. They yearned for everlasting youth. They wanted it so much that the need for it was like a pain. Of all the things that they might ever wish for, this was their greatest desire: never to grow old, never to die; no slow withering in the winter of their lives; always the smiling springtime, always young and happy. Oh, the longing for it! How lucky the People of Danann were! How blessed was Glasán. Glasán! He was still waiting beyond the gates, ageing at this very moment.

'Why don't you drink?' repeated the boy.

'Because other people need it more than we do,' replied Niamh.

The boy looked steadily at her with a quiet serious face. Then he smiled and his face shone with such brilliance that the children could not see him properly. When the wonderful light faded away he was no longer there.

'Who was that?' whispered Rónán.

'I don't know,' replied Niamh, 'but I think we have passed an important test.'

As they returned through the beautiful flowers Niamh plucked three of them and put them in her belt. At last they stepped between the white pillars again.

'That was a lovely place,' said Niamh, looking back through the gateway, but all she could see was the smooth grassy island as it had been before. She looked down at the flowers in her belt. 'It was almost like a dream,' she sighed.

They hurried to where Glasán was waiting. His face looked tired and his fair hair had grown dull, but he smiled with pleasure when Rónán held the container of water out to him and removed the lid.

'By this I owe you my life,' said Glasán. He plucked a blade of grass and dipped it into the precious liquid. Then he shook one drop from the grass into the shellful of drinking water.

'Sláinte na nÓg!' he said, raising the shell to his lips and drinking every drop of it. When he had finished, he sighed deeply. Then suddenly his eyes grew bright, his face shone and he sprang up from the grass. He took Niamh by both her hands and spun her around in a merry dance while Daire and Rónán laughed happily.

'Oh, I am a young stag in a spring forest, an eagle on its first flight, a squirrel on a quivering branch!' he declared. 'Indeed I feel almost as young as you are, my wonderful friends! Now, come with me.'

Chapter 17: Escape to Cahershee

GLASÁN BROUGHT THEM BACK to the cliff above the beach. Looking down they saw a fire glowing in a circle of stones. There was something cooking on the fire but they could not see it clearly from where they stood. The sand bore the mark of wheels and hooves.

'I think we've had a visitor,' said Glasán, as they descended to the beach.

There was a copper pan on the fire and four whole salmon were sizzling on it. On a flat slab of stone there were four freshly-baked brown loaves. Four silver goblets and a full beaker had been left on a folded blue cloth beside the fire.

As the children stood looking at all this and wondering what it could mean, Niamh noticed that the Lir-Stone was throbbing softly with a blue light.

'You didn't tell me you had been talking to Manannán,' said Glasán.

'But we weren't,' replied Niamh. 'We met a beautiful boy at the Well but – '

'That was Manannán!' laughed Glasán. 'He has many disguises. He is the Guardian of the Well and these are his gifts to us – royal salmon for his seals.'

'He must have known we were hungry,' said Daire.

'He knows most things,' Glasán replied as he set about serving them open-air lunch. The beaker contained a drink that Glasán called Sea-Wine. It was wonderfully refreshing and tasted just right with fresh salmon and brown bread.

When their hunger was satisfied they relaxed quietly, watching the glassy waves breaking gently on the sand.

'What's that in the water?' Daire asked, pointing to where a dark head was ducking and rising half-way between Inis Óg and the coast. 'I think it's swimming towards us.'

'It could be a seal,' replied Rónán.

'There's another one!' cried Niamh. 'And another.'

Glasán stood up and shaded his eyes against the sun. 'There are six of them,' he said, thoughtfully.

'They seem to be surrounded by something dark,' said Daire. 'Is it seaweed?'

'No, it's not seaweed,' Glasán replied. 'It's hair.'

The heads swam closer. Now the children could see them clearly. They had broad cold faces and large fishy eyes. There were gill-slits behind their ears and their long black hair rippled out along the surface of the water like the legs of giant sea-spiders.

'Formorians!' cried Daire in alarm, as the children leaped to their feet. Glasán calmly picked up the folded blue cloth and spread it on the sand. It was decorated with spirals of gold and had a golden fastener at each end.

'That's Manannán's blue cloak!' gasped Niamh.

'Yes,' replied Glasán. 'He knew we would be in need of it.'

The Formorian Giants were wading through the shallows at the mouth of the bay. Water streamed down from their long black hair over their polished fish-scale armour. They called

to each other in hoarse throaty voices and their large eyes stared greedily at the children.

'What are we going to do?' cried Rónán.

'Let's give them a surprise,' said Glasán steadily. He stepped onto the cloak and sat down in the centre of it with his legs crossed. He beckoned calmly to the children. 'Come and sit beside me.'

They looked at him doubtfully.

'Come quickly!' he urged. 'They'll soon be upon us.'

The children stepped onto the cloak and sat close beside Glasán. The Formorians were striding swiftly through the water, churning up the foam with their large webbed feet. Each one drew a long knife from its belt as they approached the shore.

'What do we do now?' asked Rónán, nervously.

'Look at the cloak and think of Manannán Mac Lir,' said Glasán.

As he spoke, the edges of the blue cloak began to flutter as if a stiff breeze was blowing along the ground. Suddenly the beach and the sea seemed to fall away as the cloak rose swiftly into the air.

The children were so surprised that they clung to Glasán in case they might slide off and fall to the sea that was now far below them. Glasán looked at their astonished faces and laughed his deep soft laugh. He put his strong arms around them to reassure them.

'You're not the only ones to be surprised,' he chuckled, looking back at Inis Óg. The Formorians were standing in the water, shaking their knives uselessly in the air.

The cloak sailed rapidly above the rolling waves towards the Ardán Mountains. Startled seagulls wheeled away before it, protesting with harsh ringing cries. As the children became used to it they began to enjoy the thrill of rushing through the sunny air with the wind in their faces. They passed above sea-cliffs where waves foamed white against dark rock, then they rose rapidly towards the mountains. The cloak passed smoothly between two high bare peaks. The children could feel Glasán steering it by the power of his mind. They entered a long narrow mountain valley, sailing along above the pointed tops of fir-trees, then over a lake that reflected the pale blue of the sky. The shadow of the flying cloak flickered across the gorse and heather on the northern side of the valley.

'This must be Glen Scál,' said Rónán. 'There's the mountain path we followed when the Shadow People were chasing us.'

'And there's the place where we met Bird-Head,' said Niamh, as they came to the end of the lake and flew over the woods and up above the gap of Maam Ard.

Now they could see the Green Road twisting its way through the forests of Glen Maam and soon they had passed out of the mountains and were gliding over stony lands, where glittering streams chattered on their way down to the Plain of Danann.

'There's the three pine trees where we rested,' said Daire, 'and where those hooded crows were lurking.'

Grazing sheep, looking like small balls of wool, scurried away as the cloak passed over them. They passed the bridge over An Sruthán and now the wide Plain of Danann lay spread out below them, misty green beneath the brightness of the sky. In the distance they could see a long patch of darker green.

'That will be the Enchanted Forest,' Glasán said, with a note of gladness in his voice. The children's hearts leaped for joy at the thought of returning to Cahershee with the water of the Well of Youth.

As the outline of the forest grew clearer, Daire noticed something moving quickly along the Green Road.

'Is that a herd of animals running ahead of us?' he asked.

Glasán looked keenly at them for a moment. 'Horses and riders,' he said.

The blue cloak soon closed in on them. There were twelve black horses galloping together. They were being whipped mercilessly by heavily armed riders. A little way in front of this group, three saddled but riderless horses were fleeing at full speed. One was chestnut, one black and one dapple-grey.

'Fir Bolg!' exclaimed Glasán.

'That's Gasta, Taca and Cróga they're chasing,' said Niamh angrily.

The blue cloak sped silently closer.

'How can we save them?' asked Rónán, his hand tightening around the hilt of his sword.

'There's no need for swords,' answered Glasán gently. 'You have already saved your horses by restoring me to my full powers.'

He stretched out his hands, palms downwards, and fixing

his eyes on the horses, said, 'Trí chapall mar aer!' For a second nothing happened. Gasta, Taca and Cróga still raced along with flying manes. Then they slowly grew transparent so that the children could see through them to the grass and stones of the roadway. Finally, they disappeared altogether.

The Fir Bolg and their horses continued to gallop along the Green Road for a few seconds. Then those in front began to shout and pull hard on their reins. Those behind rode into them and riders fell off and got trampled on. Everyone was waving their arms about and shouting angrily. None of them noticed the blue cloak hovering softly above their heads.

Glasán turned and stretching out his arms once more said, 'Aer mar thrí chapall!' Slowly the shape of three horses appeared behind the Fir Bolg, galloping back the way they had come. There were cries of amazement and curses from the riders as they tried to turn and give chase. There was a lot more angry arguing and even a few swords drawn before they all set off back along the Green Road.

'What will happen if they catch the horses?' Niamh asked anxiously, as they vanished into the distance.

'Nothing will happen,' Glasán replied calmly. 'Those are not your horses. Look!' He pointed to the ground beneath the cloak and said, 'Trí chapall mar thrí chapall arís!'

The children looked over the edge and saw Gasta, Taca and Cróga quietly waiting below them.

'Oh, well done!' cried Niamh, clapping her hands with delight.

'But what are the Fir Bolg chasing?' Rónán asked.

'Air,' replied Glasán with a chuckle, as he guided Manannán's cloak gently to the ground.

Once everyone had stepped off it, the cloak folded itself neatly into a square and rose a little way up from the road. Then it floated sideways, vanishing into the air as if it had slid itself into an invisible post-box.

'Don't be surprised,' said Glasán, when he saw the children staring at the place where the cloak had vanished. 'We had the cloak on loan. It has returned to Manannán.'

Gasta, Taca and Cróga came cantering up and the children kissed the horses' faces and hugged their necks. Niamh was sure she could hear Gasta's strong mind saying, 'I told you we would be all right.' Then Gasta raised his nose to Glasán's face to greet his old friend.

'He has invited me to ride with you,' said Glasán to Niamh, 'but he says it must be "the lady's choice".'

'The lady will be delighted,' smiled Niamh as she ran her fingers through Gasta's mane.

They rode easily down into the fertile lands, past the flowering orchards and the empty farmhouses and soon came to the edge of the Enchanted Forest. Once again they entered the vast waiting silence that filled the grassy spaces between the towering grey tree-trunks. Before Glasán could chant his greeting to the trees an excited whisper rustled across the high leafy ceiling and all the branches began to move.

'Listen to that!' exclaimed Glasán. 'They're calling you "The Children of Manannán" and are singing their welcome to you.' The message of joy spread into every corner of the forest as the children rode among the rejoicing trees. The branches opened overhead to send shafts of sunlight slanting down to the forest floor where seas of bluebells raised their heads and breathed out their most delicious fragrance. Flocks of birds fluttered in the air around them, twittering their delight, landing playfully on the children's arms and heads, then flying off again. Squirrels darted along the trembling branches chattering the good news to each other, while along the forest floor rabbits ran races or played hide-and-seek among the trees. It was a journey through enchantment and the children laughed merrily as they rode along. A herd of deer emerged from the shadows and escorted the travellers until, at last they came out of the trees onto the smooth green lawns that slanted down to the glimmering lake. There, splendid in the evening sunlight, with flags and pennants fluttering from every tower and spire, stood Cahershee.

Chapter 18:
The Feast of Age

'CAHERSHEE AT LAST,' BREATHED GLASÁN.

A magnificent fanfare of trumpets rang out from the walls of the city and suddenly people were crowding along the battlements. The lake surged and foamed as the roadway rose from below the water.

Niamh tied the golden purse around the Lir-Stone. Glasán dismounted and walking at Gasta's head, he led the horses and children across the lake to the Great Western Gate.

Again and again the fanfare echoed across the water. The Great Gate opened and the Blue Guard moved quickly out. They were immediately followed by the members of the High Council. Imbas, Córtas, Órga and Donnán came to the top of the steps. Behind these the gateway and the courtyard were crammed with people.

The children dismounted when they reached the bottom of the steps. A murmur of astonishment ran through the crowd and Glasán's name was whispered over and over again. But he drew the children to him and said, 'This is your moment of honour. I shall walk behind you'.

Rónán unhooked the silver flask from his belt and carrying it carefully he began to climb the steps with Niamh on his right and Daire on his left. As they reached the top a great silence fell over the crowd.

'We bring you the water of the Well of Youth!' announced Rónán in a clear ringing voice.

A mighty cheer burst from all the people. Everyone danced up and down, waving their arms and hugging each other, while horns and trumpets sounded again and again from the walls.

Imbas accepted the silver flask with a low bow and a happy smile. Then he raised his hand and the crowd grew quiet as he began to speak.

'By this you have saved the lives of all the People of Danann. From this day on, our people are your people, our city is your city and you are for ever under the protection of everyone in Tír Danann.' Then he turned and holding the flask on high, he called out, 'Tonight we celebrate the Feast of Age!'

Everyone cheered again. Imbas shook each of the children by the hand and embraced Glasán with great gladness. Then everybody gathered round to congratulate and thank the children.

Amra came running from the gateway and flung her arms around Niamh. 'I was really afraid you wouldn't return safely,' she said.

'So was I!' laughed Niamh. Then she took the three flowers from her belt and gave them to Amra.

'The Flowers of Youth!' breathed Amra, her eyes shining with pleasure. She looked at Niamh with great affection. 'Now I have what I always wanted,' she said. 'A sister!'

Niamh smiled, remembering how often she had longed for the same thing. 'So have I,' she replied.

The Blue Guard formed an escort on both sides as Glasán and the children entered the city. All the streets were lined with cheering waving people and from the windows of all the houses showers of multi-coloured flower-petals were thrown down to greet the heroes who had saved Cahershee. Suddenly, as if at an unseen signal, everyone began to sing. It was a song of great gladness and thanksgiving and the glorious sound of it swept through the city streets like a wave from a joyous sea. Niamh, Daire and Rónán sang along with all the People of Danann.

* * *

There had never been a Feast of Age like it in all the years since the building of Cahershee. The whole city became a huge carnival. Red and yellow lanterns were hung across every street. Every tree in the woods around the Great Hall was ablaze with lights. Long oak tables were set out on the grass in the parkland beside the wood. Every table was hung with garlands of flowers and covered with such a banquet of food and drink as can scarcely be imagined.

As evening came on, all the people gathered for the Feast. They wore their brightest clothes and their loveliest

ornaments and had flowers set in their hair. Niamh, Daire and Rónán, freshly bathed and wearing wonderful tunics of gold and red thread, were given the place of honour at a special table on a raised platform. Glasán, Imbas, Córtas, Órga and Donnán sat with them. At Niamh's request, Amra was brought to the high table and allowed to sit beside her.

Three huge cauldrons of water had been placed on the grass in front of the high table. When everyone was seated, Imbas, resplendent in a special robe of silver and gold and with a long crimson cloak about his shoulders, rose in his place. A quietness like the dying away of the wind settled over all the city. Imbas asked Niamh, Daire and Rónán to stand behind the cauldrons. An attendant gave each of them a special silver goblet, decorated in the same wonderful way as the silver flask that Imbas held. He opened the flask and poured the Water of the Well of Youth into each of the goblets in turn. Then the trumpets sang out a stately fanfare and on a signal from Imbas, the children poured the precious liquid into the cauldrons. As it entered the water the children saw it divide into millions of tiny liquid jewels, each flashing rainbows of light like miniature Lir-Stones. They swirled through the water and the cauldrons bubbled, giving off a delicious scent. When the fanfare ceased the children returned to their places.

All the People of Danann stood up, each carrying a small silver cup and quietly approached the cauldrons. The members of the High Council poured a few drops of the saving liquid into each cup and with the words 'Sláinte na nÓg!' everyone drank. As the vast crowd moved towards the cauldrons, the musicians began to play on flutes, harps and pipes, and everyone began to sing the Song of the Feast. It was a lovely solemn song that told of all their years in Tír Danann since Manannán Mac Lir had set up the Feast of Age. The beauty of the music, sung under the starry sky, filled the children with the deep happiness of these people so that they could scarcely speak for joy.

Imbas drank last of all. Then he called out in a loud voice, 'People of Danann, rejoice in the Feast of Age and give praise to the Children of Manannán who have made the Feast possible!'

The cheers of the people rang out loud and long. Then the feasting began. Whether or not there was an enchantment on the food, the children could not tell, but each bite they ate tasted better than the one before it, and no matter how much they ate, they did not feel too full.

Glasán told Imbas of all that had happened to him and the children described the adventures of their journey to Inis Óg. Then a harper stepped in front of the high table. All the laughing and talking ceased as he began to sing:

'Beneath the slopes of Giltspur Wood,
In the Seed Field a scarecrow stood.
While Scrags complained at the dying day
The wind blew life through the Eve of May.'

And so, to the children's astonishment and delight, he sang the story of their Battle Below Giltspur.

There was a great round of applause when the song ended. Then the pipers and fiddlers struck up a merry tune and troops of young girls and boys all dressed in flowers, danced on the grass before the high table while the people clapped and sang.

So the night passed in merry-making while the stars moved across the sky and no one grew tired or felt the need for sleep. But as the first light of dawn appeared in the east the children began to feel a strange lonely longing awakening inside them.

'Someone is calling to us,' said Daire.

'Yes,' replied Rónán. 'I think I hear a horn blowing, far away.'

The need to answer the call grew so strong they could not resist it.

'It's time I returned the Lir-Stone,' said Niamh in a quiet voice.

They turned to Glasán. He was looking at them out of deep kindly eyes. 'Do not worry,' he said. 'You are feeling the call of Manannán. I have felt it many times in the past. It is a strange disturbing feeling.'

Imbas had heard it too. 'Let us return to the Great Hall,' he said. 'We have unfinished business to deal with.'

The members of the High Council rose quietly and began to walk through the wood. Niamh turned to Amra.

'I feel that our time in Tír Danann is almost over,' she said.

'I know,' replied Amra. 'I shall always remember you. You will be my sister in the other world.'

'And you will be mine,' whispered Niamh.

The girls embraced. Daire reached out to shake Amra's hand, but to his surprise she leaned forward and kissed him on the cheek.

'Take care of my sister,' she said.

'Of course I will,' replied Daire.

'Goodbye Rónán,' said Amra, as she kissed him also. 'Somehow I feel sure that we shall meet again.'

'I hope we do,' replied Rónán.

Glasán led the children through the wood to the lake at the Great Hall.

'There are others here who want to say farewell,' he said.

Gasta, Taca and Cróga were waiting by the edge of the lake. The children ran to them and threw their arms around their strong warm necks.

'Oh Gasta,' sighed Niamh. 'I'd love to take you with me.'

'That would cause some excitement at home,' smiled Glasán.

He brought them across the bridge into the Great Hall. All the members of the High Council rose to their feet as the children entered and stood before the great oaken table.

'What you have done for our people will be remembered in song and story for many thousands of years,' said Imbas. 'By saving the Feast of Age you have also prevented a huge and bloody battle. Just after the Feast began, I sent our swiftest scouts to spy out the land. They have brought back good news. The Formorian Giants have returned to their island kingdom and the ships of the Fir Bolg are sailing north to their own coast. They have abandoned their plan to attack us. Enchenn, the Bird-Head has fled to the south. The Morrigan and her son Scarnán have been seen returning to the east. You have frustrated their plans for battle slaughter.'

'What will you do about the seaweed?' asked Daire.

'We have enough Folnamara to deal with that, now that we are free to travel out of Cahershee,' replied Imbas, as he took a small crystal bottle from a pocket in his robe. The precious red liquid gleamed through the glass. 'Your work here is finished but you still have a task to perform in Ireland. Cast this phial into the sea at Greystones. It will destroy the seaweed that has crossed between the worlds.'

As he said the name of Greystones, the children were sure they could hear the echo of a distant horn calling to them and for a moment they felt as if they were rising dizzily through the air.

'Manannán is calling to you,' said Imbas. 'You must answer that call.'

The children turned to Glasán.

'The last time it was you who had to leave us,' said Niamh. 'Now we have to leave you. Will we always be leaving each other?'

'Perhaps,' replied Glasán softly. 'Always parting and always meeting again.'

They hugged each other warmly, then at a signal from Imbas, Glasán led them down the steps to where the golden masks guarded the cavern.

'Doras slán idir dhá aghaidh!' called Glasán.

The rock-face parted and they walked between the blue-green pillars onto the gold-encircled floor. When everyone was in place, the High Council began to chant softly in deep rich harmony, a song of thanks and farewell. Niamh lifted the Lir-Stone from her neck and gave it to Glasán. He untied the string of the golden purse and drew out the marvellous crystal. The chant grew louder and more urgent. Glasán held the Lir-Stone before the children's eyes for the last time. It shone with the brilliance of the rising sun and all the cavern was filled with its glory. Niamh, Daire and Rónán could see nothing else but the wonderful light that was flowing into their very minds and bodies.

'Farewell my good friends,' said Glasán's voice. 'Slán agus beannacht.'

As his voice faded the children realised that they were already rising at great speed. The light of the Lir-Stone vanished below them. Now they were soaring into a dark sky where silver stars flashed and fell away. After a time they saw another brightness above them. Shining coins of light were raining down upon them. The children were moving more slowly now. Gradually the coins became pink and white petals floating gently onto their hair and clothes. Sunlight was streaming down through blossom-laden branches high above their heads. They stopped rising. There was petal-covered grass beneath their feet and a fragrant scent in the air.

Daire looked at Niamh. Her face was shining in wonder. 'I know where we are!' she whispered. 'This is Manannán's country!'

They walked quietly through the sunlit orchard listening to the song of blackbirds rejoicing among the branches. Soon they came out of the apple-trees onto a green lawn that slanted gently down to a golden beach. Great glassy waves were rolling in from a pale green ocean and crashing on the shore in a rush of snow-white foam. A rainbow glowed in the sky above the heaving water and below it the children saw a chariot pulled by two white horses speeding towards them over the waves. The sea spray rose in a fine mist from the chariot's wheels and the long white manes of the horses streamed out behind them. A great flock of white birds was flying behind the chariot.

The children raced down onto the beach and across the sand to where the white foam ran hissing about their feet. The chariot and its driver drew nearer.

'Is that Manannán Mac Lir?' asked Rónán, with a slight tremble in his voice.

'Yes,' replied Niamh quietly. Now that they were about to meet Manannán face to face a sudden shyness had come over her.

The horses and chariot splashed onto the sand and swung to a halt. Out stepped the towering figure of Manannán Mac Lir in his white tunic and the long blue and gold cloak on which the children had flown from Inis Óg. His thick curling beard and long golden hair flowed about him in the fresh sea-breeze and his face shone with a fierce joy. A large gold-tipped horn hung from his belt.

'Welcome again, Beauty and Oak Wood and especially welcome Little Seal!' he called in a voice that shook the earth and air. 'You have done much good to the People of Danann and also to yourselves. I have a little surprise to show you before you return home. Behold!'

He pointed along the beach. The children turned and saw a tall smiling figure dressed in long white robes walking towards them.

'Foras!' cried Rónán and the children ran delightedly to their old friend. They threw their arms around him, almost knocking him over and he swung them round and round and ran his fingers through their hair, laughing happily with them.

'Foras, oh Foras!' gasped Rónán, hardly daring to believe that he was really there alive before them. 'So this is where you vanished to. No wonder you said you were glad in the end.'

'I knew Manannán was calling me,' replied Foras. 'Answering the call was easy.'

'All harms are healed in the end,' said Manannán, 'but you have some healing to do in your own country before your task is completed.'

'Oh, must we leave so soon?' pleaded Niamh.

'Your turn to stay will come at its proper time,' replied Manannán. 'If you delay now your people may suffer harm.'

A sudden gust of wind sent the blue cloak swirling up from his shoulders. It fluttered and billowed, growing and spreading until it hid both sea and sand. Then it changed into a glowing blue mist and as the faces of Manannán and Foras faded, the children found themselves sinking slowly through the blueness. At last their feet came to rest on solid ground. The blue mist grew paler and gradually melted away.

They were standing on the hillside below Giltspur Wood, with the grove and the Cairn behind them. They were back in their anoraks and jeans and Rusk was racing up the slope from the Sheep Field.

'Rusk, you little rascal' laughed Niamh, as the dog ran up to her. 'You've just missed the most incredible adventure.'

'Incredible is the word,' murmured Rónán. 'Nobody is going to believe us.'

'Then we shall tell nobody,' said Daire. He put his hand into his anorak pocket and his fingers closed around a small crystal phial of red liquid.

'We still have this!' he said quietly, holding up the Folnamara.

* * *

After much pleading and many promises of being extra careful on the roads, the children were given permission to cycle down to Greystones that afternoon. The tide was fully in and all the brimming water from the harbour to Bray Head was alive with the dreadful seaweed. The three of them climbed onto the rocks beside the harbour. Daire drew the phial from his pocket. The seaweed wriggled violently as if it could feel the threat of the Folnamara near it. Daire raised the phial above his head and flung it into the sea.

There was a sudden loud hiss. A flash of red flame sped across the surface of the water. The seaweed churned and boiled madly, then it dissolved and vanished in a rush of bubbles.

'That's the end of it all,' sighed Daire.

'Look!' cried Niamh, pointing at the sky. 'It's Manannán's birds!'

A flock of shining white birds were circling overhead. They spread their broad wings and swept low along the sea, passing the children in a last salute. Then they soared swiftly upwards and vanished in a flash of white light.

* * *

Niamh, Daire and Rónán really enjoyed their Easter Holiday and their parents were delighted at how well they got on together. They never told anyone about their adventure and no one suspected that anything strange had happened. But it was a cause of great wonder to their parents, when they visited Presentation College Pool in Bray, that Rónán was suddenly able to swim.

'He's just like a seal!' his father remarked afterwards.

Niamh, Daire and Rónán looked quickly at each other and smiled happily.

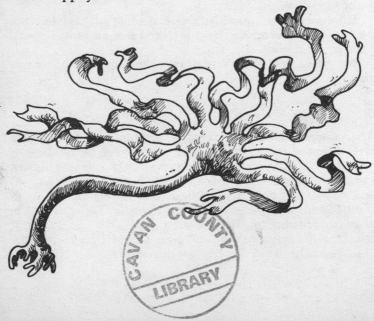

Laura Delaney's Deadliest Day

Ann Carroll

POOLBEG

Published 2001
by Poolbeg Press Ltd.
123 Grange Hill, Baldoyle
Dublin 13, Ireland
Email: poolbeg@poolbeg.com

3 5 7 9 10 8 6 4 2

A catalogue record for this book is available from the British Library.

ISBN 1 84223 031 X

Typeset by Patricia Hope in Goudy 11.5/15
Printed by Cox & Wyman,
Reading, Berkshire, UK.

www.poolbeg.com

About the Author

Ann Carroll is married with two children and lives in Dublin where she teaches English in Killinarden Community School. She is the author of the successful *Rosie* series.

Also by Ann Carroll

Rosie's Gift
Rosie's Quest
Rosie's Century
Rosie's Troubles
Rosie's War
Amazing Grace

Chapter 1

It was Monday morning and Laura Delaney was stuffing Flabby, the cat, into her schoolbag. Flabby groaned a little but didn't open his eyes. And once she'd stopped pushing and shoving he settled happily.

Sam, six years old, wasn't a bit happy. "Why are you putting him in there? It's dark." Sam hated the dark.

"Flabby doesn't want to see," Laura told her brother. "Listen to him, he's grand."

The large cat was purring like an engine.

Sam wasn't satisfied and his voice rose, "Flabby won't like school! He can't look at books!"

"Sshh! Mum and Dad'll hear."

But she knew there was little chance of that. Dad was, as usual, wondering where he'd left everything for work and Mum was, as usual, looking for his papers and keys. Soon their father would go out the door, then come back a couple of times because he'd forgotten something else. By the time he'd finally gone, Laura would be on her way to school.

This was what happened every day, and during those ten minutes before Dad at last managed to leave, Laura and Sam could have blown up the house and their parents wouldn't have noticed.

"Flabby can't write. He won't like school!" Sam was beginning to sound quite shrill.

"Shut up!" Laura hissed. "He won't even know he's in school. You're just being silly!"

"I am not." Her little brother's lip went out and his eyes grew round. Oh God, Laura thought. If he cries they *will* notice.

"Do you want to hear a secret?" she asked and at once Sam smiled.

"Our teacher, Ms Pim, said we could bring in our pets today, with our parents' permission. But if I ask Mum and Dad they'll say no, because they think Flabby doesn't like strange places. But he does really. Or he would if he stayed awake more. Cos then he might notice he was in a strange place and he'd like the change. And anyway, if he's asleep it doesn't matter where he is. D'you see?"

Sam didn't, but he nodded and smiled, delighted his sister was being nice.

"So I have to put him in my schoolbag to hide him. Promise you won't say anything to Mum and Dad."

"Promise!" Sam was very solemn. Then he ran out to the kitchen where his mother was searching through drawers and shouted, "I have a secret! I have a secret!"

As fast as she could, Laura put on her jacket and hitched the odd-shaped schoolbag onto her back. There was some moaning from Flabby, who didn't like being bounced around. Laura ran up the hall and out the front door, shouting, "Bye everyone!"

She knocked for her best friend, Joe Jameson, who came out carrying a cage with a cloth over it. Laura lifted the cover. "Hi, Pasty," she cooed.

"Get lost!" Pasty shrieked.

She laughed, "Ms Pim will love you."

"Buzz off! Buzz off!" screamed the parrot.

"Are you going to talk like that to the teacher?" Laura asked.

"Drop dead!" said the parrot.

Joe was anxious. "Maybe I shouldn't bring him. Ms Pim mightn't like his language. It's Dad's fault. He spends ages teaching him new words, none of them very polite. I don't want to get into trouble."

Laura was definite. "You won't. Ms Pim thinks you're great. You always have your homework done and you never give cheek. She won't blame the parrot on you."

Joe sighed, "You think I'm a lick, don't you?"

"I don't! It's handy the way Ms Pim likes you. You're always getting me out of trouble and she never sees it. Anyway I know you don't want to upset your dad."

Joe's mum had died two years ago and his dad had stopped bothering. He'd be late for work didn't go in at all and after a while he'd lost his job. Ever since he'd had only two moods, sad or angry. So Joe made sure there were never any complaints home from his teacher. Not wanting to upset his father was the measure by which he behaved.

But recently, Joe thought, his dad seemed to be always annoyed with him, no matter how good he was. When he'd asked to take Pasty into school, Mr Jameson had almost exploded, "Of course you can take him! Why are you asking? Why do you have to be so flamin' polite? He's your parrot, your birthday present!"

Joe had gone white and muttered, "Thanks."

Mr Jameson had stared at him a moment. Then he'd said quietly, "You're not afraid of me, are you?"

Joe had shaken his head. He wasn't afraid of him in the way he meant. He knew his dad would never hit him. But he was afraid of the way he could get so furious. He would rage at someone on the telly or go on and on about stupid milk cartons and how they never opened properly. Once when the milk had splashed out he'd dashed the whole carton onto the floor. And when he'd tripped over a chair he'd behaved as if the chair had done it deliberately – actually put out a leg to make him fall – and he'd called it all sorts of names and kicked it.

Worse than his rage was his misery. Sometimes Joe came in from school and his dad would be sitting, staring into space, lost. He wouldn't see or hear his son for a some minutes. Joe always had to say things a few times before he'd sigh and look at him.

And though he wasn't in fear of his father, he couldn't talk to him either. Mr Jameson wouldn't speak about his wife and he'd put all her photos away. Joe was eight when his mum died and he was having trouble remembering exactly what she'd looked like. When he'd asked his dad about the colour of her hair Mr Jameson had been very abrupt. "Time to move on, son. No dwelling on the past!"

Except he knew his father *did* dwell on the past, and there was nothing he could do to help, just not make things worse by getting into trouble. But Joe often thought it would be nice, just once or twice, not to have to be so good.

Now as they walked into the school, Laura studied his frowning face and said, "Don't worry, Joe. Ms Pim will laugh at Pasty. Now if it was me who brought him in she'd give out. She'll give out to me anyway and find some fault with poor old Flabby, cos she hates me."

Joe stopped. "You're not bringing Flabby?"

"I am. Why not?" Laura stopped too.

"Because she said we're only to bring in caged pets, not cats or dogs, that can run around the room."

"Oh God!" Laura moaned. "She'll kill me. Are you sure she said that? I never heard her."

"She said it three times," Joe was patient. "You never heard her cos you weren't listening."

"I was too. I knew we could bring in pets. But she says things so often I get bored." A thought struck her and she brightened. "Anyway, if she said animals that run

5

around the room, she doesn't mean Flabby. He hasn't run for years."

"She said no cats or dogs. Anyway, where is Flabby?"

"In my schoolbag. I can leave him there for the day. The only time he wakes up at home is for food and when Sam is practising on the piano. He hates that." She paused, thinking about her small brother's piano-playing. "Everybody hates it, except Mum. Even the neighbours try to tell her he can't play a note, but she thinks he's a genius!"

"Ms Pim is bound to notice Flabby," Joe told her.

"She won't even know he's in school. Except he has to be fed at twelve. He goes mad if he doesn't get his food."

The boy grinned to himself. Laura always managed to cheer him up. She had to be the only person in the world who thought she could feed a cat in a classroom without the teacher noticing.

In Fifth class, cages and baskets of varying sizes and shapes rested on the long table at the back of the room. Rabbits nibbled, hamsters ran around wheels, budgies chirped, Pasty was silent under his cover; a small snake snoozed and one pigeon made a terrible mess.

Miss Pim was in a good mood. Her weekend had been relaxing. For once she'd had no correcting to do. And now she could see the idea of having a pets' day was a good one. Not one person in Fifth class had that 'Monday-morning-depressed' look. In fact there was a buzz of excitement in the classroom as the bell went.

Everyone was eager to get the work done and move on to the important business of the animals.

Even Laura Delaney was quiet. Perhaps this would be the one day the child would not torment her. Perhaps she'd have all her homework done. Perhaps she'd pay attention. Perhaps she wouldn't give cheek. Perhaps a flying saucer would land in 5th class.

She sighed. It wasn't cheek exactly. But sometimes Laura said such outrageous things. Like the time Ms Pim had been driven to the end of all patience because the girl had been gazing out the window for ten minutes instead of doing her maths work.

"What are you daydreaming about?" she'd snapped, when she could bear it no longer.

"I was just imagining, Miss."

"Imagining what, girl?"

"I was imagining what it's like in prison, Miss. It must be like school, not able to get out, shut in a cell. I wonder if prisoners have to do Maths too?"

Miss Pim was indignant. "School is not a bit like prison! You're here for less than six hours a day, not locked up for months on end. This room is not a cell. And no, most prisoners don't have the privilege of doing Maths!"

"They are *so* lucky!" Laura said with genuine feeling.

Then the others started. "What do prisoners do all day, Miss?"

"Can they watch telly?"

"Do they get lots of visitors? When I was in hospital I got lots of visitors."

7

"Could we visit them, Miss? That'd be deadly!"

"No, you can't visit them!" Miss Pim had to shout to be heard and became quite sarcastic. "People aren't in prison to be tortured by the likes of you."

The Maths work had gone out the window along with Laura Delaney's daydreams.

Never a day went by, Miss Pim thought, without the girl upsetting lessons and sending the class astray. But perhaps today would be different. Laura was certainly very quiet.

"Now, Fifth class," Miss Pim smiled. "Let's get the homework sorted before we get on to the pets. I see you've put them on the table at the back, as instructed. Are they all happily settled?"

Danny Smith put up his hand. "Sometimes Smoothy hisses, Miss. But it doesn't mean anything."

"Smoothy?"

"My snake. He's Smoothy cos he's real smooth to touch. People always think snakes are slimy and greasy, but they're not. You can hold him Miss. He's nice. And he can coil around your neck. Once he went down the back of my jumper –"

"Later, Danny!" Miss Pim hastily interrupted, shuddering. Maybe a pets' day wasn't such a good idea. Not if she was expected to hold snakes and let them wind around her neck. The teacher fingered her throat with a choking sensation.

The morning passed uneventfully enough. Laura was lucky to be asked easy spellings in English. Irish was more difficult, though Joe tried to tell her every word she didn't know. He said them out of the side of his mouth. Then when he felt Miss Pim was looking at him, he put a hand up, pretending to cough.

"What's the word for 'meat', Laura?" Miss Pim asked.

"Fe – hegmmm – oil," Joe said.

"Fehegmoil," Laura was confident.

"Pardon?" Miss Pim frowned.

Laura tried a variation, "Fegehemoly."

"Miss Pim glared at her, "I don't know what language you think you're speaking, but I can assure you it's not Irish. Spell the word!"

"F," Laura said.

Miss Pim began to get excited. "F. Yes? F!– F what, please?" Her voice was rising.

Joe slid across a piece of paper. Laura looked as if she were really concentrating and glanced down. "F-e-o-i-l," she said clearly and breathed a sigh of relief as Miss Pim relaxed.

Maths homework should have been much trickier, as Laura had forgotten her copy. But today the teacher did not go from desk to desk, looking at the sums. She knew everyone was eager to move on and so she corrected from the board. Perhaps she felt in need of a break, because she didn't ask Laura to work out any of the problems.

The girl hoped there was no more homework due. With Flabby in her schoolbag she'd had to leave most of her books and copies at home. But the teacher was looking at her watch. "Time for Small Break. After that

I'm really looking forward to all the pets and hearing from their owners!"

The schoolbag under Laura's desk was gently snoring. "Maybe I should feed Flabby now," she thought as the others trooped out. She took the packet of cat-crunch from the side flap and shook a generous amount in. Some fell on his head and back, rising and falling as he slept. "Oh well, at least he has them for when he wakes up," she thought. "No one will notice him eating them in the bag. She pulled the string close and tied it, then followed the others out to the playground.

"What is that dreadful pong?" were Miss Pim's first words back in class. "I noticed it before we went out, but it's definitely worse now!"

"It's Porridge," Cathy Henderson said. "My pigeon. Sorry, Miss, but he's after – he's done a – he's gone to the toilet."

"Does that mean we have to stick the smell for the rest of the day?" When Miss Pim had suggested a pets' day, she'd never thought of the disadvantages and now she was dismayed.

"No, Miss. I can empty the tray. I brought in a plastic bag and a small shovel and some toilet paper. The shovel is for any that won't come off with a shake. The plastic bag is to hold the stuff and the toilet paper is for wiping –"

"*Please!*" Miss Pim was feeling faint. "We do not want all the awful details."

"I was only going to say," Cathy muttered, "that the toilet paper is for wiping the tray."

When she had cleaned up and brought the plastic bag out to the big bin, Miss Pim led the way to the back of the class.

The rabbits and the hamsters were cuddled and stroked. The two budgies loved their audience, twittering with excitement. With so many standing at the back of the class, desks had to be pushed forward to make room.

Danny Smith took his snake out. "Let me hold it!" "No, me first, Danny!" they clamoured. But Danny was adamant. "Miss is first, aren't you, Miss?"

He was so proud of Smoothy that the teacher hadn't the heart to refuse. Gingerly she put out her hands and closed her eyes, smile fixed. But Danny was right. The snake felt nice, sort of dry and smooth. Miss Pim stopped shivering and opened her eyes.

"*Aaaagh!*" she shrieked, not expecting to see Smoothy's face so close to her own. Alarmed, the snake drew back, slid swiftly out of her hands and down onto the floor.

"*Ohmygod!*" Miss Pim was hysterical. "Get him back quickly. We can't have snakes slithering around the classroom!"

But no one could see where he'd gone. There was no sign of him on the floor. Children peered under desks and in the waste-paper basket.

"*Yeeeaaaaaouw!*" There was a terrible screech from Laura's bag. It might have gone unnoticed in the pandemonium, except it was followed by another and

11

another and the bag rolled and heaved of its own accord. Then it actually leapt right off the floor.

The class gaped, suddenly silent, Smoothy forgotten.

Miss Pim was appalled.

Laura couldn't think what was wrong. Flabby couldn't be *that* hungry. He must be hurt.

She rushed to the bag and opened it. The cat leapt out, followed by a very indignant snake, who swayed and hissed until Danny took him up and stroked him. Slowly he quietened.

Laura coaxed Flabby from under a desk.

"Laura Delaney! You had no right bringing in that animal. Cats and dogs are strictly forbidden. I've never heard such a racket!"

"But, Miss, he was very quiet until Smoothy got into his bag. Anybody'd be upset if they were in a bag with a snake. It's not his fault, Miss."

"You're right!" Miss Pim said, but she was glaring. "It's not his fault. It's yours! You can never follow the rules, Laura Delaney. But this time you've gone too far. I've a good mind to bring you straight to the headmistress and have you suspended."

Joe intervened, "She didn't mean any harm, Miss. Flabby isn't like other cats. He never moves. Well, unless he meets a snake or something. Look at him, Miss. He's harmless."

Miss Pim looked. From his owner's arms the Persian gazed at her, his long hair still slightly on end, his expression pitiful.

"Well, I must say he *is* a beautiful cat." In spite of herself she patted him and Flabby purred. Then she stroked his coat and the cat closed his eyes, crooning with contentment. Miss Pim was crooning along with him until she noticed the children staring. Quickly, she stepped away. "Yes. I suppose he is an exceptional cat. But that does not mean an exception can be made for you, Laura. I will give you a note for your parents and you'll stay back tomorrow on detention. In the meantime, you are not to put that wonderful animal in your bag. He deserves better! He can sit on your desk."

All in all, Laura thought she'd got off lightly.

Back at their desks, every owner gave a little talk on their pet. Joe was last.

"My parrot's name is Pasty. I don't know why. That's the name he had when my dad got him."

"Can he talk?" Someone interrupted.

"Why don't you show him to us? Is he horrible-looking?"

"Why won't you take the cover off?"

"Maybe it's just an empty cage."

Joe hesitated. Miss Pim said, "Go on, Joe. Let's see him. No point in bringing him in otherwise."

"He doesn't like a lot of people around him, Miss," Joe said.

"Well, we'll all stay in our seats. You go down, take off the cloth and lift the cage. That way we'll have a good view."

13

Joe did as he was bid and there were gasps of admiration. The cage was very big and Pasty stood on his perch majestically, his beak in the air, his feathers a wonderful mixture of bright yellows and blues.

"Oh, wow!" they said.

"He's deadly!"

Pasty suddenly turned upside-down on his perch. Tired of holding the cage, Joe set it down.

"Oh, I must have a closer look," breathed Miss Pim.

In a second she was in front of the parrot who righted himself. "He is just magnificent. Such a splendid creature! Pretty Pasty, Pretty Pasty." The bird ruffled his feathers and squawked. Miss Pim beamed. "He likes me. Oh you are a pretty, pretty parrot. S-o-o-o pretty."

Pasty pecked fretfully at his perch, then screeched, "Buzz off! Buzz off!"

Fifth class could not believe their ears. "What did he say?"

"Buzz off! Buzz off!" Pasty was shrill and the class went into fits.

"What did that bird say to me?" Miss Pim asked as soon as she could make herself heard. There was a dangerous glint in her eye.

Before Joe could answer, Pasty shrieked, "Get lost! Get Lost!" Then he stuck his head under his wing.

"That's not very nice," Miss Pim said.

The bird's head emerged and he cackled.

The teacher was furious. She turned on Joe, "Did you teach him to be so rude?"

"No, I didn't," said Joe.

"Drop dead!" screeched Pasty, and as the teacher retreated, the words followed her up the classroom, "Drop dead! Drop dead! Drop dead!" Hastily Joe threw the cover over him and the noise stopped.

Looking at the boy's concerned face, the teacher softened. "I suppose he learned all that before you got him," she said. "Don't worry. I know it's not your fault."

On the way home, Laura was very quiet. Joe too was lost in thought, remembering the events of the day.

Laura shook her head as if she were having some argument with herself. Then she burst out, "I don't know how you do it! I just don't."

"Do what?" Joe was mystified.

"Get away with it. I mean, your parrot insults Miss Pim up to the two eyeballs and what happens? She smiles at you and says not to worry. My Flabby almost gets a heart attack because of that mad snake and what happens? I nearly get suspended! It's not fair."

Joe didn't know what to say. He was a bit fed up always being in the right with his teacher.

Then Laura grinned, "Anyway, I didn't get suspended, thanks to you. And it was worth getting into trouble just to see Miss Pim's face when that snake gave her a fright. And when Pasty told her to drop dead. That was the best day ever in school. Even if I do have to stay back tomorrow."

They parted company at Joe's house. As he turned the key in the lock, his expression became grim. He wondered how his dad would be and the day at school faded.

Laura too was not looking forward to going home. Her parents wouldn't like the note from Miss Pim at all.

Chapter 2

Sam went to small school, was learning to write his letters and was home early every day. He thought his sister, Laura was great. She went to big school where they let in cats and she had lots of important books and copies. She didn't like writing in her copies as much as he did. Sam tried to help her with her homework by covering pages with her pen and couldn't understand it when she got very cross.

He had tried to help when Laura complained that her school books were too thick and too heavy. But when he tore pages out, she wasn't a bit grateful.

Sometimes his questions drove her mad. "Why is that horse black?" he'd asked once.

"Because his mum is," Laura told him.

"Why is his mum black?" he'd said then and she knew this question would stretch back in history to the first horse. So she ended up saying crossly, "It's black because it's black. That's the why!"

Sam tried another tack, "Why is he a horse, Laura? Why is he not a dog?"

But although he could be an awful nuisance, sometimes Sam made her feel really important. Like the first time he'd seen snow. It had covered the trees and shrubs in the garden and laid a thick carpet over the lawn, creating a silent wonderland. Sam had stared at it, awestruck, then turned to her, "How did you do that, Laura?" He'd looked at her as if she were magic and she'd told him, "Oh, I just cast a little spell."

That day he'd informed everyone he'd met that his big sister had made all the snow.

Today, as always, he ran down the road to meet her coming home.

"I'm big," he said. "I'll carry your bag."

"No. Mum says it's too heavy. You can't."

"Can so. I'm strong."

"No. Your chin would be touching your toes."

He bent down to see if it were possible and fell over.

"*Please*," his sister said. Then she added darkly, "I hope you've finished your piano-practice!"

He nodded and asked eagerly, "Will I play for you, Laura?"

"Not today! I don't want a headache."

The small boy was not at all insulted. "Can we go to the circus, then?" He asked.

She shook her head, "There is no circus."

"Can we go to the panto?"

"Don't be daft. There's no panto. It's over months ago."

He was desperate. "Can we go to the – to the sun?"
She couldn't say there was no sun. He could see it clearly.

"Too hot. You'd burn your feet. You'd have to walk
like this." She started leaping up and down on her toes.
"That's called the Sun-Walk," she told him. His face lit
up and he copied her. From the window Mrs Delaney
watched her offspring spring up the garden path as if the
ground were on fire.

Laura tumbled Flabby onto the sofa and gave her
astonished mother Miss Pim's note:

Dear Mrs Delaney,

*This is to inform you that your daughter Laura will be
detained on detention after lessons tomorrow. Cats and dogs
have no place in the schoolroom and Fifth class was told this
quite clearly. Laura, however, chose to ignore the rule, and
your Persian gave a severe shock to Danny Smith's snake – a
nervous and highly-strung creature.*

*For this reason she will do half an hour's punishment-work
after school tomorrow.*

Yours,
P. Pim.

Mrs Delaney felt bewildered, not an unusual feeling
where her daughter was concerned.

19

"I know cats shouldn't be in class," she said, "but since when are snakes allowed in? And how could our Flabby upset one so badly? I mean look at him!"

All three gazed at him. He was snoozing on the sofa. Mrs Delaney shook her head, "He won't even stand up to the crows in the garden. How could he leave a snake in shock? I don't understand it."

Laura opened her mouth to explain, but her mum held up a hand. "Don't! Please! Whatever happened I don't want to hear. It's bound to give me a headache. I'm sure Miss Pim is in the right of it and if she wants snakes in the class, well who am I to question? Times change and just because they weren't allowed in my day doesn't mean there's not a perfectly good reason for having them now. But I don't want to hear it. Nor do I want you to bring poor Flabby into school again. He's too old."

Mrs Delaney stopped talking, but her daughter knew the silence was temporary. Her mother was cross. The way she was frowning it was clear she'd start giving out very soon. So after she'd gulped down a sandwich, Laura asked if she could call round to Joe.

"You can if you take Sam with you," her mother said, then added, "Of course you should be grounded for what you put poor Flabby through today!" And Laura hastily swallowed her objections to bringing Sam.

Mr Jameson opened the door in a grumpy mood. "Joe's in there," he said, indicating the TV room. Then he plodded down the hall into the kitchen, leaving them to close the front door. Sam had never met Mr Jameson and was not used to being ignored by grown-ups. Usually they gave him sweets, were nice to him and sometimes swung him in the air. This grown-up was a mystery and so, while his sister went in to Joe, Sam followed Mr Jameson down the hall.

"Hello," Sam said.

Mr Jameson did not reply. He sat at the kitchen table, lifted his newspaper and flapped it open, hiding his face. Sam sat down opposite.

"Are you cross?" he piped.

"Only when someone's disturbing me!" Mr Jameson did not lower his paper.

"Laura says you're always cross." This got no reply. "My mum says it's rude to read when someone's talking," Sam tried again, but again he got no answer. He stared at the hairs on the back of Mr Jameson's hands. "Do you like Guinness?" he asked.

"Why? Are you going to buy me a pint?" came the voice behind the paper.

"Do you have hairs on your chest?" Sam continued, very interested.

"Yes. Do you?" This time the paper lowered an inch.

Sam's face was serious. "No. My mum says Guinness puts hairs on your chest."

"Is that a fact?"

"It is. My granny must have a lot of hairs on her chest cos she loves Guinness."

This time Mr Jameson put the paper down on the

21

table and stared at the child. His face wasn't so cross anymore.

Now that he'd got his attention at last, Sam pressed on, "My mum says Granny has to cut down on the Guinness."

"Is that so?" Mr Jameson said. "Is it because she has a *very* hairy chest?"

"No, it's because she gave out to a policeman when he stopped her for going too fast."

"Good Lord! Well, I suppose we can't have grannies driving around breaking the speed limit."

"My granny doesn't drive. She's too old. She was on her bicycle."

Mr Jameson blinked rapidly and the corners of his mouth turned up slightly.

"And was your granny arrested?"

"The policeman let her off. My mum went to the police station to get her and she was drunk in charge of a bicycle. That's what the policeman said."

"Oh dear, oh dear, oh dear." Mr Jameson put a hand to his mouth.

"I know. My mum says it's shocking."

Mr Jameson seemed to need some time to get over the terrible story. He said nothing for a while, his hand tight over his mouth. When he did eventually speak, his manner was quite friendly. "Would you care to join me in a cup of tea?"

"I would." Sam didn't like tea, but he was chuffed to be asked in such a grown-up way.

A good while later Laura knocked on the kitchen door. She crossed her fingers. She had put off rescuing Sam for as long as she could and wouldn't have been surprised to find the six-year-old in tears and Mr Jameson bursting with rage at his questions.

Her mouth fell open when she saw the two of them. Her brother was finishing a cup of tea and Mr Jameson was leaning back in his chair, smoking a pipe, legs stretched in front of him, arms crossed. As she watched, Sam tilted his chair, stretched his legs and crossed his arms, nodding at whatever it was the man was saying.

Mr Jameson made a point of leaving them to the door, a thing he'd never done before. As Laura said goodbye to Joe she was astounded to hear his dad say, "It was a pleasure to meet you, Sam!" And he solemnly shook his hand.

"What did you two talk about?" she asked on the way home.

"Granny and Flabby and why he's always cross like you said and he has two teeth he can move in and out and he can make a big noise cracking his fingers and —"

"Hang on! You didn't really tell him I said he was always cross, did you?" Laura was horrified.

"I did so. And I told him you said he was a terrible pain."

"Oh my God!"

"And you said he should get a life. I told him that too."

"Oh my *God!* Did he not eat the head off you?"

23

"He ate some biscuits and I did too."

"I bet he'll eat the head off me when I go back there!"

Sam looked at his sister's head. "No he won't, silly. It'd be horrible."

Next day, school was the same as usual. Laura got into minor trouble for messing, chewing gum, not concentrating. Joe was looking a little less strained. He kept his mind for the most part on work, yet even he was caught daydreaming once. But Miss Pim was much nicer to him than to Laura. "Penny for them, Joe," she'd broken his thoughts quite gently, not roaring at him as she usually did at Laura.

Joe had gone red, muttering, "It's nothing, Miss," and concentrated on his book. How could he tell the teacher he'd been thinking about how his dad had been in much better form for a while after Sam's visit. His good humour hadn't lasted, even though Joe had tried to stretch it out, clearing up the dishes, asking if his dad wanted any messages done, sitting quietly during dinner so he couldn't upset him in any way. After a couple of hours, his dad's face was as tight as ever. Still, at least for a while he'd been different. Maybe if Sam came around again . . .

Miss Pim never mentioned detention next day and Laura, who had a very optimistic nature, thought she'd better not mention it either. Probably the teacher had forgotten all about it. Or maybe she'd changed her mind and decided to be nice and forgotten to let Laura know. So when the last bell rang the girl was on her way out of the room when the teacher's outraged voice stopped her. "Just where do you think you're going, Laura Delaney?"

Innocence was called for. "Home, Miss. The bell rang."

"Aren't you forgetting something?"

Laura made her face look extremely puzzled, studying her desk as if she might've left something behind. Then she shook her head, "No, Miss. I've got everything."

Miss Pim gritted her teeth, "Isn't there some unfinished business you have to do?"

Laura thought hard, "No, Miss. I don't think so, Miss."

"Well, think again," the teacher's voice was soft with menace. "Otherwise you'll be getting an extra ten-page essay on 'Memory Loss'. Do I make myself clear? Now what are you supposed to be doing at this minute?"

She was tempted to say, 'Going home,' but one look at Miss Pim's face changed her mind.

"I'm supposed to be doing detention, Miss."

"Exactly!" The teacher breathed hard. "And you've wasted five minutes of my time and five minutes of your time trying to get out of it. So you can stay on an extra ten minutes. Sit down at once and write an essay on 'How we ought to behave in school.'"

Laura sat. Ten more minutes! It was Miss Pim's fault. Asking her a load of silly questions when she knew the answers. Why did teachers always do that? Now Laura had to do this stupid essay. How we ought to behave in school! If Miss Pim had her way she'd be sitting there, not talking, not moving, *not breathing*.

For the next forty minutes Laura chewed her pen,

thought and wrote, for once engrossed in what she was doing. "Time up," Miss Pim said and took up the girl's copy. "I look forward to reading this."

Laura groaned inwardly, sure that her ideas on school behaviour would not be the same as Miss Pim's. She shouldn't have let herself get carried away. She'd only written what she felt but the more she thought about it the more worried she got.

That night she did her homework carefully, on neatly ruled pages, with proper headings and made sure Sam got nowhere near her copies. At one stage Mrs Delaney put a hand on her forehead and asked was she feeling all right.

To avoid as much trouble as she could, Laura was in early next morning – so early she was first after Miss Pim, who was sitting at her desk, exactly the same as when Laura had left the day before. The girl was wondering if the teacher had stayed there all night when she noticed Miss Pim was wearing a different jumper and a different skirt. And from the face on her Laura knew she was reading her essay.

Miss Pim saw her and narrowed her eyes. There was silence while she stared coldly and accusingly. Feeling a tremor of fear, Laura could not hold her gaze. What would happen? Would she be hauled up in front of the head? Would she be suspended?

Miss Pim took a deep breath and said, "I've never come across the like of this before. Now you read this out to me while I figure out what punishment you deserve."

Laura read. At first her voice quaked, but as she went on, it became firmer. She believed in what she'd written:

Behaving in School.

I don't think we should have to be quiet all the time in school. Miss Pim says there has to be silence when we are working, else we will make mistakes. But yesterday another teacher came into class when we were writing and Miss Pim and her talked and laughed and they were not a bit quiet. But when we do it we get punished.

I think we should be allowed to eat in class. Sometimes you get very hungry and it is a long time to Small Break. Eating or drinking would not stop you working. Miss Pim often has a cup of coffee while she is correcting or taking the roll.

We should be allowed chew gum. Miss Pim says we're not because we stick it under the desk and on the radiator, but if it was not against the rules we would put it in the bin. A lot of people eat it anyway so this rule doesn't work.

Teachers are always saying things ten times and more. They say, 'I will only say this once and once only,' and then they go on and on saying it and your mind goes deaf and then you get the rules to write ten times cos you're not listening and I don't think it's fair.

Teachers should not be allowed to ask questions like do I look like an idiot? or am I wasting my time? Because if you say 'yes' you are in terrible trouble. And they tell you that you're lazy and careless and other insults but you can't tell them they're grumps and moans or you're killed.

27

If I was a teacher (which I hope not to be) I would let people talk sometimes and eat sweets and chew gum. I would let them say things and I would not be always giving out.

The end.

Laura looked up, caught Miss Pim's eye and looked away again. She was for it now. The copy shook.

The teacher was silent, thoughtful. She had thought the girl would read the essay defiantly, but it was obvious Laura hadn't intended to be brazen. The tone was fed-up, not cheeky, though you had to hear her to realise that. She sighed and said, "Look, I don't agree with your point of view. Teachers have to keep order and there have to be rules. If you could all drink while you were working, somebody would be bound to spill some and copies would be ruined. But I am prepared to accept that you didn't intend any cheek. So I'm going to take those pages, tear them up and forget that essay was ever written. All right?"

Laura couldn't believe her luck. She wasn't going to be suspended! She wasn't even going to get lines. Hastily she handed over the copy and Miss Pim tore up the offending pages. Laura never wanted to see them again anyway and Miss Pim certainly didn't want her showing them around the class.

As more people came in, Laura and Miss Pim smiled at each other warily, both glad the unpleasantness was over.

Chapter 3

Miss Pim did not want Laura to think she'd gotten away with anything, so she checked her homework carefully. In spite of herself, she was impressed. The girl's written work was neat and tidy and her learning was perfect. Looking at her Irish copy, the teacher found herself saying, "You know, this is very good. You've made a real effort."

Laura was delighted until the teacher added, "Try listening today. Then maybe I won't have to repeat myself so often." But her smile took the sting out of her words and after a moment Laura smiled back.

Just before lunch, Miss Briteside, the principal, arrived into class. As usual, she was full of enthusiasm. "Now boys and girls, stop whatever you're doing, put down all pens, close all books. I have something *very* important to say."

Glad of a break in routine they sat back.

"Fifth class, I want you to put on your thinking caps. What would be the best present this school could get?"

They thought for two seconds.

"A half day, Miss."

"A full day off? More holidays?"

Miss Briteside shook her head. "Not at all. Those are foolish desires. I mean something lasting!"

"A half day off every week, Miss. Forever."

"Or a school cinema. That'd be deadly."

Miss Briteside frowned. These were not the answers she wanted. "No, no, no. I see I shall have to tell you. The best present this school could get is a new school gym! Isn't that true?"

The class struggled. A school gym might be all right, but it wasn't as good as a cinema or half days.

"Isn't that true, Fifth class?" There was an edge to the principal's voice.

"Yes, Miss," they muttered.

"Of course it is. And that's why I'm here. I want you to do some fundraising."

"Not again!" Laura spoke without thinking. Miss Briteside was always getting them to raise money for school projects – a minibus, a soccer pitch, a school library.

"Yes, again." Miss Briteside said. "And why not again?" Her voice was a little acid.

The class looked decidedly unenthusiastic.

"Now, who will volunteer?" No one raised a hand.

"Of course there will be a prize for the person who raises the most money," she added. A little bribery might work wonders. This time they did not fall for it.

"What kind of prize?" Danny Smith asked.

"Probably a set of hardback copies," Cathy Henderson groaned. "Or a dictionary. That was the prize last time."

Miss Briteside did not give up. "I see. Methinks you have fundraising-fatigue. Nevertheless we need a school gym and the Department of Education has no money to provide one at the moment. So, I shall have to come up with a really interesting reward. Now I'm going to my office, to have a good thinking session and after lunch I'll be back with the best prize you ever dreamed of." She beamed at them and went. Outside she leaned against the door. "What on earth can I give that will make them want to raise oodles of money?"

Inside the class buzzed. "Maybe the prize will be a holiday to Disneyland."

"No it won't! That'd cost too much."

"It'd be worth it," said Joe dreamily. "I'd remember a prize like that forever."

Laura was gloomy, "When she says a really interesting reward, she probably means two dictionaries instead of one!"

The others had to agree. In the past Miss Briteside had promised wonderful rewards and they'd always been a total let-down; The dictionary wasn't the worst. Not when you compared it to the photograph of the school building; or the framed map of Ireland; or to the Book of

31

World History in three volumes, magnifying glass included because the print was so small. And each time she'd behaved as if she were giving the winner a gold crown.

And not only had the prizes been a disaster, but their parents had been roped in as fundraisers too, an experience some of them never forgot – or let their children forget.

Laura's dad had organised an outing for the neighbours. Much as she loved him, it was Laura's private belief that her father couldn't organise his shoelaces, never mind the mystery tour he'd planned. The neighbours paid five pounds a head for Mr Delaney to drive them in a hired bus to an unknown destination. Only the destination was unknown to Mr Delaney too. When the bus broke down he hadn't a clue where he was. Everybody had been happily singing, paying no attention to signposts. When the engine coughed and died they were surrounded by mountains and bogland and while they had mobiles galore, they couldn't give any directions.

In the end the whole lot of them walked ten miles to the nearest village. The one daily bus to Dublin had long gone. Eventually they hired taxis – twelve of them – to come out from the city and bring them home. It was very expensive, as they kept telling Laura's dad any time they met him afterwards. He took to sneaking about and if he glimpsed a neighbour he broke into a run. He blamed it all on Laura. "Never get me involved again in any of your daft schemes!" he told her. Often.

Joe's dad had insisted on having a coffee morning to raise money. "It'll give me something to do," he'd told his son, "make me feel useful for a change." He'd been very enthusiastic, putting leaflets through letterboxes and spending a lot of his dole money on cakes, biscuits, 'real' coffee and new china.

The day arrived and Mr Jameson had everything ready. At eleven o'clock he was nervously waiting for the first arrival. At half eleven he was still waiting, a little disappointed. By twelve he realised no one was going to turn up and his good humour disappeared. The poor man was convinced everyone disliked him and he swept all the food into the dustbin. He snapped at Joe and ranted about the neighbours and their rudeness. "I put on the leaflet that they need only reply if they couldn't come and they hadn't even the decency to do that!"

Next day he was still so upset he didn't bother clearing up after breakfast, just went back to bed and buried his head under the covers. And later when the bell rang he didn't answer it for ages, until it was so loud and insistent it got on his nerves and he leapt out of bed and rushed down in a rage. About twenty neighbours were on the doorstep, rather surprised to see Mr Jameson in his pyjamas and dressing-gown, looking ready to shoot them.

"No, it was definitely today," they said, showing him the date on the leaflets. Joe's dad nearly died again. No food, a messy house and himself not dressed!

The neighbours were very understanding:

"Not to worry. Could happen to anyone. Easy mistake to make. Another time!" they said as they left.

But Mr Jameson was raging; at himself and at the fundraising that had got him into this mess. "Never again!" he vowed and he flung one of the china cups on the tiled kitchen floor.

Cathy Henderson's mum had decided on a ten-mile sponsored walk. She'd got as far as the end of the road when she tripped over a dog and sprained her ankle. She was lying on the ground moaning, unable to struggle to her feet – or at least to her one good foot – because the dog was sitting on her chest, licking her face. And while the dog wasn't exactly a Saint Bernard, he was pretty hefty. Mrs Henderson, who always exaggerated, said she'd had to endure, "two hours with a flamin' bear crushing me to death!" Cathy said it was more like ten minutes, but it had put her mum off fundraising for life.

Danny Smith's parents had had a terrible experience. They had a bottle auction at their house. The idea was that everyone gave a bottle of whiskey or vodka or whatever and Mr Smith sold it to the highest bidder. The auction took place in the Smith's back garden on a bright Saturday afternoon in Spring. About sixty neighbours turned up and it was such a success that Mr Smith decided to open the bottle he'd bought and share it around. Everyone thought that was a great idea and opened theirs too. Glasses, cups, mugs, plastic containers, even a small vase were brought out from the house to drink from.

There was an air of celebration because so much money had been raised and everyone drank a toast to the school. Then there was a toast to Miss Briteside, another to all the teachers, one to Mr Smith for having had such a great idea, and to Mrs Smith for being married to him and one to all their family just for being Smiths. As the afternoon and evening wore on chairs were brought out to sit on, and a few stools, a couple of rugs, then a sofa and armchairs and even a duvet.

Danny said everything was grand until someone produced a guitar and a neighbour started singing "Pretty Woman" to a lady who wasn't his wife. The lady who was his wife got very annoyed and threw her glass at him, only she hit someone else who thought it was deliberate and went for her. The husband tried to rescue his wife and got a wallop for his pains. The lady who wasn't his wife decided to join in. Then *her* husband felt obliged to help and very soon everyone in the garden was involved. Sofas and chairs were overturned, bottles smashed, noses bloodied and shirts ripped. There was such uproar nobody heard the sirens. It took six policemen half an hour to restore peace. The garden looked like a war zone. Everyone was totally ashamed of themselves. "I can't believe it, such a nice, quiet, respectable neighbourhood!" they said afterwards, as they chipped in to replace the wrecked furniture.

Mr and Mrs Smith had had to go to bed for a couple of hours and it was only when they came out later to look at the damage that they heard moaning from behind the bush and rescued the last neighbour who'd managed to get tangled up in the duvet.

Never again, they'd all said.

Laura's dad commented, "Any fundraising to do with your school is jinxed!" And he was right. Sales of work, pub-quizzes, bingo – all of them had been disasters. Yet the money was always raised for whatever project Miss Briteside had in mind. "Well, of course it is!" Laura's dad said. "Everyone feels so sorry when things go wrong for the poor fundraiser, that they give far more than they usually would. But never again!"

Fifth class shared their parents' view. Never again. There was no prize Miss Briteside could come up with that would make them interested.

But they had underestimated their headmistress. After lunch she was back, beaming, crackling with enthusiasm. "I'm going to put the *fun* back into *fun*draising," she announced, rubbing her hands.

There was a groan.

"Didn't I say I'd think of something interesting?" she continued. Another moan was taken for agreement. "Well, this prize is not only interesting, but unusual in the extreme."

A few rolled eyes and sighs greeted this.

"And the beauty of it is, boys and girls, it will cost absolutely nothing – not a penny!"

Typical! they thought. How could it be any good?

"So. What do you think it is?" she asked brightly, obviously expecting enthusiastic curiosity.

"Dunno, Miss." Cathy Henderson stifled a yawn.

"Not much, that's for sure, since it's worth nothing," Danny Smith murmured.

Miss Briteside heard him. "Now, that's where you're wrong, Danny. I said it cost nothing, not that it was worth nothing. In fact it's worth a great deal to any schoolchild."

And in spite of themselves they wanted to hear more. Miss Briteside smiled to herself and was silent, until someone said, "Go on, Miss, what's the prize?" Then they all clamoured. Did someone give her free tickets for Oasis? Or a year's free supply of chocolate?

Miss Briteside raised a hand, "Yes, I did get tickets for Oasis and I got lots of boxes of chocolates, but they are going to be raffled in aid of the gym. And anyway, what I have for you is much better! Now I realise you'll never guess, not in a million years, so I'm going to tell you!" She paused.

They hushed each other into silence, hardly breathing.

"This is the prize of your dreams, boys and girls. A magnificent reward for whoever raises the most money. That person will get –" she paused, savouring their rapt expressions, then repeated in ringing tones:

"THAT PERSON WILL GET TO BE TEACHER FOR A DAY!"

Well! Miss Briteside let it sink in. Fifth class thought about it. Teacher for a day. What did that mean exactly?

Would the winner really be in charge? Would he or she be able to tell everyone what to do? Give homework, punishment work, detentions? Send people on messages? Give out, shout, send troublemakers to the principal's office? Or have a day without schoolwork? Maybe declare a fifth-class party-day? A fancy-dress day?

As the possibilities occurred to them, each member of the class became more and more interested in being the winner. It was very tempting.

But where would Miss Pim be on that day? Would she be there, really in charge, ready to take over at a second's trouble? Miss Briteside always promised more than she delivered and the suspicion grew that she would not really let an eleven-year-old be the class teacher.

As if she knew what they were thinking, Miss Briteside said, "Of course the winner will be fully in charge!"

Up to this, Miss Pim had said nothing, probably because she was in a state of shock. Now she was galvanised. "Miss Briteside, I must protest! There will be chaos!"

"Not at all." The principal was blithe. "This will give the class and the winner a chance to show how responsible they are."

"And what will I be doing?" Miss Pim felt weak.

"Oh, you'll be one of the pupils. You'll take the winner's desk and you'll have to do as you're told." Noting the teacher's horrified face, Miss Briteside frowned. "Surely you see this as a wonderful opportunity?"

"Opportunity?" Miss Pim squeaked, taking a copy from the desk and fanning herself with it. This was a nightmare.

Her principal spoke firmly. "Yes! Opportunity. Not only will this brilliant idea of mine cost nothing, it will raise pots of money for the school and give you the chance to see things from your pupils' point of view for a day."

Miss Pim did not think this new point of view would be particularly good for her health, but before she could say so, there was a mighty cheer from the class.

Smiling, the principal turned to them, "Now of course there cannot be mayhem. Nothing dangerous allowed. Your safety must be guaranteed. Is that fair enough?"

By this time the class was swept away by the whole idea and shouted their agreement.

"But otherwise the winner will be in sole charge," Miss Briteside went on. "Of course he or she will have to sign an agreement to keep order, and there will be a little penalty to pay if there *is* mayhem. And if things get really bad then of course Miss Pim will have to take over, but *only*, and I stress *only*, if the winner asks her to. Does that meet with your approval?"

Miss Pim tried to protest, but she was drowned out by the class who hardly noticed the word penalty, but clearly heard the rest. Which of them in their right mind they thought, would ask for Miss Pim's help? Anyway, they wouldn't need it. The day would be great fun, which didn't mean they were all going to go mad, did it? And

the idea of their teacher having to be a pupil for a day –
well that was the icing on the cake! Miss Pim having to
sit in a desk, follow orders, do boring class work while one
of themselves stood at the top of the class giving orders –
that was deadly!

Never in the history of education was a principal
cheered the way Miss Briteside was cheered that
afternoon by fifth class.

Chapter 4

The minute the last bell went, Fifth class emptied. Everyone was eager to discuss the 'Teacher for a Day' prize, not least Miss Pim, who made a beeline for the principal's office. She had thought of nothing else since it had been mentioned, and now she gritted her teeth and knocked on the head's door.

"Come in and welcome," Miss Briteside sang out, obviously in great form.

The Fifth class teacher on the other hand was almost weeping. "I cannot go through with this," she told her superior.

"Of course you can. Cheer up, woman! It's for the good of the school."

"For the good of the school!" Indignation gave the teacher courage. "The school will run amok! Fifth class will, anyway. I cannot be a party to it."

Miss Briteside tried her most soothing manner, "You don't give your class enough credit. I mean, you've done wonders with them. They can easily handle this."

"No they can't. And neither can I, Miss Briteside. My nerves are in shreds just thinking about it. I want early retirement!"

"Don't be ridiculous!" the head said. "You can't have early retirement. Not at twenty-five!"

"Twenty-six – and rapidly ageing." The teacher was almost hysterical. "I wouldn't be surprised if my hair went grey in the next day or two. Miss Briteside, I don't think this is a good idea at all. Does the Department of Education know about it?"

"Sure if the department had given us funds in the first place, I wouldn't need to be raising money. Now, you know we need a gym, don't you?"

"I suppose so. Certainly, it'd be nice for the children to have indoor games and athletics."

Miss Briteside was her most persuasive, "And you know that we can't afford a decent prize that costs money and we have to offer something that will make the children interested in raising funds. This is it. Of course, if you have any other ideas, I'd be glad to consider them."

The teacher shook her head.

"So it has to be 'Teacher for a Day'," said the principal. "Anyway, the prize is open to all children from second class up, so there's only a slim chance that one of your pupils will win."

Miss Pim brightened. Of course! The competition

would have to be open to more than her class. Why hadn't she thought of that? Giving herself a nervous breakdown when the odds were at least two hundred to one against somebody from Fifth winning. No longer depressed, she left the office, relief making her beam idiotically.

On the way home, Laura and Joe discussed plans. "We'll have to think of something really different, so we can make loads of money." Laura said.

"I don't want to win," Joe said. "I'd hate bossing everyone around."

"I wouldn't!" Laura was certain. "I'd love bossing Miss Pim – giving her a taste of her own medicine."

Joe looked a bit nervous. "It's only for a day, Laura. She'll be in charge again after that. Anyway, she's not so bad. She was quite nice to you today."

"Once in a blue moon!" Laura was bitter. "And that's because I was perfect. No one else is given out to every time they get things wrong. She's always picking on me and it's not fair! I'd love to win this competition."

"Well, I'll help you. We'll do it together and if we raise the most money, you can have the prize."

They decided on a garden-gate sale. Laura would design a leaflet on the computer and Joe would make a big placard for her front garden, advertising the sale for the following Saturday. In the meantime they would go through all their belongings for items to sell.

Mrs Delaney was a bit reluctant. "I'm not so sure about

a sale in our front garden. Your father's right, you know. Every fundraising effort for that school has gone wrong. What with Mrs Henderson's sponsored walk, your dad's mystery tour and everything else."

"Oh, Mum!" Laura pleaded. "It's for a good cause. And anyway, not everything went wrong. Cathy says her mum got really fond of that dog who sat on her. She brings him for a walk every day now for the old lady who owns him. She's got really fit and is going in for the women's marathon. And Mr Smith formed a 'whiskey appreciation' club after his bottle party. So that wasn't a total disaster. And Dad hasn't got lost since the mystery tour, has he?"

Her mum was thoughtful. "No, he hasn't. Perhaps it taught him a lesson. He seems to actually look at signposts these days."

Laura pressed home, "And what could possibly go wrong with a sale in the garden?"

Mrs Delaney looked at her sharply, "I've never known you to be so keen. What's the prize?"

When Laura explained, her mum was horrified. "Teacher for a day? That principal is daft! Children your age need a grown-up in control. Otherwise they run wild!"

"Not like adults!" Her daughter was sarcastic. "Adults always behave themselves. They never have mad bottle parties and the police never have to stop them fighting. I still have that photo of you and Dad being led away by the sergeant."

Her mum was scarlet, "It's a pity we ever gave you that

camera. I told you before, the three of us were just walking down the garden path together."

"Huh! I don't think so. The policeman's gripping you and Dad by the arms and Dad has no buttons on his shirt and your jacket is torn. It's all in the photo. Anyway, Fifth class won't be like that. Miss Pim will be there the whole time." Laura did not say Miss Pim would be a pupil.

Mrs Delaney at last agreed to the sale and to a sign in the garden. Laura went to make a notice on the computer, helped by Sam, who was highly excited at the idea of a shop in his front garden.

"We could pick flowers and sell them," he said, looking out the window.

The flowerbeds were full of irises, daffodils and mgnificent crimson tulips, their mother's pride and joy.

"Sam, that is a brilliant idea!"

Her brother was chuffed. "I'm very clever, aren't I? I'll go and tell Mum."

He was almost out the door when Laura caught him by his jumper. "No, don't do that. I need you to give me some more brilliant ideas for my leaflet."

With this encouragement Sam made a million suggestions, "I'll sell my swimming togs. You can put them in the leaflet. And remember my crutches? For when I broke my leg. You can sell them, Laura. Crutches are useful."

His sister did not want his help, but neither did she want him to tell their mother she intended to sell her flowers. Her mother's garden was the envy of the neighbourhood and Laura reckoned people would pay a lot for a bunch of tulips or daffodils. In the end she kept her brother happy by letting him add the last two lines to the poem she made for the notices, though she thought his lines didn't match the rest.

Please do not Fail

To come to the Sale

At Delaney's Gate

– Saturday's the Date

Books and Toys

For Girls and Boys

And Comics Galore

Don't Forget

Come round at Four.

And we're selling loads of big huge flowers
That are nearly as high as enormous giant
Towers.

"Would you not just say, 'as high as towers'?" Laura asked him.

"But I like the other words!" Sam looked so pleased with himself she said no more. She let him do the decorations and he put pictures of wardrobes all around the edges.

"Why wardrobes?" Laura asked him. "We won't be selling any."

"Cos I have a new wardrobe in my bedroom," he said, and that was that.

Laura printed off a stack of notices. She didn't want her mother to see them and called from the hall, "Can I take Sam around to Joe, Mum?"

"As long as you're back before six," her mum shouted.

"Will you help me put these leaflets in letterboxes?" she asked Joe as soon as he opened the door.

"I made up the last two lines," Sam told him proudly.

Mr Jameson heard Sam's voice and came out. The little boy gave him one of the fliers. "I did that part there," he pointed out the end.

"Excellent! I love all the words in the last line," said Mr Jameson.

"Will you come to our shop?" Sam asked. "I'm going to sell my crutches."

"Oh, I bet there'll be a run on them." Mr Jameson smiled and Joe looked astounded. He couldn't remember when his father had last made a joke.

"And I'm going to sell my togs," Sam went on, "They're too small and there's hole in them. Can people sell anything, Mr Jameson?"

47

Mr Jameson considered the question seriously. "I suppose you can sell anything if someone wants to buy it. Why, what else were you thinking of?"

"I thought we might sell my granny's bicycle," he said. "Then she wouldn't get into trouble for speeding."

Mr Jameson thought a bit, then said, "You'd have to ask your granny, get her permission. She might be very fond of that bike. You think of your favourite toy, Sam. Would you like it sold without being asked?"

"No, I wouldn't. I think you're very good at answering questions."

"And you're very good at asking them, my boy."

He watched as the three set off. Joe and Laura put the fliers through the letterbox, but Sam knocked at his first door and then engaged in conversation with the woman of the house. Mr Jameson could see the smile on her face. "He'll get them all coming to the sale," he chuckled.

Next evening, Joe arrived at Laura's with the placard. Onto a rigid sheet of orange plastic he had painted the words:

SALE

GARDEN-GATE

SATURDAY 4PM

And he had nailed the sign to a long pole. Laura fetched a spade and dug a hole in the front garden. She held the pole steady while Joe packed the soil around it. Pleased with their work they stood back as Sam did a Red-Indian war dance around the pole. A passing neighbour stopped, "Very nice indeed. I got your flier in the door and I can't wait to buy some of those beautiful tulips." Laura prayed no one would mention flowers to her mother.

Joe was concerned, "Did you ask your mum about selling her flowers?"

"No need," Laura said airily. "She's not going to miss a few here and there."

Mr Delaney arrived home from work that day a bit tetchy. Nobody had thought to mention the sale to him and the large orange sign in the garden took him by surprise. "Why are you selling the garden gate?" he asked his wife. Mrs Delaney was making the dinner and listening to the radio. She vaguely kissed the air near her husband's cheek. "Hello, dear. Did you have a nice day?"

He kissed the air back and turned down the volume, "Reasonable. But I want to know why our garden gate is up for sale. It's been there for years. Nothing wrong with it. If we're selling it I'll have a job getting it off the hinges."

Mrs Delaney stared at her husband, thinking maybe more than the garden gate was unhinged. Where did he get this crazy idea? "Are you sure you had a good day, dear? No crisis at the office? Nobody going mad asking daft questions?"

For an answer he gripped her arm, rushed her up the

hall and out into the garden and stood her in front of the sign. She looked at it and looked at her lawn. "My God, I'll kill that girl! I thought she was going to put a sign on the gate. Look at that flamin' big hole. She's ruined the garden!" And she ran inside roaring for Laura, with Mr Delaney running after her shouting, "I want to know about the garden gate!"

Sam thought he'd be safer in his room and disappeared upstairs. Laura had to face the music alone. Eventually her parents calmed down, though not before her mum said she could do two hours weeding as a punishment for vandalising the lawn. Her father on the other hand was relieved no one wanted to get rid of his old gate. And Laura for the first time wondered whether the fundraising was worth all the hassle.

She had more doubts next day in school. Everyone discussing their plans to make money didn't do Miss Pim's humour any good. She was so grumpy Laura asked to go to the toilet just to get a break.

"You're allowed one minute, that's all," the teacher snapped. Laura was going to point out that it would take more than that to walk down to the toilet block, which was at the end of the long corridor, but one look at Miss Pim's face changed her mind.

As she zoomed down the corridor, she heard a faint tinkling noise. It was coming from the yard. Laura looked out the window. Two very old lanterns stood beside a large dustbin. The glass in one of them was loose and the breeze made it tinkle against the brass.

About to move on, Laura had a sudden brainwave. "I bet I could sell those on Saturday. Better than throwing them out." It occurred to her that if another pupil saw them, they might get the same idea, so she ran out the side door and picked them up. Where to put them? Miss Pim would have a fit if she brought them back to class. She wasn't supposed to be in the yard. And her minute was well up.

Without time to plan, Laura brought them to the girls' toilet, held up the cistern lid and put one down on either side. Not very large, they fitted quite neatly. Having closed the lid, she raced back to class and arrived gasping. Miss Pim glared at her, but said nothing.

Twenty minutes later the voice of an agitated Miss Briteside came over the intercom:

"Has any student or teacher seen two small antique carriage lamps? They are more than one hundred years old. I was carrying them across the yard from the storeroom to my office when I saw through the window that Miss Simmons needed some assistance with books she was taking to Fourth class. I set the lamps down in the yard and was gone for less than five minutes. In that time they disappeared.

"Now, boys and girls, this is a serious matter. Those lamps are worth a small fortune and would help significantly in the raising of funds for the gym. If any of you saw anything – caught a glimpse of the thief who stole them – please let me know at once!"

Laura was stunned, unable to move. Around her the class was buzzing. Then the voice was on the intercom once more, this time on a different matter.

"I must ask all girls not to use the toilets on the long corridor. The caretaker has just informed me that there is considerable flooding in the area."

Closing her eyes, Laura moaned.

"What's wrong?" Joe asked, "You look terrible."

Springing from her seat, the girl pushed her way along the row.

"Laura Delaney! Sit down at once!" Miss Pim could not believe it when Laura ignored her and ran out of the room.

Outside the girls' toilets, the water level was an inch and rising. Miss Briteside was mopping the floor and Laura could hear the caretaker shouting from inside, "I'll have to check all the loos. There's some blockage causing the water to go the wrong way when the toilet is flushed. I"ll have a look at the cisterns."

Laura came to a halt, "It's the antique lanterns!" she gasped. "Oh Miss, I put them down the toilet."

"I beg your pardon?" was all Miss Briteside could manage.

Laura wailed, "It's my fault the toilet is blocked. I put your antique lanterns down the back of one. Only I didn't know they were yours. And I didn't know they were valuable. I thought they were rubbish, Miss."

"How on earth could you think they were rubbish?" Miss Briteside was furious. "And may I ask if it's a habit of yours to put rubbish down the cistern instead of in the bin?"

"But that's just it, Miss. Those lanterns were beside the bins. That's why I thought they were rubbish. And I put them in the toilet because I wanted to hide them."

The caretaker emerged with two wet lanterns, which were otherwise non the worse for wear. Miss Briteside sighed. "I really don't wish to know why you wanted to hide them, or why you picked a toilet as a suitable place. But I suppose I must ask."

Bit by bit, Laura explained her actions.

When she'd finished the head handed her the mop and took the lanterns from the caretaker.

"You created this mess," she told Laura, "so you may clear it up. And I don't want to see a drop of water on the floor when I come back."

When the bell rang and the students poured out, they were much amused to see Laura, sleeves rolled up, wringing out the mop and cleaning up the floor. Some of them even wondered if it was a way of raising money for the gym.

Laura felt sick.

But at least when she went to get her schoolbag, Miss Pim had already gone.

Chapter 5

Next morning the teacher wasn't at all pleased with Laura. She started on her immediately she came through the door. "How dare you carry on as you did yesterday!"

Not sure which part of her carry-on Miss Pim was referring to, Laura said, "What do you mean, Miss?"

"What do I mean? What do I mean?" She almost choked with rage. "Have you no idea how badly you behaved? You committed *three* major offences. One, you went to the yard without permission; two, you took what didn't belong to you; three, you hid it in the toilet; four, you caused a flood and five, you ran out of here without asking."

"But that's five, Miss."

"Yes. It is. Five major offences!"

"But you said three, Miss."

The teachers eyes glittered, "Don't you get cheeky

with me, Laura Delaney. Five hundred offences is nearer the mark where you're concerned. Now you can stay back after school, write the rules out twenty times. I can't be here to keep an eye on you, but Miss Briteside will be in her office if there's any emergency. And if I don't find those rules on my desk in the morning, there will be H.T.P. What will there be?"

"H.T.P. Miss."

"And do you know what that means?"

Laura hadn't a clue but tried her best, "Is it some sort of sauce, Miss?"

"No, it isn't. There's enough sauce in this class from you, Laura Delaney, without me providing any extra. H.T.P. stands for 'Hell to Pay' and that's what there'll be in here tomorrow if you don't do as you're told. Is that clear?"

Laura moaned, "But Miss, I've to do some gardening after school."

Miss Pim snorted, "A likely story. Only a maniac would let you near their garden."

"My mum wants me to do some weeding," Laura was indignant, "and she's not a maniac!"

Miss Pim looked doubtful, but said only, "You'll be staying here after school. Of course I will give you a letter home, explaining matters."

Joe smiled sympathetically when Laura sat down. She whispered, "What am I going to do? The rules take up an A4 page. I'll be here for weeks. If I don't get home I'm in

55

real trouble. And if Miss Pim writes everything that happened in a letter, I'll be grounded forever."

"Don't worry," Joe said and could add no more as the teacher was frowning at them. But soon he slipped across a note:

Every spare second we have we can write out the rules. That way you'll have them done when the bell goes and you can leave soon after Miss Pim. I'll ask Danny and Cathy to help as well.

But Laura saw a major problem with this idea and wrote back:

She'll notice the different handwriting!

Joe smiled at her and shook his head. As soon he could he sent the message:

No, she won't. Not if we number the pages. She always says punishment work is for us, not for her. She'll only read a small bit, check the number of pages, then put the whole lot in the bin. That's what she always does.

So anytime they got written work during the day, the four friends finished it quickly and wrote as many rules as possible. Small-Break and lunch were spent writing and it was half-way through the afternoon before the last set of rules was completed.

After the last bell went, Miss Pim satisfied herself that the girl had paper and pen in front of her, ready to settle down to a couple of hours' work, then she left.

Laura waited a few minutes, then arranged the sheets of rules on Miss Pim's desk, her own handwriting on top. She was flying out the main door when she had to turn on her heel and fly back in again.

Heart in her mouth, she peered out. Miss Pim was just about to get into her car. One second later, with the teacher in the driving seat, Laura wouldn't have seen her. She'd have been caught. She'd have been dead!

As the car drew away, she sighed with relief. This time she moved more cautiously, just in case Miss Pim came back for something.

Joe and the others were waiting for her at the corner.

"Thanks a million," she told Cathy and Danny. "You got me out of a real hole." She turned to Joe, "You're a genius! If you hadn't thought of a way to help, I'd be in terrible trouble. Now I don't even have to show Mum her letter."

Laura spent a backbreaking two hours weeding. She could hear Sam practising on the piano through the open sitting-room window. He really was desperate, she thought.

By the time she was finished, every muscle and every joint was creaking. She had done her best. Mum came to check her work and stared frowning at one particular corner. "It looks very baldy," she said.

Laura felt her tone was a bit unfair. "It's because I took out every single weed, like you told me."

"I think you took out more than the weeds. I could've sworn there were some bedding plants here!"

"Well, I didn't see them. I only saw weeds!" Laura could have wept. If her mother went through the rubbish bag and found any of her precious plants, she'd probably have to spend another two hours putting them back.

Mrs Delaney looked at her daughter's exhausted face. "Well, there are certainly no weeds left. So I suppose it's a job well done."

The weeding had been made worse by having to listen to Sam banging away at the keys.

Until recently, Sam had had a music teacher, a Miss Hartigan. She was highly strung and Sam's playing had not improved her temperament. "He doesn't listen to instructions," she moaned at Mrs Delaney after the first lesson.

"That's probably because he's so creative," Mum had said with pride.

Miss Hartigan was somewhat sharp, "Yes, maybe. But even the great composers played with their fingers. Sam used his elbows!"

"He's just trying out new ideas." His mum was unshaken. "He'll probably compose something great one day."

"Like 'Sonata for Elbows'," snapped the music teacher and flounced off.

Laura tried telling her mother that Sam had no

musical talent. After all, where would he get it? The family on both sides were tone-deaf for generations. Laura herself, in spite of many lessons, hadn't mastered even the simplest tune.

But Mrs Delaney dreamed on. Sam would succeed where the rest of them had failed. And it was true he loved the piano and practised whenever he could. Except he definitely seemed to have something against using his fingers. "They're too small," he'd told his mother. "I can't do proper sounds with them."

Laura had seen him playing with his nose, only giving up when it got a bit raw. Another time he wanted to get at some music sheets on top of the piano and knelt up on the keys to reach them. He liked the sound so much, he kept doing it.

Then he discovered he could make a wonderful rolling clang if he swept his arms along the keys and that occupied him for days.

The music teacher came every week for ages, getting paler and more strained all the time. But when she arrived early one day to find Sam trying to play with his bare toes, she gave up.

"He's awful! I've never heard anyone so atrocious!" She told his disappointed mum.

"But he's only six. Give him a chance," Mrs Delaney pleaded.

"When Mozart was six, he could play beautifully," sniffed Miss Hartigan, then added testily, "but then *he* used his fingers. *He* knew his nose was for blowing and his feet for walking. *He* knew his elbows were for leaning on, his knees for kneeling and his teeth for chewing. *He* did not try to play the piano with these parts of his body!" She was getting hysterical, her voice rising, "You should lock that piano away, Mrs Delaney." She sniffed. "Better still, lock that child away!" With this parting shot she practically ran down the garden path.

"I'm sure he didn't play with his teeth," Mrs Delaney murmured. "The woman is exaggerating." Sam was so creative, she'd convinced herself, he didn't need a teacher. He would discover music for himself.

"Yes, Mum, he'll learn to play by ear – that's if he hasn't tried his ear already," and Laura collapsed in giggles.

But Mrs Delaney didn't give up for a long time. Not until that day.

She allowed Sam to play any time he wanted and on the afternoon Laura was weeding he played for the full two hours, jangling on and on, every horrendous sound throbbing with his sister's aching muscles. He'd gotten louder and louder and the house had vibrated until even his mother had had enough. She strode in, lifted Sam away and locked the piano. "That's it," she said. "No more."

"Oh thank God," said Mr Delaney when he came in from work. He had taken to using his Walkman whenever Sam made for the front room.

"That's wonderful news," the next-door neighbour said when he heard.

"All my prayers are answered at last!" the woman on the other side exclaimed.

That night in the local paper, Laura saw a large notice:

VERSE COMPETITION

1st Prize 300

2nd Prize 200

3rd Prize 100

> *Take the time, compose a rhyme*
> *On anything new, it's up to you*
> *Funny or sad, thoughtful or mad*
> *Make up your minds, do 24 lines*
> *You've 14 days in which to amaze*
> *The judges' eyes and win a prize.*

"Mum, you can write poems, can't you?"

"Well, I'm not bad at rhymes," said her unsuspecting mother.

Laura seemed to change the subject, "If you won money, would you give some of it to the school fund?"

Her mum didn't have to think twice. "Of course I would. But it's not likely, is it?"

Laura pounced, "It might happen if you entered this competition." She waved the paper. Mrs Delaney looked at the ad and said, "I couldn't enter for this. I don't have the time and there's no chance I'd win."

But Laura noticed she was studying the paper carefully. "You wouldn't be doing it just for yourself," she said persuasively. "It's for a good cause."

"I'll think about it," her mum said. Later, Laura noticed her writing away at the kitchen table.

"I've got an idea for a poem," she told her daughter. "And maybe I'll send it. And if I win the school can have half. But that's on condition you don't mention it again until the results are out in two weeks' time. I don't want to be badgered."

Which meant Laura couldn't ask her what the poem was about or even whether she'd entered it.

Next day in school, Miss Pim did exactly what Joe predicted. She glanced at the top of the pile of pages, then put them in the dustbin. Laura felt aggrieved. "It's not fair, giving twenty pages of punishment work and not reading them," forgetting that she didn't actually write them all herself and how relieved she should be that the teacher didn't look at them more closely.

Punishment work was soon forgotten. The class was buzzing with ideas for fundraising: raffles and quizzes; odd-jobs and messages; sponsored walks and cycles. Miss Pim could not get them to concentrate. Which of them had the best chance of winning it, they wondered? And was it cheating if those who were better off got their parents to chip in?

Then Miss Briteside came on the intercom. Everyone quietened down, straining to hear:

This announcement is to tell you the competition is over three weeks from Friday. Each Monday the names of the top ten fundraisers will be posted on the notice board in the long corridor, together with the amount of money they've collected to date. On the last Monday, the first name will be the winner and that person will take over as class teacher two days later, subject to the conditions I've already mentioned. Now, boys and girls, the best of luck to everyone of you. Remember, even if you're not the winner, the school is.

After she spoke the noise in Fifth class was worse than ever. "I'd need a megaphone to attract their attention," Miss Pim thought after a few unsuccessful shouts. Finally she resorted to banging on her table with the duster. The chat died away except, she noticed, for Laura Delaney. The teacher spoke softly, "If anyone of you mentions fundraising again in this class, they will be fined tenpence for every word they utter. Is that clear?" The tone was menacing and they all nodded except Laura who was chatting away to Joe, not noticing his frantic faces.

"Laura Delaney!" Miss Pim roared and Laura stopped. "What were you talking about?"

"Fundraising for the school gym, Miss." At least the teacher couldn't accuse her of wasting her time, Laura thought.

"Fined sixty pence!" snapped Miss Pim. "Bring it in tomorrow." The girl looked at her sullenly as Joe whispered an explanation.

"She is so mean!" Laura thought. "I've got to win this competition. I've just got to. Then I'll show her!"

Chapter 6

Saturday afternoon was warm and sunny. Joe and Sam and Laura opened the garden gates and lifted out the kitchen table. Flabby wandered into the sunlight, found a warm spot on the table and curled up. Around him they set out books, comics and toys. Mum provided home-made lemonade and crunchy chocolate biscuits. Dad gave them an old music box he'd found in the attic. Laura persuaded Sam not to sell his togs or crutches. "Nobody wants togs with a hole in them. And the crutches aren't really yours. The hospital might want them back."

Within half an hour they were doing a roaring trade. The books and comics went quickly, though there were a few hiccups. One girl kept trying to read a whole book on the spot without buying, until Joe said, "We don't do rentals. You have to pay for it if you want to read it. It's only fifty pence."

And Sam changed his mind about a bunny after it was

sold. Suddenly bereft, he tore after a small child and swopped the bunny for two teddy bears and a water pistol.

Then there was the boy who insisted on trying out the skateboard before buying it and was never seen again.

Children came back a number of times to buy the lemonade and the crunchy chocolate biscuits and one mother offered a good price for the recipes, but Mrs Delaney refused, saying they were a family secret.

A fierce argument started over the old music box. Three neighbours wanted it. Laura couldn't see why. She felt obliged to tell them it was very old-fashioned with its dark wood and hand painted flowers. She pointed out where the hinges were broken. And there was something wrong with the spring so that instead of playing a tune, the box coughed its way through the notes. But the more faults she showed, the more the neighbours wanted it. They thought it was beautiful and there was an angry debate over who had seen it first.

Mr Jameson, who'd come because he'd promised Sam, had the brilliant idea of auctioning it. One neighbour protested, "I had it first and only put it down to take out my purse. It should be mine."

"Sure the money is for the school," said Joe's father. "You wouldn't want to do the kids out of the best price they could get for the box, would you?"

Reluctantly she agreed to an auction and the three bidders got so carried away, vying for ownership, that Laura made eight pounds. She wished she had a few more boxes that were falling apart.

Her mum's flowers sold well too. Gradually the irises and the tulips and the late daffodils thinned out. "Just a few more," Laura told herself. She forgot how crowded the flower beds had been and sent Sam to pick another bunch.

A boy wanted to buy Flabby. "He's not for sale," Laura told him.

"Yes, he is," the boy said. "The notice on your table says '*Name your price. Everything here for sale*'. So that includes the cat."

"No, it doesn't. Look, Flabby does nothing but sleep. You'd be as well off buying the rubber duck. It has as much life as Flabby and you wouldn't have to feed it. You could have the rubber duck in the bath. You couldn't put Flabby in the bath."

But the boy was adamant. "A rubber duck isn't the same at all. I want the cat. The price I'm naming is ten pounds. It's all the money I've got." And he put a tenner on the table.

Laura was tempted. She looked around. Joe was helping a child put skates on, Sam was picking more flowers and chatting to Mr Jameson. "Go on then," she told the boy.

He swooped Flabby off the table and ran, afraid she'd change her mind. Laura saw the cat's face bouncing up and down over his shoulder, his expression shocked. He began to wail before they disappeared around the corner. Laura felt a little guilty. He had never wailed before.

"Where's Flabby?" Sam asked a few minutes later.

"Oh, he went that way," Laura casually pointed.

"But he never goes anywhere!" Sam said. "Was he walking? He hates walking."

"Flabby is perfectly all right. We haven't got time to worry about him. Mrs Lynch wants eight tulips, Sam." And for a while the little boy forgot about the cat.

Joe's dad stayed to help them pack up and Mrs Delaney came out to see how they'd done. Unfortunately her eyes fixed on the garden. All that was left of her glorious display were a few forlorn flowers, some loosened soil and a number of petals. Mouth open, she stared. Then she advanced on Laura. "What happened to my flowers?" Her voice was grim.

"We sold a few. People said they were lovely, Mum." For the first time Laura took stock and her heart sank.

Joe's dad looked at the shrubs, the apple-blossom tree and the smooth lawn (except for the patch in the middle where they'd put the notice) and said, "Your garden is lovely, Mrs Delaney."

"*Was*, Mr Jameson, *was* lovely. Until this nitwit robbed everything in it. Now it's bald!"

"I didn't realise we took so much, Mum. People kept asking to buy. Mrs Walsh said your tulips are perfect and Mrs Tobin thinks you should be in garden shows."

Somewhat mollified, her mum said, "Well, I'm glad they like my flowers. And I suppose it's good other people can enjoy them too. But I wish you'd left a few more. You picked far too many."

"I'm really sorry, Mum, " Laura meant it. "But at least they raised a lot of money for the school."

Mr Jameson was studying the lawn intently, "What feed do you use to get the grass looking so silky?"

Mrs Delaney looked pleased and much to Laura's relief was soon chatting away to Joe's dad about the garden.

They packed the few unsold items, brought in the table, then all three tackled the money, Sam sorting the different coins out into rows, the others counting.

"Oh, there's a ten-pound note!" Sam was impressed. "Who gave you that?"

Laura swiftly put it in her pocket. "I'll keep it safe," she said, then added, "Don't interrupt the counting, Sam. Now I have to do this pile over again." But she reddened, wishing she'd never been mad enough to sell Flabby – or all her mum's flowers. She'd got carried away and thought of nothing except how much money she'd make. Those flowers were her mum's pride and joy. She was bound to be furious.

The longer Mrs Delaney stayed in the garden, the more worried her daughter became. She could imagine her looking at all the bare spots and getting very angry. She was sure to think up some suitable and horrible punishment. And she, Laura, really deserved it. And what would they all say when they found out about Flabby?

"We made seventy-five pounds," Joe said, "counting the tenner in your pocket. That's brilliant. You'll probably be in the top ten this week."

"I don't care," Laura moaned. Joe's eyes widened, but before he or Sam could say a word, Mrs Delaney told Joe his dad was looking for him and the boy had to leave.

To Laura's amazement her mum was smiling. No mention was made of her flowers. "Mr Jameson knows an awful lot about gardens," she told them. "He used to work for a small landscaping company. Then it went out of business and before he could look for another job, Joe's mum got sick and he stayed at home to care for her. He says when she died he tried for one or two jobs but then he lost heart. Such a pity! It's so obvious he loves gardening. He gave me some wonderful advice."

Her mother droned on and on about the wonderful advice and Laura stopped listening, just so grateful the flowers had been forgotten.

At tea-time Mrs Delaney sat lost in thought while Mr Delaney heard about the music box with amazement. "It couldn't play a decent tune and the wood was coming apart at the corners! And the hinges were broken."

"Well, Mrs Walsh got it in the end," Laura told him, "and she gave eight pound-coins for it."

Then Sam suddenly wailed, "He never came back!"

"Who didn't?" Mum was startled out of her daydream.

"Flabby! Laura said he went for a walk. That was ages ago!"

Mr Delaney frowned at Laura, "That cat has never in his life gone for a walk. Sometimes he strolls as far as the garden gate – with a good few rest periods – but he's never gone beyond it. Last time I saw him he was asleep on your table and –" His eyes narrowed. "You didn't sell the poor creature, did you?"

The three stared at her accusingly. Beetroot, Laura was about to confess all when there was a sudden flurry on the windowsill and a very upset Flabby was mewling in at them.

At the same time the front-door bell rang, long and loud. Glad to escape Laura rushed to answer it.

The boy who'd bought Flabby stood on the doorstep, arms folded, very angry. "Your stupid cat won't stay with me. Three times he ran off, but the last time I couldn't catch him cos he whizzed up the road like a rocket. So I don't want him. And you can give me my money back!"

Even before he'd finished, Laura had taken out the tenner, stuffed it between his arms and closed the door.

No one asked her who it was, they were too busy trying to comfort Flabby, who was now sitting on a chair at the table, miaowing indignantly. Laura sat opposite and shifted uncomfortably. He sounded as if he were doing his best to tell them what happened. He certainly wasn't a bit pleased. If he could speak Laura thought he was probably saying something like: "She's *a such a mean person! Selling me to a total stranger, nearly giving me a heart attack! I've never had to move so fast. Look at me! I'm in a state of collapse. So mean!*"
And on and on he went, staring straight at Laura, moaning and mewling. It must have been ten minutes before he finally stopped giving out. Then he sniffed as if there was nothing more to say. When Laura tried to pat him, his tail

71

went up and he jumped away from her onto the floor, where he settled on the rug and went to sleep.

"I don't know why he took it into his head to go for a walk," Mrs Delaney said. "But he obviously isn't the better of it yet."

Laura's dad gave her a funny look. "Who was at the door?" he said.

"Oh, just someone who was owed money from the sale. I paid him." Laura went beetroot and her dad studied her face till it was boiling. Then he looked at Sam and looked back at Laura. "Some people would be very upset if they knew what had happened," he said, so softly no one else heard. Laura nodded and swallowed. She thought her face must be in flames it was so hot.

"How much did you make today?" Mum asked and Dad let it drop.

For the rest of the weekend Laura felt mean about Flabby. It was a while before he was friendly again. It wasn't until she'd bought him a carton of cream and some cat biscuits that he was coaxed back to his old self.

She noticed her mum was spending a good deal of time on the computer and hoped she was working on the poem. But there were a lot of numbers on the screen, then pictures of flowers and she told Laura there was some fascinating information about landscaping on the Internet. Her daughter didn't enquire too closely. No doubt Mum was looking up what to put into the bare patches in the garden and the less said about them the better.

On Monday morning, Laura handed in her money at the head's office. "Results this afternoon," Miss Briteside told her. The head was extremely cheerful. Outside her office a long queue of boys and girls waited to hand over cash. Her scheme was proving a success.

That afternoon on the intercom she congratulated everyone on the amount of money raised and reminded them to look at the noticeboard after the last bell and see if they were one of the top ten fundraisers. Of course, if they weren't, not to fret. Anyone of them could catch up depending on how much they raised this week. They had another three weeks and the race to be prize-winner wouldn't be over until the last Friday.

Still, Laura could hardly wait. When class at last was finished, she joined the surge of bodies at the notice board. Joe was standing in front of her. He turned around, beaming, "You've made it this week, Laura. You're number five! And next week we're going to do better. Wait and see!"

Chapter 7

Nobody lost heart. The school was buzzing with fundraising ideas and talk of the great prize. People went to extraordinary lengths to raise money. One boy challenged his class mates to an arm-wrestling competition, with bets of fifty pence. He made three pounds fifty. A girl raffled her pocket money, making five times the original amount. Others sold everything interesting they had. Everyone was so caught up in the desire to win, that soon nothing else mattered.

Besides doing odd-jobs for the neighbours, Laura got her father to do a sponsored bungie jump even though he'd sworn never to have anything to do with fundraising again.

The poor man hadn't taken proper excercise for ten years. He had a very busy job in an office, so busy that he took work home and often didn't listen when his family spoke to him. Which was probably how he came to agree to do a bungie jump when Laura asked him in front of two witnesses, his wife and Sam.

Sam was so delighted he went round telling all the neighbours. "My dad is going to jump off a very high building," he said proudly.

"Oh my God!" exclaimed the woman next door. "He must be feeling rotten. Is he working too hard?" She hurried around to see if she could help and was relieved to hear about the bungie jump from Mrs Delaney.

Days before the event neighbours and friends called to congratulate Mr Delaney on his daring. At first he didn't know what they were talking about. "What do you mean, 'daring'?" he said.

"Well, maybe you don't think it's daring," said one, wondering if he'd insulted the man. "But I think you're very brave! I'm telling you, I wouldn't bungie-jump at your age. It could give you a nasty turn."

Mr Delaney went white. "Bungie-jump! Me? God Almighty. Where did you hear that ridiculous rumour?"

"Laura and Sam said you promised – for the fundraising." The other man looked very disappointed, "Ah now, don't tell me you're backing out. The entire neighbourhood has sponsored you. And the whole lot of us will be there. Of course, you'll need all the support you can get, at your age."

Mr Delaney was highly indignant. "Listen here," he said, "that's the second time you've mentioned my age.

I'll have you know I am in my prime. At the height of my powers."

"That's great. A spot of bungie-jumping will be no bother to you so." The man grinned and went away, whistling cheerfully.

Which is how, when the day came, Mr Delaney found himself himself on top of the university water-tower, strapped into a kind of harness. He thought he might have a heart attack. How had he allowed himself to be talked into this madness? Really, he must concentrate more in future before saying yes to those wretched children! Now he was staring down from a great height and the ground was miles away. His family and neighbours were cheering him on. He had never liked flying in an aeroplane, never mind dropping into thin air on his own, like a bird.

Someone gave him a hearty pat on the back and he found himself plunging, screeching his head off, eyes closed. The wind whistled past his ears and he felt braver than he'd ever felt in his life. He was jerked up, then bounced in the air a few times like a rubber ball. Someone ran over and steadied him. When the harness was unstrapped his legs gave way and he was helped to his feet.

"Dad! Stop roaring, Dad. You're safe. You can open your eyes!"

"Well done!" His wife said. "I never thought you'd do it."

He opened his eyes and gripped his wife's hands emotionally. "That was wonderful!" he said.

"You made two hundred pounds for the gym!" Laura was jubilant.

"I feel like Superman," her dad was shouting with excitement. "I don't know why I've been sitting in that stuffy office when I could be having adventures like this. We could start a neigbourhood club! I wonder what sky-diving is like?"

But in spite of the two hundred pounds, Laura found herself in seventh place the next Monday.

"I'm first," a snooty voice beside her drawled. "I was first last week and I bet I'll be first next week." Laura looked at the smug face and then at the list:

"Mona Jones, Sixth class. Five hundred pounds."

Her heart sank. She'd never catch up. Was there any point trying?

"Yes, there is," Joe told her. "You might be seventh, but you're only one hundred pounds behind her. Mona's first because her dad wrote a big cheque. That's a once-off. She wasn't even on the list last week and she's not doing anything herself to get money.

Laura felt comforted. Then she frowned as another worry occurred. "But how will we raise anything this week? All the neighbours sponsored dad. We can't ask them again."

"Well, we could help my dad," Joe was hesitant.

"Your dad?" Laura didn't want to say that since his dad did nothing he'd hardly need help, but her tone said it for her.

"He's doing Mrs Malone's garden. You know the one on the corner that looks like a jungle. She has arthritis and can't do it herself, so Dad offered."

Joe didn't say how much courage it had taken for Mr Jameson to approach the elderly lady. For days beforehand he'd gone on about it. "She'll probably say 'no'," he'd told Joe over and over. "I bet she doesn't care about the garden now. And anyway, why would she want me to do it? Probably reckons I'm a lazy good-for-nothing who won't work for a living. What do you think, son?" He looked at Joe in such an argumentative way that the boy knew no matter what he said, his dad would snap at him. He didn't answer.

"Maybe you agree with her!" said his dad, snapping anyway.

Mr Jameson went out for a walk, still brooding. He stopped at the house on the corner and studied the tangle of brambles and shrubs, the high grass and the flourishing weeds. Dead leaves from the previous autumn were caught in the new growth. He sighed. It could be a beautiful garden. But he couldn't bring himself to knock and so had continued his walk.

Sam was out on his bicycle and when he saw Mr Jameson, his eyes lit up. "Where are you going?" he asked. Somewhat to his own surprise, the man told him about Mrs Malone's garden.

"She bought lots of flowers at our gate-sale," Sam told him. "She said she missed having flowers in the garden."

That decided Mr Jameson. "Right so. I'll talk to her. And if she says 'no', it won't kill me."

Mrs Malone had been delighted. "I always meant to hire someone to keep the garden in order," she told him. "But I lost heart after Tom died. You know how it is." Mr Jameson knew very well how it was and nodded in sympathy.

"And I'll pay you what I would have paid anyway," the old lady told him.

He protested, "I don't want money. It'd be a pleasure to put the garden to rights again – as a neighbour."

An argument followed, but she insisted and since Mr Jameson very much wanted to do the garden, seeing in his mind exactly how it would look, he at last agreed to payment.

Now every day that was where he was and when he saw Joe coming home from school, he'd take a half-hour break to share a bite to eat and tell his son how the work was going. Joe didn't want to upset this cheerful mood and so he listened seriously and nodded politely. Yet it seemed to him that by the time he went back to work, his dad was his old grumpy self again.

Maybe he was overworking, Joe thought, which was when he had the idea of lending a hand and helping Laura's fundraising. But would it be mean to ask for money? Maybe his dad wasn't earning that much.

"Well if he doesn't want to pay, we'll help out anyway," Laura said when Joe explained about Mr Jameson's job.

"I will indeed pay you. It's for a good cause. But only on one condition. You have to bring young Sam with you. I think he'd fancy gardening with all the dirt and the digging."

It was then Laura had *her* bright idea. As soon as she got home she said, "Mum, if I take Sam out for two hours every afternoon, will you pay me for baby-sitting?"

"I'm not a baby!" Sam was offended.

"Indeed you're not," his mum said, and to Laura, "Indeed I will! That'll give me time to do my own work."

Laura was so pleased at the idea of being paid twice, that she never asked what work her mum was doing.

Sam loved working with Mr Jameson, digging the cleared flowerbeds with a small spade while Laura and Joe were bent double weeding. It was hard dirty work and they all went home filthy, fingernails clogged, faces streaked, jeans muddied. For the first few days Laura managed to sneak her brother into the house, upstairs and into the bathroom and keep him there till they were both scrubbed, clothes changed.

The third day she was too tired to hang onto Sam and he ran into the kitchen to see his mum.

"What on earth were you doing?" she heard her mother's shrill voice and then, "Laura. Laura! Come in here at once!"

Mrs Delaney got another shock when she saw her daughter. "What happened? Were you caught in a mud-slide? You're filthy."

"We're gardeners so we are!" Sam was proud.

"You must be digging a tunnel! Laura, explain please." Laura did her best, then waited for her mum to explode. But Mrs Delaney was smiling, "I'm proud of you, working so hard to make money that's not even for yourself. And guess what? I'll be keeping the promise I made. Look!"

She took up the evening newspaper and showed her children. Laura looked, then snatched the paper from her mum's hands. "This is deadly! Sam, Mum wrote a poem about you and your piano playing and she won first prize. Listen." She read it aloud.

> *Please Don't Play It Again, Sam.*
>
> *"Please don't play it again, Sam*
> *It's a terrible noise!" said his mam.*
> *For nothing could shatter the calm*
> *Like the piano-playing of Sam.*
>
> *Oh, music is catchy and lingers*
> *When the piano is played with fingers*
> *But Sam always got the fidgets*
> *When he used those particular digits.*
>
> *So he ran up the keys with his toes*
> *Then tried out a tune with his nose,*
> *And 'The Banks of My Own Lovely Lee'*
> *Was unusual, played with one knee.*

When the lid fell he shed a sad tear
For he had to stop playing by ear
Still he managed to tinkle intently
When proudly he practised al dente*

Alas it all came to an end
In a manner Sam didn't intend
For the piano collapsed with a crash
When his forehead gave it a bash.

"At least you can't play it again, Sam,
'Twas a terrible noise," said his mam.
But his gran went and bought him a trumpet
– And his family just have to lump it!

*with his teeth

Laura giggled and Sam said, "Gran never bought me a trumpet. I'd love a trumpet."

"Well, you can't have one!" his mother and sister spoke together and Mrs Delaney added, "I've a treat that's better than any trumpet. Guess what it is?"

Sam pondered. What would be louder than a trumpet? "An elephant," he said hopefully. "I'd like an elephant."

His mum sighed. Sometimes she had doubts about Sam. Did he really think they could have an elephant in the house? "No, not an elephant. We're going out to a nice restaurant, just to celebrate my win. Isn't that nice?"

"It's not as nice as an elephant." Sam seemed to think he'd been promised one.

"You can have a burger and chips and chocolate-chip ice cream instead," his mum told him.

"Scrummy!" Sam jumped around yelling, "Choc chip! Choc chip!" When he'd calmed down he told them, "I can get a trumpet for my birthday, so I can. And then I'll be louder than an elephant."

Mrs Delaney rolled her eyes. She handed an envelope to Laura. "Half my winnings," she said. "A cheque for one hundred and fifty pounds."

Between her mum's money, the baby-sitting and the gardening, Laura was second the next Monday. Mona Jones was still first. "My dad wrote another cheque," the girl said airily.

"That's not fair!" Joe told her. "You should raise the money yourself."

The girl laughed, "Why should I? There's no rule that says I have to."

Laura nudged him, "Mum gave me a cheque too, remember?"

"That's different. You got her to enter the competition. And you're babysitting and gardening. Mona doesn't do a tap. Just sits back and lets Daddy do it all."

The girl reddened. "You're a sap!" she told Joe. "And so's your pal. When I win, you two better watch out. It'll be a pleasure giving you detention!"

"Huh! You can't. You won't be our class teacher."

"No, but I'll be a teacher. And any teacher can give any pupil detention. So get ready, you!" She strode off.

"Joe, I'm never going to make it. I'll never beat her."

"Yes, you will. Her dad won't give her another cheque. He'd have to be rolling in money!"

"He *is* rolling in money! And you said the same thing last week. I haven't a hope, have I?"

"You've got to win," Joe said. "If only to beat Mona Jones. She'll make our lives miserable, probably have us cleaning toilets for hours. She's horrible. You've got to be top of that list next week, Laura!"

Chapter 8

That day, Miss Briteside visited every class for the final push.

"Well, girls and boys, you're a credit to the school," she told Fifth class. "One of your number is second on the top-ten list." She smiled at Laura. "Miss Pim must be proud."

Miss Pim groaned inwardly, but managed a weak smile.

Miss Briteside continued, "I'm sure she's giving you every encouragement, Laura. Isn't that so?"

"Well – no, it's not." Laura couldn't think of one word of encouragement the teacher had given her. She suspected the last thing on earth Miss Pim wanted was to have her in charge of the class.

"You know my views on the matter," Miss Pim told the headmistress.

"Nevertheless the school needs a gym and Laura has done remarkably well," Miss Briteside was steely. "And the least we could do is give credit where it's due. Isn't that right, Miss Pim?"

The teacher's reply was spirited, "Oh, we should never forget who deserves credit!" She became a little emotional, "And especially for ideas that don't affect the person who thought them up, but leave another person to suffer the consequences. Oh, credit where credit is due alright! Credit for madness and mayhem!" Miss Pim's voice was by now extremely shrill. "Credit for insanity!" she went on. "Credit for lunacy, if you ask me."

"I'm very sorry I *did* ask you," the Head murmured, so that only the teacher and a few in the front row heard. "Pull yourself together, please Miss Pim!" Then loudly and brightly she added, "One more week and we should have enough money to satisfy the Department of Education. And please, boys and girls, even if you've no hope of winning the top prize, don't give up." Her voice was pleading now. "It would be a shame to lose out on the gym. Imagine what it would mean to the school. Indoor soccer and basketball. Gymnastics, aerobics – even some disco-dancing. I'm sure you can see the benefits?"

They nodded vigorously. Now that they were so near their target, a gym sounded great.

"And if we make our fundraising goal," Miss Briteside continued, "we will celebrate the opening of the gym with a party for the whole school. How about that?"

The class cheered, all except Miss Pim, who thought

she might spend her spare time for the rest of the week in church, praying that Laura Delaney would not win. The child was a recipe for disaster. "Anyone but her!" she thought.

And later when she snapped at Laura for asking a question, she overheard Cathy tell Danny, "I hope Laura wins. Miss Pim should get a taste of her own medicine."

She turned on Cathy, "You'd do well to remember that whoever wins, the prize is only for the day and next morning everyone will have to face the real teacher again."

It was a veiled threat and Miss Pim felt mean after making it. But she was fed up with all the class thinking it would soon be pay-back time and relishing the thought. Laura Delaney was a scatterbrain who didn't listen and therefore asked foolish questions. And she, Miss Pim, wasn't going to treat her any differently just because she might win this insane competition!

Later at break, Cathy Henderson got all of Fifth class together. "Is there anyone here who has a hope of getting onto that list, apart from Laura?" she asked.

"Well, a few of us have raised nearly as much money as the tenth person," said one boy. "We might make the list, but we won't win."

"So who do you want to win? Mona Jones, or Laura?"

"Laura, of course." They had no doubts.

"Well, why don't we make sure she does, then? All the money we collect this week, why don't we give it to Laura?"

They thought a moment, then one said, "But Miss Briteside will think none of the rest of us bothered."

"No, she won't," Cathy said. "There's no rule against giving all we collect to Laura. We can tell the Head – *after* Laura is teacher for a day. We'll beat that snotty Mona Jones at her own game. And at least we'll have made some effort to get money. And it'll be great fun if Laura's in charge. She'll probably give us a party."

They thought again and eventually someone said, "That's a brilliant idea!"

"Deadly!" They nodded in agreement.

During the week the money came in. Joe was in charge of minding it. Danny and Cathy went round collecting it each morning and on Joe's insistence, gave everyone a receipt for their amount and an updated figure on how much was raised. It was beginning to pile up and by Thursday, the friends were confident Laura would win.

Mona Jones had other ideas. She stopped Laura and Joe on the corridor. "I heard what you and your pals are up to," she sneered. "But it won't make any difference. You see, my father is rich and he's going to write the biggest cheque this week."

"For how much?" Joe asked.

"Oh, just a thousand pounds." Mona spoke as if a thousand pounds were nothing.

Joe and Laura stared at her. Everyone in Fifth class was doing their best to make money, but the most they'd have by Friday would be around seven hundred pounds.

Mona saw their disappointment and said loftily, "It's

only right I should win. After all I'm in Sixth class, so I'm a senior."

Laura couldn't follow the logic of this, but when she said so the other girl smiled and said in her most superior voice, "Well, that proves my point, really. I mean if you can't understand simple English, you're hardly fit to be class teacher, now are you?" and away she swept, leaving the friends speechless.

That afternoon as usual after school, Laura brought Sam around to help out in Mrs Malone's garden. But now her heart wasn't in it. What was the point of killing herself when she'd no hope of winning. Joe's dad noticed how downhearted she was and said, "Why don't you take a break today, Laura?" She shook her head. Joe had told her how much it meant to Mr Jameson to do this job properly and how much he appreciated their help. And she could see Sam loved being involved, loved everything to do with the garden.

"I'm fine," she said.

At that moment a small lorryload of manure arrived. Mr Jameson had to give it his full attention, supervising and directing, so that it was tipped safely onto the garden path, making what Sam thought was a beautiful large slithery heap.

"It's very smelly," he said with some satisfaction, just before he tripped on a shoelace and fell face first into the heap. His efforts to get himself up involved clutching at the stuff which slid over his shoulders and arms. Mr

Jameson gripped the back of his jumper and pulled him free. Sam looked horrible and smelled worse. There was manure in his hair and it covered the front of his clothes.

"That's a disgusting pong!" Laura said.

"I like manure," Sam sniffed appreciatively.

"And it makes the flowers grow," said Mr Jameson. Laura noticed he had a hand over his nose.

"There's a lot of it in my shoes," Sam said. "My feet might get *very* big."

On the way home, Sam squelched along the pavement, enjoying the sound so much he jumped every so often to get a really good squelch. Crossing the road, he wanted Laura to hold his hand. "Mum says you have to. I could be knocked down if you don't."

"You're not to come near me with those hands. They stink!"

"Do they?" Sam sniffed them while Laura held a clean patch on the back of his jumper as they cossed.

They met a couple of neighbours. "God, but you're very smelly," one of them said.

"I am, amn't I?" Sam was delighted.

"That's a powerful pong!" said the second. Taking it for a compliment the little boy smiled.

"Whatever happened to you?" they asked, but when Sam went into details, they hurried away, unable to stick the smell. When one of them dropped a coin, Sam picked it up and went after them. But they started running, shouting something about the bus and he couldn't catch up.

Even an old bull terrier who usually loved barking at them from behind his gate, got up with a choking noise and shuffled as fast as he could up the path.

Laura made Sam take his shoes and socks off outside the front door. He squiggled his toes, fascinated by the yellow ooze between them. She sneaked him upstairs to the bathroom where he managed to give himself a reasonable shower, and changed into spotless clothes, emerging clean though still a bit smelly.

His sister bundled his dirty clothes into an old towel and pushed them far down into the washing basket.

Later that evening when Sam was in bed, Laura sat brooding. So much effort with nothing to show for it. She'd never know what it would be like to be 'Teacher for a Day'. Still, at least there was the gym and the party to look forward to. But she would have loved to give Miss Pim just one order. Now it would never happen. She sighed.

"Laura, what exactly is this?" Her mum had appeared in the doorway, holding out the bundle of Sam's clothes, nose wrinkled in disgust. Her voice held the threat of eruption.

Laura knew she was in trouble. She was supposed to look after Sam properly. Now she'd be grounded, given punishment work, probably have to wash out all that manure from Sam's clothes. It wasn't fair. Why did she always have to take the blame for her silly brother? Before Mrs Delaney could say another word, Laura burst out, "It's not my fault! You always blame me. I'm fed up, and *sick* of fundraising and *sick* of that snotty Mona Jones who's going to win and it's a pity she didn't fall into the manure heap instead of Sam cos I can't stand her!"

Her mum's mouth dropped in astonishment. Then she turned on her heel and in a minute Laura heard the hum of the washing machine from the kitchen. She was for it now! She shouldn't have spoken like that, roaring at her mum. She was definitely for it! Tears came and, busy wiping them away, she didn't notice her mum's return until she'd sat down beside her.

Mrs Delaney patted her shoulder. "There's no need to get so upset. You should have explained what happened to Sam, instead of getting yourself into this state. You must be overtired."

Laura sniffled and her mum went on, "You know, you've done very well. I'm not talking about the money. I'm talking about all the hard work you've put in. I didn't think you'd stick it. Your dad and I are proud of you, Laura. I know winning matters, but it wasn't all for nothing. You've helped to get the school a gym."

"But I won't be class teacher," her daughter was tearful. "And that's why I did it. Not for the gym. Well, maybe a little bit for the gym. But I wanted to win."

"You might not have won," her mum said, "but look at what you've done. You've thought up a lot of ideas and you've carried them through. You've helped Mr Jameson and Mrs Malone. And Sam has stopped talking about trumpets and elephants because now he thinks gardening is the best. And he also thinks no one has a sister like you. He said so last night.

"Did he?" Laura wiped away the last of her tears, and said, "You should have seen those neighbours running away from him because he was so smelly." She giggled and Mrs Delaney smiled. Laura became hysterical with exhaustion and soon she was guffawing uncontrollably, tears starting again, this time from laughter.

It was only when the doorbell rang for the third time that they heard it. Mrs Delaney answered. Laura could hear some muffled conversation, then her mum rushed into the room, followed by Mrs Walsh.

"You won't believe it!" She was breathless with excitement, as was their neighbour who sat down, eyes gleaming.

"Remember the music box I bought at your gate-sale?" Mrs Walsh said. "Well, I took it to the jeweller's for some repair work and she said it was French, 18th century, and worth quite a bit because the mechanism is rare."

Laura's heart sank. She had sold a valuable antique for eight pounds! But Mrs Walsh went on, "Now I know it was mine by law, but I remembered Joe's dad talking about the fundraising and how the money is for such a good cause, so I've got a cheque here, made out to the school, for seven hundred and fifty pounds, which is what I sold the music box for."

"Isn't it marvellous, Laura?" her mum said. "Mrs Walsh is very generous."

Stunned, Laura held the cheque. With the seven hundred from the class she was well ahead of Mona Jones. No longer tired she stood up, did a little dance, whooping with joy, then ran upstairs to wake Sam and tell him the good news.

Chapter 9

Next morning Laura was behind Mona Jones in the queue outside the principal's office. Mona was waving her cheque. "One thousand pounds, signed by my father. I'll be heading that list on Monday. And I'll have power!"

Laura said nothing. The other girl shoved the piece of paper under her nose, giving Laura a dig at the same time. "Read that!" she said. "Look at the amount. You have no chance!"

"If you push that into my face again, I'll tear it up," Laura said.

"Jealousy!" crowed Mona, but she put the cheque away. "When I'm a teacher," she went on, "you can't call me Mona."

"How about 'Moany' then?" Laura said and the other girl frowned. "You will call me Miss Jones. In fact you might as well start this minute. Get a bit of practice at showing respect for your betters!"

There was a large queue now and Mona was playing to an attentive audience. She gave Laura a dig in the arm, "Go on then. Say it! 'Miss Jones'."

Laura looked at her. The girl was big and sturdy. Giving her a dig back mightn't be wise. She took a deep breath, said, "All right." Then she startled everyone by shouting, "Miss Jones, Miss Jones, Miss Jones, Miss *Jones*! Miss Jones, Miss Jones, Miss *Jo-o-o-o-ones*!"

Those in the queue laughed and a few even clapped. Most of them were sick of Mona's boasting. The girl herself went beetroot, especially when a teacher stopped and asked what was going on.

"Mona wants to be called Miss Jones," someone explained. The teacher laughed and Mona was raging.

"Just you wait!" she hissed at Laura. "You are going to pay for this!"

"Maybe *you* should wait," Laura told her, but Miss Briteside's office had opened and the girl was again waving her cheque triumphantly.

Later Joe asked, "Why didn't you tell her you'd collected far more than her?"

"Because she might sneak home and get her dad to write a bigger cheque. So don't you tell anyone either, Joe. Just in case she gets to hear. You're the only one in school who knows about the money for the music box."

For the first time in her life, Laura spent the weekend wishing it was over, dying to get back to school. "I'll probably win, Sam," she told her brother.

"And then you'll be Teacher for a Day," Sam said. "I know."

"Everyone knows," her father was grumpy, unable to concentrate on the paper because his daughter was so fidgety. "You've told us a million times. And I don't understand this mad desire. You don't even like teachers. I've never heard you say one word in their favour. In fact, you seem to think their purpose in life is to torture you with homework and classwork and rules and regulations. So why do you want to be one?"

To get my own back and to have some fun, Laura wanted to say. But Mr Delaney would not approve and so she told him, "I just want to see what it's like, that's all."

"If I were the teacher, I'd stand on the table," Sam said.

Mrs Delaney smiled, "Why would you do that?"

"Because then I could see everyone and I could write on the top part of the blackboard where no one writes and it's nice and clean."

"That's a great idea," his dad said. "You should give that bit of advice to your own teacher. Mr Maguire probably never thought of standing on the table. You tell him, Sam."

"I will too." Sam was delighted. "Then he won't need two pairs of spectacles."

His mum was puzzled. "Mr Maguire hardly wears *two* pairs of glasses?"

Sam was patient, "No, he doesn't. But he says he'll have to get another pair when he gets eyes in the back of his head. If he stands on the table he won't need more eyes."

"Where's he getting these eyes?" said his mum, faintly.

"In the Man United shop, of course."

There was silence as they took this in. Then Laura said, almost afraid of the answer, "Why the Man United shop?"

"Cos he likes Man United!" Sam spoke as if they were very slow on the uptake. Seeing their expressions, he added, "Mr Maguire says it's the only place you can get red and white eyes."

This time the silence was longer, broken only by some choking sounds from Mr Delaney. Laura hurriedly left the room to look for something and Mrs Delaney took a startled Flabby off the sofa, lifted him high in front of her face and said, "*There's* a handsome cat!"

"If Laura wins, she might bring me home some chalk," Sam said, to no one in particular.

She had wanted to be early on Monday, but her parents couldn't find her dad's keys. Mrs Delaney told Laura to take Sam to small school. "I'm going to kill your father," she added. "We'll have to look everywhere. I only hope he didn't throw them in the bin. He's quite capable of it! He's quite capable of throwing one of *you* in the bin, he's so absentminded. He's quite capable of –" Laura left hastily with Sam, knowing her mother could go on for another five minutes.

Mona Jones sauntered down the long corridor with a few cronies. She was smiling smugly and waved at some of her classmates who were standing silently at the notice board. "You'd think she was the Queen," Joe later told Laura. He was at the front of the small crowd, the only one from Fifth class so far.

They cleared a space for her, still unspeaking.

"Well, I'm glad to see that at least my own class know how to show respect. Though it's a bit late now for some of you!" The girl's voice was sneering.

"And why is it a bit late, Mona?" one boy asked, smiling a little.

"Because, Tony Doyle, it's payback time and you won't be smiling for long. I told you," she waved a hand airily, "but you wouldn't listen would you? Now you'll be sorry for calling me a spoilt brat and not wanting me to win!"

The boy smiled broadly now. "Sorry for not wanting to be bossed around by you? I don't think so."

"Sap!" Mona was scornful and she shoved her face into his. "Look hard at the list, you!"

"I did. You should too. Cos you're not first!"

"I don't believe you!" But the girl went pale and her eyes swivelled to the board. Her mouth dropped and she swallowed again and again, her colour going from white to purple. Then she shrieked, "This can't be true! It's a joke. Laura Delaney can't have won."

"She has, though," Joe said.

Then Mona Jones went mad. "It's not right!" She stamped her foot. "I won't stand for it. My father has given lots of money to the school!" She was roaring and people were running up the corridor to see what the commotion was about.

Eyes bulging, Mona seized the notice board and half-pulled it from the wall. "Why didn't Laura Delaney say something on Friday?" she shouted. "She's nothing but a cheat. Cheat! Cheat! Cheat!" Spitting the words out, she wrenched the board completely off.

By now Laura's friends and classmates had gathered. "You're a bad loser, Mona," Danny told her and Cathy Henderson added, "You think your dad can buy anything you want. Well, he can't."

Mona hurled herself at Cathy, kicking, clawing, grabbing hair. Everyone was shouting, mostly in support of her victim. Then the hullabaloo died down and faded. Apart from the two on the ground, no one made a sound.

"Get up at once! Mona Jones, do you hear me? Stop it!"

But the girl had gone beyond listening to Miss Briteside. It took three teachers to prise her away from Cathy. She was taken, kicking and screaming, into the office. Miss Briteside took the noticeboard and followed. Overawed by what had happened, the rest went quietly to class.

In the girls' loo Cathy fixed her hair, bathed her face and settled her jumper. Feeling weak, she sat on the bench outside the head's office. Which was how she came to see the arrival of Mona's father and, sometime later, the weeping girl being led away.

"No, no, Miss Briteside," she heard the man say. "I don't want the money back. It was given for the school gym and not so Mona could win a competition. She and I will have to have a serious talk."

Laura was half an hour late. She frowned when she saw the notice board was gone and hurried to class. Miss Pim was not in good humour. "Typical!" she snapped at Laura. "Just typical. The one who causes all the trouble is not even there to see it." The teacher was in a terrible mood, feeling life had let her down very badly and she added, "Well, you're not getting away with it. You can do a two-page essay."

"But why, Miss?" Laura was mystifed. "I did nothing."

"Exactly! That sums you up. You spend your life doing nothing."

It was very unfair, Laura thought. So did the rest of the class. "She wasn't even here," someone muttered.

"It's not her fault Mona Jones is a bad loser!" another added under his breath.

Then Joe said aloud, "Laura's just come in, Miss. She didn't start the trouble."

Miss Pim realised she could hardly punish Laura for the disgraceful episode at the notice-board.

"What did she do, Miss?" Joe asked, in such a polite way he couldn't be thought cheeky.

The teacher could hardly say that what Laura had done was win the stupid competition. Now the girl was going to make her life a misery, not least because she'd no

101

idea how to behave as a teacher. But if she couldn't punish her for winning, she could punish her for something else. "She came in late, that's what she did!" Miss Pim shouted. "And she can take a two-page essay on *Getting Up Early*."

"But Miss. I have a note. From my mother."

Miss Pim took the envelope with very bad grace and studied the note closely. Was she looking for spelling mistakes, Laura wondered. The teacher sniffed and sent her to her desk without further comment. Later, when she'd calmed down, Miss Pim felt sorry, especially when she saw how aggrieved the class felt. They sat doing the work she gave them, not looking at her and speaking only when she asked them a question. Never had they been so silent.

At Small Break in the yard, it was a different story. The class crowded around Laura, congratulating her, dying to tell her all that had happened.

"So that's why Miss Pim is in such a foul humour," Laura said, when she'd heard the story. For a moment she wished the teacher were on her side. It would be nice if she were proud of Laura's win instead of behaving as if it were her worst nightmare. "She just doesn't like me," Laura thought. "She thinks I'm useless, but I'll show her I can do this properly!"

Later she was called to the head's office. Miss Briteside congratulated her. "You did remarkably well, Laura. You're a credit to the school." The girl was chuffed. "Of course being a teacher requires a certain effort," the head went on. "You know that, don't you?"

Laura nodded. Certainly Miss Pim always made an effort, though mostly it was to give out to her.

"Now, I want you to read this document and sign it." Miss Briteside pushed across an official-looking paper. "Then tomorrow I will call a school assembly and announce that on Wednesday you will be Teacher for a Day."

Laura read:

I, Laura Delaney, shall be Teacher for the Day and do agree to the following conditions:

1. *My clothes and appearance shall be neat and respectable.*

2. *I shall carry a briefcase which will contain at least a packed lunch.*

3. *My classes will be prepared.*

4. *My lunch hour will be spent in the staffroom.*

5. *I shall behave like any other teacher with regard to the punishment and correction of pupils.*

6. *I shall have no favourites.*

7. *I accept that Miss Pim cannot come to my assistance unless she is asked by me.*

8. *The behaviour of the class is my responsibility and mine alone.*

9. *I shall not chew sweets or chewing-gum in class. Nor will I eat crisps, popcorn, or biscuits. Nor will I permit others to do so.*

10. *If I fail to keep any of the above conditions, I give my solemn word that I shall spend three weeks of the summer holidays helping to paint the school premises.*

Laura took a deep breath. The only tricky condition, she thought, was number 3. Still, it shouldn't be too hard to give sums or an essay out of the book. Anyway, she didn't intend to spend much time on lessons. As for behaviour, the class wouldn't let her down, would they? Not with Miss Pim sitting among them.

Her eyes gleamed. This was going to be one great adventure. Imagine being in charge for a whole day. How could anything go wrong when she'd be her own boss? Even if it did, no one in the class could give out to her, not even Miss Pim.

"Where do I sign?" she asked.

Chapter 10

Next day Miss Briteside made a wonderful drama of assembly. She waited for silence from the school, then called Laura up to the stage and congratulated her. She read out the document Laura had signed and with a flourish presented the girl with a copy. Thinking the ceremony was over, Laura heaved a sigh of relief and was about to leave the stage when Miss Briteside asked her to say a few words. The girl's mind immediately went blank. Petrified she stood there.

"Come on, Laura!" Someone shouted.

"Speech!" another voice called and soon this was taken up as a chant: "Speech. Speech. Speech!"

She had to say something. "Eh, I'd like to thank Miss Briteside for making me 'Teacher for a Day'," she started. Everyone cheered except Miss Pim, who moaned. Laura gathered courage. "And I'm going to do a good job and have a good time too," she continued.

Miss Pim gritted her teeth, while the girl told them earnestly, "People shouldn't be miserable in class, especially pupils cos they're the only ones who have to follow the rules, so it's not surprising, is it, if they break some of them when they have to spend years and years trying to keep them?"

The school clapped and cheered and there were even a few whistles of appreciation. Miss Briteside frowned.

Laura put up a hand and the noise died except for Miss Pim. "Oh God," she wailed. "Oh dear!"

"Is someone in pain?" Miss Briteside asked. She peered down at the school. The sound came again. "For heaven's sake!" shouted Miss Briteside. "Who is moaning?"

"It's Miss Pim," someone shouted.

"Miss Pim? Are you all right, Miss Pim?"

The teacher was lost in thought, unaware of the sound she was making. She had been gripped by Laura's comment that only pupils had to keep the rules. If that were the case, she thought, then she'd never have to insist on homework, never have to make sure her class learned anything. She needn't bother trying to interest them in good stories, or explain difficult maths, or take them out to art galleries, films and plays so they could improve their knowledge. She needn't have bothered having a pets' day.

"Laura's not being fair," she thought. "We all have to follow rules, even teachers. *Especially* teachers!"

Miss Briteside called again and Miss Pim raised her head, startled to find everyone looking at her. "Are you all right? Feeling fine?" asked the head.

The teacher nodded. There was no point saying she was ill, sick as a dog, and it was all Miss Briteside's fault.

The head gestured at Laura to finish her speech.

"All I want to say is, I can't wait till Wednesday," Laura told them. "It'll be a deadly day!"

What should she wear? Laura wondered on Tuesday night. Trousers? Fine. A sweatshirt? Too casual. None of the teachers wore sweatshirts. She tried the pink frilly blouse Gran had given her for Christmas. It was horrible, but it was very respectable. She borrowed one of her mum's cardigans, grey and sensible. It was too big but it would do if she rolled up the sleeves. She scraped back her dark hair into a ponytail and studied herself in the mirror. So neat! None of her teachers looked this boring, but Miss Briteside would have no complaints.

Dad agreed to give up his briefcase, but not without a grumble. "Where am I supposed to put my lunch," he said, "not to mention my newspaper?" Eventually he accepted Laura's schoolbag in exchange. "I'm not sure a purple rucksack goes with my suit," he said, but later she saw him checking how it looked in the mirror and smiling.

Ever since his bungie-jump Mr Delaney had a more adventurous attitude, even towards clothes. He had taken to wearing colourful waistcoats and bright ties with pictures of cartoon figures. His new hairstyle no longer resembled a badly styled wig, but was short and a little spiky.

"You look wonderful," Laura's mother had said and given him a big kiss.

"Yuck!" Laura had pretended to get sick. Sam took a fit of giggles and couldn't stop.

Mr Delaney got a shock when he saw Laura on Wednesday morning. "My God you look like my mother!" he told her.

"Well, everyone always says I look like her." Laura didn't see what he was getting at.

"Yes, but you're not supposed to look the same age as her! Not when you're eleven and she's sixty-five."

"Oh, don't exaggerate!" Mrs Delaney told him, "Laura just looks – she looks – well, she looks –"

"Horrible," Sam suggested.

"Sensible!" said her mother, firmly.

"I look the way I want to look. And anyway it's only for today."

Her dad was appalled, "You're not going out dressed like that, are you? What on earth will the neighbours say? No doubt they'll blame us for letting you out in that get-up! Would you not think of us before you make a disgrace of yourself?"

Laura stared pointedly at her dad's clothes and said, "Well, at least I'm not wearing a purple tie with a big yellow picture of Homer Simpson. And I'm not wearing a waistcoat that a parrot would be proud of!"

Mr Delaney got his own back, "That high-neck pink frilly blouse you're wearing – your gran probably wore that in the sixties. Or maybe your grandad!"

They glared at each other, then Mr Delaney said, "Tell you what, Laura. Since it's your first – your only – morning as a teacher, I'll give you a lift to school." He turned to his wife and whispered, "That way no one will see her."

"Why don't you want people to see Laura?" Sam asked, but the two were already on their way out the door.

And so at five to nine that Wednesday morning, Laura was dropped right in front of the teachers' entrance. Walking down the long corridor, she hesitated outside the staffroom but couldn't pluck up the courage to enter.

On her way to class children gaped at her. "Good morning, Miss Delaney," someone called and there were a few sniggers.

"Good morning everyone." Laura sounded so like a teacher that they were stunned into silence.

Once in Fifth class, she put her briefcase on the table and took out her class plan:

> *9 o'clock – 10. Maths, English, Irish, History, Geography and Religion.*

These subjects usually took all day, but in Laura's opinion one hour was more than enough time for the whole lot of them.

> *10 – 11. Singing, followed by Small Break.*
> *11.30 – 12.30. Football, then lunch.*

1 – 2. *General Knowledge Quiz.*

2 – 2.40. *Games.*

Slowly the class filled, each person sitting where they wanted, not where Miss Pim had put them. As they came in her classmates greeted her:

"Hi, Laura."

"This is deadly, Laura."

One or two called her, "Miss Delaney," for a laugh, but she stopped them. "I don't like it. It makes me feel silly."

Soon every girl and boy was in place, not chatting as usual before class, but looking at her expectantly. As soon as the bell rang, Laura took the roll, placing a neat X beside every name. Then she looked at notes for absences. Just as she finished, Miss Pim arrived in, ten minutes late.

Laura longed to say in her snottiest voice, just as the teacher always did, "And what is your excuse this time? Please make it one I can believe." But she hadn't the nerve.

As it happened, Miss Pim was apologetic, "I meant to be here before you so I wouldn't interrupt the class, but I overslept." The teacher didn't say she'd been awake nearly all night worrying and had only dropped off at dawn.

"There is a seat at the back beside Danny Smith," Laura told her.

Danny groaned. The class looked disappointed. An opportunity to give Miss Pim a taste of her own medicine had been missed.

"Take out your Maths' homework," Laura said, feeling she'd let everyone down. They giggled but did as they were asked, except for Miss Pim. This time Laura said in a shaky voice, "And where is *your* homework?"

Taken by surprise and annoyed by the question, the teacher said sharply, "I didn't think I had to do it."

Her tone was irritating and Laura said more firmly, "Oh. And do you think you're special in some way? Not like the rest of the class?"

These were words Miss Pim had used a million times in a similar situation, but never had she expected to have them said to her. Anyway, she wasn't like the rest of the class and she said so, very definitely.

"I'm afraid," Laura told her, spurred on by the faces in front of her, "that today you're exactly the same as every other pupil in this class. That means you should have all your homework done and it especially means you should be wearing the school uniform!"

The class sniggered at the thought of Miss Pim in uniform. The teacher's eyes blazed. Laura didn't give her a chance. "Now please don't interrupt!" If she sounded exactly like her teacher it was because she was an expert on how Miss Pim gave out. "The school uniform is a grey skirt, navy jumper, blue shirt and navy tie. It is not black trousers and jumper."

Miss Pim glared at her, but Laura was on a roll now. "And as we all know, the punishment for no homework and no uniform is detention. You can stay back after school. Is that clear?"

Miss Pim thought it was very unfair. She was twenty-six years old – far too old for a school uniform. And as for homework, she wasn't the only one who hadn't done it. "It's not fair!" she burst out. "Danny Smith hasn't done his homework either!"

"Thanks a lot," Danny muttered.

"Rat!" the girl on the other side whispered.

Miss Pim went beetroot. If there was one thing she couldn't stand, it was telling on someone else, unless of course it was over something very serious like bullying or robbing.

"Sorry, Danny," she murmured. "I don't know what came over me." The startled boy nearly fell off his seat.

Laura smiled sweetly at her, "Danny Smith has his copy open. That satisfies me. I will now call out the answers from the back of the book and you can all mark them right or wrong."

"Are you not going to go around and have a look at each copy?" Miss Pim's sense of good practice was outraged.

"I am not," Laura said. "And I will thank you not to question my authority!" She loved saying that and for good effect she narrowed her eyes and frowned.

The class was delighted. One or two cheered, though not loudly. Quickly they corrected the maths, looking forward to the next episode.

For English Laura gave a spelling test. Everyone got full marks for effort, except Miss Pim who had no pen or paper and therefore couldn't make an effort. "Well, I didn't think I'd need either today," she said, very grumpily. Laura made a great show of providing her with both, tut-tutting all the while. "And don't forget," she said in Miss Pim's own familiar cross tone, "I want the biro back *unchewed*! Otherwise there will be HTP."

Irish homework was easily corrected. Laura asked Miss Pim all the questions and said "Correct. Tick please," after each answer. Even to herself she now sounded exactly like her teacher. Her words, gestures and expressions were the same. The class was astonished and amused to see her standing at the top of the room, one hand on her hip, the other raised for attention, head stretched forward, words clipped, a copy of Miss Pim.

The first hour was up after Irish and Laura decided to skip the rest of the work and go straight to singing. "We'll start with Westlife and go through the top ten," she told them.

This was different to "Bali Hai is Calling," and "Doe a Deer" – songs Miss Pim had tried to teach them, along with a few hymns.

They sang enthusiastically.

After a while they noticed Miss Pim had joined in and was now singing the loudest of all. "Much better than those dreadful fifties' numbers Miss Briteside gets me to teach," she thought as she clicked her fingers and swayed to the tune.

Danny turned to her, "This is deadly. Not like –" he stopped, suddenly embarrassed.

"Not like the boring songs I teach," she finished for him and smiled. Danny reckoned Miss Pim was much nicer as a pupil than as a teacher.

It was actually a relief, Miss Pim thought, to have someone else in charge for once, even if that girl was supposed to be the scattiest child in school. Really, she was surprised at how well Laura was doing. In her own fashion the girl had corrected a lot of the homework and now everyone was having a good time. Not that it was very pleasant to be given out to. Especially when she could hear herself in what Laura said. It was a shock to realise that she, Miss Pim, could be so snotty. She had thought the girl never listened, never concentrated. But that wasn't true, at least not all of the time, else how could Laura mimic her so exactly?

And that business over the homework and uniform. She'd forgotten how nasty it was to be put in the wrong when she wasn't at fault. And suddenly she thought, "That's how Laura feels. She probably thinks I'm unfair. And I was *very* unfair when she won the competition. It's a wonder she hasn't been nastier. I was just so worried in case she'd make a total mess of the day!"

It was lovely not to be giving out, or having to give punishment work, set homework, teach songs no one liked. It dawned on her, as they sang 'Fool Again' for the fourth time, that being a pupil could be as much fun for her as being a teacher was for Laura.

Chapter 11

After Small Break came football.

Laura gave Miss Pim the most boring task – goalie. But soon the opposition was complaining, "It's not fair! She's too tall. She's stopping every shot." Of course this made Miss Pim very popular with her own teammates and when they won 12-3, one boy told her, "You were deadly!" and slapped her on the back. For a second, Miss Pim frowned, but seeing his delighted face, she relaxed and grinned. The team thought she was a good sport. Getting mucky hadn't bothered her. And she was very skillful, able to stop difficult shots and then kick the ball far down the field. Now they crowded around her, all wanting to know how she was so good.

"I played a lot in college," she told them. "And everyone in my family is keen. Especially my brother Frank."

"Frank? *The* Frank Pim? The one plays for Ireland, Miss?"

Miss Pim nodded, "That's right."

"He's your brother? But he's ace, Miss!" Before she could get insulted, someone said, "No wonder you're so good, Miss."

Looking at the group around her teacher, Laura thought her plan to get her own back wasn't exactly working. Miss Pim looked happy instead of miserable. But she didn't care. The teacher was far less of a moan than usual. Apart from the one protest, she hadn't whinged at Laura and she'd taken part in everything so far. Another thought struck her, "Surely she can't *like* being a pupil?" But she dismissed the idea as impossible.

Miss Pim hated the yard at Big Break. Once a week she took lunch-patrol there, giving out to pupils who threw things, raced around, pulled and tugged at each other, or played ball too near the windows. They were always up to something she considered dangerous. Eating lunch on her own there, without any control over them, was her idea of a nightmare. But as soon as she arrived in the yard, some of her teammates called her, "Sit with us on the steps if you want, Miss."

That's really nice, she thought, and in a fit of friendliness said, "Maybe you should call me Rachel, for the rest of the day."

They looked at each other. "Okay, Miss Pim – Rachel,"

said one girl, who then got beetroot and the rest giggled like mad.

"Like a sandwich?" Miss Pim asked her.

"No, Miss – eh, Rache – eh, Miss Pim! Oh God!" The girl was mortified and the rest got hysterical. The teacher grinned. "Okay. It won't work. Back to normal."

With that embarrassment over, they were all soon deep in conversation about clothes and pop-songs. As she chatted, Miss Pim idly rolled the large piece of tinfoil from her sandwiches into a ball. She inserted a small stone to give it weight, then threw it in an arc, expecting it to sail into the bin a few yards away. Instead it hit Mr Slevin, whose day it was for yard-patrol. Instinctively she ducked down.

Mr Slevin, his neck stinging, roared, "Right, you lot! Who threw this. And don't tell me you were aiming at the bin. I've heard that one too often!"

When no one answered he stormed over. "I know it was one of you! And whoever it was is going to tidy up the yard, so own up!" Then he saw Miss Pim, who looked at him apologetically. "I'm afraid it was me. Sorry." For some reason she felt like one of the children.

"Really, Miss Pim!" He spoke with mock-severity. "I know you have to be pupil for a day, but firing missiles at teachers is taking the role to extremes!" And he stalked off, grinning to himself, leaving Miss Pim wondering could he possibly be serious and the lunch group once again in hysterics. "That was deadly, Miss!" one stated, with such admiration the teacher decided against saying it was an accident. It was nice to be liked so wholeheartedly for a change.

Laura's lunch hour was completely different to Miss Pim's. She'd been very nervous at the idea of going into the staffroom for lunch. How was she going to talk to teachers for a whole half-hour? Worse still, they might ignore her completely. She had just decided to eat in Fifth class when Miss Briteside came looking for her. "There you are. Come along now and I'll introduce you to the staff."

"But I know them all," Laura quavered.

"Not as a teacher, you don't. Follow me." Horrified, Laura wondered if the head was going to insist that she call everyone by their first name.

In the staffroom, Miss Briteside clapped her hands for attention. The girl stood meekly by her side, looking at the floor and wishing she could disappear beneath it.

"Now everyone. You all know Laura Delaney," the head announced. "She is 'Teacher for a Day' and I know you'll make her very welcome in our staffroom."

Mr Evans, the PE teacher, jumped up from the table and fetched a chair. "Sit here, Laura."

Miss Simmons, who taught Fourth class, nodded and smiled. Miss Briteside poured her a cup of tea and Laura began to relax.

So this was the staffroom! She'd been in it twice before, once in second class, when for a dare, she'd run in and out again, so fast no one had known who she was.

All she'd seen was two or three startled teachers gaping at her.

The second time Miss Briteside had asked her to leave a parcel of books on the table inside the door. She could have looked around then, but she found the room eerily empty and hurried out, not wanting to be surprised by a teacher. Of course she'd often been sent on a message and got a glimpse from outside the door. But it was only a slanted, sideways view, never like this.

She wished she had a camera. Second class would love to see their teacher, Miss Henry, with her shoes off, lying back on the armchair by the window, her feet up on a stool, her eyes closed. And everyone would love to see Mr Thomas, the vice-principal, sitting on a windowsill, puffing away at a cigarette, the smoke curling away through the open window. His eyes were closed too and he was half smiling. Usually he had a grim expression.

The room was very comfy, Laura thought. Lots of armchairs at one end, some small tables and straight-back chairs the other end, where she sat now.

There were books and copies everywhere, some even stacked on the floor. One of the side tables was piled high with folders and markers and a very small coatstand was swamped with coats, jackets and even jumpers. Some of them looked as if they'd been there for years, abandoned, as if their owners had forgotten all about them.

It occurred to Laura that maybe teachers were a bit untidy.

Surely not, though! She'd never met a teacher yet who hadn't hated untidiness. Every one of them insisted on tidy uniforms, tidy desks, tidy classrooms, tidy homework. Neatness was very important to them. Laura tried to take in every detail, knowing her classmates would be full of questions later.

Miss Briteside caught her examining everything and said, "Not very orderly, is it? Of course it will be, once the new shelving is in. And we need more cupboards." She said this as Mr Thomas was opening a press. He'd had to shut it again very fast to avoid the contents falling out on him. He tried again more cautiously, the opening no more than a slit. His left hand slid in and extracted his lunch. Then he swiftly closed the door and came over to Laura's table.

Pulling up a chair beside her, he said, "Laura, maybe you can tell me something. I've a question that's been exercising my mind for quite some time and you just might have the answer!" Laura doubted it, somehow. She'd never provided solutions for teachers before, only problems.

"Now, can you tell me why it is all the pupils come in the teachers' door, when their own door is much nearer the classrooms? See, we like a bit of peace and quiet down here, first thing in the morning, but all those boys and girls racing past puts paid to that. Some of them bang at the door and run off, which is very aggravating."

"We only come in the teachers' door when it's

raining," Laura told him, glad the question was so easy.

Mr Thomas reflected, then nodded, "You're right. But why only when it's raining? Surely you'd get less wet coming in your own door?"

Laura explained, "We have to go around the side to our entrance and the ground is full of potholes. Some of them are huge and you can't jump them. Everyone gets splashed and mucky coming in that way. We end up filthy."

"Oh." Mr Thomas was silenced for a second by the simple explanation. Then he said, "Why didn't anyone say so?"

Laura remembered saying so once, but Mr Thomas had been so annoyed at the crowd thundering past the staffroom, he hadn't listened. He'd just shouted some more and Laura had disappeared as fast as possible. Now he was calm, speaking to her as if she were an adult and she found it easy to say, "Sometimes, teachers don't listen when you tell them things."

He frowned and said thoughtfully, "Mmm."

Miss Briteside suddenly asked, "Do you think that happens a lot, Laura? That teachers don't listen?"

The girl was about to say 'yes' straightaway. After all, Miss Pim never listened to her. But maybe that was because Laura didn't always listen to *her*. She remembered the close attention the teacher paid to Joe and to most other people in the class.

"No, it doesn't happen a lot," she had to say honestly. "Only when they're really annoyed, like, if someone doesn't listen or if everyone is talking at the same time. Then they start roaring and it puts people in a bad mood." She glanced at the vice-principal.

Miss Briteside noticed that everyone at the table had stopped talking. All of them were listening intently. "So what would you do?" she asked. "How would you get people to stop and pay attention if they're all talking at once?"

Laura thought hard, not noticing the silence as everyone waited. Mr Evans and Miss Simmons glanced at each other, half amused. Mr Thomas and the Head gazed at her, expressions serious.

At last her brow cleared, "I'd do what Miss Pim does sometimes," she said.

"Miss Pim?" The Head was all ears. Recently it seemed to her that Miss Pim was more inclined to whinge about her pupils than get them listening to her.

Laura nodded, "Sometimes if the class is very noisy, she stands there saying nothing."

"A recipe for disaster, surely!" Miss Simmons was disdainful. The fourth class teacher was known to be very cross. "Complete mayhem! Everyone would just get louder."

"No, they don't." Laura told her. "People start noticing. She catches their eye. They start telling other people to hush, and they catch her eye too and stop talking. It always works. Maybe it's the way she looks at people. The class gets completely quiet and everyone wishes she'd say something and when she does it's so low you can barely hear. You have to listen real hard."

"And does she do this all the time?" Miss Briteside was impressed. So were the other teachers.

"Only when people are chatty," Laura did not want to give the impression that her classmates were always out of order. "But sometimes she gets annoyed and roars." Especially at me, Laura thought, but did not say so.

The bell went and Miss Briteside rose. "It's been a pleasure having you here for lunch, Laura. Very interesting." The others nodded, Mr Thomas with great enthusiasm.

"Thank you," Laura said. "It was much nicer than I thought – " Horrified, she stopped. "I mean, none of you is as bad – as cross – er – you're more – " Scarlet, she came to a complete halt.

"Human?" Mr Thomas smiled. "Is that the word you're looking for? But surely you wouldn't go that far?" Laura saw he was joking and giggled. He added, "Tell everyone I'll have the potholes sorted in a week."

When she was gone, he turned to the others, "That child made a lot of sense, don't you think?"

The day was going well, Laura mused on her way back to class. Everyone in Fifth had been on her side and they'd had a great time at singing and football. And she'd enjoyed giving out to Miss Pim for a while. She'd taken it well enough too. And it was nice too the way people had listened in the staffroom. Though Laura couldn't see what teachers were on about when they complained about pupils. After all Fifth class had behaved perfectly for her. All she had to do now was avoid trouble for the afternoon. In fact, she decided, being a teacher was an absolute doddle!

Chapter 12

Mona Jones was not happy. It seemed no one in the school could talk about anything except Laura. It was all she heard in her own class. At Small-Break people hung around to get a glimpse of her as if she were someone important, but she'd stayed in the classroom. At lunch time, even Mona's cronies had grouped around Fifth class, wondering what Laura was like as a teacher.

"Deadly!"

"Great fun!"

"A laugh! We sang all the top ten."

Mona was irritated. "But can she teach?"

"Don't be daft!" Joe told her. "She doesn't have to teach."

"So she can't do proper work with you!" The girl was at her snootiest.

"Yes, she can. She corrected homework, did singing

and brought us out for football. And after lunch we're having a general-knowledge quiz."

Mona changed tack. "Boring!" she drawled. "I mean, what's the point of her being your teacher if all you do is the same boring stuff? A general-knowledge quiz! That is *so* naff! Sounds like hard work to me. Now if *I'd* won, the day would be one long party. She should be giving you a good time. After all, you helped her win, so you should get some kind of reward."

"You're just jealous," Joe said. But the others were silent, even Cathy and Danny. Seeing she'd scored, Mona moved off, drawling, "Not much of a day, is it? No party. Still, as long as you're happy, swotting away . . ."

Cathy said, "She's right, you know!"

"I brought in crisps and coke, thinking we'd have a party – more than I could eat for lunch," Danny said.

Others chimed in, "So did I. And sweets. I've still some left."

"So have I. And Laura promised we'd have one, didn't she?"

"She must have. She loves parties!"

And so they convinced themselves. The quiz was conveniently forgotten and they thought it would be nice for Laura to come into class with everything set out for a feast. Even Joe got carried away and was sure his friend would love a party.

Most of them were back in class before the bell rang. Packets of popcorn, sweets, crisps and bottles of coke were loaded onto the desks. By the time Laura arrived, some of them had started drinking and munching.

"Get the tape-deck, Laura. We brought in tapes!"

"What about the general-knowledge quiz?" The girl was dismayed.

"Boring! We want a party. We want a party!" Everyone took up the cry, "Party! Party! We want a party!" Some clapped hands in time to the chant. Others pummelled the desks and stamped their feet.

A couple of minutes later, Miss Pim arrived with her lunch group. There was a brief silence and everyone looked at her. She opened her mouth, then closed it again, remembering she could not intervene. Quietly she went to her place.

The noise resumed, worse than ever, "We want a party *now*! We want a party *now*!"

As she had seen Miss Pim do, Laura stood there silently, staring at the class. But since they didn't really think of her as a teacher, this had no effect. As far as they were concerned, Miss Pim was the only one they had to worry about and she was saying nothing. Anyway, Laura *owed* them a party. They'd put her where she was and they'd gone along with her all morning, not because she was in charge, but because she was their friend. Now she should go along with them. And so the shouting and banging got louder.

Desperate, Laura shouted. Her voice was lost. Taking up the duster she went to bang it on the table for attention, when a boy in the front row leaned forward and snatched it out of her hand. Quick as a flash he threw it on top of the press.

The uproar stopped for a second and everyone glanced at Miss Pim. The teacher stared at her desk, grim but silent. Then someone threw a bag of crisps to a pal across the room. It split open, scattering the contents all over the boy. A girl unscrewed the top from a bottle of coke she'd been using to beat time on the desk. The liquid exploded and she was covered in sepia foam.

Then one girl thought it would be very funny to pull the chair from under the boy beside her. He was sitting on the edge and tilting forward when she deftly tugged and he disappeared from sight. Not too pleased, he scrambled up and pushed her onto the floor. People around them cleared a space as the two bodies struggled, kicking at table legs. Miss Pim stood up and seeing no one was in real danger, sat down again. The din increased.

Noticing how miserable Laura looked, Danny stopped shouting, got out of his chair and carried it up to the press. Maybe he could help by getting the duster back. Standing on the chair, he could barely see over the top of the tall press and he certainly couldn't reach the duster. He hoisted himself up by his hands and accidentally kicked away his support. He was left clutching the press which began to tilt over. The noise in the room was louder than ever. Laura felt like weeping. The day was going horribly wrong. Now she'd have to ask Miss Pim for help. She tried to catch her teacher's eye, but Miss Pim didn't look up.

"Watch out, Danny!" roared Joe, starting to climb across his desk in order to help his friend. But Danny jumped clear and Laura stepped sideways as the press crashed onto the teacher's table.

At that precise moment the door opened and Miss Briteside surveyed the scene. For once she was struck dumb. Not so the man who suddenly appeared behind her. "What on earth is going on here?" His voice was stern.

"Oh my God!" the Head thought. "Not him. Not now!"

"Well, Miss Briteside? Why is this class in uproar?" He peered over her shoulder. One boy had just scrambled over a desk and was helping another boy and a girl to push upright a very tall press.

He could see no teacher. What he could see among the desks was a boy picking crisps out of his hair and a girl covered in a dirty, sticky-looking foam and wailing – or maybe she was roaring like the rest. Two others were rolling around the floor. No one was paying any attention to the headmistress who turned to face the man, immaculate with his dark suit, tiny moustache, short hair and fine leather briefcase.

"Good afternoon, Mr Matthews." Her smile was shaky.

"No it isn't," the man snapped. "In all my years as department inspector I have never witnessed such uproar! What is the meaning of this?"

Inside the classroom the press was finally upright and

the class at last noticed the principal. Fright brought sudden silence. Now they were for it! There was a sudden mad scramble as everything was swept off desks and into bags. The boy with the crisps hurriedly brushed them off his hair and clothes, then dived under the table and did the biggest clean-up ever. The two on the floor noticed the hush and stopped trying to whack each other. Sheepishly they got to their feet, fixed their desks and chairs and sat down. The girl covered in coke did the only thing possible. She jumped up and ran out of the room, muttering, "Excuse me, Miss. Sorry, Miss." Better to spend the afternoon in the toilet block, cleaning herself up than stay in the classroom, looking as though she'd stuck her head and face into a giant pot of foam.

In minutes the room looked reasonable. Danny was back in his seat, but Joe stayed at the top of the class. He thought Laura might need his support.

Miss Briteside tried to be her regal best. "What is the reason for these shenannigans?" she thundered.

"Yes, I'd like to know that too," said the inspector, but his words were addressed to the Head. By this time they were both inside the classroom.

Laura swallowed, "We were having a party."

"A party!" echoed Miss Briteside.

"Looked more like a riot to me," boomed Mr Matthews.

"It was only a bit of fun," Joe said.

"Fun!" said the Head.

"More like mayhem!" the inepctor said severely.

130

"Well, things got a bit out of hand," Joe tried to explain.

"Out of hand? Out of hand?" Miss Briteside was incredulous.

"Totally out of control, if you ask me," sniffed the inspector before he turned on the Head. "And will you please stop sounding like a demented echo, repeating everything." Turning back to Joe, he glared at him and said, "It's obvious to me that you're the ringleader here! Climbing over desks. Pushing presses around. Not going back to your seat! Oh yes! It's easy to see who's the troublemaker!"

"Well, it's not me," Joe was fed up. He'd only been trying to help.

But the inspector was in no mood to listen. "Don't you give back-answers!" he said. "I don't like your cheek. I know what I saw!"

"No, you don't," Joe's voice rose. He was sick of adults, sick of his father, sick of being good and getting nowhere. "You don't know what happened, so you needn't blame me!"

The inspector went white. Miss Briteside was unable to speak, so surprised was she. The class was agog. Joe had some nerve! Laura felt afraid for him, as did Miss Pim, who had long thought the boy was unnaturally good. Now he was going to boil over if the inpector said another word. But Mr Matthews decided to ignore him. There were more pressing matters on his mind for the minute. "Just *who* is in charge here?" he asked in an ominously quiet voice.

"I am," Laura told him.

"Don't be ridiculous!" Mr Matthews felt he might burst. Miss Pim kept quiet, mindful of the agreement. The inspector had not yet noticed her. "I ask again! Who is in charge here?"

"I am," Laura said again. "I'm 'Teacher for a Day'."

Miss Briteside groaned and Miss Pim realised the Head had never mentioned the competition to the department.

The inspector was paler than ever. "What sort of hairbrained idea is this? Who would put a scatty schoolgirl in charge?" He was looking at the principal. "It's obvious this child isn't fit to look after half a dozen chicks, never mind a classroom of eleven-year-olds!"

Miss Briteside couldn't think of anything to say. Laura, distracted by the idea of looking after six chickens, was also silent.

But Joe sprang to his friend's defence. "She is so, fit! Laura is a deadly teacher."

Enraged, the inspector turned on him, "And who asked for your opinion? I have your measure, young man! You are a troublemaker of the first order, cheeky and insolent. I think your parents should be contacted!"

That was it. Joe had had enough. His father would be called in over nothing and the atmosphere at home would be worse than ever. What was the point of being good?

"You can contact who you like!" he said. "I don't care. It won't make any difference to my dad!"

"Oh, won't it? We'll see about that." The inspector was seething.

"No, it won't!" Joe started shouting. "D'you hear me? It won't. He's bad-tempered now. He's been bad-tempered for ages! So no matter what you tell him, he'll still be bad-tempered."

In the class the silence was shocked. Everyone except the inpector realised how upset Joe must be to behave like this. But the boy wasn't finished, "And whatever you say," he told Mr Matthews, "it can't change how deadly Laura was this morning. Can it?" He appealed to the class. Startled, they nodded agreement.

"Now you listen here!" the inspector was raging. No one had ever spoken to him like this before. "Both of you!" he included Laura, but before he could say another word, Miss Pim stood up.

"I'm afraid I can't stay quiet any longer," she said. "That boy is one of the best pupils in this school!"

Joe squirmed. "Not any more," he was sullen, "I'm sick of being good!"

Miss Pim continued as if she hadn't heard, "And as for Laura Delaney," she paused and Laura groaned. Now was the teacher's chance. The girl could hardly blame her. She'd been very nasty to her this morning, insisting that a grown woman should wear the school uniform.

"The girl has done wonderfully well!" Miss Pim said, very firmly, brooking no argument. "All morning this has been a happy and a well-behaved class, due to Laura Delaney. You came in at just the wrong moment, Mr

Matthews, and you shouldn't accuse us of mayhem, just because it was noisy for a few minutes!"

The Head was listening intently, hoping Miss Pim would convince the inspector that there had been nothing wrong at all, though she thought that might take a miracle.

But the inspector couldn't believe his ears. "Came in at the wrong moment! Came in at the – Listen here! When I came in there was uproar. There were crisps and sweetpapers everywhere. Children fighting on the floor. That boy was climbing over a desk. That big press could have killed someone. There was a girl covered in some vile substance, who has now completely disappeared, and a boy over there had the contents of a crisp packet on his head. So don't tell me there wasn't mayhem!"

But the teacher stood her ground and said quietly, "Look around you, Mr Matthews. No rubbish, everyone quiet, listening politely. Joe wanted to help quickly, that's why he climbed over the desk and that girl – Laura – had been successfully in charge for hours before you arrived."

The inspector drew himself up, not at all pleased. But before he could say another word, someone in the class said very clearly, "Miss Pim's right. Laura was great!"

"And Joe did nothing wrong," another added.

More voices joined in:

"It was our fault. We shouldn't have gone on about a party!"

"No, we shouldn't. But *he* shouldn't pick on them!"

"So mean!"

"It's not fair. He doesn't even know them."

The inspector heard the bitterness and saw the resentful faces. Looking around it was obvious the room was tidy, the children orderly. Not a crisp. And the sticky child had probably gone to clean up. Maybe he'd been a bit hasty. Nobody had ever accused him of being unfair before and he didn't like it. It hurt.

In the silence that followed, Miss Briteside sighed, sure the inspector would write a bad report. Joe was clenching his fist, sorry he'd made the outburst, but determined from now on not to put up with other people's bad temper – especially his dad's. Laura was still reeling from the shock of Miss Pim's unexpected praise. The teacher held her breath, believing the inspector would think she'd shown him up in front of the class.

"Maybe I was wrong," Mr Matthews conceded at last. Everyone gaped at him. "Maybe things were not as they seemed," he told the class. "I shall sit with Miss Pim and Miss Briteside at the back of the class and I shall see if this child is as good as everyone thinks."

"Oh my God!" groaned Laura and the Head and the teacher, each to themselves.

Mr Matthews took the desk in the back corner. Miss Briteside and Miss Pim sat beside him and closed their eyes in agony.

Chapter 13

At the top of the class, Laura took a deep breath and nudged Joe. He was lost in thought and it wasn't till she spoke that he paid attention. "Joe, I'm going to do the quiz. Will you keep score on the board?"

He nodded. Swiftly Laura divided the class into teams, putting the three adults at the back with Danny and Cathy. No one in the class cared about who won, they just wanted Laura to do well. They sat like mice, in circles, each team captain with pen and paper, ready to write down the answer.

There were five rounds: TV. Pop-Music. Sport. Computer-Games. Problem -Solving.

The rounds were polite and orderly. Laura collected the answer sheets each time, quickly corrected them and then Joe put the results on the board. At the end of round three the inspector's team was first, but it was very close, only one point separating the first three teams.

People began to get excited, especially the inspector, who could be heard arguing with Miss Pim in a loud whisper about the fourth round questions. "Of course I know what I'm talking about!" he said fiercely. "My daughter plays computer-games all the time!"

"Well, so does my young brother!" Miss Pim was equally fierce. "And I'm telling you, you're wrong!"

Miss Briteside kept out of it, not having a clue. Danny and Cathy knew Miss Pim was right and said so, but the inspector had his own way.

The answers came up and the inspector's team lost two points, putting them into second place. There was a small cheer from the rest of the class. Miss Pim looked grimly triumphant. "I told you so!" she whispered. "Sorry," muttered Mr Matthews.

"This is the problem you have to solve," Laura said, then read out:

Ten women are going into a supermarket. A man doing a survey in the shopping centre wants to find out the average amount of money they have with them. None of them wants to tell him exactly what they have, because it's their own private business. How does he find out the average amount they possess? The women are each given pen and paper.

She put the problem on the board, then said, "You have ten minutes to solve it."

There was fierce whispering and scribbling. Everyone was

frowning with concentration. The leaders chewed on their pens. More paper was brought out. Laura smiled. Her dad had given her the problem the previous night and it had taken her ages to work it out. Yet the answer seemed so easy when she'd found it.

The inspector was frowning more than anyone else. His whispers grew louder and louder, until he burst out in frustration, "You're the teacher, Miss Pim. Surely you have some idea!"

"I might have," Miss Pim was equally annoyed, "if you didn't keep nattering."

A furious argument began. Danny and Cathy couldn't get a word in. Miss Briteside didn't try, still preoccupied by the report the inspector would write.

Finally Mr Matthews snapped his pen in half, "This can't be done. Not if they won't tell the man exactly what money they have!"

"It can be done," Laura smiled at him sweetly. "Time up!" she called.

"That's not fair! We're only getting into it." Then he blushed, said "Sorry," for the second time that afternoon and handed up a page of scribbles that made no sense.

Laura read out the solution before she corrected the answer.

The man doing the survey writes down a sum of money on a piece of paper. He hands this to the first shopper and asks her to add what she has to that amount. She gives the answer — and only the answer — to the next person, who adds what she's got and gives the amount to the next shopper, and so on until the next person hands back a piece of paper with the whole amount on it.

Then all the survey-man has to do is subtract the figure he wrote first, then divide the rest by ten. That way no one knows what each person has to spend except the person herself.

In silence the class digested this. It was so easy when they heard the answer.

"Cool!" they said. "Neat!" "Dead simple!"

The inspector was very impressed. "Most interesting," he said. "A wonderful quiz." And this was *after* he knew his team had finished third.

Only one team got the answer right and Mr Matthews thought so highly of them that he insisted on giving each of them a pound. "Achievement should be rewarded!" he told them and was rewarded himself with a clap and a cheer.

He went to the top of the class and raised a hand for silence. Instantly everyone was quiet. No way were they going to let down Laura again.

"Speaking of achievement," Mr Matthews said, "I have to say this class seems to me to be a prime example of it." Down at the back Miss Briteside perked up. The inspector was looking quite cheerful, she thought. His fury at the class was completely gone, as was his annoyance at not being able to solve Laura's problem. Maybe his report wouldn't be so bad after all. In which case she might let Laura off the penalty clause.

"What I've seen today has been very unusual," he continued. "What I thought at first was serious misconduct has turned out to be part of a unique experiment. Now, I have known Miss Briteside for many years, and while we haven't always seen eye to eye, I have to admit she is a person who gets things done and who has always put this school first."

He paused and everyone turned and looked at the head. Miss Briteside went bright red.

"In fact I came here today," said the inspector, "to congratulate your principal on behalf of the department. She set out to raise a large sum of money and she achieved her goal. I'm also here to tell her that the new gym will be built during the summer holidays!"

At this everyone cheered and the inspector thought how nice it was to have people delighted with him. Usually his arrival in a school had staff and students frowning and miserable.

"But it seems that it is not Miss Briteside's only achievement. What I've seen today in this class has shown me your principal is at the forefront of education. She is not afraid to try new ways, as this unique experiment in student-responsibility has shown!"

Miss Briteside was astounded. "My goodness," she thought. "So that's what I've done – experimented with student responsibility. My goodness! Sometimes I don't know my own cleverness." And catching Miss Pim looking at her, eyebrows raised disbelievingly, she grinned.

And Laura, she thought, would defintely *not* have to spend three weeks painting the school.

The inspector hadn't finished. "I came to this class looking for Miss Briteside. The situation I found here was, frankly, awful. But the way it changed so quickly, the way everyone tidied up, settled down and did the quiz and supported Laura was absolutely wonderful. It was an achievement for the class and an achievement for this child here!"

It was Laura's turn to blush.

"And as I said earlier, achievement should be rewarded. So what I'm going to do is arrange for the Department to pay for a class-outing to a theme park, transport provided with lunch in a nice restaurant. What do you think?"

They left him in no doubt about their thoughts, shouting approval. Then Cathy called, "Speech, Laura! Speech!" They all took up the cry, only stopping when she stood beside Mr Matthews.

"I had a great day," Laura told them, eyes shining. "And I'd like to thank Miss Pim for being such a good sport." Everyone nodded vigorously. The teacher had been a real surprise.

"And I'd like to thank Miss Briteside for organising everything, and the class for all your help, but mostly I'd like to thank Joe, cos if it wasn't for him I wouldn't have won and we wouldn't be getting this reward." Everything she said came out in a rush and Laura was out of breath.

Joe was blushing and grinning, still standing at the blackboard.

"Three cheers for Joe and Laura," Danny yelled and as the last cheer died away the bell rang, signalling the end of a most extraordinary school day.

Chapter 14

It took Laura some time to get out of the school. After Miss Briteside and the inspector left the class for the Head's office, everyone wanted to talk to her about how the day had gone.

News had spread around the school like wildfire that the inpector had turned up in Fifth class just when everyone was running wild. "He's probably going to expel Laura," Mona Jones had sniffed and that rumour had made its way into every class. Now students crowded into Fifth to hear what had happened.

"What do you mean, you're all getting a reward?" Mona's voice was shrill.

"The inspector thinks we're ace," Danny told her. "Especially Laura. He said she did a great job!"

Mona flounced off, raging. Now she'd have to listen for weeks about the day Laura Delaney was teacher.

But everyone else congratulated Laura, even the

teachers of other classes, who'd heard how impressed the inspector was. Her own class basked in the unusual glow of having so many staff praise them. They wanted the day to go on forever. But eventually, one by one, everyone left. Laura found herself alone with Joe and Miss Pim. The teacher had deliberately waited behind.

"Well done, Laura," she said quietly.

"Thank you, Miss." Then she smiled mischievously and said, "You needn't do detention, Miss, if that's why you're staying behind."

"Don't go too far, Laura," the teacher said, but she was smiling. Then she added, "I think we both learned a lot, don't you?"

Laura nodded.

As Miss Pim was leaving, she turned and said, "By the way, I really enjoyed the day. Well, maybe not the bit after lunch. And maybe not the bit when you gave out to me over not wearing the school uniform. But I certainly had a great time otherwise."

"So did I, Miss. Sorry about the uniform." They smiled at each other warmly.

When she was gone, Joe said, "I told you Miss Pim was sound."

"Maybe," Laura said. This had been a special day, after all. She'd soon be in trouble again. Still, Miss Pim had seen a different side to her, just as she'd seen a different side to Miss Pim. "Maybe!" She said with more conviction.

On the way home they saw Joe's dad in Mrs Malone's

garden. He was leaning on a spade resting. Having asked Laura about the day, he turned to his son. "Are you all set to give me a hand in a while, Joe?"

"No, Dad. Not today. I'm going to play football later on with Danny and Laura. And Danny asked me to stay over this weekend. I'd like to do that. And I'll get my own sandwich today. You don't have to come over. I can look after myself."

Mr Jameson stared at his son. There was something different about the boy, he thought. Joe looked him straight in the eye and not at the ground as he usually did. But the biggest difference was that he hadn't asked permission. And he seemed to be waiting. For what? Suddenly Mr Jameson knew what it was. The boy was waiting for a row, for a fit of bad humour, and from the cut of him, he was going to stand his ground.

Mr Jameson grinned, "You enjoy yourself, son. About time too."

Joe looked disappointed and his father's heart soared. The lad actually *wanted* an argument! He was showing some spirit and Mr Jameson was delighted. Still he'd better pretend otherwise. "It's a pity you can't help me though." He made his voice cross.

"Well, I can't. I want to play football!" The boy was defiant.

"Okay, son," Mr Jameson said meekly, hoping he wasn't giving in too easily.

Joe nodded and crossed the road to his house and Laura went on home. The boy was whistling.

It's a good day, Mr Jameson thought. Not only was his son showing something of his old self, but in other ways life was looking up. That morning Laura's mum had paid him a visit, told him she was interested in setting up a landscape-gardening business. She'd had stacks of figures with her, showing what investment was needed, what profits could be made. She'd done a lot of research on the internet, made important contacts and the bank was willing to lend set-up money.

It was a while before Mr Jameson realised she wanted him as a partner. He'd spent the rest of the day in a dream, unable to concentrate properly. Life was certainly improving!

As soon as his son was out of sight Mr Jameson did a little dance around the spade.

Laura's front door was open and Mrs Delaney and Sam were waiting for her.

"Did you bring me chalk?" Sam was all excited.

"I brought you a box of coloured chalk and two sticks of white." She took them from briefcase.

"Brilliant. You're the best!" Sam looked at his sister with adoration.

"Don't be soppy," she told him. "It's only chalk." He was already examining the different colours.

"How did the day go, Laura?" her mum asked, a little timidly.

"Fine," Laura said, a bit weary of being asked the same question.

"Really?" Mrs Delaney said. She'd been worried, hoping Laura had been able for the responsibility, sure something was bound to go wrong.

At that moment the telephone rang. Mrs Delaney answered, then handed it over. "Your father," she said.

"Laura. How was your day?" Her mum was standing beside her, keen to hear.

"Fine, Dad."

"Only fine?"

She heard the anxiety in her dad's voice and saw her mum's frown. Laura realised how worried her parents had been. They'd thought it was a mad idea to put an eleven-year-old in charge of a class. Yet they'd helped and encouraged her to win because it was what she'd wanted. And she'd enjoyed it so much!

Time to put them out of their misery.

She smiled at Mrs Delaney, all tiredness gone.

"Dad," she said, "I had a deadly day!" Then she cupped the phone and turned to her mother, "Sam is drawing on the wallpaper, Mum."

In red chalk on the yellow wallpaper, Sam had written his sister's name. Underneath was a face in profile. Hair, nose, mouth were very clear. Clearer still were the eyes – two pairs, one in the front and one in the back of her head.

THE END

Rosie's Quest

by

ANN CARROLL

Dublin, Friday the 13th January 1956:
A playgroup accident affects the lives of twin girls forever.
After all, there is no way to alter the past . . .
or is there?

Rosie McGrath travels back in time to 1956.
Can she survive that harsher world?
Will she be trapped there forever?
Can she change the events of that long-ago Friday
when her mother and aunt went their separate ways?

ISBN 1 85371 281 7

Available from **www.poolbeg.com**

Rosie's Troubles

by

ANN CARROLL

*Dublin in 1920 was a dangerous, violent city.
A twelve-year-old girl on her own could easily
disappear without trace.*

Was Catherine Dalton caught up in the mayhem
of Croke Park on Bloody Sunday? Was she murdered
and secretly buried?

Rosie's gran still wonders what happened to her
best friend. To find out, Rosie must travel
once more to the past, putting her own life
and future at risk.

ISBN 1 85371 681 2

Available from **www.poolbeg.com**

Rosie's Gift

by

ANN CARROLL

*What was it like to be a skivvy in 1870, slaving away in
a big house at everyone's beck and call?*

For time-traveller Rosie McGrath – used to the
dishwasher and central heating of modern times –
it is a horrible shock. But she must suffer on if she
wants to save her ancestor Joseph and foil the
plans of a powerful enemy!

ISBN 1 85371 875 0

Available from **www.poolbeg.com**

Rosie's Century

by

ANN CARROLL

A letter from the past, a set of clues, the threat of murder – these bring Rosie back to the gas-lit streets of Dublin 1900 for another great adventure.

It is April and Queen Victoria is about
to visit the city.

Rosie has learnt nothing in school about this event
and she's amazed at the Dubliners' enthusiasm
for the queen.

But beneath the holiday atmosphere evil lurks . . .

ISBN 1 85371 972 2

Available from **www.poolbeg.com**

Rosie's War

by

ANN CARROLL

Time-traveller Rosie finds an old newspaper, dated
19th July 1943, and spots a report on the arrest of one
Edward O'Neill for murder. Rosie is horrified: this is the
Edward she met on her trip to 1900, son of her
great-great-uncle Joseph!

Remembering the brave, fun-loving boy, Rosie has no
choice: she must time-travel to 1943 in the hope
of helping him.

She takes her rollerblades - and a few snacks like popcorn
and chocolate. She might have packed differently if she
had known that food was rationed in Dublin in 1943!
Ireland is in a state of 'Emergency' as the Second World
War rages in Britain and Europe . . .

But Rosie has survived harsh conditions before.
The important thing is: can she save Edward?

ISBN 1 84223 073 5

Amazing Grace

by

ANN CARROLL

Grace's great-aunt Josie is cool – but she expects a stay in Josie's big old house will be mega-boring – and that's before she finds out there's no TV!

Boring it is. Then she explores the attic and finds an amazing comb – a comb that, at a wish, can turn a dog's coat into a haystack and a teacher's hairdo into a bird's nest!

Grace and her comb soon make sure that the locals will never forget her visit! If she teaches some geeks and freaks a lesson along the way and presents her lucky fans with their hearts desire, it's all in a days work for *Amazing Grace!*

ISBN 1 85371 980 3

Available from **www.poolbeg.com**